egends

Godfrey's Crusade

Mark Howard

D1096500

Godfrey's Crusade is a work of fiction. Similarities to real people, places, or events are entirely coincidental.

GODFREY'S CRUSADE
First edition. July 23, 2021.
Copyright © 2021 Mark Howard.

ISBN: 978-1-0879-8204-5
Written and published by Mark Howard 2021.

www.thegriffinlegends.com

To my wife, who never stopped believing.

The Nordslands

Troll Lands

Cyclops Tribes

Wyrmwind Peaks

The Bosvian Sea

Vasag

Sigtun

The Five Clans

Zemel

Westronorg

Drammon

Orcish Tribes

Brismarik

Gorgon Heights

Olsa

Vorni

Kirnu

Hydra Gulf

Northern Marches

Mendelpov

Yskov

Pavik

Oblarv

Skasgun

Korkul

Friodlad

Epsberg

Novod

Tisga

Asgald

Helsirki

Blighted Lands

Smasten

Vartelad

Mirtus

Odsha

Troms Mountains

Eastern Marches

Austlad

Vindholm

Durstfold

Royal Domains

Gotlad

Sval

Taht

Biorkon

Smalad

Kalscony

Mirborg

Sudvall

The Freezing Sea

The Griffin Legends
Godfrey's Crusade

Chapter One

Ominous dark hills surrounded the valley through which the tattered, battle-hardened knights rode. The valley descended deeper the farther they went. Cheldric signaled the riders to stop, giving the infantry a chance to catch up to them. Ahead, Cheldric could see a distant column of Sudman warriors marching inexorably towards a head-on collision with his forces. Armor and weapons gleamed in the fading light among the Sudmen. Cheldric's friends, Odo and Bishop Reginald, rode on either side of him.

Cheldric turned to the Bishop and Odo. These men had saved each other's lives on countless occasions through the years on campaign. The Battle of Illipia, the Siege of Sargutun, Kurka; on what coast did they not spill blood for each other? Cheldric knew they would be with him every step of the way from this nameless dusty valley to the Abyss and back home again.

Behind the three, a retinue of knights awaited Cheldric's command while their spear-and-shield-armed infantry drew nearer to the knights. Cheldric knew every knight here by name. He smiled at the memory of past jokes, pranks, and other moments of buffoonery he had shared with those in his inner circle; the sort of thing he could not let the common soldiers see. Then tears welled in his eyes at the thought of those who were not with them. The warriors he had buried at Illipia, Sargutun, Kurka, and a dozen other battle sites. But there was no time for sorrow now. There was work to be done.

Are you sure? Odo's words from earlier raced through Cheldric's mind. *How can you know?*

Now they knew.

Odo removed his flat-top helmet, revealing dark wet hair sticking to his red forehead. He gave Cheldric a look that betrayed both his surprise and repentance at having questioned his friend. Odo did not take being wrong lightly. Smiling at his friend, Cheldric gave a deferential nod. All was forgiven.

"We were being followed after all," Bishop Reginald spat.

"You were right," Odo mumbled. "King Ibrahim broke the truce."

"That is why I was entrusted to lead the rearguard," Cheldric acknowledged, patting his steed, Onyx.

"You'd think they would have had enough war already," the Bishop sighed.

"That's what you told the cyclopean minotaur at Kurka," Odo jibed. "And how did he respond to *Have you had enough war already?*"

"He gored me." Reginald put his hand to his side where the old wound still troubled him from time to time.

"And you screamed so loudly your mother heard it back at Roun." Odo smirked.

"I'll gore your sister next time we're at Harv." The Bishop grinned.

Odo quickly turned a deep shade of purple as he spat out an increasingly incoherent retort about celibate clergymen. Poor Odo was so easy to get worked up. Cheldric had to put a stop to this before they forgot themselves entirely. There was about to be a battle after all.

"And *then* you cleaved the beast's head clean in two with your battle ax." Cheldric pointed to Reginald before he could deliver another remark about Odo's family. "May this battle yield many more such tales."

"Shall we signal King Lambert of the enemy's approach?" Odo asked as he looked at the horn hooked to Cheldric's belt.

"What is a rearguard for if it must call on the main army at the first sign of danger?" Cheldric reprimanded Odo. "No, I swore that my sword would spill blood before I call for help."

"This is Ganelon's doing," Odo brooded. "Surely he provoked Ibrahim into chasing after us."

"That traitor deserved execution over exile," Bishop Reginald cursed. "This is how Ganelon repays us? I will kill him myself if I find him down there!"

"They will all know the Bishop's infamous fury," Cheldric reassured him.

Signaling the infantry to hurry, Cheldric frowned as the Sudmen continued their approach. The infantry marched in double time to close with the knights as quickly as possible. They stopped, awaiting their lord's command after they reached the cavaliers. Years of campaigning had hardened these soldiers from young farmhands and laborers into grizzled veterans. Shields were dented. Scars disfigured faces. Links were missing from chainmail hauberks. Surcoats were stained with years of dirt and blood from countless battles and long sieges. Despite all this, determination burned in their eyes underneath the mismatched spangenhelms, kettle helmets, and whatever else the peasants could scrounge up to protect their heads. Allowing himself a humorless smile, Cheldric saluted his men.

"Ostmen of the glorious army of King Lambert," Cheldric addressed the rearguard, "you can see that the Sudmen of Iberland have broken the peace treaty and have chosen battle once again."

Cheldric paused for a moment. As he thought of the inevitable carnage ahead, his expression changed to a defiant grimace. There was glory ahead, certainly. It would be glorious no matter the outcome. He would not shirk his duty.

"And may the gods grant it to us," Cheldric continued. "After this final battle, your homes in sweet Lortharain are just beyond the mountains. You shall have rest. But we must fight once more before then. Justice is on our side, and it is our duty to be here for the King. Now let each man strike great blows, so that no one may sing a shameful song about us!"

Raising his lance, Cheldric cried out, and the rearguard cheered in reply. Odo put his helmet back on as the knights formed into a wedge at the front of the Ostman infantry column. The Sudman army had advanced as close as they dared without engaging, and were forming their lines. Awaiting his signal to charge, Reginald and Odo turned to Cheldric.

"We're outnumbered," Reginald warned.

"By a lot," Odo added bleakly.

"They have no cavalry," Cheldric assured them. "We will smash through their ranks, and our infantry will cut them down before they can reform."

"And the Sun is with us." Reginald gestured to the sky. "I saw a good omen from the birds during my morning prayers."

"Let's hope so," Odo grumbled.

Odo was always grumbling, complaining, or moaning about something. Under other circumstances, Cheldric or Reginald would have made some joke in response, but not now. The killing was about to begin.

Shouting war cries to their gods, the Sudmen began to draw exotic curved swords, axes, and maces. The sound of hundreds of men's feet charging across the dry ground thundered through the valley. Death was about to descend on the battlefield.

Cheldric gave a broad smile. They were now at the perfect distance and position for a cavalry charge. Onyx was a strong, noble steed and would not fail him.

"Once more, old friend?" Cheldric scratched his horse's ear.

Onyx snorted in reply.

"The glory is yours, of course," Cheldric said. "Let's send them to the Abyss!"

Tensing his muscles, Cheldric took a deep breath. His heart was beating with excitement. He dared not let the Sudmen get any closer before the charge. It was time.

"Attack!" Cheldric bellowed, spurring Onyx down to the foe.

With Cheldric leading the charge from the center, at the point of the wedge, the other knights followed a mere second behind their lord, maintaining their wedge formation, while the infantry rushed behind the knights at a full run. The Sudmen braced themselves, but the knights trampled over several ranks, plunging into the middle of the enemy force. Skewering a Sudman, Cheldric's lance cracked and snapped in half from the impact. He drew his sword and began slashing at the enemies around him.

Joining the knights, the Ostman infantry crashed into the Sudman ranks. The Sudmen fell back farther into the valley but were not routed. Hundreds of Sudmen died or were gravely wounded in the first few minutes of fighting, compared with only dozens of casualties from the ranks of the rearguard.

No matter, Cheldric thought as he slashed through another enemy. *They will break. We hold the high ground.*

The killing continued.

Cheldric kept slashing and hacking at the enemies around him. Several of his knights, including Reginald and Odo, now fought on foot with the infantry. The three friends all drifted away from each other as they pursued the enemy deeper into the valley. Personal bravery and feats of arms meant more than order and discipline to these warriors. Yet Cheldric kept a close eye on his friends just as he knew they were watching him. They would not let any harm come to each other.

Narrowly avoiding several strikes and blocking many blows, Cheldric concentrated all his energies on the defense. Even so, a stinging slash throbbed across his knee from an unknown source. Cheldric parried another blow from an enemy blade, but his horse stiffened in the same instant. Onyx gasped one last time and died on the spot.

Hitting the ground with a terrible thud, Cheldric rolled away as his horse fell. With the taste of blood filling his mouth, tears blurred Cheldric's vision. It was not because of his own pain but from the slumped mass that was his dead horse. Huffing with rage, Cheldric got to his feet. With a bloody yell, he cleaved through the Sudman who'd dealt the blow to his horse, and then he dispatched a second and a third enemy. He thirsted for vengeance.

"You killed him!" Cheldric screamed with hot tears streaming down his face.

Cheldric's vision turned red with gore. His fury could not extinguish his pain. He was no stranger to this madness. He gave in willingly.

How many times had Onyx saved his life before? At least as many as Odo and Reginald. That horse had been no ordinary steed. That was how he justified letting the rage consume him.

Both remorse and reason faded. His rage was reckless. Death became the sum of Cheldric's thoughts. All the Sudmen would die at his hands. Or Cheldric would die trying to satisfy his thirst for blood.

The clanging of steel against steel and the cries of the wounded and the dying filled the air as the Sudman army was pushed farther back. Ignoring the bite of a glancing blow to the torso, Cheldric yelled in frustration as he killed another enemy. Even then, he was still agonizing over the loss of Onyx. Yet the Sudmen did not break. Only with that realization did he notice the blood beginning to seep through the tear in his tabard and down his chin. His knee ached from another cut. All his injuries protested at once. His vision clearing, Cheldric winced with each movement. Looking about, his mind began to process the flow of battle. It did not make sense.

The rearguard has the advantage, Cheldric thought; *we did from the very beginning. Why do they still fight?*

"Stubborn lot," Cheldric said as Odo fought his way towards him.

"We are both without horse," Odo replied. "It seems the enemy is under orders to kill all our steeds."

"Why would they do that?" Cheldric asked.

"Could this be a trap?" Odo asked in turn.

Furrowing his brow, Cheldric looked to the valley walls on either side of the battlefield. They were high and steep but not impassable. A chill ran down Cheldric's spine as the enemy's plan dawned on him. Now there was no way to undo what had been done.

Not without heavy casualties.

"We need to withdraw," Odo said, stiffening in apprehension. "We can't go any farther."

"Hold position!" Cheldric shook his head, shouting. "Rally to me!"

Falteringly, the rearguard halted their advance and began to take a defensive stance around Cheldric. The Sudmen stopped withdrawing down into the valley, but did not push farther up either. For a moment, the fighting grew less intense as both sides tried to maintain their positions, each side daring the other to advance.

"Why do we not press forward?" Reginald asked as he approached Cheldric, his voice hoarse.

The Bishop removed his helmet. Wiping sweat from his brow, Reginald leaned against his tall wooden kite shield. His face was pale from the loss of blood from several small wounds covering his body. After a couple deep breaths, he replaced his helmet and stood with his sword and shield at the ready again. Cheldric knew the Bishop was growing more fatigued than he let on. They all were.

The momentary pause was broken by the sound of rushing cavalry above the valley. Orders were shouted in the strange exotic tongue of the Sudmen. Cheldric did not need to know the meaning of their words in order to understand the exchange.

"Because of them!" Cheldric pointed up to the Sudman cavalry that appeared on either side of the valley walls.

Ululating, the Sudman cavaliers galloped into the valley and brandished their swords and lances. Odo and Reginald both looked to Cheldric in desperation as their lord resolutely planted his feet where he stood.

"Spears to the flanks," Cheldric ordered coldly. "Assume square formation."

"We're dead!" Odo exclaimed, watching the enemy cavalry cut into their men.

"Cheldric," Reginald shouted with wide eyes, "blow the horn. Call for reinforcements!"

"No," Cheldric shot back. "Not yet."

The Sudman infantry rushed forward to join the cavalry as they tore through the midst of the rearguard from either side. The Ostmen turned about in confusion as they were attacked from three directions at once. Lashing out at the foe, Cheldric bellowed for his men to keep fighting.

Cheldric bawled. Something had hit him hard in the shoulder, probably a mace. He did not see it. Cheldric's left arm hung limply. His shield only remained attached to him thanks to its enarmes.

Swinging his sword in a wide arc, heedless of the pain, Cheldric sliced through the neck of an enemy steed, causing the rider to fall off. Hot blood and foul stenches covered Cheldric as he stepped past the fallen mount. With a downward thrust, he ended the Sudman rider before the enemy could stand.

Cheldric's mouth grew dry and rancid. His muscles begged for rest, but Cheldric could not yield. Not now.

Another Sudman cavalier charged past Cheldric and sent Reginald spinning as the enemy's lance struck him. Time stopped. For a moment Cheldric lost all feeling in his body as his mind refused to process what he was seeing.

Shocked, Cheldric's gaze would not move from the Bishop's sprawled body as blood oozed from his lifeless form. Not Reginald. Not the Bishop. The image of the

Bishop's sweet old mother back at Roun swept through his mind. What would he say to her?

He would say he avenged her son after he fell gloriously in battle. Cheldric gritted his teeth as his eyes flashed, seeking the culprit. Only more blood would suffice.

Was that Ganelon? Cheldric could have sworn the Sudman cavalier who just rode past bore the traitor's heraldry on his shield. Sure enough, the rider wore Ganelon's armor as well. Cheldric could do nothing. He and Odo were completely surrounded by Sudmen.

"For the gods' sake," Odo pleaded with Cheldric. "Blow the horn!"

But Cheldric no longer heard Odo, nor did he notice his friend wrenching at his tabard. Completely oblivious to the rearguard falling and beginning to scatter in every direction, he continued his attack against the enemy despite his limp arm. Cheldric's eyes were fixed on Ganelon, who seemed to take little interest in the knight's attempt to cut a path to him as Ganelon himself struck down more of Cheldric's men. His pleas ignored, Odo fell in beside his friend and resumed fighting.

"Father?" Godfrey tugged on the Duke's tunic, pulling the man out of the bard's story.

"Yes, Godfrey?" the Duke whispered, leaning toward his son as the bard continued to sing of Cheldric's exploits.

Duke Ulric smiled at his five-year-old son. Godfrey was a thin boy with hazel eyes, pale skin, and brown hair. He was the old Duke's only surviving child. He looked much like Ulric had at his age.

"Why doesn't Cheldric blow the horn?" the boy whispered back with wide eyes. "Won't the King hear it?"

Stroking his greying beard, Ulric pondered his son's question for a moment. He surveyed the banquet guests gathered in Fuetoile Keep's great hall around him. Some were plucking at various trays of food on the tables while others chattered among themselves. It seemed only the youngest and the oldest at the Duke's banquet followed the bard's story with any real interest. Most present had already heard several versions of the story from minstrels, bards, and troubadours who invariably accompanied such feasts.

With a bemused smile, the Duke remembered asking the very same question to his uncle when he was close to Godfrey's age. Some children darted past a servant bringing in a pitcher of wine. Ulric thought perhaps they were playing out the scene the bard was now describing. Or maybe they were wrapped up in a game completely unrelated to the tale. Ulric could not tell. He leaned even closer to his son, so much so that their noses almost touched.

"Are you not learning about chivalry?" the Duke asked. "You tell me."

Godfrey pulled back from his father for a moment. The boy scrunched his face in concentration. He looked to his father, the banquet guests, and then to his mother, who sat with a number of other noble ladies at a distant table. Lost in their own world, they laughed at some joke the Duchess had made. Godfrey's attention then turned to the tapestries hanging from the castle walls.

The tapestries bore the image of a blue shield with a white griffin rampant emblazoned upon it. It was the same symbol that emblazoned Ulric's shield, and would one day emblazon his son's when he became a knight. As Godfrey pondered the tapestry, Ulric vividly recalled the details of how his mother had gone to great lengths in explaining why the griffin was the symbol of his house, House Cretus. Distant ancestors of Ulric's had performed the heroic feat of taming griffins and riding them into battle. It was a dark, barbaric age one of those ancestors fought against before becoming the first duke of Bastogne. The griffin had been the symbol of Ulric's house ever since.

The other armored knights present also wore tabards or surcoats over their chainmail. Their personal heraldries were emblazoned upon them, and the colorful symbols each bore told stories of noble deeds and virtues in addition to familial ties. In that way, each coat of arms represented the legacy of a distant family hero.

"He wants glory?" Godfrey asked, forgetting to whisper.

"Yes," his father hushed Godfrey. "But that's not why he won't blow the horn."

Another befuddled expression crossed Godfrey's face. He was about to ask another question, but the Duke raised his hand, silencing him. True, only a few people were paying the bard any attention. However, Ulric knew that refusing to let a conversation get too loud helped everyone involved— child or adult—pay closer attention to what was actually being said. Giving his son a fleeting smile, Ulric continued to explain the answer to Godfrey.

"Duty," Ulric whispered. "It is Cheldric's duty to fight as hard as he can for the King before he asks for help. How else can Cheldric say he fulfilled his oath?"

Godfrey scrutinized the various banquet guests. At the other end of the table Godfrey and his father sat at was the Duke's lord, Theodoric, the King of Lortharain. The King's retainers and a few other members of the royal family surrounded Theodoric, including a boy about ten years older than Godfrey. That was Prince Wilhelm. Wilhelm seemed to be ignoring something one of the King's retainers was telling him as his eyes lasciviously followed a young maiden.

"Shall it be my duty to fight for Prince Wilhelm?" Godfrey asked hesitantly.

"Your duty shall be to fight for whoever becomes King," the Duke said, as he frowned at Wilhelm's poor efforts to conceal his lust. "But remember this—though you may need to use your sword against your lord's personal enemies as the need arises, above all, use it to destroy the monsters of this world."

"I promise to slay a hundred dragons before I die," Godfrey swore.

"I'm sure you will," his father beamed.

Ulric paused for a moment as his expression grew more serious again.

"Some monsters are easy to see, like trolls or dragons," the Duke continued. "Other monsters look like men."

"How will I know which men are the monsters?" Godfrey asked.

"The men who act like monsters are the monsters," the Duke firmly replied.

Godfrey still appeared confused by this answer, but refrained from asking more questions. The father and son turned their attention back to the bard's story. It had progressed well past Cheldric's heroic death. In fact, the bard was now singing of King Lambert's final lament after avenging his favored vassal's end.

"And when the angel said to Lambert he must now fight the demon-worshipping Nordsmen," the bard sang as he strummed at his lyre. "King Lambert thumped at his breast and replied to the seraph, 'O gods, how weary my life is!' So ends the Tale of Cheldric."

A muffled applause filled the great hall as the performer took a bow. With the bard moving to one of the tables to enjoy some refreshments of his own, the conversation in the great hall grew louder. The striking of pipes, harps, and other musical instruments from the loft only forced the competing speakers' voices louder still.

Friends moved from table to table to learn the latest news from lands both near and far. Young knights flirted with damsels. Old men told their own war stories to capture the attention of some of the children.

For some of the smaller children, the sitting had become too much. They rushed off to play with other children who could not manage to sit through the entirety of the Tale of Cheldric. The smell of roasted meat permeated the hall as servants brought more food in for the feast. King Theodoric stood and began to mingle with the lords and ladies he had not had the chance to speak with before the entertainment had started.

Eagerly, Godfrey tugged at his father's arm once again. Forgetting the conversation he was about to start with one of the King's knights, Ulric turned back to his son. Some things were more important than court intrigue.

"King Lambert will do what the angel told him to?" Godfrey worried.

"Angels are messengers from the gods," Ulric said patiently. "And that is as good as the gods themselves giving Lambert a command."

"But King Lambert sounded tired," Godfrey noted. "Will he be strong enough?"

"King Lambert will do the right thing," Ulric reassured his son. "Just as Cheldric had a duty to the King, so too does the King have a duty to the gods."

Contented with this answer, Godfrey ran off to play with some of the other children his age. Godfrey's mother approached Ulric from the table she had been sitting at. She subtly gestured to Ulric, who rose from his seat. He followed her from the hall into an empty corridor, unnoticed. A servant gingerly stepped past the Duke and the Duchess with a bow, and proceeded into the kitchen for more food and drink. Seeing that he was now alone with his wife, Ulric stepped closer to her.

"Regana." Ulric touched his wife's face, kissing her. "What news from Azgald?"

"Nothing good." Regana shook her head. "The Nordsman clans have been united under a single king."

"And when that king dies they will return to their old ways." Ulric waved dismissively. "We have seen this before."

"Maybe," Regana conceded. "But this new king has also secured the loyalty of some of the orc tribes in the North."

"How do we know?" Ulric set his jaw.

"Because a combined army of orcs and Nordsmen just razed the fortress of Skasgun." Regana tearfully bowed her head. "Matilda d'Artois heard it directly from a herald at the King's court."

"Orcs?" Godfrey cut in.

Ulric and Regana turned in surprise to see their son standing next to them. The Duke and Duchess glanced at each other and then turned back to Godfrey. The boy's expression was mildly curious as it so often was with children his age, but his ability to retain the answers to questions about the world seemed above average for one so small. Ulric knew the sages and monks would love to tutor such a mind and train Godfrey to be a scholar. But as the Duke's only child, Godfrey's formative years would be best spent learning to ride, to fight, and eventually, to lead.

"Orcs are a race of monstrous creatures," Ulric said, with only the slightest strain in his patience showing. "They helped kill off most of the elves and dwarves, and they are only friends with wicked men."

"Then most of the orcs should die since they killed most of the elves and dwarves," Godfrey reasoned. "Why did the orcs kill the elves and dwarves?"

"Because the orc gods only believe in strength." Regana seemed to have difficulty hiding a growing bitterness in her voice. "The orc gods, the Nordsmen gods, and all the other dark gods are in an eternal war with our gods."

"The War in Heaven?" Godfrey asked, apparently remembering the term from a priest's sermon some weeks previous.

"Yes," Regana flatly answered.

Ulric shot Regana a mildly concerned look before turning to Godfrey. The boy would learn of the fate of Skasgun soon enough, but Ulric could see his wife wanted to talk with him about it alone first.

"Godfrey," Ulric began. "I think it is best that you go play with your friends now. Your mother and I need to talk."

Slowly but obediently, Godfrey turned down the corridor back to the great hall and disappeared into the crowd of guests. Ulric and Regana walked farther away from the center of so much activity, in hopes of not being interrupted again.

"Skasgun was no small castle," Ulric murmured. "And Theodoric's reply to that message?"

"The King of Lortharain says he has enough trouble with the orcs in his own lands," Regana reported in a flustered tone. "The Kingdom of Azgald cannot expect Theodoric's banner to go north anytime soon."

"Orcs," Ulric grumbled. "Theodoric is more concerned that half of the duchies would rebel against him while he is away."

"But that fear is not groundless," Regana whispered, as she turned to make sure she and her husband were still alone.

Another servant clattered from the kitchen through the hall with a full tray of beef radiating the scent of herbs and spices mixed with the meat. Subconsciously holding their breath, the Duke and Duchess watched him pass. The Duke trusted both his knights and common servants, but spies were not unheard of in Lortharain.

"The King of Lortharain has nothing to fear from the Duchy of Bastogne," Ulric inflexibly whispered after the servant had passed. "I sadly cannot say the same for all the duchies."

"You do not think Theodoric will really let Azgald fall to orcs and murderous barbarians?" Regana gasped.

"Azgald has been slowly declining for many years." Ulric scowled.

"Azgald does not have enough knights." Regana became more defensive. "It is because there are too many cowards in this world who will not help their nominal allies. Perhaps if a crusade were called…"

"Even Skasgun's destruction is not a loss catastrophic enough to stir much enthusiasm for a crusade these days," Ulric grimly confided.

He took a step forward and embraced her as she began to sob into his shoulder. Her body shook violently as she cried, though the Duchess' weeping was all but silent. Ulric stood there, holding her until she pulled away, staring at him with reddened eyes.

"I am sorry about your brother." Ulric caressed Regana's face. "He was a very strong and brave knight. Skasgun could have asked for no better castellan. I am sure the fortress did not fall easily with him leading the defenses."

"With Badian gone and you getting old, I am afraid there will soon be no brave men left." She bit her tongue, visibly fighting back more tears.

The two stood silently for a moment. Ulric remembered seeing his wife for the first time up in Azgald. She was so young and fair then; no worries to spoil her beautiful face. He caught a glimpse of a small griffin pendant on a silver chain around her neck. It was an ancient family heirloom. Ulric had given it to her early on in their courtship. So much time had passed since then. Happy memories had been made in those years, but there had been much sorrow too.

Ulric was sure Regana had never forgiven him for taking her from her home, even after all this time. Her brother, Badian, and her mother had been less than thrilled with the news that Ulric was taking his new bride back south to Bastogne. No number of gifts could soften that blow.

Azgald needed knights like Ulric. He knew this. He had been told as much in years past. Azgald's enemies were many and her friends few, but that was not enough to convince Ulric to stay in Azgald with his bride. Instead, Regana came to Lortharain, bringing along only her beautiful Azgaldian accent from her native land. Ulric's inheritance was in Lortharain. Bastogne was home.

Once, Azgald had been a large and prosperous realm to the north, but those days only lived in the memories of Ulric's oldest peers, he mused. And even they were young when that was true. Wars were lost and good kings died. Azgald never fully recovered. It had so few knights and men-at-arms even at the height of its power. Ulric brooded over the thought of no brave men left.

"You should see our son's eyes light up when he hears stories like the tale of Cheldric." Ulric half-smiled. "I would not say the world is without hope yet."

Chapter Two

Twelve Years Later...

Swinging his sword, Godfrey parried the blow of the older knight before him. The man advanced on the young squire, striking a second, third, and fourth time. Narrowly dodging each attack in turn, Godfrey lashed out at his attacker. The man easily sidestepped Godfrey's blade and struck the back of Godfrey's head with the pommel of his own sword.

Falling forward, the squire tumbled to the ground. Godfrey silently cursed. This was not the first time this had happened to him today, and Godfrey had no one to blame but himself. Why would he expect a different result if he kept falling into the same trap again and again?

Godfrey breathed heavily, rolling onto his back. Trees reaching towards the sky filled his vision. The ground was cold and wet. He attempted to stand as quickly as he could, but the knight's sword was at his neck, freezing him to the spot.

"That's enough for now," the knight said, sheathing his weapon.

The scent of damp decaying leaves infused Godfrey's mailed gloves as he pushed himself up off the ground. He removed his spangenhelm, panting as sweat beaded on his forehead. He handed the sword he had been drilling with to one of the men-at-arms who had been watching him spar, but he refused to meet the other man's eyes. The man-at-arms was an older warrior named Bruno with scars from dozens of battles dominating his features. Though Bruno was a common soldier, Godfrey respected the veteran's wisdom and had been stung by his keen rebuke more than once.

Perhaps sensing Godfrey's embarrassment, Bruno withheld his criticism. Godfrey was already silently rebuking himself enough for both of them. Bruno could see that much, Godfrey was sure.

The other man-at-arms observing the sparring match was equally barrel-chested, but a good twenty years younger than Bruno. His name was Fulcher, and if he lived another twenty years he would probably look just as Bruno did now. Godfrey had come to believe that aside from age, the only thing that distinguished Fulcher from Bruno was Fulcher's uncanny hunting skills.

In front of Godfrey, his cousin Fallard, the older knight he had been sparring with, watched dark billowing clouds approach from the distance. Fallard was a man in his early thirties with dark hair and pale skin who always wore a serious expression around Godfrey. He had grown accustomed to this over the last twelve years, first as Fallard's page then as his squire.

"Your technique is still sloppy," Fallard commented distractedly as he watched the clouds slowly grow darker.

"It grows sloppy through fatigue," Godfrey refuted. "Anyone would begin to feel tired after so many hours of practice."

"And that is exactly when an enemy sword will find your neck," Fallard answered. "You must always be on your guard. Training is as much about perseverance as it is brute strength and skill with weapons."

"You are right," Godfrey grumbled, bowing his head. "I should have exercised more caution."

"Try to watch your opponent's movements more carefully." Fallard pointed to Godfrey's eyes. "Anticipate where he will step, notice how he holds his weapon, imagine where he will try to strike."

"I know." Godfrey waved his hand in annoyance. "I know. I just get tired. That's all. I know what to do."

"Bruno…" Fallard turned to his retainer. "What should a young impetuous squire do in the heat of battle when he grows tired?"

"Well lord," Bruno replied thoughtfully. "It depends on the course of battle. If the battle goes well, it would be practical for the squire to retire to the rear of the line. Though it may be without glory he will at least be alive."

"And if the battle goes poorly?" Godfrey asked, rolling his eyes.

"Then he will fight to the last breath," Fallard answered, meeting Godfrey's gaze in a stern reprimand. "Neither will he take one step backwards. That is where both duty and glory lie. Understood?"

Godfrey nodded meekly, recognizing his error. Thinking back to all the poems and tales he had been told as a small boy, he knew how closely linked the concepts of duty and glory were. Even as a squire he had witnessed these concepts put to the test. He had seen Fallard in the midst of a group of mounted knights smashing through a horde of shambling zombies. He remembered how one knight fell from his horse and his squire rushed in to the rescue. That squire was knighted the same day at the battle's end once the necromancer controlling the undead had been slain.

Other images from that same battle against the necromancer made Godfrey's hand tremble. He wished he could forget those sights. Biting his lip, Godfrey forced his hand to stop shaking, and his mind concentrated on the present. There was no sense in talking about those memories. He needed to focus on the present and the future, not the past.

More than anything, Godfrey wanted to discard the red tabard and shield of his cousin, and replace it with the blue of his father's line. Though his cousin's shield and tabard also bore the white griffin rampant like Godfrey's father, Duke Ulric, Godfrey could not wear the heraldry of his father until he was knighted. As a squire, Godfrey was required to wear the colors of his cousin, signaling his subordinate role to Fallard just as Fallard's men-at-arms did.

"When shall we know when I have trained enough to become a knight?" Godfrey asked. "I have seen battle. I have even defended castle walls. When will I have proven myself?"

"I think that day will come soon." Fallard nodded. "You have a stout heart and are coming of age. When a suitable quest presents itself; that is when you will face your final test."

Godfrey's spirit immediately lifted. All this time, all this training, and all the journeying across the whole of the Kingdom of Lortharain; Fallard thought Godfrey had learned enough to soon be knighted. All that remained was one final test.

"What will that test be?" Godfrey asked.

"Some things we cannot know until they are upon us," Fallard conceded. "But we will know when the time comes."

Godfrey frowned. Maybe he would not be knighted so soon after all. With a sigh, he put the idea to rest for the moment.

"Well," Fallard said. "The Sun is beginning to set. We should find a place to sleep."

With that, Godfrey and the men-at-arms began to load up their belongings in satchels, packs, and saddlebags. Putting the saddlebags on Fallard's horse, they themselves carried the smaller packs and satchels. Fallard mounted his horse as he fastened his own satchel to his belt. Not every aspect of life as a knight and his entourage was filled with romantic adventures, Godfrey reminded himself through these mundane chores.

The group wearily made its way from the outskirts of the woods to a nearby gravel road. The path was well-used, but its paving stones had been broken up through centuries of neglect. It was an ancient ruin from a time long forgotten during the reign of the elves. Though most of the elves had long since retreated to distant forests and the far North, some of the remains of the buildings and roads of their old empire still endured.

Fallard's horse's hooves clopped rhythmically against the road as the group moved on. The slow steady beat reminded Godfrey of the breathing of a cyclops he had once faced in a castle siege. He envisioned the creature in his mind's eye. It was nine feet tall with tusks as thick as spear shafts. Only a ragged loincloth covered any of the beast's body. Its thick skin was protection enough. The monster had him pinned to the ground with its massive forearms after killing two other men defending the castle. Its putrid green flesh stank of filth Godfrey did not care to think about. Its rancid breath wafted down to Godfrey's face in short puffs like the clopping of horses' hooves.

Godfrey was lucky. Just as the cyclops was about to smash in Godfrey's skull, a trio of soldiers fired their crossbows at the hulking beast. Two of the bolts found their way into the cyclops' neck as the other stuck harmlessly out of the meat of its shoulder. One would have been enough to bring down the cyclops after striking its comparatively vulnerable neck. It was only through the actions of those commoners that Godfrey was still alive. He would be slow to forget the debt he owed them. Could Godfrey handle such a monster if he was asked to face one alone?

Most squires were customarily given the task of slaying dangerous beasts such as trolls, hydras, or other such creatures as their final quest before becoming knights. There was no shortage of monsters in the world that needed to be brought down. Many squires died in the attempt. Many other squires elected to remain in their positions indefinitely rather than face such trials. Could he succeed where so many others failed miserably or flinched?

A gust of wind picked up, pushing the distant clouds closer and closer. What little sunlight remained disappeared behind the clouds as rain began to patter against Godfrey's chainmail and spangenhelm, chilling the steel. The cooling rain soothed Godfrey's aching body after the day's training.

"Who says the rain god is fickle?" Godfrey sighed, stretching his arms out to catch as much of the rain as he could. "Broxe, shower us with your blessings."

Thunder rumbled overhead and the downpour intensified. Godfrey lowered his arms and began to sulk as the whole group was drenched from head to toe.

"Well you did ask for it, didn't you?" Fulcher jibed at Godfrey.

Everyone chuckled at the irony of the moment as they continued down the road.

They walked another hour or so in the dark storm. Though at first Godfrey welcomed the cool rain, he was not enjoying it nearly as much now. His soaked feet were growing cold and numb. His mind turned to brooding, and he only just kept his complaints to himself. Finally, he saw the lights of a town set on a hill not far off, and breathed a heavy sigh of relief.

"Not much farther now," Fallard assured his cousin.

A wooden palisade encircled most of the buildings of the town. A few huts and shops sat on the outside of the palisade near the road, but the majority of them were crammed inside the walls. Drawing nearer to the town, Godfrey figured that the owners of those few buildings on the outside of the wall must have been brave, foolish, or both if they were not simply too poor to afford housing within the safety of the town walls.

"This place is called Harv, right?" Godfrey asked.

"You have been studying your geography." Fallard raised an eyebrow. "Can you tell me who the lords of this town are?"

"No, sire." Godfrey blushed.

"The clergy." Fallard pointed to a shrine at the top of the hill. "You can always tell who or what is most important in a place by its position."

"Because the center of the town is most secure," Godfrey noted.

"Exactly." Fallard smiled in agreement.

The shrine at the top of the hill did not appear nearly as impressive to Godfrey as the great temples of the Southern duchies of Lortharain. True, Godfrey's home was in these Northwestern realms of Lortharain, but his travels across the kingdom had opened his eyes to just how varied the wider world could be.

The shrine was built of plain grey stone which lacked the highly polished columns or intricate gilding of the Southern temples. However, the columns, gilding, and statues of the Southern temples only concealed the fact that the structures were ancient, and in some cases in a greater state of disrepair than the more modest rural shrines of the North like the one overlooking Harv. Perhaps things were not better in the South, but each region just had different problems, Godfrey mused.

"But the priests don't hold lands or titles in my father's estates." Godfrey gave Fallard a puzzled look.

"Ah but they do," Fallard answered. "Maybe not Uncle Ulric's personal chaplain you've seen at the castle, but some of your father's vassals are priests who command knights of their own. That's in addition to any lesser priests and acolytes that might also fall under them."

"It all sounds so complicated," Godfrey said. "How does anyone keep it all straight?"

"Courtly matters can be complicated sometimes," Fallard admitted. "Sometimes a knight might even have more than one lord of equal rank. Things can get very complicated should those two lords ever be at odds with each other."

"I think Lortharain's lords would do better focusing their energies on fighting monsters than worrying about each other." Godfrey kicked a rock for emphasis.

"So do I." Fallard shook his head.

"But some men are monsters," Bruno cut in. "They need to be dealt with just as much as the orcs do."

"My father told me that same thing once," Godfrey said, recalling a banquet back home many years prior.

"Dukes are rarely fools," Fulcher added. "They usually either serve a monster or have a few monsters of their own in their service."

Godfrey frowned at this thought. He knew it was true, but he did not like to think that any of his father's knights or the barons and counts who paid homage to the Duke of Bastogne were bad people. Other barons, counts, and knights in Lortharain might be monsters, but not in Bastogne. Certainly no knight of Bastogne would ever prove disloyal.

The group had reached the gate to the palisade. A pair of sentries atop the wall pointed lantern light down on them before Bruno could knock on the gate. Another pair of guards atop the wall rushed over to the first before Godfrey even noticed their approach.

"Not another step closer!" one of the sentries shouted as he aimed a crossbow down at the group.

"Who goes there?" asked one of the other guards as he drew his own crossbow.

"Sir Fallard," Godfrey's cousin answered in a measured tone. "These are my retainers and my squire. Why are you so wary tonight?"

"There have been some disappearances," one of the sentries with the lanterns started. "A couple of unusual deaths have happened here too. Rumor has it there is dark magic afoot."

"One of those deaths occurred just yesterday," added the first sentry with the crossbow. "The Bishop has been called in from Vosg to help investigate."

"Please," Fallard said. "I am Duke Ulric's nephew, and his son, Godfrey, is my squire. Let us talk with the Bishop and see what we can do to help."

The sentries muttered to themselves for a moment. At the exciting news of death and dark magic, Godfrey quickly forgot how tired he felt. Looking to Fallard, he tried to gauge what his cousin was thinking, but his expression was hard to read in the dark. Fulcher huffed impatiently while Bruno squinted as rain dripped from the brim of his kettle helmet onto the bridge of his nose. They were all beginning to shiver with cold.

"All right," the lead sentry with the lantern finally said after consulting with the other guards. "They are at the shrine now. Make straight for it."

The gate opened with a creak, and Godfrey followed his cousin and the men-at-arms. The homes and shops glowed in eerie hues of yellow and orange from the dim light of the occasional lantern in town. The gravel road had given way to a slick muddy path as the group climbed the hill to the top of the town.

Upon reaching the shrine, Fallard dismounted his horse and handed the reins to Bruno. The men-at-arms led Fallard's horse to a nearby stable, and Godfrey followed his cousin up to the doors of the shrine. As Fallard opened them, light flooded out into the night from the shrine's interior, and murmuring voices echoed from inside. To Godfrey, the voices were muffled. He was not sure what to expect inside.

"Hail, Bishop." Fallard announced his presence as he entered the shrine.

Following just behind Fallard, Godfrey bowed his head before he even saw who it was he was bowing to. Upon raising his head, Godfrey saw several people inside the anteroom of the shrine. Some wore fine clergymen's robes while others wore the armor and heraldry of the town guard. Godfrey thought a third group appeared to be a family, based on their similar appearances. He guessed they must have been part of the local aristocracy, since they were neither dressed as the clergy nor in the uniforms of the town guards. The Bishop, dressed in the most ornate of the clergymen's robes, beckoned Fallard towards him from beyond the anteroom as he was speaking with what looked like some other clergymen and soldiers.

"Wait here," Fallard told Godfrey as he brushed past the people gathered in the anteroom.

Somewhat at a loss for what to do, Godfrey stopped in his tracks. He removed his spangenhelm and tucked it under his arm before looking around to the others gathered around him. Most were soberly talking among themselves and paid little attention to Godfrey. After a moment, he caught the eye of a blonde boy in a simple tunic and acolyte's robes, not much younger than Godfrey.

"What's going on here?" Godfrey whispered to the boy as he approached him.

"They're getting ready for a funeral tomorrow," the acolyte replied. "A girl was killed last night."

The boy gestured over past the Bishop in the shrine's chapel. A closed wooden casket lay in front of the altar. An older man and woman stood near the coffin, silently staring at nothing in particular. Wanting more details, Godfrey stepped closer to the acolyte.

"How was she killed?" Godfrey asked.

"I think it was a vampire," the acolyte whispered.

"Why do you think that?" Godfrey whispered back, turning to face the coffin again.

"I saw a bite mark on her neck," the boy said, barely able to conceal his excitement. "The Bishop wouldn't tell me he thought so too. But I've been studying undead. Every acolyte has to know about that stuff before they become priests or priestesses; and the mark looked just like the drawings in the books I've been reading. I think the Bishop just doesn't want to cause a panic in the village or something."

"He might be right about that," Godfrey replied after thinking it over. "I am Godfrey, by the way."

"Walaric." The acolyte shook Godfrey's hand. "You are a squire?"

"For a little longer at least," Godfrey answered. "My liege says as soon as I complete my final quest as a squire, I can be knighted."

"What quest is that?" Walaric asked with apparent interest.

"I don't know yet," Godfrey admitted. "I have not been given it yet."

"Maybe you could find the vampire," Walaric suggested. "Then you could destroy it and save Harv from any more attacks."

"Vampires have all sorts of black magic." Godfrey shifted his weight nervously. "They couldn't expect a simple squire like me to kill one of those things."

"It was just a thought." Walaric shrugged dismissively.

"You said you were studying to become a priest?" Godfrey changed the subject. "What god did you claim as your patron?"

"I haven't picked one yet," Walaric answered. "It would have to be one of the celestial gods or goddesses. Nature deities tend to stay neutral in the War in Heaven unless provoked. And I'd rather not be neutral. Fortune is a fickle goddess, and I have been unlucky enough in my life… Do you have a patron deity or do you just worship the celestial pantheon as a whole?"

"My family venerates the whole pantheon but we have always worshipped the Sun god, Loxias, in particular," Godfrey explained. "He and his sister, Luna, are the greatest champions against evil."

"I have always liked Luna," Walaric added. "The Moon is ever a light in otherwise dark places."

"Amen," Godfrey and Walaric said simultaneously as they crossed their hearts.

"Perhaps she will be my patroness." Walaric considered the possibility aloud.

The squire nodded his approval. Fallard signaled for him, and Godfrey turned to join his cousin. The Bishop was talking to the other clergymen with him while the soldiers listened with interest. The older couple had moved towards the group as if to join in the conversation, but they remained passive observers. As he remembered Walaric's suggestion about destroying the vampire, Godfrey's heart raced and his hand began to twitch. He tried to calm himself. How could he be sure Walaric actually saw what he thought he did? Walaric was just an acolyte and could not know if it was really a vampire.

"Good to meet you," Godfrey told Walaric as he briefly turned back to the acolyte.

"You as well," Walaric answered with a wave.

The squire's head was still spinning as he approached Fallard, the Bishop, and the others. Fulcher and Bruno had also made their way to Fallard's side while Godfrey had been speaking to the acolyte, but he had not noticed them until now. How was he going to kill a vampire? The more Godfrey tried to talk himself out of believing he would have to face a vampire, the more convinced he became that was exactly what he would have to do.

"Bishop…" Fallard gestured to Godfrey. "This is my squire, Godfrey. He is the son of Duke Ulric. Godfrey, this is Bishop Clovis."

"I know your father well." Bishop Clovis stepped closer to Godfrey. "He was a fierce warrior in his day and is still renowned as one of the most chivalrous dukes in all of Lortharain. Sir Fallard tells me his son lives up to his father's reputation."

"My lord boasts." Godfrey awkwardly bowed. "I am still a simple squire."

"Not for much longer," the Bishop interjected. "As you know, I have been called down here to investigate a series of unusual murders. The daughter of Lord and Lady Eist is only the latest victim."

The Bishop gestured to one of the soldiers, who then stepped forward. In addition to the heraldry of the town guard, he wore the badge of a constable. His grey hair and piercing eyes marked him as a nocturnal predator ever patrolling the shadows.

"Disappearances among the farmers that live outside the palisade are an unfortunate but regular occurrence," the constable started in an icy, calculated tone. "It's usually no more than a few every year. A monster wanders out of the forest and eats an unsuspecting shepherd watching his flocks in the night. A bandit sneaks into a peasant's hut and murders him in his sleep. There's not much anyone can do about those incidents. But for the last few months, not only have the murders and disappearances outside the wall increased, we have also had about a dozen deaths inside the town. Increasing patrols both in the town and along the palisade have not yielded a culprit yet."

"Pardon me for asking," Godfrey inquired hesitantly. "But why hasn't anyone searched the surrounding woods or marshes and swamps yet?"

"Normally my authority does not extend beyond the wall," the constable explained.

"We were discussing the possibility of authorizing a patrol to be sent out of Harv," Clovis added. "Then you came, and Sir Fallard made an alternate proposal."

"Godfrey," Fallard spoke up. "Bishop Clovis believes that a vampire is what has been killing the townsfolk."

"That is what the acolyte I was talking to thought," Godfrey answered, finally accepting Walaric's insight.

"Walaric is a smart boy," Clovis acknowledged. "He will make a fine priest one day. But his future is not what we are talking about now."

Straightening up to his full height, the Bishop took a few steps back from Godfrey. The entire shrine went silent with a wave of his hand. All eyes were on Clovis. Godfrey's heart was pounding. He had to focus all his thoughts on his hand to stop it from shaking. Now that the moment was here, he was unsure if he could survive the attempt at all, much less fulfill his quest.

What other response could Godfrey give? Could he refuse this quest? If he somehow could say he was not ready yet, there would not be any guarantee that the next potential quest would be any easier. Then there was the dishonor of turning down the chance to fight against evil. He could not back down. Monsters were to be destroyed.

"Godfrey," the Bishop pronounced with a loud voice. "Son of Ulric, the Duke of Bastogne, a great evil is upon the town of Harv. A vampire has killed the fair damsel, Gwen, the daughter of Lord and Lady Eist, and is believed to be responsible for the deaths of many other innocents. Do you accept the charge to find and vanquish the monster that has caused so much pain and suffering?"

Godfrey hesitated for a moment; his tongue felt heavy. Words refused to form in his mouth. Everyone's attention had turned from the Bishop to Godfrey. A moment passed in silence. Then, Lady Eist stepped forward with tears streaming down her face. It was the first time Godfrey had seen her or Lord Eist broken from their trance-like state.

"Please, young squire," Lady Eist begged. "No mother should have to endure what I have. No father should have to go through what my husband has. If you can avenge my daughter's death, how many parents will you have saved from such grief?!"

Godfrey solemnly nodded. There was only one response to this charge. He could not back down. How could he have ever thought differently, even for a moment?

"I accept this charge and vow to fulfill the proposed quest," Godfrey answered for all to hear.

A cheer erupted through the shrine. Lady Eist found her husband's embrace. The constable nodded approvingly to Godfrey, and Walaric raised his fist with a broad grin. Bruno and Fulcher started a round of applause that filled the shrine. Fallard, however, maintained his sober demeanor even as he applauded Godfrey. Bishop Clovis once again waved for silence.

"Having accepted this quest," Clovis said, "you will be released from it only upon successful completion or death."

"I understand," Godfrey replied. "And I set out for death or glory at first light."

Another wave of congratulations washed over Godfrey. When it had died down, the crowd began to disperse. The town guard left for their posts and the nobles left for their manors. The small group of priests briefly remained to speak with the Bishop and Fallard before they too retired. Still beaming with excitement, Walaric approached Godfrey.

"I am to show you to your room," Walaric said. "Your party will be lodging here in the shrine tonight."

Walaric led Godfrey out of the chapel to a set of stairs. Torches filled the stairwell with the smell of sweet oil. Chattering about how he had never witnessed a squire receive such an incredible quest before, Walaric ascended the stairs at a meandering pace. Those who slew monsters of such power were considered living legends. Godfrey's mind, however, hovered around one question no one seemed to think to tell him the answer to.

"That's all well and good," Godfrey said, dismissing Walaric's last comment, which he was not really listening to anyway. "But how am I going to kill this vampire after I find it?"

"Oh…" Walaric paused as they reached the top of the stairs.

Caught off guard, Walaric stared from Godfrey to the hallway on the upper level they had reached. It was lit by soft yellow candles. The hall was narrow but long, with several doors leading into bedrooms on either side. The smell of recently burned incense lingered in the corridor. Apprehensively waiting for a reply, Godfrey watched Walaric ponder the question.

"There are loads of ways you could destroy a vampire," Walaric answered at last. "Anything arcane like a spell or a magic weapon could easily do the trick. I'm not exactly an expert though. I'm still an acolyte."

"But I'm not a wizard and I don't have any magic weapons," Godfrey protested. "I don't even know anyone who knows a wizard or has ever seen a magic weapon. Do you?"

"No," Walaric confessed. "But the Bishop knows lots of people in the kingdom. Maybe he knows a wizard. Vampires also fear holy relics. Do you have anything like a blessed medallion or amulet?"

"No." Godfrey bluntly shook his head.

"That would be a problem," Walaric said as he started down the hall. "But your lord would not have proposed this quest if he didn't think you could do it. There must be another way. You'll see."

"Maybe he and the Bishop are discussing a plan downstairs right now," Godfrey thought aloud, following Walaric. "Or they're searching through the shrine's reliquaries for some magical item. You're right. They wouldn't send me to certain death."

The thought was desperate. Godfrey was not entirely convinced it was true, but he could not rationalize another alternative that saw him surviving a horror like a vampire. Vampires were supposed to be stronger and faster than mortal men. Each was a practitioner of dark magic. They were rare but rightly feared. Even those well-prepared to face a vampire were still at great risk.

"See…" Walaric stopped in front of a door, ignorant of Godfrey's troubled expression. "You were worried over nothing."

Opening the bedroom door, Walaric motioned for Godfrey to enter. The room was small and sparsely decorated with only a single table, chair, and a plain unadorned bed, but Godfrey was not concerned with the austere trappings of the room. With weary footfalls, he stepped into the room.

"I'll pray for you all the same," Walaric added while closing the door.

"Right," Godfrey replied as the door shut in front of Walaric.

Godfrey was alone now. The rain still pattered against the roof above. He stared blankly at the alabaster wall, taking in the evening's events. He nodded to himself, his confidence growing. He could do this. By the gods, he could do this.

May no one sing a shameful song about me, Godfrey thought.

Chapter Three

Godfrey woke up early the next morning. His senses were heightened in apprehension of what was to come. What was Fallard's plan? Could Godfrey slay the vampire even with the best plan possible? He could not go back to sleep if he wanted to.

Dressing quickly, Godfrey pulled his hauberk over his tunic. He put on his arming cap then threw his chainmail coif over it. Next, he slid his tabard over the hauberk, and then he tied his belt over the tabard. He hoped he would have more than his armor to protect him.

The room was cool in the early morning light, but was also sticky with humidity from the previous night's rain. Kneeling, Godfrey silently muttered a quick prayer for protection and success, to Loxias and whatever other gods might be listening to him. He was going to need the gods' help more now than at any other time in his life so far.

Slinging his shield over his back, Godfrey then put on his mailed gloves and boots, and grabbed his spangenhelm. Taking one final look around the room, he made sure nothing was left behind. His satchel was still sitting at the foot of the bed. He grabbed it, undid the knot in his belt, and ran the satchel's loops through the belt before retying the knot. Now he had everything.

Godfrey stepped back in mild surprise as he opened the door. Bishop Clovis stood in the doorway waiting for him. The smell of incense from the morning prayers clung to the Bishop.

"Ah yes," Clovis said, nodding to himself. "I was hoping you would be up by now. I would like to have a word with you before you embark on your quest."

"Of course," Godfrey replied as he came into the hall, closing the door behind him.

Clovis led Godfrey to the opposite end of the hall from the stairs he had gone up the night before. A million possibilities fluttered through Godfrey's mind as he wondered what the Bishop wanted. They reached the end of the hall. Clovis opened the door in front of him, revealing a small sanctuary. Its walls were lined with bookcases and shallow alcoves containing numerous holy texts. A musty smell filled Godfrey's nostrils, suggesting just how old many of the books were. Would one of these tomes tell Godfrey how to slay a vampire?

Some of the texts included common prayer books, the creation myths, and the deeds of the great heroes. Other books had more obscure titles, including the hagiographies of minor saints, proverbs of ancient prophets, and the philosophical musings of long-dead theologians. If there were an answer about how to destroy vampires in one of these books or codices, Godfrey would not have the slightest clue where to begin looking.

There was a single small, round window high up on the opposite wall from the entrance to the sanctuary. From it, a shaft of light poured down onto an altar in the center of the room. A brass basin filled with water sat on the altar. Holy water. Every building dedicated to the gods had a limited supply—from the grandest temple to the smallest shrine.

"Bishop," Godfrey asked, "how am I going to kill the vampire when I find it?"

"Courage and faith," Clovis answered sagely. "It is how all great deeds are done."

Godfrey was not satisfied with that answer.

"But the great heroes and the saints and prophets," Godfrey started. "They were all so strong and had the help of the gods or magic, while I am just a squire."

"Is that so?" Clovis smirked. "Every hero has a beginning. You must learn to trust in your own abilities eventually."

"But against a vampire," Godfrey protested. "I am not sure if I'm ready. I don't think it will be a fair challenge."

"Much in life is not fair." The Bishop shook his head. "I often reflect on how unfair Cheldric's lot was in the bards' songs. Yet he did not complain or shrink from his duty."

"Yes…" Godfrey flushed at the reprimand. "But Cheldric also wasn't real."

"Perhaps not." Clovis absently scratched his ear. "But you are real even if Cheldric is not, and you have the power to emulate his good deeds. Name a squire or knight who has not been inspired by such stories."

Godfrey thought on this for a moment. The Bishop was right. Godfrey had a duty. He had to trust himself and the gods. He could do this.

"I suppose you are right." Godfrey smiled.

"Even so," Clovis continued. "The gods do not abandon the faithful."

Clovis moved to the other side of the altar and faced Godfrey. Beckoning him forward, the Bishop gestured for Godfrey to kneel at the foot of the altar. The squire reverently complied.

"This is holy water." Clovis stressed each word as he dipped his finger in the basin. "It has been set apart to bless the gods' servants, and protect them from corrupting influences as they set out to do the will of the divine. Do you believe the gods can bless you?"

"Yes," Godfrey answered without hesitation.

The Bishop drew a horizontal line with his wet finger across Godfrey's forehead as he began reciting an incantation in an ancient language Godfrey did not understand. It was the celestial tongue. Few outside of the clergy knew it anymore.

At first, Godfrey did not feel any different, but near the end of the ritual, peace washed through the squire's mind. His doubts about the quest receded to the back of some faraway corner. What remained was clarity of purpose.

"Thank you, Bishop," Godfrey said, rising to his feet at the end of the incantation.

"Now go forth and conquer in the name of all that is just and true," the Bishop commanded Godfrey.

Godfrey's chainmail hauberk grew increasingly heavy as he sloshed through the foggy swamp. His feet sank into mud past his ankles with every step, and he almost fell into small pools of murky water a couple of times thanks to unseen tree roots. The putrid smell of something rotten permeated the air. The walk had left him soaked, raw, and tired, but he did not complain to Fallard, Bruno, or Fulcher.

Fallard rode his barded horse just ahead of Godfrey, and Bruno and Fulcher followed on foot behind the squire as they carried their spears. The day's journey had caked them all in mud, and everyone's agitation was obvious to Godfrey. He tried to recall how he felt during the Bishop's blessing. But the memory of how he felt then was elusive in this miserable place.

Monolithic trees cast dark shadows through the mist. They gave Godfrey the impression of people standing in the middle of a field at random intervals. Godfrey's heart jumped once or twice as he mistook a tree for some monster reaching through the mist, furthering the feeling that the swamp was alive and that they were being watched or followed.

"What are we searching for?" Godfrey asked.

"A castle," Fallard replied. "The Bishop told me that some years ago a mad lord built a castle in this swamp. It is believed that he fell to worship of the dark gods before killing himself and his household. Such a being in league with the darkness could have risen again as a vampire."

"That doesn't sound like a bad place to start looking at least," Godfrey answered. "But once we find it, how am I going to kill it?"

Fallard did not respond. A knot in Godfrey's stomach began to twist and his hand began to shake. He was unsure when his hand first began to tremble like this. It was some days or weeks after that first battle he had taken part in. He was fourteen or so at the time. There was a lot that had happened there that he could not purge from his memory. He had gotten used to the sights, sounds, and smells of battle. Blood and gore did not move him. The screams and moans of the dying could be tuned out. The undead, though, had shown Godfrey how terrifying the unknown and unnatural could be when the smell of living flesh brought them to frenzy.

Did Fallard not have a plan after all? Godfrey looked to Bruno and Fulcher, who also acted as if he had not said anything. Why were they all ignoring this question? Godfrey stopped in his tracks and was about to voice his concern when Fallard tensed.

"Hold." Fallard raised his hand as he stopped his horse.

The others waited just behind Fallard as he peered into the mist. The dark rectangular stone keep made Godfrey's heart begin to pound in his chest. There were gaps large enough for Godfrey to walk through in the crumbled wall. Its towers were in ruins, but it was what lurked inside that he dreaded. Turning around, Fallard gave his cousin a humorless smile.

"Squire," Fallard addressed Godfrey, waving him forward.

Calming his nerves, Godfrey took a few steps toward his cousin. He could do this. He knew he could. He remembered the Bishop's blessing. After this he would be knighted. Harv would be saved, and he would be the one to do it.

"Yes, sire?" Godfrey replied.

Godfrey and Fallard's tone was formal in this exchange. Even now, in this fetid swamp, there was a certain amount of ritual to be observed. It was an ancient tradition. The knight was to give his final instructions and send his squire to conquer or die.

May no one sing a shameful song about me, Godfrey repeated in his mind.

"You can feel the evil of this place?" Fallard asked, pointing to the keep.

"Yes, my lord." Godfrey nodded, clearing a lump in his throat.

"It was twelve years ago that I took you from your father's hall to train you as a knight," Fallard said. "Now look at you, a squire as worthy as any I have ever seen. If you return from that castle alive with the vampire's head, your quest for knighthood will be complete."

Godfrey's face went pale, and though he wished to be brave and go inside the castle, his feet remained firmly planted where they were. That nervous twitch ran through his hand again. By the gods, how he hated that twitch. He could not move, and his mouth was completely dry.

Fallard watched his cousin for a moment. The knight closed his eyes and slowly exhaled. Godfrey's embarrassment burned almost as hot as his fear was cold. He knew Fallard had expected this. The shame. Godfrey cast his own eyes down at his feet, willing them to move. They would not. He could not bear to look at either of Fallard's retainers. Reluctantly, Godfrey's gaze found Fallard again.

Opening his eyes again, Fallard dismounted his horse. He pulled a sword in its scabbard from his saddle pack. Godfrey flinched, but Fallard handed the weapon to the seventeen-year-old squire. The squire's fear vanished, and was replaced by curiosity.

"This sword has been enchanted by a great wizard," Fallard explained. "It looks like an ordinary blade, but against the undead it holds great power. Use it to cut off the vampire's head, and you will have saved countless lives. I cannot do this for you. Now may the gods bless you. Go."

Godfrey took the sword, and slipped its scabbard through a leather frog on his belt. He breathed a sigh of relief. There was a plan. Fallard was not sending him off to die. Bruno and Fulcher both nodded to Godfrey, and he returned the gesture. He walked towards the castle's keep awkwardly at first, but as he did he gradually found his courage. He thought on his cousin's words as he got closer. This was not just about becoming a knight. This was about being brave, saving people, and doing the will of the gods.

"But then that's what becoming a knight is about," Godfrey said to himself aloud as he reached the castle wall.

Fallard and the two men-at-arms were now obscured by the mists as Godfrey walked through a large gap in the wall. The earth was firmer inside the castle courtyard, and it was only then that he realized the keep was on a small hill. Despite the castle's advantageous position, it still only overlooked a fog-covered swamp. Godfrey wondered if its purpose was not to lay claim to this decayed land, but instead to remain hidden where few would venture.

The sound of toads croaking and insects buzzing, which had surrounded Godfrey in the swamp up to this point, was ominously absent inside the castle walls. Yes, this castle was meant to hide fell deeds from prying eyes. The twitch returned to Godfrey's hand, but he kept walking regardless.

The entrance to the keep was located partway up a tower that jutted from the side of the structure. A set of stone stairs ran roughly halfway up the side of the keep and ended at the entrance set in the tower. The keep's door had rotted off long ago, leaving only rust-stained hinges behind. The entrance to the keep opened into a dark alcove.

As he looked inside, a chill ran up Godfrey's spine. There was nothing visible inside the entrance, but dread filled him all the same. This was a place of evil.

Drawing the magic sword from its scabbard, Godfrey could not see anything but shadow inside the keep still. He unslung his shield from his back. Taking a few deep breaths, he took a moment to look at the blade. Fallard was right. It looked just like any other longsword, but with magic, appearances were often deceiving. Or so Godfrey was told. He pondered the blade a moment longer, wondering why so many people were terrified of magic. Perhaps it was because blatantly magical things were so rare and dangerous. The moment was surreal.

"My first magic sword," Godfrey said in disbelief.

Climbing the stairs as quietly as he could, Godfrey glanced over the courtyard several times to be sure it was still empty. Every time he looked, he saw only the same mud and patchy grass that was there when he first entered the castle grounds. He decided it was best to focus his attention on the stairs in front of him so if he were to meet a grisly end, it would not be at the hands of a misplaced foot. Out of all of Godfrey's irrational fears, his fear of falling was the one he himself least understood.

As he drew closer to the keep's entrance, Godfrey's skin began to crawl. The feeling intensified until his heart began to pound again when he reached the top of the stairs. His hand was shaking uncontrollably now.

Pausing, Godfrey prayed silently to the gods for their protection. After a moment, his hand stopped shaking. The fear did not leave, but the clarity of purpose he had felt during the Bishop's blessing overrode that fear. He released a long breath and stepped inside the keep.

The air inside the keep was frigid even though it was only early fall. Godfrey let his eyes adjust to the dark. He took a step forward inside the alcove, and was shocked to see a pair of skeletal arms swinging a sword directly at his face. Godfrey instinctively raised his shield just in time to block the blow, but before he knew it, a long spear thrust towards him from the other side. Narrowly dodging the spear tip, he realized there were two skeletons attacking him. The one on his left had a cracked helmet and a two-handed greatsword while the other one carried a spear and shield.

Godfrey thrust his sword at the skeleton with the spear, while planning to block the other monster's attack with his shield again. The spear-armed foe stopped Godfrey's attack with its own shield as the other attacker swung its greatsword at him. Godfrey's shield clanged at the sword's impact, but he knew he could not fight both of these creatures for long. As the spear-wielding monstrosity jabbed its weapon at Godfrey, he parried it with his blade, and in a single fluid motion bashed in the abomination's face with the cross-guard of his sword. The creature's jaw fell off as its body crashed into the alcove's wall, and it collapsed into a heap of bones.

The other skeleton made a downward swing with its sword, and Godfrey stepped back. The heavy blade deflected off the flared nose guard of Godfrey's spangenhelm, and slashed diagonally across his cheek. He yelped more in alarm than pain, but the attack threw him on his back all the same. He felt warm blood drip from his wound as the monster leered over him. As it raised its sword for the killing blow, Godfrey desperately swung at the horrid creature's legs. He cleaved through the bone and the skeleton fell beside him.

Godfrey jumped to his feet and snapped the skeleton's neck with a stomp from his boot. He watched the scattered bones lie inert where they were for a moment, to make sure they would not reanimate. Wiping the blood from the scratch on his face, Godfrey was relieved to discover the wound was superficial.

Satisfied, Godfrey turned from the alcove into the keep's hall. It was familiar in the sense that there were long feasting tables with benches and serving dishes placed upon them, just like in the hall of any castle keep, but the fire of the hearth had long since died, and the furniture was scattered as if there had been a great commotion. Upon the walls hung faded tapestries with heraldic devices obscured as much by the moldering ravages of time as by shadow.

A sudden movement caught Godfrey's attention. Towards the back of the hall, a figure sat on a throne set atop a large dais. The figure wore tattered robes and armor stained with rust. Withered skin stretched across its face but where eyes should have been, empty sockets stared back at Godfrey. The squire involuntarily stepped back as the figure rose and set a tarnished crown on its head.

Another pair of spear-armed skeletons appeared from the shadows. One creature lunged at Godfrey with outstretched claws. Godfrey raised his shield to block one clawed hand while he slashed his sword down on the other. The monster recoiled at the loss of its hand, but gave a piercing screech as it struck at Godfrey with renewed fury. The noise dazed Godfrey, and he was pushed back as his helmet and shield were pummeled by the undead creature. Parrying the thrust of an oncoming spear, Godfrey then cleaved through one of the skeletons, but the other skeleton's spear pierced Godfrey's side. He cried out in pain, but managed to smash in the attacker's skull with the pommel of his sword.

The crowned undead monster stepped back, regarding Godfrey with interest. Its jaw slackened, revealing a gaping mouth with only a few loose cracked teeth set in its rotten gums.

"You trespass, boy." The words hissed from the monster though its mouth simply remained open. "I am Kurl, lord of this swamp. Tell me who you are before I kill you."

"I am Godfrey de Bastogne," Godfrey answered between painful gasping breaths. "I am the son of Ulric, Duke de Bastogne. I came to slay the monster who has been murdering the people of Harv."

Godfrey hesitated.

"But Bishop Clovis said you would be a vampire." Godfrey frowned. "You seem to be a wight instead."

"Fool," Kurl laughed. "You are a young and stupid squire sent on a quest to destroy vampires. That won't happen today. Instead, I will sacrifice you to Belnor, and devour your flesh on his altar!"

Breathing heavily, Godfrey willed the pain down, but the wight was not about to be lenient. With a snarl, Kurl ripped into Godfrey's tabard and lifted him off the ground by his hauberk. Regaining his wits, Godfrey slashed his sword through the wight's neck, severing his head. Kurl collapsed in a heap, releasing Godfrey, who plopped on the ground beside the monster's ruined form. Coughing, he blinked tears from his eyes as he felt the wound on his side. It was not bad, he told himself even as he cringed with pain.

The air around Godfrey immediately grew warmer as the wight's dark magic began to dissipate. Godfrey laughed in elation as he realized what he had accomplished in that moment. The feeling was cut short.

Something still did not feel right. The cold was gone but the sense of unease would not leave the pit of Godfrey's stomach. He sat where he was for a moment to see if it would simply take longer for the sensation to leave him, but it remained constant despite coming to grips with the evil of this place. His eyes were drawn to the floor, and the feeling of despair intensified. It was below him.

Godfrey looked around the hall and could make out more details now that his eyes had adjusted to the dark. Sure enough, there was a set of spiral stairs in one of the corners leading both to the keep's upper levels and down to what Godfrey assumed would either be the storage rooms or dungeon. He had no torch but pressed for the stairs anyway, keeping his sword drawn. He was sure whatever evil was still in this place could be found down those stairs.

As Godfrey neared the stairs, he noticed a faint glow coming from the bottom. At least he had that in his favor.

He walked down the stairs and his unease grew worse as he passed the landing to the ground level. This evil, this monster or whatever it was, lived below the earth. The evil presence in the basement emanated despair just as the wight had in the keep's hall. Godfrey braced himself as he reached the bottom of the stairs and looked into the chamber in front of him.

With white stones used in its walls, the room had the appearance of a chapel. Black candles placed on tables adjacent to the walls and atop chandeliers glowed softly, giving the room a slightly yellow hue. In the center of the room sat a large wooden statue of a creature with the head of a beast and the body of a man. The statue's arms were outstretched in a welcoming gesture before a wide altar set in front of it, but its face leered as if to signify the unworthiness of those in its presence. Godfrey's discomfort at seeing the statue grew to the point that nausea began to grip his stomach.

"Belnor?" Godfrey asked aloud as he entered the chapel.

"That is the god's name," a girl's voice answered petulantly.

Godfrey spun around to see a girl with auburn hair in a corner of the room behind him. She was thin, looked about his age, and her pale features gave her an ethereal allure. Enthralled by her beauty, he stood there, staring at her for a moment with his mouth half-open. She looked back at him with an annoyed expression as she ruffled her dress.

"Have you never seen a damsel before?" the girl asked in a mocking tone.

His hand giving a slight twitch, he involuntarily stepped back a pace. Her rebuke stung him. Apparently, this damsel's beauty only went skin-deep.

"I did not expect to see one in a place like this," Godfrey said, regaining his composure. "I destroyed the wight and four skeletons. Do you know if there are more monsters in the keep?"

"No," the girl flatly replied. "There are not."

"Good," Godfrey said, slightly puzzled by her tone. "We need to destroy this idol, and then I will get you out of the swamp."

"I don't need you to save me," the girl protested.

"What?" Godfrey shrank back at this completely unexpected response.

"You invaded my home," she spat. "You killed my father, and now you are going to destroy the unholy image of my god!"

Godfrey was frozen in place, completely dumbfounded. None of this made any sense to him. His mind began to race as he tried to put the pieces together.

"If you are responsible for creating undead and worshipping dark gods, it is my duty to slay you," Godfrey replied, keeping his sword gripped tightly in his hand. "I shall not allow that to continue."

The girl hissed at Godfrey, revealing a pair of large fangs. His eyes went wide as he realized what she was. She leapt at Godfrey, but he dodged her attack with ease. Then the wound in his side ached, and Godfrey gritted his teeth. Wincing, he kept back from her. He knew what he had to do, but he still hesitated. She looked nothing like what he had imagined a vampire to be.

"How could such a fair damsel be the vampire terrorizing Harv?" Godfrey asked as the two circled.

"My father," the girl explained. "Lord Kurl always worshipped Belnor. When I grew sick, he prayed for his god to spare my life. I was granted immortality at the price of continuing Belnor's work here in the mortal realm more than a century ago."

"Why have you only attacked Harv more recently?" Godfrey asked with genuine interest.

"I turned the unsuspecting servants here into my first acts of devotion," the vampire answered with a defiant grimace. "The remainder fled when they realized what I had become, leaving just my father and me at the castle. We slowly built up our strength in that time. He taught me death magic, and I used it on him in his sleep. For the last hundred years I have ruled this swamp and its surrounding villages. Your petty lords only think they do, but now that my strength has grown to its fullness I will overthrow them. As long as I feed on fresh blood, I will never die."

"Was your father one of those petty lords who only *thought* he ruled even in undeath?" Godfrey asked, incredulous at the venom in her words.

"He promised to always protect me," the girl said with misty eyes that quickly flared in anger. "That was his responsibility. Mine is to rule. And you will not ruin it!"

"Your abomination destroys innocent life," Godfrey answered. "My sacred duty is to end that horror."

The vampire jumped at Godfrey again. His wound slowing him, Godfrey was unable to avoid her strike. Her fangs caught on the coif around his neck as she knocked him on his back. She tore out several chainmail links as she ripped her fangs free from his armor.

With Godfrey still on the ground, the vampire pounced on top of him. She pinned him before he could react. Her eyes blazed wildly as she repeatedly gnashed and chomped at his neck. Yet for all the animalistic ferocity of her attack, the vampire was silent as death as her fangs ripped more links from Godfrey's coif. The next bite would tear into his now exposed neck. Despite her diminutive form, she was incredibly powerful. Godfrey's efforts to buck her off him proved futile. Panic almost overcame him entirely as he realized he was about to die.

At that moment Godfrey saw his opportunity. Summoning all the strength he could muster, he shoved the vampire off to the side with his sword arm. She was on her back beside him, momentarily disoriented. She made to pin Godfrey again, but his arm was free to swing his sword in a wide arc. The stroke severed the girl's auburn head from her body as she momentarily hung over Godfrey's prone form. Instead of blood, a thick black ichor oozed from the stump of the vampire's neck, covering Godfrey in reeking filth as the vampire's corrupted corpse fell on top of him.

Shaken but resolute, Godfrey brushed the headless corpse to the side and climbed to his feet. He sheathed his sword and looked to the unblinking idol of Belnor. How many people had been slain on that altar? There was only one thing left to do now.

Suddenly, dozens of skeletons emerged from an anteroom at the back of the chapel. They were armed with swords and spears. Knowing he could not destroy them all, Godfrey looked to the statue of Belnor. His skin prickled as he felt the malice pouring from it. The skeletons charged Godfrey from the other end of the chapel.

Godfrey knocked over several candles on one of the tables, catching a rug on fire. The blaze quickly spread to the tablecloth, then to the table itself. A moment later, flames began to lick the tapestries on the wall and the base of Belnor's idol also caught fire. It was only at that moment that the sickening feeling of the evil presence began to dissipate. As the wooden statue burned, the skeletons crumbled to dust and their weapons clattered on the ground. Grabbing the vampire's severed head, Godfrey realized half of the chapel was now ablaze. He dashed back up the stairs as fast as his aching wound would allow.

Smoke and flame followed up the stairs after Godfrey. Heaving with great pain, he raced to the keep's entrance as he felt a cold sweat covering him from all of his exertions. He stumbled as he began to choke on the fumes, and his vision blurred with tears. The fire spread into the hall with frightening speed. With a desperate gasp, Godfrey ran through the keep's entrance and tumbled down the slippery stairs.

Both of Godfrey's feet flew in front of him for a moment. This was how Godfrey was going to die? Sharp pain struck him again and again as he hit each step. All of that, and he was going to die falling down stairs.

Finally, Godfrey stopped and found himself lying in the mud, bruised and bloodied. His wounds seared in agony, and Godfrey could not stand, but at least he was alive. He was spared an ignominious death for now.

Fallard and the two men-at-arms were standing over Godfrey before he knew it. He was dazed and hardly aware of their presence. Coming to himself, Godfrey saw that they were torn between watching the flames lick the sky from the keep's roof—as if awaiting a great demon to burst from the flames—and attending to his own battered form. Fallard reached down to pull his cousin off the ground, but stopped and stared incredulously at the vampire's severed head lying next to Godfrey.

"You did that with only an ordinary blade?" Fallard's mouth gaped.

"An ordinary blade?" Godfrey repeated dumbly. "You said…"

"I said what would give you the courage to continue your quest," Fallard interrupted, pulling Godfrey to his feet. "That you completed it as such renders all the more glory to you."

Though confused, Godfrey felt his anger at Fallard's deception subside. He was right. Godfrey had done something few others could boast of. That his situation was more perilous than he imagined was beside the point.

"How was I able to slay the vampire if the sword was not enchanted?" Godfrey asked.

"Most creatures will not survive a decapitation, regardless of the instrument used." Fallard shrugged.

Now it was Godfrey's turn to have his mouth gape open in surprise.

Chapter Four

By the time Fulcher and Bruno dressed Godfrey's wound and cleaned him up, the flames consuming the castle had put themselves out. He kept telling himself the wound was not so bad, but his body begged to differ. Still, it was not the first time he had been wounded in combat. He knew it would heal.

"Now back to the town," Fallard said, handing Godfrey the reins to his horse. "You will ride into Harv and receive a hero's welcome there after they hear what you have done."

With a deferential nod, Godfrey mounted the horse. They set off through the swamp back to Harv. Godfrey could hardly believe what he had done as he looked back on the smoking castle. Yet the vampire's head still lay in the mud where he had left it. He bit his lip, still wondering how he had even survived; yet he had prevailed against the vampire.

Turning back to the direction of Harv, Godfrey spurred Fallard's horse forward at a slow walk. He thought of all the glory he would gain from this deed, but tried to temper those thoughts with humility. By slaying the vampire, he was serving all the people and, by extension, the celestial gods.

Still, his heart swelled at the expression he imagined on his father's face upon hearing the news of Godfrey's triumph.

Duke Ulric would knight Godfrey, and then Godfrey would serve as one of his father's retainers until he inherited the duchy. The thoughts of what was to come filled Godfrey's head so much that he hardly noticed as the mud of the brown dead swamp and marsh gave way to the more solid ground and green breathing pine trees of the forest. Neither did he ponder the old elf road as they made their way across it again. Nor did he even notice the Sun begin to set. It was only as they approached the gates of Harv that Godfrey's mind turned to what was directly before him.

The guards at the gate immediately brought Godfrey and his companions to the shrine they had stayed at the night before. Heralding Godfrey's arrival, the shrine's bell tower tolled in the fading light for the whole town to hear. Bishop Clovis, the constable, and a few other priests and town guards from the previous night were waiting for them, in addition to a curious crowd of townsfolk. Walaric stood wide-eyed beside the Bishop as he saw Godfrey come into the chapel. Lord and Lady Eist entered just a moment after Godfrey did.

"The vampire is destroyed," Godfrey announced. "The quest is complete; Harv will be troubled by her menace no more."

"I, Sir Fallard, witness to the truth of this matter," his cousin added. "Be it known that Godfrey slew the vampire with a mundane blade given to him by my own hand. He brought me the foul creature's head as evidence of this act."

"Well met," the Bishop replied. "Your father will be proud, Godfrey."

"Thank you," Godfrey answered with a stiff bow as those gathered cheered.

"Now," Clovis said, silencing the crowd. "I shall join your company on its journey to your father's keep, where Sir Fallard and I will both give our recommendations for your elevation to knighthood."

Another burst of applause filled the chamber. The congratulations Godfrey received were even more enthusiastic than what he had experienced the previous night on having taken up the quest. Even the constable seemed to give Godfrey an almost genuine smile. The guards asked questions about all the details while the priests took up a hymn to victory. Walaric started to talk Godfrey's ear off, but cut himself short at a reproving look from Bishop Clovis.

A feast was brought in. Savory meats, sweet wine, hot bread; Godfrey was obliged to eat well more than he thought he could manage, and he was only able to refuse when he felt his stomach was about to burst open. Toasts and laurels were offered to Godfrey well after he had grown too weary to stand and receive them. Minstrels and jongleurs came to hear Godfrey tell the tale of how he had defeated the vampire, and when he had grown too tired to repeat the story, they began to hear it from others in the room. The details became exaggerated with each telling, but Godfrey was growing too tired to correct the inaccuracies.

After hours of this praise and attention, the excitement slowly died down and, just as the night before, the crowd began to disperse. Thinking on this, Godfrey realized that perhaps glory was fleeting after all. For the moment he was glad for the reprieve though. More glory could come some other time.

"Godfrey," Lady Eist whispered in the squire's ear as everyone else seemed to be distracted with other conversation.

"Yes?" Godfrey whispered back, a bit surprised at Lady Eist's sudden proximity to him.

"You have avenged my daughter." Lady Eist's expression was far livelier than it had been the night before.

The Lady was focused, determined, and regal. Godfrey doubted any detail could escape Lady Eist's attention in this state. He pitied whoever dared to get in this woman's way now that she was roused from the depression that had previously overcome her.

"I will not soon forget it," Lady Eist continued. "If misfortune should ever befall Fuetoile Keep or Bastogne at large, Harv's loyalty will be to the son of Duke Ulric, no matter who or what threatens it. I will make sure of it."

Godfrey nodded slowly as he processed the full implications of what Lady Eist was saying. No matter *who* or what? Godfrey was not sure exactly *whom* Lady Eist had in mind, but he knew now that he was a knight in all but name, he was in the adult world. That world was full of dangers that were less obvious than dragons. Some of those dangers were far more destructive than even the largest of the elder dragons. His father had taught him that lesson years previous.

The next morning, Bishop Clovis and a trio of his retainers also joined Sir Fallard, Godfrey, and the men-at-arms outside the shrine as they prepared to leave Harv. The Bishop's retainers wore flat-topped helmets that fully enclosed their faces except for narrow vision slits in front of their eyes. They also wore heavy mail hauberks, and were armed with longswords sheathed in gilded scabbards. Their white tabards were each marked on the front with a large blue circle in the center with four flame-like points emanating from it.

Godfrey easily recognized the star that adorned the retainers' tabards and shields. It was the symbol of the celestial gods with its four points symbolically facing north, south, east, and west, but he was surprised to see Bishop Clovis dressed in similar attire. Godfrey had never known a cleric to wear vestments other than the finery he had seen the Bishop wear during their previous meetings. Though stories like the Tale of Cheldric frequently featured clergymen in martial roles, Godfrey had only rarely witnessed a cleric actually take up arms and armor. After staring for a moment, Godfrey realized the Bishop was perfectly right to dress in armor while traveling. The world outside the walls of towns and castles was dangerous.

Thinking about it, Godfrey also recognized that he was wrong about something else. His father's chaplain, Turpin, was a cleric too, and Godfrey had rarely seen the grizzled man dressed for anything but battle. Even those who walked the divine paths could vary greatly in their personalities.

The only way Godfrey could distinguish the Bishop from his retainers was that Clovis only protected his head with a mail coif instead of one of the face-concealing helmets that his retainers wore. Apparently, the Bishop felt confident enough in what protection he had. Godfrey would never allow himself to go into danger without wearing his spangenhelm.

"We cannot expect you to make the long journey back home on foot," Clovis said, leading a black horse with a white blaze to Godfrey. "The injuries you received will slow you down quite a bit."

"I can manage," Godfrey replied dismissively. "It wasn't that bad."

"Perhaps not," Clovis answered, undeterred. "Then accept this horse as a gift for your bravery and the magnitude of the deed which you accomplished. The people of Harv are grateful and the gods smile upon you this day."

"Thank you." Godfrey smiled graciously.

"His name is Baruch," the Bishop told Godfrey as he handed the reins to him.

"Baruch?" Godfrey repeated as he took the reins.

"It means *holiness* in the celestial tongue," Clovis explained. "Baruch's father and mother were both fine steeds, two of the fastest and strongest I have ever owned. I suspect Baruch will serve you just as well as his parents served me."

Godfrey bowed his head in a gesture of gratitude. Wincing slightly, he clambered into Baruch's saddle. The pain was forgotten as Godfrey beamed at the horse, and patted his neck. Satisfied, the Bishop went back to his men. Fallard, Bruno, and Fulcher approached Godfrey as they inspected the horse.

"He's a fine steed," Fallard said as he circled Baruch. "He looks young and strong."

"The product of good breeding." Fulcher began following just behind Fallard, taking in every detail of the animal's physique.

"You'll get many good years out of him," Bruno added sagely. "This horse is a very fine gift indeed."

"I was going to wait until after you were knighted," Fallard continued. "But since the Bishop has already given you his gift in honor of saving Harv, I will give you mine."

Fallard handed Godfrey the sword he had used to slay the vampire. Godfrey hefted the blade in his hands for a moment, appreciating its weight.

"Thank you, cousin." Godfrey grabbed the sword and secured its scabbard to his belt. "It's still not actually magical though, right?"

"No." Fallard frowned. "Not unless you bewitched it behind my back."

Bruno and Fulcher chortled while the faintest smile betrayed Fallard's amusement. Knowing that the blade was not magical hardly diminished its value to Godfrey. There was a sentimental value that came from his experience in the vampire's castle. This was the sword that saw him through that trial.

Mounted atop his own horse, the Bishop approached while his retainers followed on foot. Fallard mounted his horse as well, which then began a slow trot towards the palisade. Godfrey followed just behind Fallard, Bruno and Fulcher fell in behind Godfrey, while Clovis and his men took up the rear.

Godfrey had a steed and a sword of his own now. He knew his sword well enough though he had no name for it yet. His steed, Baruch, however, had a good enough name, though he knew nothing of the horse yet. Both deficiencies would be corrected in time, Godfrey assured himself. For now he was content just to have them.

The journey to Duke Ulric's castle, Fuetoile Keep, had taken the better part of a week thus far. The distance was not so great, but the path was difficult, and Godfrey's wounds had not fully healed yet. The old elf road entirely disappeared for lengthy stretches. The paving stones that should have been in place had long ago been removed to build walls for some lord's estates or other less altruistic building projects. Thick forests and steep hills also slowed down the group's progress.

Then there was the danger of brigands, orcs, and other monsters that lurked in the woods. They had yet to come across anything thus far, but unwary travelers who stumbled upon a challenge they could not meet were rarely shown mercy. Caution meant delay.

On the sixth day of their travels, the group struggled through a particularly dense patch of woods. They wandered for hours trying to find a path clear enough for them to lead the horses through. Eventually, they stopped at the bank of a large stream where there was a bit more of an opening. Bruno started a fire while Fulcher began skinning some rabbits he had caught earlier in the day.

"That will make for a nice meal." Clovis gazed at the catch longingly. "We would all be a lot hungrier without your talents."

Fulcher acknowledged the Bishop with a deferential bow, and continued with his work. Godfrey had grown to appreciate Fulcher's knack for hunting. He himself was not so gifted with the patience, stealth, or sharp eyes required for the trade. Fulcher's ability to cook more than doubled his value in Godfrey's mind.

Godfrey skipped stones down the stream, his mind wandering. The wound in his side only occasionally bothered him now, and the scratch on his face had long since been forgotten. So he took the opportunity to enjoy this simple pleasure he had rarely found the time for as a squire. He wondered if there would be more time for such games after he was knighted. Thinking on this, he concluded that the duties of a knight were probably far heavier than even a squire's, if his experience with Fallard was any indication. Still he skipped the rocks, enjoying what idle diversion he could for the moment.

An argument broke out among the group about the best way to get back to the road. They should have reached the castle by now, but no one seemed sure about the right way to get there. Godfrey wished he could help, but if these well-traveled men did not know the way, what could he contribute to the conversation?

"The rabbits are ready," Bruno cut into the debate.

"Yes, thank you," Fallard said, accepting a bowl of stew from Bruno.

"Right." the Bishop offered a conciliatory smile, taking a bowl. "Forgive me. Hunger always puts me in a bad mood."

Godfrey detected the faint aroma of the meal up in the camp mingling with the smoke from the fire. He salivated as the smell teased his senses. But however tempting Fulcher's cooking was, Godfrey was not quite hungry enough yet to be diverted from his game.

"Godfrey?" Bruno asked, gesturing toward the stew in the kettle.

"Just a moment," Godfrey answered, picking up one final rock to skip across the stream.

Godfrey found a large, flat stone perfect for skipping. With an enthusiastic flick of the wrist, he threw the stone downstream. The rock bounced once, twice, but abruptly stopped on the opposite bank as it hit a log Godfrey had not noticed before. There was something familiar about the log he could not put his finger on. He scanned the log and the bank opposite from where he stood. All at once, a memory from long ago flashed in Godfrey's mind.

"I know where we are!" Godfrey called up to the others.

Everyone turned to Godfrey with curious looks, waiting for his explanation. He climbed up from the bank, and pointed down to the log.

"You see," Godfrey started. "That log down there. It was an old dead tree on the other bank. I snuck out of the castle one night years ago looking for monsters to fight."

Clovis and Fallard both gave Godfrey chastising looks that made him blush. Godfrey swallowed a lump in his throat from embarrassment, but continued.

"I know it was just a silly game," Godfrey attempted to justify himself. "I was only five years old at the time though."

Though Godfrey knew perfectly well that his actions as a small child were hardly worth getting embarrassed over, he hated admitting them all the same. He believed he should have known better, even at that age.

"Anyway," Godfrey stammered through his confession. "I climbed that tree, but it collapsed under my weight into the river. I didn't get hurt, but it left me so wet and scared that I never forgot about it. Father was pretty furious with me at the time."

Though Duke Ulric's scorn for his son after Godfrey's return to the castle that night was short and well-meaning, and his father never spoke of the incident again, Godfrey never forgot it. The hot flush of humiliation at having disobeyed his father and mother in the first place came back fresh every time Godfrey remembered it or one of the few other events like it. It stung him now, especially as he had to confess the transgression to others. It was probably also why he held onto his irrational fear of falling, now that he thought about it.

"Anyway," Godfrey began again. "If we follow the river downstream for another five minutes, it will lead us out of the woods and we should be able to see Fuetoile Keep."

"Well that is certainly good to hear," Fulcher answered. "I would have hated to wander around the woods for another week."

The group packed their things after everyone had finished eating. No one commented on Godfrey's obvious chagrin over confessing his childhood misadventure. He could pretend it never happened. Godfrey preferred it that way.

As Godfrey had suggested, the group followed the water downstream. It took somewhat longer for them to get out of the woods than what Godfrey had recalled, but once they did, the sight of Fuetoile Keep was unmistakable. The whole structure was built of massive stones, and was set on a hill with a commanding view of the surrounding country. Banners with the Duke's heraldry fluttered high atop the towers at each corner of the castle's crenelated outer walls. The keep itself rose from behind the inner wall, which sat somewhat higher on the hill than the outer wall did.

"This is your home, Godfrey." Fallard turned to his cousin. "You should lead us in."

Godfrey smiled in recognition of his cousin's noble gesture. Spurring Baruch to the front of the procession, he led the way to the open castle gates, which were large and cut from a heavy dark wood. Behind the gates lay the outer courtyard and a glimpse of the inner wall. It had been a long time since he had been here. Yet it was familiar. Nothing had changed, at least on the outside. That gave Godfrey comfort.

A herald spotted the group as they approached, and he announced their arrival with a blast from his horn. Waiting by the outer gate, Godfrey soon spotted his mother and father rushing to the gate from the courtyard. How much they had aged since Godfrey last saw them.

Godfrey's mother, Regana, was a thin, greying woman with a delicate face and brown eyes. She had been gentle to Godfrey in his younger years, but her devotion to the gods was fierce. She spared no efforts in instilling that same reverence in Godfrey.

Duke Ulric stood about a head taller than his wife, and his thick silver beard covered his slightly rounded face. Where age had diminished the figure of Godfrey's mother, it had merely slackened the full muscular features of his father.

Godfrey's father had had a reputation as a fierce warrior years ago. Ulric had done much to enhance the prestige of Bastogne in his prime. Though age had begun to weaken the Duke's body, the fire of a younger warrior still burned in his green eyes.

The Duke and Duchess embraced Godfrey as he dismounted Baruch. Ulric acknowledged Fallard and his men with a nod, while Regana gave the Bishop and his retainers a bemused smile. Looking from his parents to the entourage that had escorted him thus far, Godfrey cleared his throat.

"I've done it," Godfrey sheepishly explained.

"Indeed he has," Fallard added. "Duke Ulric, Duchess Regana, the time of your son's training to be a knight is at an end. He has become a man, and in that time I have developed many good qualities in him; the rest were gifts bestowed by his parents and the gods."

"The Town of Harv was plagued by a vampire," Bishop Clovis interjected. "Your son took it upon himself to save Harv from the vampire, as well as its undead thralls, including a powerful wight. And, having successfully completed his quest, Sir Fallard and I both recommend that Godfrey be dubbed a knight."

"And so he shall," Duke Ulric announced, beaming at his son. "The ceremony will take place at dawn tomorrow."

Godfrey's spirits swelled at the praise. It was him Fallard and Bishop Clovis were talking about like the hero of a bard's tale. The pride in his father's face was a sight Godfrey would never forget. That meant more to Godfrey than any words someone else might say.

Regana made a grateful gesture towards the heavens and embraced her son again. The Duke and Duchess led Godfrey and his company up to the keep while the horses were put in the stables. Godfrey explained to his parents all the details of his quest to slay the vampire, as well as many of the other adventures he had been on with Fallard since the last time he was home. Most of Godfrey's time with Fallard had been spent training in Fallard's estates in Tyrol. However, Fallard had been called to war against the orcs twice in the last year by his own lord, the Duke of Tyrol. Those two campaigns and the previous war with the necromancer had given Godfrey plenty of practical experience with the sword. The memories of Godfrey's last visit home before those wars seemed far distant by comparison.

"We were fortunate not to come across any orcs in the woods on the way over here," Fallard commented.

"I think they have had enough fighting for one year," Clovis thought aloud. "They and their troll kin took quite a beating already, and are probably licking their wounds back in their filthy hovels. Their dens are too deep in the forest for most of us to just stumble upon, fortunately."

"We may yet see a few raiding parties before winter sets in," Ulric noted grimly.

"I pray not." Regana shot her husband an accusing look.

"As do I," Ulric answered with a defensive gesture. "We will be ready all the same. But we will speak more on that later."

"For the moment…" Regana turned to her son. "I believe Godfrey should prepare for the ceremony at hand."

"Yes," Clovis agreed. "The dubbing of a knight is a ceremony the gods take a keen interest in. Godfrey, I advise fasting and prayer until we commence with the ritual."

"Of course," Godfrey replied.

The group passed through the inner curtain wall's gatehouse to the main courtyard. A few wooden buildings hugged the interior of the wall; a barracks, the stable, a couple of storehouses. Upon reaching the keep, Godfrey went to his room while Fallard, Clovis, and the others were shown to various guest chambers.

Godfrey's room had few personal belongings in it, as he had not really lived there for most of his life. His time with Fallard had always left Godfrey feeling transient. Fuetoile Keep, though an infrequent destination, was at least a place where Godfrey had always known he was welcome.

Surveying the room, Godfrey wondered what he would actually fill it with now that he would be home more or less permanently. A large comfy bed filled a good portion of the room while a desk, a mirror, and an armoire occupied three walls. Perhaps he would get a shelf and start filling it with books. He had little time to read as it was, but that might change one day. The wisdom of ancient writers intrigued Godfrey, during what little exposure he had to them.

Remembering why he had isolated himself from his family and friends, Godfrey knelt in prayer, facing the window. The Sun was bright in the midafternoon sky, though a few large billowing clouds rolled towards the horizon. Concentrating his thoughts, Godfrey began his prayer in earnest.

Loxias, Godfrey silently addressed the Sun God. *Lord of light and ruler of the skies, help me to be strong. Help me to be a worthy knight, and help me to always put my sword to good causes. As the Duke's son, I am afraid others may try to manipulate me for their own ends. Help me to be wise so that I may not fall into such traps. Help me to be both brave and wise.*

Silence was the only immediate answer Godfrey received as the clouds began to obscure the Sun's light. Still he knelt, repeating requests and adding more as he could think of them. His thoughts eventually trailed off, and he began pondering his life as he stared out the window.

After some time, the Sun broke through the clouds, and somehow made Godfrey feel everything would be okay. It was inexplicable how a bit of light could reassure him that his future would work out and that the gods were pleased with him. He felt it all the same.

"Thank you," Godfrey concluded his prayer, rising to his feet.

A herald down at the outer wall's gate blew his trumpet, signaling the arrival of some new traveler. Peering down into the courtyard, Godfrey saw his father hurrying to greet his second unexpected arrival of the day. Godfrey did not recognize the knights who saluted his father, but he quickly spotted the royal banner among them. Sure enough, the knights' tabards and shields all bore the royal heraldic eagle. One of them wore a golden eagle displayed against a red field on his tabard and shield, just as the royal banner did. That, Godfrey was sure, was King Wilhelm if the crown fitted onto the man's spangenhelm was not indication enough. Though the new King made regular visits to his dukes and counts since his ascension three years ago, Godfrey nervously bit his lip as he considered the timing of Wilhelm's arrival. Surely, this was no coincidence.

<u>Chapter Five</u>

Alvir of Clan Black Dragon stood breathlessly in the cold dark bed chamber of High Warlord Ivarsson. He strained his ears, listening for signs of his lord stirring in the bed. Only the heavy breathing of one in deep sleep could be heard.

Slowly Alvir's eyes adjusted to the dark. The furnishings were ornate, the best a high warlord could demand of his subjects in the frigid Nordslands. High Warlord Ivarsson had united the five Nordsman clans in his younger years, a long and bloody affair, and now spent his latter days in the material comforts won by his previous conquests. High Warlord Ivarsson's vision of uniting the clans had been grand, but not as grand as Alvir's ambitions were now.

Gripping the ax in his hand tightly, Alvir inched closer to the High Warlord. Ivarsson was under the blankets on top of the bed directly in front of Alvir.

Fill me with the ferocity of a dragon, Alvir silently pleaded. *Yoan, goddess of cunning and war, make my ax strike true. We know what is at stake. The survival of the clans depends on this. Grant me the power to see your will through.*

Stopping just in front of Ivarsson's bed, Alvir looked down at his lord's face. He almost jumped as Ivarsson's eyes flashed open. For one tense moment, the two just stared at each other. Alvir was young and ambitious like so many lords in the five clans. Ivarsson was old and immediately knew full well that Alvir could not have come this far without making sure there would be no help for the High Warlord should he cry out.

"Alvir," Ivarsson noted grimly as he sat up in his bed. "Make it quick then."

Alvir hesitated for a moment, at once surprised and disappointed that Ivarsson had somehow expected this. A hundred reprimands raced through Alvir's mind, but only his clenched teeth betrayed any such feelings. Then, without a word, he struck the High Warlord's face with the head of his ax. Accepting his fate with regal stoicism, Ivarsson died with barely a sound.

Alvir stood there in the dark, taking in his fell deed with relish. His work had just started. Now it was on to the second act. The third act would undoubtedly prove to be just as easy as the first for Alvir to pull off if the second act went smoothly. Yet if he did not play his part well in the second act, he would die as the traitor he was, well before he could set the third in motion.

Opening the door to the bed chamber, he entered a dimly lit castle hallway, where he saw two guards with relieved expressions on their faces. The poor fools had no idea what their treachery would cost.

"The High Warlord is dead?" one of the guards whispered.

"It is as the Great Witch of the North instructed." Alvir grimaced. "She saw Ivarsson's fate in her runes. His end leads us to a better fate."

"Then we shall attack Azgald?" the second guard asked. "Will it be soon?"

"Yes," Alvir answered with a dark nod. "No one has come by since I went in?"

"No one." The first guard shook his head.

"Good." Alvir gave a cruel smile. "Remember how I said we could leave *no* witnesses?"

Before either of the guards could reply to this, Alvir sank his ax into the first guard's chest, and the man dropped with a thud. The other guard was momentarily stunned with disbelief by this abrupt attack. He tried to draw his sword, but was too late. Alvir hacked into the side of the second guard's neck. Gurgling blood, the second guard fell to the ground with the ax still embedded in his neck.

Alvir stepped over the guard's body as the wretch took his last choking gasps. Taking a casual glance over his shoulder, he frowned at the now dead guard, and walked down the hall to his own chambers. Sacrifices had to be made for this plan to work. There was no room for regret.

The next morning, Alvir was awoken by a loud pounding on his door. He stretched, smiling. He briefly glanced out the window, watching snowflakes float down from the clouds. What a perfect start to winter, he thought as the person on the other side of the door pounded again.

"Yes?" Alvir called out.

One of Alvir's warriors opened the door. The warrior gave a brief bow as Alvir sat up in bed. Alvir gave him a puzzled look as the warrior rose upright. The warrior's expression carried a combination of suppressed rage and grief.

"Well?" Alvir asked. "What is it?"

"High Warlord Ivarsson was murdered last night," the warrior stated, trying to filter the emotion from his voice.

"By the gods," Alvir cursed. "Did they catch the murderer?"

"No, lord." The warrior shook his head. "They believe the ax used to commit the murder was left behind in his haste to escape. A council has been called for all the remaining lords in the castle."

"Let's hurry then," Alvir said as he got out of bed.

"Lord Alvir," the warrior started. "There's one more thing."

"Go on," Alvir encouraged the warrior, setting his jaw.

"Your brother, Vitigis, was in charge of the night guard," the warrior explained. "It was his neck the ax was found in."

Alvir turned his back to the warrior. He brought his hand to his face as if to wipe away tears. The warrior bowed his head in a sympathetic gesture. Alvir's brother had proven instrumental in arranging Ivarsson's assassination, but Vitigis did not foresee that Alvir had no intention of bringing his brother any further along in the conspiracy than that, at least not as a living participant. This warrior knew nothing of the conspiracy, and with Vitigis dead, Alvir was the only one in the castle who knew what had really happened. The loss of Vitigis was a heavy price, but one worth paying by Alvir's calculations.

"All right then." Alvir gravely turned back to the warrior after a moment. "Let's get to the bottom of this."

Four long tables were arranged in the council chamber in a roughly square shape so that those seated could easily talk with one another. However, instead of friendly discourse, the lords present in the council chamber buzzed angrily as they shot each other suspicious glances while muttering to their confidants. All were dressed in full armor and cloaks, and their personal guards lined the walls of the chamber. There was little pretense at civility. Hands still gripped the hilts of swords or the handles of maces and axes, even if no weapons were drawn at the moment.

Alvir noted that he and his guards were among the last to enter, and he seated himself near the end of one of the tables. Sullenly sitting with his arms crossed, Alvir gave each of the other dozen or so lords a glance while trying not to catch too much attention.

Finally, a golden-haired druidess in black robes entered, and slipped through an opening in the tables, silencing the murmurs as she stood in the center of the room. She drew back the hood that had hidden her face, and held aloft the ax Alvir had used the night before. The blood from the ax's victims had dried over the blade, giving it a grisly appearance.

"I have examined the victims and the instrument of death," the druidess solemnly began. "Much is obscured in this matter. The victims' bodies tell me nothing while the blood splatters on the ax only tell me that the power of the dark gods was invoked just prior to the murder. Whoever did this had the blessing of one of the dark ones."

A tumultuous outburst erupted from the gathered lords as each shot out accusations, counter-accusations, or otherwise reacted to the druidess' pronouncement. Alvir continued to sit where he was, pretending not to be moved by any of this. The next few moments would be critical to his plot. The most important part of the second act would unfold here and now.

The druidess gestured for silence, and the lords complied.

"You can see here," she explained as she traced a triangle along three flecks of dried blood on the ax. "It is the mark of Yoan. Either this deed was done by cunning, or perhaps by cunning this mystery may yet be solved."

Alvir's heart began to race. Had his patron goddess betrayed him? No one looked at him. Besides, there were so many flecks of dried blood on the ax that Alvir could have traced any of the dark gods' marks upon them. He calmed himself in that knowledge even as the druidess' eyes fell upon him for one long moment. Did the druidess know? She was from Clan Black Dragon like Alvir was, but Ivarsson too was of that clan. Where did her loyalties lie?

The druidess dropped the ax to the ground with a clatter and left the room as quietly as she had entered. Alvir concluded either the gods did not reveal as much to the druidess as he initially supposed, or the druidess was not going to intervene and would instead let fate decide.

One of the older warlords, Widemer of Clan Hydra, looked to his peers on either side of him, and rose from his chair. He cleared his throat while giving the ax on the ground a sideways look. Alvir held his breath as his heart pounded in his chest. His plan would either succeed here or he would shortly be executed.

"So much for the High Warlord's feast," Widemer scoffed while pointing at the murder weapon. "Our only clue to Ivarsson's murder is this ax here. Plenty of lords and warlords have had the opportunity and the means to pull this off, so no one is above suspicion. There are only two questions to ask: Who would gain the most from Ivarsson's death, and how do we connect him to this ax?"

"Or her," Alvir added thoughtfully.

A few of the lords chuckled, thinking Alvir was trying to make light of the situation. However, the gravity of his expression quickly suppressed that laughter. Widemer's gaze turned to Alvir as if he now was seeing him for the first time.

"Do you have any information you would like to share with us?" he asked suspiciously.

"No," Alvir fretted. "You just said that no one was above suspicion. And there *are* womenfolk in this castle as well."

"We're trying to narrow down suspects." Widemer stamped his foot dismissively. "What would a woman be able to gain by killing the High Warlord, even if she could get past the guards first?"

"But the ax was found in the neck of one of the guards," another lord from Clan Frost Lion shot out. "Would that not mean that he—or she—killed Ivarsson and then the guards?"

"It's possible," Widemer conceded, furrowing his brow. "Does anyone know if Ivarsson was with a maiden last night?"

"The only people who could tell us that are also dead," Alvir noted.

"Which brings us back to the ax," another Clan Black Dragon lord at Alvir's table confirmed.

All the lords stood and leaned over their tables to examine the ax more closely. Widemer shoved past his table and picked it up. He held it close to his eyes, taking in every detail.

"Dwarvish make," Widemer concluded. "And it has orcish glyphs."

"Who has connections with the orcs or dwarves?" someone from Clan Behemoth asked.

"Alvir does!" another Clan Hydra lord cried.

"Don't be stupid," someone from Clan Owlbear cut in. "Alvir's brother was one of the men killed last night."

"Funny how he does not show sorrow," Widemer said slowly, observing Alvir with the same skewed glance he had given the ax.

"But Warlord Hedin also has connections to both the dwarves and orcs," one of the other lords shouted. "And he's Ivarsson's heir!"

With that, all eyes focused on the previously unnoticed Warlord Hedin. Hedin, though neither short nor frail by the standards of most men, was clearly a runt in comparison to his fellow Nordsmen. And runts were despised in every Nordsman clan.

Clearly taken by surprise, Hedin's defense quickly broke down as the other lords twisted his words in their unrelenting cross-examination of his alibi. Watching the frenzied spectacle, Alvir breathed a sigh of relief. The Nordsmen hardly needed a pretense to dispose of such a mewling weakling. Men like Hedin never lasted long in the clans, especially if they were likely to inherit positions of importance. A Nordsman had to either grow large and strong very quickly, or cunning and duplicitous in an even shorter time. Hedin had done neither. Alvir had done both.

Widemer considered the ax in his hand. With every word Hedin spoke, Alvir knew he looked weaker and weaker in the eyes of the other Nordsman lords. All Alvir really had to do was watch the events unfold before him.

"Warlord Hedin of Clan Black Dragon," Widemer solemnly proclaimed as the room came to a hush. "You have been found guilty of murdering High Warlord Ivarsson in a conspiracy to usurp both his title and leadership of the five clans. This council hereby strips you of your title and privileges. You are disowned from your clan, and you shall receive execution by the very blade you used to kill the High Warlord."

Two of the Clan Frost Lion warriors standing guard forcefully grabbed Hedin, and thrust him into the center of the room. Though Hedin was still trembling as Widemer hefted the ax in his hands, he managed to put on a brave, defiant face. Alvir shook his head in disgust. This fool did not have the vision to lead.

"Wait," Alvir called out as the cries for Hedin's execution reached a crescendo.

Another pause filled the room as Alvir pushed his way to Widemer. Alvir gestured for Widemer to hand him the ax. As if sensing a thirst for vengeance in Alvir, Widemer handed the weapon to him. Hedin's eyes peered into Alvir's, and suddenly the accused appeared to realize this had been intended all along.

"For Vitigis," Alvir breathed before Hedin could say anything, taking off Hedin's head with one stroke of the ax.

More shouting erupted from the lords as Hedin's corpse hit the floor. Alvir stared down at the body and severed head of poor innocent Hedin. Alvir frowned as he pondered the deaths of the two lords he had killed in the last few hours. He was disappointed in both Ivarsson and Hedin for not showing the least amount of resistance to him. They were small-minded. They lacked his vision. Neither of them was worthy of the title of High Warlord, Alvir reminded himself. Alvir had the vision to unite all the clans, not just the five largest as Ivarsson had done.

As the excitement died down, all eyes in the room began to seriously consider Alvir. He had difficulty containing a cruel smile as he watched it dawn on the other lords. With Ivarsson and Hedin now dead, Alvir was next in the line of succession for leadership of Clan Black Dragon, and therefore the five clans as a whole. The second act was complete. Now, on to the third act.

Nera's eyes flashed open as she heard the crowing of a raven somewhere in the distance. Drawing her robes close around herself, she got up from her bed, and moved to the window on the far side of her room. She briefly looked over herself in the mirror to her right side. She did not care that her dark hair was unkempt. Neither did she notice the twigs remaining in it from her dark rituals the previous night. She only looked in the mirror to see if any omens would present themselves to her. Nothing in the mirror alarmed her at first glance.

Quickly, Nera turned her focus to the sky outside her tower window. She easily spotted the black raven silhouetted against the light grey morning clouds. It crowed again, but fluttered low out of Nera's view. A moment later, a hawk swooped in from the clouds in the direction of the raven. The raven gave out an anguished cry, and Nera turned to see the hawk feasting upon the still-struggling raven down in the castle courtyard below.

Nera smiled in satisfaction at the sign. The dark gods had acknowledged her prayers. She knew without a doubt that Ivarsson was now dead and that her husband, Alvir, would very soon be made High Warlord over the five clans.

"If all goes well…" Nera wistfully glanced back at her star charts, half-brewed potions, and divination tomes scattered about her room. "We will soon rule not just the Five Clans but all the clans, and then we can push Azgald into the sea."

Nera changed from her night robes into one of her dresses and climbed down the stairs of her tower. She purposefully strode into the great hall of Bergred Citadel, where many of her husband's retainers were just coming in to eat their breakfast. As the retainers took notice of Nera's entry, the usual morning chatter of the warriors died down to complete silence.

Nera thought she heard a hushed whisper: the Great Witch of the North. She smirked at the fear her title inspired in everyone she encountered. Few would dare act against the wishes of such a nightmarish being.

"Warden Tarik," she called out to Alvir's most senior retainer.

"Yes, Lady Nera?" Tarik warily responded.

"Assemble three hundred cavalry and six thousand infantry from the villages," she ordered. "We march to Drammon. My husband is in danger."

Nera knew this retainer well. Tarik knew better than to question his lady's orders. The witch could invent tortures worse than death for any disobedient subjects. Men who did question Nera eventually found themselves dismembered and pickled in her potions, cursed, or otherwise meeting some ghastly fate. If she said that her husband was in danger, then the majority of Alvir's warriors were to be called on a two-week march to High Warlord Ivarsson's castle in Drammon without hesitation. No one dared question the will of the witch. But fear was not Tarik's only motivation. He was a veteran soldier and no stranger to court intrigue. Any gain for Alvir's house frequently proved to be for his own benefit too. He was loyal to Alvir and would follow the witch's commands. Nera knew Tarik would die in her service. She read it in the runes.

With a bow, the warden immediately left the great hall with his bowl of porridge sitting on one of the tables untouched. Nera smiled to herself as the tone of the warriors suddenly shifted from dread silence to preparations for war. She did not know which she was more excited about: her imminent ascension to royalty or the possibility of even greater power which teased at her thoughts. She was glad her husband was equally ambitious and required little persuasion in accepting her plan. With luck, an elder evil she had long sought would soon be bound to Nera's service, making all these schemes successful.

Spotting one of her slaves, a maiden in her late teens, Nera gestured for her to follow, and made her way back to the tower. The slave followed closely without saying a word. Upon reaching her room, Nera motioned for the slave to enter. The slave complied as she nervously brushed her hair out of her face with her hand.

"Yoan has been kind to our house," Nera said as she reached for her gilded wooden staff, which was propped against the wall.

The slave weakly nodded. Nera had trained her slaves not to say anything at all unless asked a direct question. Control meant exact obedience from all her subjects. She would not allow for anything she could not predict.

Nera eyed the pyramidal crystal at the top of her staff and drew it close to her face for inspection. The crystal sparkled a deep purple in the morning light. It hungered for blood.

"Get my things ready for the journey," Nera commanded her slave. "It will be a two-week march to Drammon."

The slave busied herself collecting Nera's belongings. She began packing clothes into a chest, along with some of Nera's spell books and thick corked glass vials filled with strangely colored potions. The slave kept her eyes low, obviously afraid of what else the witch might require of her. Nera smirked at the thought. The slave knew her place.

"How do the people of your lands honor your gods?" Nera asked the slave as she leaned over her cauldron.

"In the Ostlands my people built great temples and shrines," the slave explained, still trying to pack quickly without breaking anything or appearing careless. "Pilgrims would travel for many weeks or even months to worship at the largest and most beautiful temples. Sacred Vindholm attracts many pilgrims to Azgald, even with the city being so far north."

"Vindholm is a blight to the Nordslands which will soon be destroyed," Nera snorted as she gestured for the slave to come and view the contents of her cauldron. "The gods of the Nordslands are not so vain."

The slave stepped closer to the cauldron and almost retched at the stench of the soupy contents of the potion. Large bubbles broke through a thick green film covering the surface of the putrid potion. The slave had no desire to stand so close to this vile concoction, but she had little choice. Nera knew her slave's thoughts. She could see the disgust written across her face. Yet she stood where she was told. This was control.

"Our gods only demand sacrifice to honor them," Nera continued. "A sacrifice can be made anywhere by anyone, shrine or no. And as we honor the gods, they bless their worthy patrons in turn, which binds us to serve them all the more faithfully."

"But the dark gods are fickle," the slave noted with a hint of fear in her voice. "They can turn on you when you no longer serve their needs."

"They have helped me this far," Nera countered, annoyed that the slave had spoken out of turn. "And they will take me further than they will take you."

Nera drew a knife from the folds of her dress with the speed and dexterity of a trained assassin. The slave screamed and tried to deflect the blade with her arms, but Nera's knife still found the girl's neck. With a hard jerk, Nera removed the knife from the slave's throat and pulled her head over the cauldron. Blood gushed from the wound of the dying girl into the foul potion.

"Blood is the most worthy offering we can give the gods." Nera stroked the cold limp corpse. "The blood of young virgins is especially so."

Nera called in another slave to dispose of the body as she stirred her victim's blood into the potion with her staff. The concoction began bubbling more violently. Nera wafted the fumes into her nostrils. Exhaling in satisfaction, she ceased stirring the potion as the bubbling slowed to a simmer. She observed how the crystal on the end of her staff had changed from a deep purple to almost black while stirring the potion.

I am coming, Nera directed her thoughts toward her husband while pointing her staff in the general direction of distant Drammon. *Our army will set out before the day is through. No one will contest your claim to the throne once we arrive and I am at your side. Remember, vengeance against our foes and control over all the Nordslands will soon be ours.*

The crystal at the end of the staff had changed from almost black to light purple while Nera delivered her telepathic message to Alvir's mind. This signified to Nera that the magic had been drained from it, and there was little to do except continue as planned. Not that Alvir could have responded to her anyway. He was not magically gifted like she was. All the same, Alvir could hold his own until she arrived.

<u>Chapter Six</u>

After a moment of wondering what to do, Godfrey marched out of his room and made for the stairs. He was going to find out just why the King was here and put his suspicions to rest. He nearly collided with his mother, who was coming up the stairs just as he was about to go down. The look on her face told Godfrey she had come to find him.

"The King is here," Regana told him.

"I know," Godfrey replied. "What is he doing here?"

"He has come to dub you a knight," she answered with a weak smile.

"But father should do it," Godfrey protested. "If King Wilhelm performs the ceremony, I will have to swear fealty directly to him instead."

"You will still be your father's retainer," Regana reassured her son. "And your father is the King's vassal. So it doesn't really matter who performs the ceremony. The King can't expect you to pay homage to anyone but your father. All will be as it should. You will see."

"Then why did he come all the way out here?" Godfrey asked. "Who told him I would be knighted tomorrow?"

"I don't know who told him." Regana shook her head. "It would have taken him time to get word, but that doesn't matter now. As to why the King thinks it's necessary for him to personally knight you: King Wilhelm has not been on the throne long. He feels he needs personal assurances that those directly under him are loyal. Bastogne is a powerful duchy, House Cretus has many friends, and you are next in line to be Duke."

Godfrey nodded in understanding, though he still did not like it. He had never personally spoken with the King, and he had only seen him on a few occasions, but there was something in the King's eye that Godfrey did not like. He thought about this for a moment.

What it was he did not like about the King, Godfrey decided, was that there was a calculating, acquisitive glimmer in Wilhelm's eye. It was not anything the King actually said or did, but it was how he looked at castles, treasures, women, and especially his vassals that made Godfrey feel uncomfortable. It was as if everyone and everything King Wilhelm saw were a resource to be gained, positioned, and spent in some world-spanning game of strategy.

But maybe Godfrey was too quick to judge the King's character. After all, Godfrey reminded himself, they had never really spoken face to face. Perhaps actually meeting King Wilhelm would change Godfrey's mind.

"Shall I go and see King Wilhelm then?" Godfrey asked his mother.

"Aye." Regana nodded. "He did come on your account, after all."

With Godfrey following close behind, Regana led the way down the stairs into the keep's great hall. A juggler had been summoned for entertainment as the Duke's guests mingled.

The Bishop and Ulric's chaplain were intensely discussing something about just war theory; whatever that was. The chaplain, Turpin, was a rough-looking man who had gained considerably more grey hair since the last time Godfrey saw him. As holy men, Turpin and Clovis were cut from the same cloth, but Turpin's mission in life was to see to the spiritual needs of soldiers rather than pursue theological concerns in more academic spheres as bishops tended to do.

Fulcher and Bruno were playing chess at a table in the corner while some of the other men-at-arms watched with mild interest. Though commoners, Godfrey had come to see that men-at-arms were no less intelligent than nobles. Nobles, however, were destined to lead, whereas commoners were duty-bound to follow.

Standing aloofly near the stairs to the dungeon was a ranger named Varin. Godfrey did not know the ranger well. Varin was often employed by Godfrey's father to scout the woods of Bastogne. It was a vocation that was as dangerous as it was solitary. Only lone wolves such as Varin were attracted to that line of work.

Fallard was speaking with one of the King's retainers, and Godfrey's father was speaking directly to King Wilhelm. The King's responses to Ulric's queries appeared dull and automatic, and his eyes wandered around the hall. Godfrey guessed by the bored expression on his father's face that Ulric himself was losing interest in his attempts to entertain Wilhelm. The two were merely exchanging formalities and did not really want to talk to each other.

Regana stepped to the side, urging Godfrey forward. Taking a deep breath, Godfrey approached the King. He was unsure exactly what to expect, and tried to reason away his worst fears. King Wilhelm turned and noticed Godfrey walking towards him, and Godfrey quickly stopped and knelt before the King. For a long moment, Godfrey stared at the rug in front of his face. Then Wilhelm gestured for him to stand. In a slow, deliberate manner, Godfrey rose to his feet. It was just as he had been trained to do as a page while in the presence of someone of high rank.

The King embraced Godfrey a bit too tentatively, as if neither of them were sure of the other's intent. The moment was awkward. It lasted far too long for Godfrey.

"Word of your exploits has spread quickly," King Wilhelm said as he finally released Godfrey from the embrace. "You have become something of a local hero at Harv."

"I am sure the details of my quest have become greatly exaggerated," Godfrey countered.

"Modesty," Wilhelm noted with a bemused smirk. "I like that quality in a knight."

The King was sizing him up, Godfrey had no doubt about that. He could see it in Wilhelm's eye. Godfrey shot a quick glance at his father, but the Duke gave Godfrey a reassuring smile. The smile put Godfrey at ease for the first time since Wilhelm's arrival.

"Thank you, lord." Godfrey bowed his head.

"It will be a pleasure to knight you." Wilhelm looked into Godfrey's eyes.

This was a highly calculated statement. Godfrey knew it. The King wanted to see if he would show any sign of resentment at this. Traditionally, fathers dubbed their sons knights if the former were alive and in good standing with their lords. When Godfrey inherited Bastogne, he would be expected to pay homage to the King. But that was not what this was. Wilhelm assuming the responsibility in the ceremony himself was an intrusion that made Godfrey grind his teeth. However, Godfrey was ready for this, and he held his irritation in check.

"The pleasure will be mine," Godfrey replied smoothly.

Godfrey thought for a moment. Dare he ask it?

"My lord," Godfrey began. "How is it you happened to arrive here on the same day as I? Had you come even a day later, my father would have already knighted me, and you would have missed this opportunity."

Now discomfort flashed across King Wilhelm's face, but only for the briefest moment.

"As I said," Wilhelm answered, "news of your exploits has traveled quickly."

The King's tone suggested that Godfrey should not press the issue further.

"You will have to tell me how you slew the vampire before I continue visiting the other duchies," King Wilhelm said, changing the subject.

"Of course," Godfrey agreed while secretly hoping to avoid entertaining the King any more than he absolutely had to. "It was an honor to finally meet you, my lord, but I feel I must return to fasting and prayer before the ceremony tomorrow."

"Indeed." King Wilhelm dismissed Godfrey with a gesture. "May the gods bless you."

Duke Ulric gave Godfrey an approving look as he left. His mother subtly repeated the Duke's gesture to Godfrey, though she pretended to be involved in conversation with some of the other ladies present. Returning to his room, Godfrey was unsure what exactly he had accomplished by his interaction with the King. The whole thing felt as brief as it did foolish. He knelt in silent prayer once again.

Several hours passed in complete boredom for Godfrey as everyone else celebrated downstairs. He had given up on prayer shortly after returning to his room, since divine manifestations were lacking at the moment. He just sat in a chair staring out the window for a while. The entertainment down the stairs grew louder as a feast was held in honor of

King Wilhelm. Godfrey's stomach gurgled. His last meal was so long ago. Finally it grew dark, and the noise from the great hall quieted down. Godfrey lit a few candles in the room, more to give himself something to do than for any other reason, and returned to his chair. He took solace in the fact that at least he would soon be able to pass the remainder of his fast sleeping.

A knock at the door swept Godfrey from his thoughts. His father entered the room and closed the door behind him as Godfrey stood. There was so much Godfrey wanted to tell his father, but most of it would just sound like unwarranted whining. Aside from that, he doubted there was much his father could do anyway.

"You handled yourself very well down there," the Duke said. "Your mother and I think you were quite diplomatic."

"I don't like King Wilhelm," Godfrey confessed.

"No," Ulric answered, shaking his head with a humorless smile.

"It's the way he looks at people," Godfrey explained. "It's like every word he says has a hidden meaning or he's testing people or something."

The words rushed out of Godfrey's mouth. Having had nothing to do but think for the whole afternoon, Godfrey's complaints were well-rehearsed, in his mind at least. His father listened patiently, apparently expecting this reaction.

"You know how dangerous it is to be my son?" Ulric asked at last.

"Of course," Godfrey answered, unsure why this question had been asked. "Lots of people would try to get me to do what they want instead of what is best for the Duchy."

"Some of them might even try to take you hostage or kill you if it suits their purposes and they have the opportunity." Ulric belabored the point. "The same is even truer for the

King. There are many men who could be king. Some of them even have legitimate claims to the throne. Any king is always in danger of being overthrown by someone within his kingdom, just as much as he is in danger of foreign invasion. Perhaps King Wilhelm means his subjects harm, but perhaps he is bad at concealing his own fears of the sword that always hangs over a king's head."

"Oh." Godfrey considered this possibility for the first time. "But I don't want to be king. Bastogne has more than enough riches for me. I don't need more power or money than what the Duchy has to offer."

"You could tell that to him," Ulric acknowledged. "But if he is particularly paranoid he may never know that for himself until his dying day."

"I see," Godfrey said after thinking over his father's response.

"That is why so much emphasis is put on homage and vows of fealty," Ulric explained. "Without these public promises of loyalty, it would be a lot harder for a lord to know whom he can trust."

"But it is still all based on trust," Godfrey pointed out.

"Right you are," Ulric answered. "And that is why our ancestors believed chivalry was so important. If and when that trust is betrayed, others will not stand by idly. Now get some sleep. We have an early morning tomorrow."

Leaving Godfrey once again to his thoughts, Ulric left the room. His father was right. If the King did not act with honor, there could be serious repercussions. Godfrey decided worrying would be useless at this point anyway. He was overthinking this entirely. He would take this whole thing one step at a time, he advised himself.

After undressing, Godfrey slipped into bed. The bed was soft but somewhat cool due to the gradually falling temperatures at night. He slept heavily for several hours, but awoke with a start. What had awoken him? He had dreamt of a ship, snow, blood, the clash of blades, but the details were rapidly escaping Godfrey. Maybe there was a girl involved too?

The image of a damsel with dark brown hair, grey eyes, and a fair white face slowly faded from Godfrey's mind, slipping away as he tried to recall her features. He heard a soft knock at the door and realized it was a similar knock which had initially awoken him. Yawning, he rubbed his eyes and stretched.

"Coming," Godfrey groggily called from his bed.

Jumping to his feet, he quickly threw on a tunic and some trousers. He briskly made for the door, and opened it to see a small boy holding a tabard and shield with Godfrey's father's heraldry emblazoned upon them. The boy was a page maybe seven or eight years old at most.

"You are to wear these, sire," the page answered in a squeaky voice.

"Thanks," Godfrey said as he took the items from the boy.

"And I am to take the sword you are to be knighted with to the King," the page explained.

"Right," Godfrey said as he went to fetch the sword Fallard had given him.

The room was dark, and only a single candle remained lit from the night. Godfrey rummaged through his clothing and armor, which he had lazily left scattered on the floor. He found his sword and unsheathed it from its scabbard. Yes, he definitely wanted to be knighted with the sword he had slain both the wight and vampire with.

For a long moment, Godfrey pondered the weapon in his hand. It had started its service to him destroying creatures of darkness. That was a good omen in his mind. He had thought long on what to name his sword. Thunder? Fang?

Menace? He wanted to dedicate the blade to righteousness, and its name should reflect that.

I will call you Uriel, Godfrey thought as he stared at the weapon. *Fire of the gods is a fitting name for such a blade.*

Godfrey did not really know the celestial tongue, but he had caught enough words in his dealings with the clergy to understand short phrases or individual words when recited at service or in prayer. Ur meant fire or light, he thought. And el meant gods. So together the terms meant fire of the gods or fire gods. He was pretty sure they meant the former. Godfrey would have to ask a priest or scholar before he started calling the blade Uriel out loud.

"Here you are," Godfrey said, stepping out into the corridor as he handed the sword to the page.

Godfrey smiled at the boy as he remembered doing similar tasks for Fallard when he was first taken in as a page. It seemed so long ago, and yet the time had gone so fast. The boy looked back with a tired but quizzical expression.

"Do you need anything else, sire?" the page asked, hefting the sword in both hands.

"No," Godfrey quickly answered. "But thanks again."

The page left down the hallway without another word. Godfrey meant to ask the page's name, what house he had come from, and express other pleasantries before he left, but at the moment Godfrey became distracted as he looked over his new shield and tabard. Forgetting the page, he examined these new possessions.

The shield was made of solid wood encased in a thin layer of steel, and was of the slightly more compact heater design as opposed to the longer kite shields which were older but still popular. Aside from the differences in heraldry, it was very similar to the one Godfrey had used while training with his cousin.

He brought the items to his room and dressed in his armor with only the aid of the single candle that had not burned out during the night. Finally, he slid the new tabard over his chainmail. He looked at himself in the mirror, admiring his father's heraldry emblazoned over his own chest. This was how it should be.

Pre-dawn light began to filter into Godfrey's room through the window. Blowing out the last candle as he left his room, he hurried downstairs to the great hall. The light of the fire from the hearth flickered against the walls. He only had a few minutes before the ceremony was supposed to start. His father and mother, as well as the Duke's chaplain, were already in the great hall when he arrived. They were all whispering about something Godfrey could not make out.

"Good," Regana said as she noticed Godfrey, abruptly ending the previous conversation. "We were just about to get you. Hurry, everything is set up in the courtyard."

A pair of guards unlatched the doors to the outside of the keep. Godfrey passed through the opening, followed by Ulric, Regana, and Turpin. King Wilhelm stood in the center of the courtyard, with Bishop Clovis and some of the King's kin standing a few paces behind with Fallard, Bruno, and Fulcher. It looked like everyone in the castle had gathered in the courtyard, even the aloof ranger, Varin. But of course they all had. This was the most significant day of Godfrey's life thus far.

Godfrey recognized some of the knights and men-at-arms in their shining chainmail and freshly cleaned tabards as retainers who had been in his father's service for as long as he could remember. Karl the Hammer, Sir Rodair, and Sir Malbert were among the faces Godfrey knew from his earliest years. Other faces he did not recognize. He guessed some were sons who had taken the place of fathers. Some were husbands who had married the daughters of older retainers.

Like the men, Godfrey recognized some of the women in their colorful wool and linen dresses as maidens he had grown up with, or the wives of some of the members of Ulric's household. Sadly, some of the maidens Godfrey had found more attractive were missing, though he wondered how they would compare to the girl in his dream. That was if she were real. Smiling ruefully, he figured the missing girls must have been married off to other lords and now resided in distant estates.

Ulric, Regana, and Turpin took their places behind the King, and Godfrey knelt at Wilhelm's feet just as the Sun began to rise. Bishop Clovis stepped forward and offered an invocation in the celestial language. Godfrey did not understand the prayer in the slightest aside from the word *Ur*. Perhaps that word meant Sun? He regretted that he had only picked up a few words from the holy tongue. His father's tutors had taught Godfrey the basics of reading and writing, and enough about other subjects to make Godfrey curious about them, but Fallard's pragmatic training regimen had not left enough time for Godfrey to really learn much about academic topics growing up. He had only been taught enough about languages and letters to one day manage the affairs of Bastogne.

After the Bishop's prayer, King Wilhelm touched Godfrey's left shoulder, right shoulder, then the top of his head with the flat of the blade of Godfrey's sword. Elation clouded Godfrey's mind. His bitterness towards the King was forgotten in this moment. Though he hoped he would not forget the part he was supposed to say in the ritual.

"With this sword which has been consecrated for the purpose of destroying evil and preserving that which is holy," King Wilhelm began, "I dub you, Godfrey de Bastogne, knight of the Kingdom of Lortharain."

"I, Godfrey de Bastogne swear fealty to you, King Wilhelm," Godfrey replied. "Furthermore, I pledge my services to the Kingdom of Lortharain for as long as I shall live."

"In return for that service," King Wilhelm answered, "I grant you place in your father's household as his retainer until such time as the needs of the kingdom require your services in another office. Take your sword and arise a knight."

Godfrey stood and took his sword from the King's hands. He returned it to the scabbard on his belt as the crowd applauded. King Wilhelm briefly embraced Godfrey, then his mother and father repeated the gesture, but with the sincerity of those who actually loved him. He was now a knight in both name and fact.

<u>Chapter Seven</u>

Baruch snorted impatiently in the cold starless predawn. Godfrey soothingly patted his steed as he sat atop the horse. As he waited for the sign, his eyes skimmed through the trees and he gripped his lance more tightly. The thin layer of snow covering the ground reflected the diffused light beginning to fill the sky, while the trees of the forest stared back, grim and menacing. Winter had come early this year.

Godfrey gave a small shiver. He hated winter. The cold bit his nose, and clear watery mucus threatened to run down his face from his nostrils. Sniffling, he fought back the dripping mucus. This task was too important to leave until spring.

The twenty mounted knights around him also gripped their lances in anticipation. Just thirty or so yards ahead of Godfrey and his father's knights stood the scattered hovels of a small orcish encampment. The structures were crude. To say that they were designed more with function than aesthetics in mind would have been a vast understatement. Several tree stumps studded the ground around the camp, attesting to how recently the outpost had been constructed. The figures of a few orcs began to stir among the encampment, but they did not notice the human knights yet.

Ulric's chaplain, Turpin, gave Godfrey a nod as their eyes met. The chaplain sat atop his own steed next to Godfrey. He had no doubt his father had the chaplain escorting Godfrey to make sure things did not go wrong. The thought comforted Godfrey, as he knew Turpin would keep him out of danger, but it also made Godfrey keenly aware that his father did not entirely trust his son to a position of command yet.

Godfrey muttered a silent prayer to Loxias in hopes that he would not get too many of his father's men killed in the battle about to take place; and more importantly, that they would win. His heart began to race at the possibility of somehow failing in his first command. His hand twitched nervously.

Thoughts of potential failure quickly vanished from Godfrey's mind as a few small hovels caught fire in a storm of flaming arrows. Brutish bellowing started up from the orc camp as more and more of the hovels began to burn. A moment later, Godfrey could hear the clashing of weapons and the shouting of men and orcs on the other side of the encampment as the battle commenced and the firestorm of arrows ceased.

"Now!" Godfrey shouted as he spurred Baruch onward.

The other knights followed just behind Godfrey as he couched his lance. They closed in on the encampment as the horses galloped onwards. The hunched figures of orcs raced towards the fight on the other side of the camp as Godfrey and the knights drew closer to them. The creatures' grey mottled skin gave their bodies the appearance of slimy marbled stones with wispy black hair and orange molten gems set in deep pits for eyes. The orcs' eclectic combination of leather and chainmail armor only added to their barbaric appearance. They were running in the direction of the burning huts, still unaware of the mounted knights closing in on them.

Godfrey skewered one of the brutes with his lance just as the orc turned and noticed him. Giving an anguished howl, the orc toppled as it died. The knights slaughtered more orcs unawares as they rode through their midst. Confusion overcame the orcs as they noticed the human knights amongst them and to their backs. Some turned to face the knights. Others pressed on to their original destination. Most fled in panic or died as they were trampled.

Godfrey thrust his lance into an orc as it charged him while Baruch trampled another monster under his hooves. A third orc snarled a challenge to Godfrey as it brandished a two-handed ax. Godfrey spurred Baruch towards the orc, which bellowed as it raced to meet him. Godfrey thrust his lance, but the orc jumped out of the way. It swung its ax at Godfrey, shattering the haft of his weapon. The shock of the blow sent pain racing up his arm. Godfrey urged Baruch back a couple of steps as he dropped the splintered fragments of the lance that were still in his hand. Ignoring the pain throbbing through his arm, he drew his sword.

The orc lunged for Godfrey with another swing of its ax. He deflected the blow with his sword, anticipating it better than the last one. The orc raised its ax again, but Godfrey plunged his blade down into its chest. The monster gurgled a low bloody sigh before keeling over into the snow. Godfrey felt no pity for the creature. It deserved such an end.

The knights advanced through the hovels to the center of the encampment. Their horses crushed orcs with their hooves as they galloped over them, or the knights stuck them with lances as the brutes burst out of their huts. Many of the orcs did not even take the time to put their armor on in their haste to join the fight. Godfrey shook off the subsiding pain from his arm and soon forgot about it. Adrenaline kept him sharp.

From the center of the encampment, Godfrey spotted where his father's footmen had engaged the majority of the orcish warriors. Spears, swords, and axes clashed against shields and other weapons while other blows found their marks and killed their opponents. The two masses of troops appeared to be at a standstill. The men were better equipped and more skilled, but the orcs were naturally stronger and in greater numbers.

"There!" Godfrey pointed his sword at the rear of the orcish horde. "Form up. While their backs are to us, destroy them!"

Charging as fast as their steeds would carry them, Godfrey and the other knights crashed into the backs of the orcs. Dozens of the brutes were trampled while others were skewered with lances and swords. Godfrey swung Uriel indiscriminately into the mass of the orcs, felling a monster with each strike. At this, the orcs began to panic and scatter. The footmen and knights cheered as one while the orcs fled.

"Run them down," Godfrey ordered. "Leave none alive."

The knights and footmen chased after the orcs, cutting them down as they overran the monsters. Some of the footmen took torches to the remaining hovels, ensuring complete destruction of the orc camp. Dawn was now fully upon them, and not a single orc remained standing. It was over.

"A well-executed attack." Turpin trotted his horse in Godfrey's direction.

"Indeed," Godfrey replied as he surveyed the scene while stroking Baruch.

All of the orc buildings were either burning or only remained as smoldering heaps of ash and debris. Some of the footmen lifted their fallen comrades from the dead, while others jabbed their spears into the gasping bodies of still-breathing orcs. The archers who had commenced the battle by loosing their flaming arrows into the encampment from afar now walked freely among the spear- and sword-armed infantry. From the dead orcs they plucked arrows that had fletching that matched the arrows' in their quivers. The archers tallied their kills aloud to their friends. The ranger, Varin, was apparently in the lead. It was a macabre contest, but Godfrey understood how the bowmen found honor in it.

"I'm surprised they didn't even have a wooden palisade to protect this encampment," Godfrey noted to the chaplain.

"It should have been the first thing they built," Turpin agreed. "They might not have wanted to build a wall until they had determined the boundaries of the encampment. Or maybe they just never expected us to find them this deep in the forest."

"That orcs might consider themselves so secure living within the borders of Bastogne," Godfrey huffed contemptuously. "If we could scour every cave and glen in the forests, we might be rid of their filth entirely."

"You speak more and more every day like your father used to." Turpin smiled ruefully. "He still shares in your idealism, but there are a lot of caves and glens in the forests of Bastogne, perhaps too many for the son of one duke to find in his lifetime."

"And then there are the great orc fortresses in the mountains," Godfrey conceded. "Perhaps it is too much work for us, but we will do what we can while we can."

"So we shall." Turpin wiped the sweat and grime from his face. "I trust this will not be the last time your father entrusts his soldiers to you for a punitive strike."

Smiling to himself, Godfrey basked in the chaplain's praise. Godfrey had mostly known Turpin as a quiet brooding man. Like Fallard, Turpin's compliments were rare, from what Godfrey had seen of the chaplain.

Godfrey dismounted Baruch and made his way towards the dead among the human footmen, and Turpin silently followed suit. Ulric's soldiers had lined them up in a row. A quick count from Godfrey put the human dead at fifty or so. Were those *acceptable* losses?

Splattered blood stains covered the tabards of both the living and the dead. Godfrey did not recognize any of the dead as soldiers he had personally known. Fifty, of the twenty knights, hundred men-at-arms, and fifty archers Ulric had given Godfrey for the task of destroying the orc encampment. There were hundreds more stationed in the castle back at home, and that only represented a fraction of what Bastogne could muster in a true emergency.

Still, it occurred to Godfrey that these dead men lying before him were fathers who would not return home to their children, and sons who would not see their mothers again. He put his hand to his face, holding back the tears that threatened to fall from his eyes. One of the men-at-arms standing over the dead gave Godfrey a curious glance.

"Sire?" the footman inquired.

"We will bury them here," Godfrey ordered the footman. "But leave the orc dead where they lie. Let it serve as a warning to their kind."

Godfrey took a shovel from one of the men-at-arms, and began to dig in the cold, hard earth. Several of the knights gathered around him, watching him from their steeds. The knights watched Godfrey, seemingly perplexed, as he helped the footmen bury their dead. Turpin also took a shovel and began to dig. Seeing Godfrey help with so menial a task, the men-at-arms dug the graves more energetically. Soon, all the Bastognian soldiers and knights were occupied with the task of digging the graves.

"Nobility is not just in a name," Turpin told Godfrey after they had finished.

"They died in the service of my father," Godfrey answered as both the knights and infantry listened in. "What greater honor could I bestow upon them?"

Turpin gave a brief but heartfelt eulogy over the graves, speaking of sacrifice and ridding the world of evil. The rest of the army listened respectfully, and when the chaplain had finished, Godfrey ordered them to march back home.

About an hour or so into the march, Godfrey noticed Varin approaching him from the rear of the column. The man did not meet Godfrey's gaze, though Godfrey was certain Varin intended to speak with him. Godfrey slowed Baruch, allowing the ranger to catch up.

"That was a kind thing you did back there," Varin said as his eyes scanned the trees.

Godfrey suspected Varin was always looking for danger in the shadows, ready to pounce at a moment's notice. Rangers were not generally the best-mannered, but Godfrey ignored Varin's eccentricities. The man obviously had seen too much, and was broken because of it. It was best to just take the compliment in stride.

"The men are impressed," Varin continued. "Most lords would consider burying the dead to be beneath them."

"Do you talk much with the men?" Godfrey could not help but wonder.

"No." Varin shrugged. "But I hear what they say. Many of them were unsure of your abilities before today. Now many of them would die for you."

"And what's your assessment?" Godfrey pressed.

"I would be willing to go on another patrol with you." Varin's eyes still had yet to meet Godfrey's in this exchange. "I would be willing to join you on a longer campaign, maybe share a meal with you. But I die for no man."

"Fair enough." Godfrey did little to hide his amusement at the ranger's blunt response.

With that, Varin fell back in with the archers, not saying another word to anyone.

Upon returning to the castle, a footman took Godfrey's and Turpin's horses to the stables as they made their way to the citadel. Godfrey's mother rushed out to meet the two in the courtyard before they could even reach the keep. Mothers always seemed to worry like that.

Regana embraced her son as tightly as she could. It was as if she were releasing all the anxiety that had built up inside her since he went out on the patrol. The embrace did not seem as strong to Godfrey as it had even when he first got back to the castle a few weeks prior. She gave a weak cough as she caught her breath in the crisp winter air. Godfrey's father followed close behind, giving his wife a look of concern.

"Are you all right?" Godfrey asked.

"It's nothing." Regana took a step back and sniffled. "You are home safe, and that's what matters."

"The patrol?" Ulric anxiously inquired.

"We discovered the orc encampment and burned it to the ground," Godfrey reported.

"It appeared to be a new settlement," Turpin added gruffly. "They did not even build a wall around it yet."

"That's not good." Ulric frowned. "Sending out settlers this late in the year could only mean that the larger fortresses are overcrowded."

"But," Godfrey interjected. "We've killed thousands of them this year alone. How many more orcs could there be?"

Regana gave a deeper cough than before. She tried to suppress it, but the fit grew worse. Again, Ulric shot her a worried look. She stopped coughing and regained her composure, but Ulric's grim expression remained. Godfrey frowned at this. His mother was sick and doing a bad job at hiding it.

"I think it's best that we all go inside," Ulric said as he put his arm around Regana.

Ulric led his wife back to the keep, and Godfrey followed with the others. A fire crackled in the great hall, and Regana gained a bit of color back in her face as she sat down at a table near the hearth. Ulric sat next to her, and Godfrey and Turpin also sat near the fire. Glad to be inside where it was warm, Godfrey removed his spangenhelm and set it on the table. Next, Godfrey took off his gloves and stretched his hands out over the fire. He began to unwind but thought better of it when he saw the sober look on his father's face.

"How many men did we lose?" Ulric asked.

"Fifty-four men-at-arms," Turpin grumbled. "No archers or knights were lost. The orc dead numbered over three hundred."

Ulric huffed. Godfrey was unsure whether this was in assent of how few casualties they had taken in comparison to the orcs, or if it was in disapproval that he had even lost that many men. Ulric's expression was unreadable, which made Godfrey's insides squirm.

"It was Godfrey's idea to attack the encampment from two fronts," Turpin explained. "We would have lost many more otherwise."

Thoughtfully, Ulric nodded. Godfrey released a breath he did not realize he was holding. Ulric approved of how

Godfrey handled his first command after all. Somehow, Godfrey thought his father should have appeared more pleased with the results.

"You'll have to forgive your father for not appearing more enthusiastic about your success," Regana said, seeming to read Godfrey's mind. "We were not expecting to hear that you would find a *new* orc encampment."

"Right," Ulric said, snapping back to the present. "You've done well, Godfrey. However, if there was one such encampment out there, there must surely be more just like it hidden in the woods."

"My thoughts exactly, lord," Turpin agreed. "They must be stronger than we thought. Perhaps this year's wars were merely testing their strength."

"Or ours," Ulric answered. "We cannot afford to wait until the spring to find out. Turpin, send out a call to muster new soldiers. We need to *at least* replace our losses. Godfrey, return to Harv. Purchase as much arms and armor as you can so that we might have a stockpile here in case of a siege in the spring. Then, the three of us will lead separate patrols and cover as much of the woods as we can."

Godfrey's heart surged. He was working with his father. He was being entrusted with something very important. His reservations about the attack on the orc encampment were cast aside as quickly as they had formed.

"But do not venture into the Black Iron Mountains," Ulric cautioned. "We know the orcs are there, and even Bastogne cannot afford to squander its strength against those fortifications. Understood?"

Godfrey and Turpin nodded, but Regana frowned. She let out another weak cough as Ulric looked at her. With a somewhat puzzled expression, he returned the frown. Godfrey's enthusiasm receded at the exchange. He ground his teeth, knowing his parents were not being open with him. He could guess what it was. He was not a child anymore.

"Let's not get so carried away with playing war that we do not even let Godfrey sit for a good meal," Regana protested. "The orcs and the end of the world can wait for another hour at least."

Ulric smiled wearily, and Regana returned it. Servants brought out a simple meal of bread and salted meats while a page waited on each of them. As Turpin and Ulric began to methodically dig into the pork, Godfrey noticed the page attending him was the same one who had presented him with his new tabard and shield the morning he was knighted a few weeks prior.

"I didn't catch your name," Godfrey prodded the page as he took a slice of pork from a serving dish.

"Corbin," the page replied. "I am Corbin de Ghend, sire."

"How many other pages are here at the castle?" Godfrey asked.

"Six," Corbin answered after thinking for a moment. "The other three are helping their lords."

"And who is your lord?" Godfrey inquired as he began to bite into a small loaf of bread.

"Sir Malbert," Corbin replied.

"He is one of my father's best knights," Godfrey noted. "Pay close attention to what he teaches you."

"Oh I will," Corbin gave a squeak.

Godfrey's thoughts turned away from the page as he looked across the table to his mother. His expression creased into a frown. She was so old and frail. Remembering that she was sick, Godfrey grew frustrated that she did not bring it up in conversation. However, he reluctantly decided to not ask about it. His father did not mention it either, which meant Godfrey really should not ask about it.

After the four had finished with their meal, the pages and servants cleared the scraps and dirty dishes away. Ulric gave Godfrey a sack of gold coins with which to purchase the weapons and armor from Harv, while Turpin excused himself to go on his way recruiting more footmen from nearby villages. Regana embraced her son as he made to leave the great hall.

"I'll be back in a couple of weeks," Godfrey reassured her.

"It's just that you're growing up," Regana tearfully explained. "You're becoming a man, and you're going off on your own."

"Mother," Godfrey interjected awkwardly. "Are you sick?"

"It's nothing." Regana shook her head. "Do not worry about it. You have an important mission to fulfill for the Duchy."

"Right." Godfrey bit his lip as his mother hugged him again.

"Hurry back now, son." Ulric patted Godfrey's shoulder.

<u>Chapter Eight</u>

Mounting Baruch, Godfrey set out from the stables of Fuetoile Keep. No longer did he accompany Sir Fallard or some other lord. Godfrey was by himself now on his father's business. It was a strange feeling. As Fuetoile Keep grew farther away, he kept looking back, expecting someone, anyone, to come and announce that he would escort Godfrey the rest of the way. With the castle now hidden by the trees, Godfrey came to terms with the fact that no one was coming to hold his hand. He really was being trusted with this great responsibility. Alone.

As darkness fell, Godfrey stopped to rest for the night. It was miserably cold out. However, he did not light a fire, as he was alone and there was no one else to take watch. Even if there were not any orcs around, there were still wargs, brigands, and other foul creatures whose attention Godfrey did not want to attract while he slept. He simply wrapped himself tightly in his cloak, only taking off his spangenhelm. He knew it would be harder to sleep in his armor, but he had to be ready if some sudden danger woke him up.

He tossed fitfully in his sleep, his dreams filled once again with violence, snow, and the maiden with grey eyes and dark brown hair. He could not make much sense of it when he woke up, but he grew so tired as the day wore on that he decided he would risk sleeping without his armor on for the rest of the journey. Even doing so, by the end of a week, Godfrey was stiff and exhausted from traveling so long. Occasionally catching a whiff of his own repugnant body odor, he grew eager for the chance to bathe. He breathed a heavy sigh at the sight of Harv's palisade, and even Baruch seemed relieved.

The sentries at Harv's gate did not notice Godfrey's weathered appearance. They waved down at him from the parapet when they recognized him, and talked excitedly to each other. Wondering if the guards were still in awe of the tale of how Godfrey slew the vampire, he stopped Baruch just at the gate and looked up at the men.

"You should go to the town square, sire," one of the guards called down. "Bishop Clovis has an announcement that he wants everyone to hear."

"Right," Godfrey replied, dismounting from Baruch.

Important men like bishops regularly held councils, recited decrees, or otherwise made use of open communal spaces, but Godfrey rarely found these events to be worth getting excited over. A new law might be pronounced concerning grazing on royal pastures, the clergy might vote on some theological matter well over Godfrey's head, or any number of equally mundane or dense topics could be brought up in these forums. On more rare occasions, a lord or clergyman might warn travelers not to use a certain road because a cyclops was spotted on it eating pilgrims, and volunteers were needed to drive it off, or some similar threat might need to be dealt with. Those sorts of announcements had a way of leaking out before the official message was given. And that got people excited like they were now.

The snow was wet in the cloudy, grey afternoon. It was partly melted, leaving large odorous puddles in the mud. Godfrey left Baruch at the stables by the gatehouse, patting the steed's nose in farewell. Splashing mud up to his ankles, Godfrey made his way to the town square. There was a large crowd. Peasants, nobles, merchants, it seemed the whole town had come to satisfy their curiosity. Bishop Clovis stood atop a recently erected wooden platform with some of the local clergy and a few other bishops Godfrey did not know. A few knights wearing heraldry with white four-pointed stars set against black fields also stood near Clovis.

Spotting Walaric near the front of the crowd, Godfrey made his way towards the acolyte. Clovis was just starting into a speech, but Godfrey was more interested in catching his friend's attention. He tugged on Walaric's tunic, and the boy jumped.

"Godfrey." Walaric gave a surprised smile.

"It's good to see you." Godfrey shook Walaric's hand.

Most of the crowd was rapt in Clovis's speech. Turning his full attention to the platform, Godfrey realized he had no idea who these black-clad knights were. He frowned at this revelation. He should have recognized the heraldry of all the major houses within Lortharain at least. They wore the same four-pointed star as Clovis's retainers but the colors were wrong. Perhaps they were the retainers of another bishop?

"Who are they?" Godfrey indicated the knights in the black tabards.

"The Knights of the Silver Sun," Walaric curtly explained. "They are one of the orders that defend Azgald from the Clans."

Nodding appreciatively but not fully understanding, Godfrey now began to listen to Clovis's speech in earnest. It did not sound like he had missed much, mostly the pleasantries and formalities that came with addressing large crowds of varying social status. Gesticulating towards the crowd, Clovis now got to the true purpose of his return to Harv.

"The Kingdom of Azgald was founded at the end of the first great crusade into the Nordslands." Clovis stretched out his hand. "It has only been their efforts, their sweat and blood that have prevented further Nordsman invasions into the Ostlands. Even so, Azgald's strength has dwindled through the years."

Godfrey searched his memory. His mother had spoken of family in Azgald. An uncle, grandparents, a few more distant relations had once lived there but were now long dead. He had never been that far north, nor did he ever think about going. A traveler had to cross the Freezing Sea to get there.

"The Silver Suns here with me bring most dire news," Clovis continued. "The Nordsmen have resumed the war with Azgald under a new High King. He is both a fearless warrior and a cunning strategist. Many castles have burned under the banner of Alvir. Countless valiant knights have been slain by his hordes. The entire County of Fhunlan has been desecrated by his wrath. He has not spared children from his rage, and what his armies have done to the women they have captured is best to pass over in silence."

Hanging on every word the Bishop said, Godfrey clenched his teeth at the injustice of it all. Walaric's fists were balled. The Bishop went on to enumerate many more Nordsman misdeeds. He spoke of how the Nordsmen were servants of the dark gods, and were among the foulest men alive. There was no honor in these Nordsmen, and their name was a byword for treachery. So the Bishop said.

Many in the crowd were equally agitated. Some grimaced. Some were on the verge of tears. These Nordsmen sounded even worse than orcs. According to the Bishop, this High

King Alvir was even allied with some of the larger orc tribes of the North now.

Godfrey vaguely remembered being told about the crusades sent north. Most of them were long ago and were passed down in bards' songs like the Tale of Cheldric. Yet only a fool could not see what all of this was leading to.

"The Silver Suns and the other orders are strong," Clovis said in a raised voice. "But their strength added to the lords and knights of Azgald is not enough anymore. High King Alvir has more orcs, cyclopes, and dwarves under his command than any Nordsman lord has ever had before. He has the loyalty of more Nordsman clans than any Nordsman High King in three centuries."

The crowd grew increasingly agitated with every word the Bishop uttered. Walaric's fists were clenched so tight now he appeared to be losing circulation in his hands. Someone had to do something about this Nordsman threat. Then Godfrey realized that he was someone.

"Who is better qualified to lead a new crusade into the Nordslands than the knights of Lortharain?" the Bishop asked, pointing to individual knights in the crowd. "After all, it is your lands that they protect. Remember, the War in Heaven is eternal and it is mirrored here in the mortal realms. The gods will bless those who join this crusade. The hardships you face along the way now are nothing compared to the reward you will see in the afterlife. Who will join? Who will join the crusade?"

Shouting erupted from the crowd. It was indiscernible. Without thinking, Godfrey found himself atop the platform. He had drawn his sword and raised it in the air.

"I, Godfrey de Bastogne, pledge my blade, Uriel, to the crusade." He brandished his weapon for all to see. "I saved Harv from the terror of the undead, now I will be on the first ship to the North to save Azgald."

Emboldened, Walaric jumped atop the platform too. He knelt before Bishop Clovis in supplication. Nodding solemnly, Clovis gestured for him to stand.

"With the permission of the holy priesthood," Walaric said, rising. "I also pledge to be on that first ship."

Others, mostly knights, also gave their pledge to join the crusade. A few pledged to renounce their lands and join the Silver Suns or offer money to the temples and shrines to help fund the crusade. Walaric turned to Godfrey, almost shaking with excitement. Elated, Godfrey slapped his friend's shoulder before embracing him. It was good to know Godfrey would not be going alone. He nodded to himself reassuringly. Suddenly, Walaric furrowed his brow as he contemplated his friend.

"So what brought you back here?" Walaric asked.

Thinking for a moment, Godfrey remembered why he had traveled through the woods alone for the last week. Blushing with embarrassment, he looked at Bishop Clovis, who was in deep discussion with the Silver Suns. He flinched as he looked back to Walaric, unsure of what to say.

"I think I might have made a mistake," Godfrey divulged as a wave of embarrassment washed over his face. "I was supposed to come here to buy weapons and armor for my father's soldiers. He is worried that orcs are going to besiege Fuetoile Keep in the spring."

"If they do that, all of Bastogne will be in danger," Walaric gasped. "Harv, Vosg, Menz, all the towns and cities in the Duchy will be vulnerable. Does the Duke really think they'll try to attack Fuetoile Keep itself?"

"He seems to think that," Godfrey said, rubbing his chin. "We were going to go out on more patrols, try to see if we could find more camps or villages hidden in the woods."

"Well you can't go on crusade then." Walaric frowned. "It sounds like you're needed here. Your father will be furious when he hears that you've joined the crusade."

"That's what I'm afraid of," Godfrey confessed as his hand began to shake.

Lady Seda Eist studied Godfrey with a bemused smile. He was standing in the middle of the parlor of the Eist manor, and the floorboards creaked as Godfrey shifted his weight from one foot to the other. The air was musty. Account ledgers lay sprawled across a large desk near the back wall. Lady Eist hefted the bag of gold coins Godfrey had given her, and she poured them out over the desk. They clattered across the wooden surface, and Lady Eist quickly counted then recounted the coins.

"Yes..." Lady Eist nodded as she scooped the considerable number of coins back into the bag. "That should be enough to equip your father's men. I'll tell the servants to start loading the wagons immediately. Is it for the crusade?"

"Possibly." Godfrey was hardly convinced by his own answer.

He still was unsure how his parents would react to the news that he had joined the crusade. His stomach sank at the thought, and his hand randomly twitched even hours after he pledged to go on crusade. Staring out the window, he frowned.

"There are a lot of dangers here too," Godfrey added as casually as he could manage. "My father is very concerned about the orcs coming down from the mountains in the spring. They might already be gathering in the woods."

"Even after all their losses this year?" Lady Eist bit her lip thoughtfully. "The Black Iron Mountains do not just spawn orcs on their own."

Godfrey did not reply.

Though he refused to look directly at Lady Eist, Godfrey watched her reflection carefully in the glass. He pretended to be very interested in the movement of people outside, but he guessed Lady Eist was not fooled by this ruse. She examined the bag of gold coins again, then looked back at Godfrey. She shifted in her seat as if debating what to say to him. Finally, she let out a long breath.

"Not many people actually go on crusade when one is called." Lady Eist absently toyed with a quill and ink bottle on the desk. "Many might vow to join in the beginning, but few follow through. Most are too concerned about affairs at home to listen to the gods' call, but you're youthful and idealistic. I don't think you will let petty day-to-day concerns or fear stop you from doing something great with yourself."

"Thanks," Godfrey said, meeting her eyes for the first time since she mentioned the crusade. "You're right. The crusade is too important. It doesn't matter what other people think. The problems here at home will work themselves out."

"The gods will protect you on their errand," Lady Eist continued. "You've done my family a great service as well. My husband and I have not forgotten. He will not mind if I lend you some of his guards to escort your caravan back to

Fuetoile Keep. Just be true to your word now like you were to us then."

"I will," Godfrey promised.

There were only five wagons in the caravan, but ox teams were slow and had to stick to wide and well-used paths. Godfrey thought about leaving the caravan behind. Baruch could make much better time than the wagons and take shortcuts the oxen could not. In the end, Godfrey's sense of duty told him he could not simply leave the caravan to its own devices, even if it was well-guarded by others. This task had been entrusted to him by his father, however tedious it seemed.

It took nearly twice as long for the caravan to reach Fuetoile Keep as it took Godfrey to make the initial trip on his own. He had nearly forgotten how painfully slow traveling like this could be. He had only occasionally seen to escorting caravans with Fallard, and the experiences were hardly memorable. Caravans needed escorts because they attracted both brigands hungry for loot and monsters hungry for flesh. Godfrey's previous experiences escorting slow, creaking wagons were not nearly so adventuresome though. At least it gave him plenty of time to think about how he would break the news to his parents about joining the crusade. It made the journey seem to last all the longer.

At last, as Fuetoile Keep appeared in the distance, a lump formed in Godfrey's throat. However, the agony of waiting was growing worse than the fear of whatever his parents

might say. Deciding he would prefer to face his parents
sooner rather than later, he spurred Baruch onward ahead of
the wagons laden with arms and armor. He stopped for a
moment at the head of the caravan.

"You have things under control?" Godfrey asked the lead
guard.

"Yes, my lord," the man answered with a quizzical look.

"See that the wagons make it to the keep safely," Godfrey
ordered.

With that, Godfrey spurred Baruch forward, leaving the
caravan behind. They were in sight of the castle now. The
caravan was safe. Godfrey had little reason to worry about
that now.

Approaching Fuetoile Keep, Godfrey was met at the gate
by his father. Ulric's expression was grave as the snow began
to fall from the clouds overhead. At first, Godfrey was
afraid his father was about to reprimand him for abandoning
the wagons, but he realized it was not anger in the Duke's
eyes. His expression was numb and distant. It was as if the
Duke was looking through his son rather than at him.

"Father?" Godfrey apprehensively asked as he got off
Baruch.

"Your mother," Ulric replied, gesturing for Godfrey to
hurry after him.

Ulric turned and ran back to the keep faster than Godfrey
had expected. Godfrey quickly removed his spangenhelm
and tucked it under his arm. Rushing after his father through
the outer and inner courtyards, Godfrey struggled to ask any
coherent questions. The two made their way through the
keep up to the Duke's bed chambers before Godfrey could
register any of it. Serfs, knights, and footmen readily parted
in the halls for Ulric and his son. Godfrey caught bleak
expressions on their faces as he passed. He was horrified to
think what awaited them.

"What's wrong with mother?" Godfrey gasped.

Turning to his son, Ulric shook his head. The Duke's half-formed words barely crossed his lips as some barely audible expression of suffering. Godfrey had never seen his father so distressed. It was unnerving.

The Duke hesitated for a moment, then he burst into his bed chamber. Godfrey followed him in, still panting from his flight through the castle. Choking on incense as he entered the room, Godfrey tried to make sense of the scene before him. Turpin was muttering an incantation as he swung a censer near the Duke's and Duchess' bed. Lying in the bed, his mother gave several harsh coughs before taking in gasping breaths, and repeated this several times. Sir Rodair, Karl the Hammer, Sir Euric, Varin, and a handful more of Ulric's closest retainers stood vigil at a respectful distance from the bed.

Ignoring them all, Godfrey bounded to his mother's bed. She was damp with sweat and kept her eyes closed. Godfrey caressed his mother's face. She was so weak right now.

"Mother?" Godfrey said, gripping her hand.

"Godfrey." Regana opened her eyes.

"What is wrong?" Godfrey asked feverishly. "What is going on?"

"The sickness," Regana managed between coughs. "The infection has gotten much worse. I am dying."

"No," Godfrey pleaded.

Yet the truth was written on her face. Godfrey could not deny it. Tears began to fall freely from both mother and son.

"You have to be strong," Regana urged her son. "This is the will of the gods."

"The gods?" Godfrey shook his head.

"We are here for a short season and then we go to their celestial realm." Regana closed her eyes again. "The gods have work for our spirits there after we die."

"I pledged while at Harv to go on crusade, and this is how the gods repay me?" Godfrey spat bitterly.

Silence filled the room except for the crackling of the fire in the hearth. Godfrey stood as if to leave, but Ulric put his hand on his son's shoulder. Godfrey stopped and looked into his father's eyes. They were red and swollen from crying, just like Godfrey's. He had never seen his father cry. The thought that his father could cry had not entered his mind before now. He squirmed uncomfortably at this revelation.

Seeing his father so vulnerable blunted Godfrey's rage. He was frustrated and scared, but he knew there was really nothing he could do. What good would becoming bitter against the gods do?

Turning back to his mother, Godfrey saw her sitting upright in her bed. A small silver pendant rested in her palm. The pendant hung on a thin silver chain and was fashioned in the image of the griffin rampant Godfrey knew so well from his family's heraldry.

"This pendant was a gift from your father when we were courting in Azgald." Regana held the pendant out for Godfrey to take. "It had been in his family since before there was a Duchy of Bastogne. He said it was a symbol of vigilance and strength. Those qualities are especially needed on crusade. I think you should take it with you to Azgald. That is where the crusade is going?"

"Yes." Godfrey bowed his head meekly.

"Then it is settled." Regana dropped the pendant into Godfrey's hand in between coughs. "Grant your mother her dying wish. Go and defend the home of her fathers. Wear this pendant around your neck until you fulfill your crusading vows. Remember vigilance and strength."

Obediently, Godfrey clasped the pendant's chain around his neck. The metal griffin slid over his tabard and rested atop his breast. Kissing her son on both his cheeks, Regana gestured for him to stand back.

Regana entered another deep coughing fit, which lasted for what seemed like an unreasonably long time. When it ended, the Duchess was lying down in obvious pain.

"Now everyone but Ulric get out," Regana ordered, sitting up again. "Yes, even you, Chaplain Turpin. I have a few words for my husband before I die."

Turpin bowed his head, and set the censer down on a nearby table. The time for incantations was at an end. Godfrey and the others shuffled out of the Duke's and Duchess' chambers and began to disperse. Unsure of where next to go, Godfrey started walking towards his room. Darkness had fallen outside, and the hallways were always colder than the rooms with hearths. Someone grabbed Godfrey's shoulder from behind. Turning, Godfrey saw it was Turpin.

"Going on crusade is no small task." Turpin frowned at Godfrey, releasing his shoulder. "Naturally your father will want me to accompany you."

"But what about the orcs here in the borders of Bastogne?" Godfrey returned Turpin's grimace.

"There is still time for the patrols," Turpin reassured Godfrey. "It will be several months before the crusaders will be ready to go north. Spring will be the earliest that the crusade begins in earnest."

"I see," Godfrey said, relieved. "We will know if the orcs are really massing for an attack by then?"

"Exactly," Turpin replied. "Try not to worry so much. You are a faithful knight whom the gods smile upon. This is all in their hands."

"Right." Godfrey bit his lip.

"Pray for your mother." Turpin read Godfrey's expression. "There is nothing else we can do for her now."

There was bitterness in Turpin's voice during this last statement—bitterness Godfrey could not account for. It was not Turpin's mother who was dying. Yet beneath the chaplain's cold exterior, Godfrey sensed Turpin was battling against something just beneath the surface.

Godfrey went to his room and changed out of his armor into a simple tunic. He was physically and mentally exhausted. He prayed for a long time that his mother would not die. He prayed that the gods would help her recover from this infection. Feeling nothing but worry, Godfrey eventually gave up on praying.

Despite tossing himself onto his bed, he could not sleep. The crusade, his mother's impending death, orcs; all these things kept spinning through his mind. Fading in and out of an uneasy sleep, he thought he heard his father singing a funeral dirge sometime past midnight. Godfrey wept, but could not raise himself out of bed. Cursing fate, he finally succumbed to sleep for the remainder of the night.

<u>Chapter Nine</u>

The wind sweeping her hair to the side, Nera stood atop the roof of Olso Fortress's keep. Grabbing a fistful of small pebbles from her leather pouch, Nera tossed them a few feet in front of her. They made a dull clattering sound as they scattered. She hunched over the smooth stones now lying on the rooftop. Each had a rune etched upon it, which, depending on its position in relation to Nera, celestial bodies, the other runes cast, and a host of other factors, could mean any number of things.

Like most tools used in divination, runes could be ambiguous, and even the wisest druids were prone to misinterpreting their messages. Nera's skill in reading runes was good, but not remarkable. Yet in this matter she could trust no other seers. It had to be her.

The first rune Nera's eyes rested upon was *harvest*. Pensively, she bit her lip. That could be good or ill. Next was *consumption*. No, when it touched the rune for smoke it meant *burning*. Yes, *consumption* was touching *smoke* so the two runes together meant *burning*. Nera's attention darted back to the rune for harvest. She noted *harvest* was a little farther from her than *burning*, and to her left. She would try to determine the significance of that after taking in some of the other signs.

Black, *strength*, and *age* were three runes clustered together. Near these was the directional rune. It was facing away from *black*, *strength*, and *age* which could be taken to mean *under* or *above*. What the directional rune pointed to was *journey*. Should Nera take the combination to mean *flight* as in; *the old black strength flies*, or *dig* as in; *the black age digs with strength*? She was still puzzling over what to do with *harvest* and *burning*.

Nera turned away from the runes for a moment to clear her thoughts. Surrounding her and Olso Fortress were the precipitous snowy heights of the Wyrmwind Peaks. There were few birds out to consult for augury in the frigid air. Perhaps that meant what she was seeking should be sought beneath the earth. There were numerous caves throughout the mountains, and there were the silver mines as well. Yes, that made sense. She would harvest the old black strength beneath the earth. Now what did *burning* mean?

There were six letter runes scattered among the others. Nera tried to sort them out to make a discernable word. Was the word she was trying to form even in her own tongue?

"Vozzab?" Nera said aloud.

The sorceress knew that name. Songs, legends, Vozzab had his place in myth.

"Vozzab!" Nera's heart pounded in her chest.

Scooping the runes back into her pouch, Nera proceeded to one of the turrets at the corner of the keep. She barely registered opening the door and descending the stairs back into the depths of the keep as her thoughts were consumed by this revelation. She needed to tell Alvir. This was what she had been hoping to discover.

As Nera hurried down the stairs and into a corridor at the ground level, a Nordsman warrior jumped out of her way as if trying to avoid a raging bull. A small goblin slave did not notice Nera's approach as he scrubbed the floor, and she knocked the unfortunate creature aside with a swift kick to the ribs. Yelping, the pale greenish critter scurried away, dropping a few musty soiled rags from the pile in his crooked limbs as he went.

Nera passed other creatures in service to the Nordsmen; orcs, dwarves, the descendants of other races of men captured in raids generations ago. All gave way in fear of Nera, her position, and her power. Some of the orcs, dwarves, and other Nordsmen did not fear Nera so much that they refused to meet her gaze, but almost every goblin and human outside the Nordsman race who resided in the lands of the Five Clans was a slave. They knew that to look a free Nordsman in the eye was to invite the harshest of punishments.

Entering the great hall, Nera caught sight of her husband sitting on his throne atop a dais near the back of the chamber. A cyclops chieftain knelt before Alvir, a curious sight given the cyclops' hulking form, even when making gestures of submission. Glancing at Nera from between the cyclops chieftain's kinsmen, Alvir signaled the brute to rise.

"I accept your tribe's vows of fealty." Alvir gestured to the cyclopes. "I will require your aid soon, but we will all share in the spoils."

The cyclopes nodded dimly, though the chieftain appeared to grasp more of what was said than his comrades. With a wave, Alvir dismissed the cyclopes. An honor guard of heavily armored orcish oath-warriors escorted the cyclopes out of the great hall back to their own lands. Nera watched the procession with mild interest.

"You are building up the Clans' strength with astonishing speed," the sorceress noted once the visitors had left. "Orc oath-warriors, cyclops chieftains, are there any who will not kneel before your banner?"

"Envoys to the necromancers have…not returned," Alvir conceded.

This was no surprise to Nera. It was likely that the Clan ambassadors never made it past the uncaring necromancers' zombie thralls once they entered the Blighted Lands. The undead had an insatiable hunger for living flesh.

"No matter," Nera dismissed the grisly fate of the Nordsman envoys. "You have managed to win over or beat down all rivals within the Five Clans, and now you are extending your influence over others who would heed the dark gods' call."

"But is it enough to crush Azgald?" Alvir grimaced. "They are few in number, but their knights are among the best in the world. And the Silver Suns…"

Approaching the throne, Nera shushed Alvir with a consoling finger to her lips. She was mere inches in front of her husband now, and gave a sharp look to Alvir's guards in the corners of the room. Not needing any clearer instructions, the guards instantly vacated the great hall. It was just Alvir and Nera in the chamber now.

This was not the first time Nera had seen her husband like this. Alvir was cunning and ruthless, but Nera knew him to sometimes be shortsighted or to despair when the challenge appeared too great. But Nera was always there to encourage him, to help him find a way…or to make one.

"Remember how the Duke of Pavik hurt you?" Nera traced her finger across an old faded scar on Alvir's neck. "You wanted revenge right away. You wanted your warriors to launch an immediate attack."

"But you advised patience." Alvir's jaw tightened. "Tancred is a vile beast, not a man. We should have known that when he refused to give his daughter to you. You knew who Tancred's daughter really was. You could have taught her so much…"

"That does not matter now," Nera whispered in Alvir's ear as she caressed him. "The Clans and Azgald ultimately cannot share the Nordslands. Tancred has dealt these wounds to us, but he will soon regret it. All our patience and planning will be rewarded. A thousand horse-mounted knights could not defeat the great Vozzab."

"Vozzab?" Alvir repeated, comprehension dawning across his face.

"I have seen it in the runes." Nera hefted her pouch.

"Can he be made to serve us?" Alvir began thinking of the possibilities.

"I can ensnare him." Nera smiled. "With time and preparation it can be done."

"How?" Alvir wondered. "Vozzab is one of the children of the gods. You can bend such power to our ends?"

"It's more of a pact," Nera said, clarifying her earlier statement. "If an appropriate sacrifice is offered, then Vozzab may be willing to grant us a boon."

"Will that not make Yoan jealous if we abandon her in preference for Vozzab's service?" Alvir countered. "We have called on her for our help thus far, and we have seen success."

"Vozzab is a son of Yoan." Nera was ready for this objection. "To honor Vozzab is to honor Yoan. Besides, Yoan may very well be leading us to her son. In any case, we must seize what opportunities present themselves while we can."

"The sacrifice we must make," Alvir started.

"The sacrifice must be an enemy of Vozzab." Nera toyed with the dragon pendant her husband wore around his neck. "And Vozzab has many enemies in Azgald."

"The Duke of Pavik," Alvir suggested. "That would satisfy the demands of vengeance."

"It could be anyone in his bloodline," Nera added. "Perhaps his daughter might be more appropriate given her special qualities."

"Vozzab would prefer someone with her gifts?" Alvir prodded.

"Of course," Nera answered. "Tancred's daughter would make an ideal sacrifice to Vozzab."

"Where can we find Vozzab?" Alvir's excitement was beginning to show.

"The children of the gods often slumber under the earth," Nera explained. "And the runes have made clear that Vozzab is there now."

"The mines!" Alvir exclaimed.

"The omens led us here to Olso after all," Nera concurred. "But how he was not discovered here before, I cannot say."

"Perhaps no one thought to seek him out before now," Alvir mused.

"Let's find out," Nera agreed.

The two hurriedly left the great hall, making for the stairs. Down through the armories, store rooms, and dungeons they went. The industry beneath Olso fortress was almost as great as that which was above. There was the rushing air of bellows as furnaces were fueled. There was the hammering of blacksmiths as they worked on steel. There was also the scream of prisoners as torturers worked on them.

Alvir grabbed a torch straight out of the hand of a passing orc as he and Nera made their way through one of the forges closer to the mines. The orc's beady eyes narrowed in fear as he stood paralyzed on the spot. Alvir paid the brute no further attention, and Nera caught what almost looked like relief cross the creature's scarred reddish face as they walked on.

Closer to the surface, the ground was slick. The frost permeating the soil was being melted by the fires of activity that heated the air in the tunnels. However, as Nera and Alvir descended farther it grew quieter, darker, and colder. Now only the sounds of shovels, picks, and other tools mixed with the occasional grunted exchanges between miners could be heard.

Alvir and Nera did not have to go far to find the miners themselves. They were mostly dwarves and goblins, beings better suited to small, dark confines than men were. The miners busied themselves with the strenuous tasks of breaking ore from the tunnel walls, and separating it from dirt and rocks before sending the precious silver up to the forges in wheeled carts for refining. Taskmasters, mostly goblins, were set over the miners, ensuring the quality of the miners' work with sharp cracks of their whips.

"Who is in charge here?" Alvir brandished his torch.

"I am Overseer Dresk." One of the goblins with a whip bowed to Alvir.

The goblin's yellowish complexion almost appeared white in the dim torchlight. The other goblins were of varying hues, like most of their kind in Clan territory. Though the color of an orc, goblin, cyclops, or troll might tell someone what region the creature may have originated from, the Nordsmen's robust slave trade ensured a great deal of variation among their servile class. Dresk, though a taskmaster, was also a slave judging by the brand upon his neck. The best slaves were those who could be controlled by their own.

"What can you tell us about this mine?" Alvir pressed.

"Though long used, this mine still yields great quantities of fine silver." Dresk gestured at the tunnel walls around him. "Our mine shafts run deep, but the alchemists believe that there are yet greater reserves of silver to be found."

"Are there any natural caves which are a part of this mine?" Nera wondered, gazing farther down the tunnel. "Are there any which might lead to the surface?"

"There are natural caves..." Dresk thought for a moment. "Some of them are quite large. Some of them may lead to the surface. We have had tunnels near them collapse, so we have avoided those areas. I lost more than thirty slaves and two taskmasters in one cave-in a few weeks ago."

"You will start unsealing those collapsed tunnels," Nera ordered. "Use all the slaves you can spare, even if it means reducing our silver output."

"Of course, my lady." Dresk kept his eyes low. "Might I inquire what my lady is searching for?"

"Vozzab." Nera's terse response made the goblin shiver.

Dresk swallowed hard. Goblins and dwarves knew that name well. Such names were used by the subterranean races in tales of entire underground kingdoms being destroyed, or foolish adventurers meeting horrific ends. These stories were used to scare their young into behaving, to prevent them from wandering too far into unexplored caverns, or to reverence the children of the gods. Nera gave a cruel smile at these thoughts.

"My lady," Dresk's voice quivered. "I will do your bidding without question, but should we awaken Vozzab, not one stone of Olso will be left standing upon another."

"I will make sure you don't," Nera reassured the overseer. "My magic will make your miners as silent as death."

"But still," Dresk continued. "Some of the miners may be too frightened to cooperate."

"Then I suggest you do not tell the miners what it is they are searching for." Nera's words forced a grimace across the goblin's face.

Chapter Ten

Harsh, bright morning light pierced through the windows as Godfrey stirred in his bed. Turpin rapped at the door to Godfrey's room, and muttered something Godfrey barely understood as he opened his eyes. Scowling, Godfrey groggily got to his feet and dressed. He'd slept little that night, and something hollow gnawed at his insides. When Godfrey opened the door, Turpin had already left. The chaplain had gone downstairs on some important business for the impending funeral, if Godfrey understood right.

Arrangements for Regana's funeral had already been made. Godfrey suspected his father had known for some time it would come to this. He simmered at having had this knowledge withheld from him for who knew how long. He was not a child anymore. Did they think he could not handle it?

Making his way to the castle's chapel without breakfast, Godfrey said nothing to anyone who crossed his path. Incense wafted up to the chapel's vaulted ceiling from censers hung throughout the chamber. Godfrey hated the stench of the incense, and his loathing did not diminish, no matter how many rituals he attended that required the substance. At least that was what he told himself now. His mood was sour. Nothing could comfort him.

He sat in the front pew next to his father in the castle's chapel. Ulric's expression was distant. He had not commented on Godfrey's decision to go on crusade, or said much of anything, for that matter. Godfrey's anger with his father still simmered just under the surface. Shifting in the pew slightly, he wanted to put a little more distance between himself and his father, even if it was only a few inches. It was a passive-aggressive act he doubted his father even noticed, but that thought only caused him to grind his teeth.

Regana's body lay resting in a dark-stained wooden casket in front of the altar. A shaft of light penetrating the chapel through the main window fell across her lifeless form. It all seemed so cold to Godfrey. This was not the mother he remembered from years ago.

The chapel was filled with attendees for the funeral, but most of them were those either already at the castle or were Ulric's nearest vassals. Funerals and weddings were both like that. No matter how meticulous the preparations; something would not go according to plan, and people would choose not to show up.

On the altar, Turpin stood in a plain but clean habit, and somberly read the funerary liturgy. The chaplain only gave the slightest hint of distress in his voice. Godfrey hardly listened to it. What comfort could words bring?

When they removed themselves to the family cemetery at the rear of the castle grounds, Godfrey contemplated the freshly dug grave. An icy wind had swept the previous day's clouds away, sending shivers through Godfrey. The pallbearers, Sir Rodair, Karl the Hammer, Sir Euric, Sir Malbert, Sir Guy, and Borani the Bull, set the casket by the grave, and after Turpin gave a brief benediction, the coffin was lowered into the earth. A couple of serfs bearing shovels covered the casket with dirt. Once the hole was filled, the servants patted the dirt down until it was firm.

Turpin's cloak rustled as he turned away from the sight. He left without another word. Others began to disperse as well. Some offered condolences to Ulric and Godfrey on their way from the grave, but Godfrey ignored them all. Soon it was just the father and son remaining.

That was it. The whole funeral had gone by so quickly. Godfrey's stomach sank as he realized this was the end.

"You will see her again," Ulric said to Godfrey as he looked at his wife's gravestone.

"In the afterlife." Godfrey rolled his eyes.

Godfrey's contempt could not be understated. He knew the doctrines of spirits, the afterlife, and related teachings meant to bring comfort during such times. Yet none of those teachings reassured Godfrey, now that he was here.

Ulric tugged at his son's arm. Frowning, Godfrey met his father's eyes. Ulric's expression was resolute as steamy breath billowed from his nostrils.

"Yes," Ulric affirmed. "We will see her in the afterlife. But the gods have not called us there yet. There is much for us to do still here."

"But," Godfrey began to protest.

"Get your things ready." Ulric pointed back to the keep. "It is time to work now."

A few weeks later, Godfrey returned to Fuetoile Keep from his patrol with little of interest to report. His men had killed a few wargs in the woods. An old brigands' camp had been discovered, but it was long abandoned. It was all such a waste of time. Turpin returned two days after Godfrey with similar news.

"No word from your father?" Turpin asked at the conclusion of his report.

Godfrey shook his head. The two stood near the fire in the great hall. Letting out a long sigh, Godfrey watched the flames dance across a crackling log in the hearth. A few serfs busied themselves with chores, passing in and out of the hall while Sir Euric and Sir Malbert sat at a table at the far end of the hall to enjoy a hot meal. Everyone was looking for an excuse to get out of the cold. Godfrey hardly blamed them.

"Don't worry," Turpin reassured Godfrey. "Your father is a zealous man. He's not afraid to chase shadows in the forest."

Godfrey grimaced. He knew he should be preparing for the crusade, but his father still had not said a word about it to him. Though small, the weight of the griffin pendant around Godfrey's neck constantly reminded him of both his vow and his mother's death. He tried not to think about either the pendant or the vow, so that he would not have to think about his mother's last night alive. Trying not to think of those things only left emptiness.

"Father is just trying to stay busy so he doesn't have to think about mother." Godfrey's accusation did not appear to move Turpin.

"You're wrong," Turpin's reply came tersely. "You need to stop wallowing in self-pity. Don't lash out at your father for doing his duty to the Duchy."

"So he can just go out to work without spending any time grieving?" Godfrey's rage began to boil.

"He has been grieving every day." Turpin pointed a finger at Godfrey. "And he will continue to grieve every day for the rest of his life. He loved your mother more than anything. I know. I knew them when they were young, and I've known them ever since."

The truth in Turpin's words stung Godfrey. He struggled to find something to say, but his mouth gaped open uselessly. He blushed in embarrassment at his outburst. Turpin's expression softened as if he were about to apologize for being too harsh in his rebuke, but he stopped himself. Godfrey's hand began to shake. Turpin was too tough to admit he crossed the line.

"Some chaplain," Godfrey muttered under his breath.

The withering scowl Turpin gave Godfrey made him instantly regret what he had said. Godfrey himself could hardly believe he'd let those words slip from his mouth. With the sting of Turpin's backhand blow burning across his face, Godfrey only realized the chaplain had struck him as he stumbled back into a table. For a brief moment, the great hall fell silent as Godfrey and Turpin stared each other down.

"Insulting your elders is the last mistake you'll make today." Turpin grabbed Godfrey's arm, pulling him to his feet. "Get over yourself. You have duties to perform, and the world won't wait for you to realize that people you love can die too."

Everyone was looking at Godfrey. The embarrassment hurt far worse than being hit. There was no way to save face here, not in front of Ulric's retainers. Godfrey was in the wrong on every count, but he could not admit it. Fighting back tears, Godfrey stormed off to his room.

Another three days passed with no sign of Ulric's return. Godfrey spent most of his time brooding in his room. He hardly ate. His conversation was rarely cheerful, and few bothered to disturb him. Corbin de Ghend once bumped into Godfrey as the two passed each other in a hallway, and the dark look Godfrey gave the page made the boy squeal in terror as he ran back the way he had come.

On the morning of the fourth day, Godfrey heard a herald announce that Ulric and his knights had returned to the castle. Turning over in his bed, Godfrey could not summon the will to get up. He put his pillow over his head, blocking out the morning Sun. He knew his father would come up the stairs at any moment. He did not want to be confronted about moping around the castle for so long. Part of him knew this was not how his mother wanted him to spend his days, but part of him was still upset about how unfair it was to lose her. Turpin's gruff advice and sharp reprimand had not helped anything either, and Godfrey avoided the chaplain. He had prayed his mother would not die. The gods were supposed to answer prayers.

Ulric did not come up to Godfrey's room that morning. The whole time, Godfrey had been thinking of what his father would say and how he would respond to it. By early afternoon, Godfrey's stomach finally got the best of him. He had not eaten dinner the previous night, and had not eaten breakfast that morning either. Aside from that, he had finally grown tired of his father's voice berating Godfrey within his own mind. After dressing, Godfrey made his way downstairs to the kitchen.

Descending the stairs, Godfrey saw Ulric stood in the hall alone near the stairwell. Ulric looked directly up at Godfrey. Paralyzed, Godfrey realized he had no options. His stomach squirmed, and he knew he could not avoid his father any longer.

"Godfrey." Ulric gestured for his son to come to him. "Turpin tells me your patrol did not come across any more orcs."

"That's right," Godfrey said as he came to the bottom of the stairs.

"Mine did." Ulric indicated a new scar on his forehead. "It was a small camp; less than a hundred. We took prisoners."

His mind racing to keep up, Godfrey's depression was pushed to the back of his thoughts. He suddenly felt an urgency he had not felt since his mother's death. He had a desire to do something again.

"We learned the orcs up in the Black Iron Mountains had something of a succession dispute," Ulric continued. "What we have come across were simply exiles that were cast out of the fortresses. I sent out another patrol to finish off the last of the orcs."

"That's a relief," Godfrey said, gesturing his thanks to the gods.

For a moment Godfrey almost forgot his bitterness. Then, with his sorrow returning, he turned away from his father. He was not sure what to say. He did not want to say anything. There was a long pause. As Godfrey started to leave, Ulric cleared his throat.

"You're thinking about your mother," Ulric said.

"How do you not?" Godfrey asked his father accusingly, turning back to face him.

"I do." Ulric smiled humorlessly. "More than you know."

The daggers had not left the young knight's eyes. Ulric gave a heavy sigh. Gesturing for his son to follow him, the old Duke began walking down the hall. Godfrey followed his father's heavy footfalls. Ulric stopped in the great hall just long enough to grab a pair of cloaks, and tossed one to Godfrey.

Putting their cloaks on, the father and son soon found themselves crunching through the snow in the courtyard. It was freezing out, and the sunlight did nothing to warm

Godfrey's face. He realized they were heading towards the cemetery, but he kept following his father anyway.

"Here…" Ulric indicated a gravestone. "This is your grandmother. She died giving birth to me, and I never knew her."

Ulric pointed to the gravestone next to the first.

"And this here is the maiden my father married after my mother died." Ulric frowned. "The plague took her when I was ten years old. She was the only mother I have ever known. My father died the following winter. Do you know why his body is not here in the cemetery?"

Godfrey shook his head. He had never asked much about his grandparents. They had died before he was born, so he was never too interested before now. Maybe Godfrey's father and mother had told him at one point, but he was too wrapped up in himself to care at the time. He felt foolish for not remembering.

"He disappeared in the forest traveling alone." Ulric gestured to the woods beyond Fuetoile Keep's walls. "Did bandits kill him? Was it a great beast? We will never know."

Godfrey shifted uneasily in the snow. His nose and ears started to burn with cold. Ulric stood in front of him and gripped him by the shoulders.

"My uncle raised me as regent of the Duchy after that," Ulric gently reproved Godfrey. "You are lucky to have had your mother for as long as you did. Turpin can be tactless sometimes, but he's right. You can't stay like this forever."

"How do you make the sadness go away?" Godfrey asked.

"Time, mostly," Ulric confided. "In time, the pain dulls even if it never goes away, but staying busy helps too. Speaking of which; we have a crusade to prepare for."

Godfrey nodded pensively.

"Word is that ships are being prepared to go north in the spring even as we speak," Ulric added. "Bishop Clovis should be coming by within the next few days to further discuss the preparations."

"Why did mother want me to go on crusade so much?" Godfrey raised the griffin pendant from his chest up to his face, examining it.

"Crusading runs in our blood." Ulric smiled wearily. "My father and uncle both went on crusade in their younger years, and your great grandfather went on two crusades. Your mother's ancestors went on the first crusade to Azgald and settled there. Her family especially knew how important crusades can be."

Pride swelled in Godfrey at hearing this. He had been told before when he was much younger, but Fallard did not often remind Godfrey of the family history when he was his cousin's squire. Fallard was unmarried and had no children of his own, and did not think much about those types of stories.

"But your mother really wanted you to go on crusade for one reason only." The Duke pointed his finger at the pendant on Godfrey's chest. "You already promised you would go."

What was it Godfrey's mother had said the griffin represented? Vigilance and strength was it? Those were the sort of values stories like the Tale of Cheldric were supposed to teach.

"Will you come with me?" Godfrey implored.

Ulric shook his head with a sad smile. Godfrey's heart sank. His feet crunching through the snow, Ulric began walking back to the keep. Godfrey followed.

"No." Ulric's voice was low and somber. "No, crusades can last for years at a time. That is just too long for me to be away from the Duchy with orcs in the forests and mountains, and… intrigue here at home."

Ulric's voice trailed off. He stopped for a moment. The wind picked up, throwing back Godfrey's and Ulric's cloaks. Stopping to catch the Duke's eye, Godfrey suddenly realized just how old his father was getting. The wrinkles on his face looked more defined than before. His hair was becoming more white than grey.

"I want to make sure you have a duchy to come back to when this is all done." Ulric patted Godfrey's shoulder.

Bishop Clovis arrived at Fuetoile Keep almost a week later. He met Godfrey, Ulric, and Turpin in the great hall accompanied by one of the Knights of the Silver Sun. The Silver Sun was a grizzled man Godfrey guessed to be in his mid-forties. A web-like scar covered half of the man's face, and he carried a flanged mace on his belt. As the two parties grew nearer, Godfrey recognized the Silver Sun from Clovis's sermon back at Harv.

"This is Morgan the Bloodied," Clovis introduced his companion. "He is Grand Master of the Knights of the Silver Sun."

"A pleasure." Morgan curtly nodded.

"Likewise." Ulric gestured to one of the long tables in the hall. "Please sit. We have much to discuss."

Morgan and Clovis sat on one of the benches, and Godfrey, Ulric, and Turpin took their seats on the other side of the table. The Bishop's expression was genial though

Morgan's was stoic. Morgan reminded Godfrey a lot of Turpin, except Morgan wore his hair down to his shoulders, while Turpin kept his cropped close to the head. Morgan was also a thicker build than Turpin, but the two shared much in their near-constantly grim expressions.

"Food?" Ulric inquired as he was about to call a servant.

"No." Morgan raised a hand. "But thank you."

"Right." Ulric gave a slight frown.

"Godfrey," Clovis beamed at him. "Once again you amaze me. What a sacrifice, pledging to go on crusade."

"It seemed like the right thing to do at the time," Godfrey meekly replied, straightening up on the bench.

"Aye," Clovis replied. "It is going to be a long and difficult journey. The Knights of the Silver Sun have pledged to make this as easy as possible for the crusaders, but it will still be a great sacrifice for all involved."

"We are prepared to offer transport across the Freezing Sea," Morgan said, looking to Ulric. "We have ships mustering in various ports. Colaigne up north will be the closest for you. After the ships disembark, they will rendezvous at the island of Kalscony. The Baron of the island is friendly to Azgald. What we need from you is a donation to the Order to help cover the costs of transporting your son and those who will be accompanying him."

"You'll have the money," Ulric assured Morgan.

"How many of your men will be going?" Clovis asked.

"So far almost eight hundred knights have volunteered to go," Turpin answered. "A levy of six thousand men-at-arms and two thousand crossbowmen will be ready by spring. I am seeing to their preparations myself."

"Excellent," the Bishop replied. "It looks like Bastogne has not lost its crusading fervor."

"What of the other duchies?" Godfrey asked.

"Conrad the Wolf has pledged three hundred knights and six thousand footmen and archers in addition to himself," Clovis said after thinking for a moment. "Baldwin de Ghend is coming with two hundred knights and three thousand infantry."

"Who are Conrad and Baldwin?" Godfrey furrowed his brow.

"Conrad succeeded his father as Duke of Errans last month," Clovis explained. "He is actually just a couple years older than you, Godfrey. Baldwin de Ghend is the son of Sigismund, Duke of Ghend. He is also a young knight going on crusade with his father's blessing."

"Most of the duchies are contributing between one and six thousand men," Morgan added. "The other kingdoms of the Ostlands are also contributing what their counties and duchies will allow. In all, we could have a force of more than forty thousand crusaders."

"That will really help out Azgald." Godfrey whistled in amazement.

"It's probably overly optimistic." Turpin scowled.

"Aren't you supposed to be a chaplain?" Clovis reproached Turpin. "Where is your faith?"

Turpin huffed disdainfully in reply.

"What of King Wilhelm?" Ulric leaned forward on the bench.

The Bishop closed his eyes for a moment. Scratching his nose, Godfrey found the pause unsettling. He knew whatever the Bishop was going to say was not going to be good. Straightening his robes, Clovis gave a heavy sigh.

"There is an ongoing dispute between King Wilhelm and the King of Gothia." Clovis shrugged. "King Wilhelm says he does not feel that his Eastern realms are safe, and that he must remain in Lortharain to protect them."

"What a fine example to his subjects, eh?" Turpin grumbled. "He sure knows how to show his people what a champion of the gods he is."

"Enough," Ulric cut in.

"To be fair," Clovis mused. "How many kings have pledged to go on crusade, yet never did? At least Wilhelm is being honest from the start."

Turpin quietly smoldered. Turning to face Morgan, Godfrey saw the Silver Sun was also ruminating. Blinking, Godfrey cleared his throat.

"What other preparations should I be making?" Godfrey asked, changing the subject.

"You will need to bring money to buy food for yourself and your soldiers once you get to Azgald," Clovis disclosed. "It will have to be enough to last for the duration of the crusade."

"How long will it take?" Godfrey inquired.

"To be honest," Clovis confided, "a clear objective has not been decided upon yet. Killing the Clans' High King, Alvir, is a top priority. If he dies, we suspect the Clan threat to Azgald will be greatly diminished. His leadership is what unites the Clans right now. Retaking the County of Fhunlan would also certainly be a great boon. Then again, there are a number of fortresses that have been lost along Azgald's northern borders in recent years. If even a few of those could be liberated…"

Clovis thought for a moment.

"The most ambitious target, however, would be the silver mines in the Wyrmwind Peaks," Clovis speculated, scratching his chin. "Now that would be a prize that could breathe new life into Azgald."

"The Wyrmwind Peaks are perilous," Ulric said, shaking his head. "The Nordsmen have held it for generations. All manner of dark creatures live up in those heights."

"The Eastern Marches were held by the Silver Suns for over two hundred years." Morgan leaned forward against the table. "That area has some of the best farmland in all the Nordslands. I think the crusade should aim to recover the marches for the Silver Suns."

"Well nothing is decided yet for certain." Clovis folded his arms.

"Who is building all the ships to even bring the crusade to Azgald?" Morgan slammed his fist against the table.

Godfrey stared at the Grand Master with wide eyes at the sudden outburst. Grimacing, the Bishop held his tongue. Turpin rolled his eyes in contempt. Morgan made to stand, but Ulric raised his hand.

"What I think the Bishop means," Ulric said evenly, "is that the crusade should seek to do what is best for Azgald overall when it arrives. There are still a couple of months before spring, and a lot can happen before that."

"Of course," Morgan grumbled, regaining his composure. "Well, I think that settles our business for now. Your crusaders are to assemble at Colaigne by the first week of spring. I will send someone by to collect your donation for the ships within the next few weeks."

"I am proud of you, Godfrey." Clovis smiled and got up from the bench.

Godfrey also got up and clasped arms with the Bishop. Turpin and Ulric followed suit. Morgan nodded respectfully to Godfrey, Turpin, and Ulric. Then, he followed the Bishop out of the great hall. Godfrey could tell from the light in the window that it was getting to be late afternoon. Suddenly tired, he stifled a yawn. There was so much to think about.

"The cost of transporting almost nine thousand men with horses and equipment across the sea will almost empty the treasury," Turpin noted.

"I know." Ulric frowned as he looked at the chaplain.

"And bringing enough coin to feed them all for any length of time will finish off whatever we have left and then some." Turpin scowled.

"Are you just now thinking about this?" Ulric sardonically asked.

"I thought it would be a good time to bring it up," Turpin admitted.

"We could raise a toll on the roads throughout the Duchy," Godfrey suggested.

"There are not many travelers in winter, but I like the idea," Ulric said, nodding approvingly. "We could put a tax on the larger towns. If it were expressly for financing the crusade, they should agree to it."

"What about a tithe from the shrines and temples?" Godfrey's thoughts were racing.

"Yes…" Ulric considered the thought. "A tenth of all the temples' and shrines' earnings should go to the crusade. The clergy should be keen to use sacred money for sacred causes."

"We might want to consider renting out some of your estates as well," Turpin added.

"We may end up needing to sell some of the smaller ones," Ulric said with a grimace. "But how could we begrudge any sacrifice for such a holy cause?"

<u>Chapter Eleven</u>

Colaigne was larger than any of the towns in Bastogne. The great city was nominally part of the County of Savoy, but in practice it was ruled by an oligarchy independent of the Count of Savoy. Godfrey thought towns like Harv, Vosg, and Menz were big. Now he knew he was wrong.

Colaigne's streets were narrow, and filled with pungent refuse. The buildings and houses were packed so tightly together, Godfrey wondered how the people here could even breathe. So many people crowded the streets. It was difficult for Godfrey to lead Baruch through all of them, but Turpin navigated his own steed through the people with ease.

Turpin was leading the way to the docks, while Godfrey and Walaric followed closely. Godfrey's satchel was heavy with golden coins.

"How did you end up getting all that money?" Walaric eyed the bag with evident suspicion.

"It's surprising how readily people will part with their money when it's for a good cause," Godfrey answered. "Too bad fewer were willing to come along in person."

Peddlers crowded around the three of them and their horses, trying to sell their wares. Turpin had to forcefully shove some of them out of the way to get himself, Godfrey, and Walaric through the street. Other commoners stopped to point and whisper to each other about how the first of the crusaders had arrived.

A girl, about fifteen Godfrey guessed, cut through the crowd and stood directly in front of him. She was tall, and had a pretty smile and short, braided red hair. She wore the clothes of a merchant's or nobleman's daughter. Without preamble, she pressed a delicate white flower into his hand.

"Remember me when you come back," she said with a wink before going back to one of the houses just as quickly as she had arrived.

Dumbfounded, Godfrey held the flower for a moment before tucking it into one of his satchel's pouches. Walaric grinned broadly at Godfrey, and punched his arm. Annoyed, Godfrey returned the punch to Walaric's shoulder, but Turpin pressed on, appearing oblivious to all of it.

"Not much farther," Turpin assured Godfrey and Walaric.

"Good," Walaric moaned. "I don't know how many more flowers Godfrey can carry."

"Shut it." Godfrey flushed in embarrassment.

"The men should be loading onto the transports shortly." Turpin ignored Godfrey's and Walaric's exchange. "The ships should be ready to launch by midday."

"It's still too cold for spring," Godfrey noted with a shiver. "Aren't the sailors worried the seas may still be too rough?"

"The crusade has already been delayed a month." Turpin shook his head. "First the ships weren't ready in time, then this weather. If we wait too much longer, it will be winter again."

"Right," Godfrey acknowledged.

"Better to go now than not at all." Walaric shrugged.

The three continued down the street. The press of people did not diminish for a while. Godfrey had not anticipated becoming a crusader would yield this sort of popularity. Or maybe there were just a lot of merchants trying to push their wares on travelers with money. It seemed to be both things at once.

Eventually, Godfrey caught sight of the masts of some of the ships behind the buildings. Silver Sun pennants waved lazily from the tops of the ships' masts. They were tall with canvas sails furled in tight bunches. As the port itself came into view, Godfrey was overwhelmed by the salty smell of seawater.

"Wow." Walaric's mouth gaped as he took in the sight of the ships. "I have never seen so many cogs before."

Godfrey roughly estimated the ships in the port. There were two dozen or so sitting in the perfectly calm water of the harbor. Crewmen loaded supply crates into the cogs' hulls by crane. Godfrey gave a low whistle at the impressive sight.

"Twelve of those transports are for us." Turpin indicated the vessels. "One shall be for the knights and us, one for the horses, and the rest are for the infantry."

"They're huge," Godfrey said, gawking at the ships.

"They have to be to hold six hundred passengers, eighty tons of cargo, and a crew of almost a hundred sailors," Turpin replied casually.

"Who are all the other ships for then?" Walaric looked around for an answer.

As if in direct response to his query, another group of knights emerged through the streets from the other side of the port. They were distant, but Godfrey could make out the heraldry on the tabard of the lead knight. His white tabard depicted a black wolf passant across the center.

"I am guessing that is Conrad the Wolf," Godfrey mused aloud. "He has a lot of crusaders going with him too, if I remember right."

Conrad seemed to spot Godfrey, Turpin, and Walaric, but he did not approach them. Godfrey waved, but Conrad did not return the gesture. Talking with his retainers, Conrad was apparently too preoccupied to bother with formalities, or at least thought he was far enough away to pretend he did not see Godfrey. Scowling, Godfrey returned his attention to Walaric and Turpin.

"Well he's certainly a rude one," Walaric huffed.

"Let's not think too much of it just yet," Turpin advised with a sideways glance.

Approaching one of the cogs, Turpin hailed its crew. A sailor leaned over the gunwale in response to Turpin's call. The sailor was a young man, maybe a few years older than Godfrey, though his clothing was worn and tattered from years of hard work at sea. Godfrey considered the young man for a moment, wondering what his life would be like had he been born to a sailor instead of a duke. Not enjoying the conclusions he came to, Godfrey counted himself fortunate, and left it at that.

"My lord?" The sailor looked down from his work.

"We are the crusaders from Bastogne," Turpin called up to the sailor. "Which of these transports is for the horses?"

"Well that would be this one." The sailor patted the gunwale.

"And which one is for us?" Turpin asked.

"Over there." The sailor pointed to his right. "Three ships down from us here. Go ahead and leave the horses where they are. We'll bring them aboard."

Affectionately patting Baruch's jaw in farewell, Godfrey made for the ship the sailor indicated as Walaric and Turpin did the same. Baruch gave a sad snort. Grimacing, Godfrey turned back to him.

"Don't worry," Godfrey reassured his steed. "We'll be there in no time."

A group of sailors began handling Baruch and Turpin's horse by the reins. Godfrey turned and sprinted a few steps to catch up to Walaric and Turpin. They walked out onto the pier, and boarded their ship across a narrow gangplank leading up to the cog's deck. Just as Godfrey set foot on the deck, the sound of thousands of marching feet resounded through the streets. Sure enough, it was his father's knights and infantry coming through the city to the port.

"Six thousand infantry and five hundred knights all told," Godfrey said, reading the astounded look on Walaric's face.

"I thought you said there would be more?" Walaric asked as he came to himself.

"There were going to be more," Godfrey agreed. "But some could not raise enough money to go. Others changed their minds or made up some excuse. Anyway, this is what we have."

"That's still quite an army, Godfrey," Walaric admitted, leaning against the gunwale.

"Word is now there are about thirty thousand crusaders in total," Turpin added as he watched the men begin to board the ships. "There are always some who abandon the cause, but more are boarding the ships now than I expected."

"Well that's comforting," Walaric grunted, rolling his eyes.

Walaric muttered something indistinct. There was a strange rhythm to the words. Furrowing his brow, Godfrey gave Walaric a curious look. The acolyte stopped abruptly.

"*Delwyn's Five Hundred*," Walaric said. "An old poem Bishop Clovis taught us at the orphanage when I was small. It's about the Battle of Rhyl Pass."

"I know it." Godfrey frowned. "Delwyn's Five Hundred all died at the Battle of Rhyl Pass. I'm hoping we do better than that."

"They got a poem out of it for their martyrdom at least." Walaric threw his hands up. "Besides, I'm sure we'll do better against the Nordsmen than Delwyn did against the necromancer's horde."

He and Godfrey watched the men boarding the ships. Turpin eventually excused himself to go down into the hull, leaving Godfrey and Walaric to themselves. Soon after, Godfrey noticed Conrad's soldiers boarding their ships.

"How long have they been at that?" Godfrey asked Walaric.

"A while." Walaric shrugged.

"Oh." Godfrey watched the soldiers from Errans with mild interest.

Most of the knights from Errans incorporated the wolf into their heraldry. It signified familial relations to Conrad, just as most of the knights from Bastogne used the griffin in theirs because of some loose connection to Godfrey's family. Remembering Conrad's slight from earlier, Godfrey crossed his arms.

"The wolf is not really such a noble animal," Godfrey prodded Walaric.

Furrowing his brow, Walaric looked at the knights and footmen from Errans. He scratched his ear, contemplating the men from the distant duchy. Finally, he blinked and rubbed his eyes.

"No," Walaric admitted. "They're pack hunters that go after the sick and weak, but they also look out for their own."

"True enough," Godfrey conceded.

A few more hours passed, and it seemed to Godfrey that most of the men from both Bastogne and Errans had loaded onto their respective ships. The crews were preparing to cast off from the piers. A sudden exhilaration overcame Godfrey as a thought crossed his mind. After months of tedious preparation that had nearly emptied Bastogne's treasury, he was going on crusade. The moment was here at last. Despite the financial strain, Godfrey felt honored as he clutched the griffin pendant around his neck.

Turpin came up on deck, clutching a live chicken in his arms and observing the ships' final preparations.

"Why did you bring that up here?" Godfrey pointed at the chicken.

Turpin looked at Godfrey and raised an eyebrow, but he did not answer. Unsure of what Turpin was hinting at, Godfrey simply returned a puzzled expression. Walaric caught on first.

"We almost forgot to make sacrifice." Walaric punched Godfrey in the arm.

"Stop doing that." Godfrey punched Walaric back a little harder than he meant to.

"Thalatta…" Walaric winced. "The sea goddess punishes those who do not offer proper sacrifices before traveling through her realm."

"What kind of sacrifice does Thalatta want?" Godfrey asked.

"One of these." Turpin offered Godfrey the chicken. "You must offer an invocation, break its neck, and toss it over the right side of the ship."

"Okay." Godfrey took the chicken, surprised to have suddenly been given this responsibility. "I've never done an animal sacrifice before."

"You are the leader of our contingent, so it must be you," Walaric explained.

"Let's start this off right." Turpin nodded to Godfrey.

The chicken's muscles tensed as it tried to squirm out of Godfrey's grip. He held the bird as tightly as he could, but it wriggled all the more fiercely in response. Not only was the crew of the ship Godfrey was on giving him their full attention, but the crews of the ships on either side were watching as well. The bird's excited clucking only unnerved Godfrey all the more. Holding the chicken aloft, he closed his eyes.

"Thalatta," Godfrey called. "Thalatta, goddess of the sea, hear our prayer. We go on the errand of the celestial gods. Loxias, Luna, the stars, and all the other gods in the heavenly realm have called us on crusade. We, though few, have answered their call. Grant us safe passage as we cross thy domain's unfathomable depths. Please accept this offering as a token of our respect for thee and thy thralls, amen."

Those present chorused their affirmation. Opening his eyes, Godfrey put one hand around the chicken's neck and twisted as hard as he could. There was a sickening crack of cartilage underneath Godfrey's fingers, and the chicken began thrashing uncontrollably. Not wishing to hold the bird another moment, Godfrey tossed the chicken over the gunwale. The flailing chicken gave a dull splash as it hit the water.

Kneeling, Walaric examined some of the chicken's discarded feathers on the deck. He smiled at Godfrey. The acolyte rose to his feet, clutching some of the feathers in his hand.

"It is a good omen," Walaric announced in a loud voice. "Thalatta grants her blessing."

"What is a good omen?" Godfrey whispered so that only Walaric could hear.

"These feathers," Walaric whispered back. "If the chicken sheds some of its feathers when you sacrifice it, it means Thalatta accepts your offering."

"That seems like a fairly easy omen to obtain." Godfrey frowned doubtfully.

"If the gods offer a gift…" Walaric smirked. "Take it. Other good omens are not so easy to come by."

The ship's captain was already shouting orders to his crew. The sailors busied themselves with their various tasks in response, and soon the ships were all sailing out of the port. They followed the coastline, the sails of the two dozen cogs billowing in a stiff northern breeze.

Godfrey found himself peering out to the horizon from the ship's forecastle. Several hours out, the coastline drifted away to the west, leaving only the open sea before the fleet. The vastness of it all overwhelmed him. The density of the forests in the Ostlands with their numberless hills and valleys prevented most Ostmen from appreciating how expansive the world was. Godfrey had never felt smaller than he felt now.

Though the scene of the open ocean did not change, Godfrey continued to stare. Marveling at its beauty, he forgot about everything else for a while. The Sun was beginning to set before the novelty wore off. Even then, he continued as he had, though now his thoughts turned to contemplation of his place in such a vast expanse.

Godfrey was still at the ship's forecastle well after dark. The stars shined brilliantly overhead. However, he had ceased admiring the stars long ago. His posture had changed. His face was buried in his hands, and he was sniffling. He heard Walaric approaching from behind, but the acolyte hesitated for a moment. Walaric was about to leave his friend to himself when Godfrey turned to him.

"I still miss her," Godfrey confessed in a hoarse voice.

"Your mother." Walaric nodded in understanding.

Godfrey gave a sad smile. The two just stood there for a moment in silence. The cog rocked back and forth against the waves, but both of them were used to it by now. Most of the crew and other knights were below deck. The helmsman guiding the steering oars at the back of the ship was the only other person on deck at the moment.

"I wish father could have come with us, or Fallard." Godfrey rubbed his eyes.

"Why didn't they?" Walaric asked.

"Father said he had to protect the Duchy while I was gone," Godfrey explained. "He said he had to make sure nothing bad happened while I was away."

"And what about your cousin?" Walaric continued. "I thought Fallard would have wanted to be a part of this."

"I don't know," Godfrey admitted. "I didn't realize he wasn't coming until we started for Colaigne."

"Well Turpin is here with us," Walaric added optimistically.

"He's just here to make sure I don't do anything foolish." Godfrey brushed his tabard absently.

"Godfrey," Walaric said, and looked his friend in the eye. "Why are we here?"

Godfrey thought for a moment. He had focused so much on getting to this point that he had almost forgotten why he was here in the first place. Shivering, he looked out to sea. Something had been bothering him, but only now did that something finally make sense.

"It's even colder here than it was in Colaigne." Godfrey turned back to Walaric. "Could there still be snow up in the Nordslands?"

"Maybe." Walaric shrugged. "If you go far enough north, it's supposed to get so cold that there is snow all year round."

"I think we are here because I have been dreaming of the crusade." Godfrey chose his words carefully as he tried to recall the details. "Even before Bishop Clovis gave his sermon at Harv, I dreamed of snow, fighting, blood, fire. I can't remember everything, but when I heard Bishop Clovis speaking, I knew my dreams were connected to it somehow. It just felt right to join the crusade."

"It's the gods' will," Walaric hissed in amazement. "How could you doubt when you've been given such a sign?"

"I don't doubt," Godfrey corrected Walaric. "It's just hard. I don't know why the gods want me here, or why my mother wanted me so badly to go. What am I supposed to do when I get there?"

"I don't know." Walaric shrugged. "But I think whatever you are supposed to do will feel right. It will make sense in your head and your heart."

"Thanks." Godfrey blinked uncertainly.

Like so many things with religion, Godfrey was at once comforted by Walaric's answer and frustrated by it. He was comforted to know it would all be right in the end. He was frustrated by the present ambiguity.

"At least you know you are on the right path now." Walaric gestured out over the fleet. "Worry about the details of what comes next when we get there."

"Right," Godfrey replied with more enthusiasm.

The two went below deck. Turpin had laid out a pair of bedrolls on the floor for Godfrey and Walaric. Most of the knights were sleeping, gambling, drinking, chatting quietly, or otherwise wasting the night away. Turpin himself was snoring loudly as he slept. Godfrey and Walaric quickly tucked themselves into their bedrolls as they attempted to avoid the worst of the cold night air, although it was warmer inside than up on deck. Godfrey reassured himself that this expedition was the right choice as the creaking ship lulled him to sleep.

The next morning, Godfrey awoke to Turpin putting a dry, hard biscuit up to his face. Taking it from Turpin's hand, Godfrey bit into it and began to chew. The outside of the biscuit was tough and began to hurt his jaw as he chewed.

"Get used to it," Turpin glowered. "We have a few more days at sea before reaching Kalscony."

Godfrey took another bite out of the biscuit. There was nothing good about it. Walaric was eating a salted fish while trying not to gag. Some of the knights were eating hard cheeses with their breakfasts, but there was little variation from the fish and biscuits outside of that. Finishing his biscuit, Godfrey took one of the dried fish out of a barrel that had been brought up from the hold. He took a large bite. The taste of salt was so overpowering it blocked any hint of the fish's original flavor. He had to try hard not to spit it out.

"I love the food already." Godfrey smirked.

"Me too." Walaric cringed, tossing aside the tail of the fish he was eating.

Godfrey washed down the rest of his fish with a jug of water. It was a mistake. The salty flavor in Godfrey's mouth washed away, but the aftertaste of the fish itself was left behind. Godfrey took a hunk of cheese, and put the whole thing in his mouth. At least he could tolerate the cheese.

The next few days passed much like the first. Godfrey mostly kept staring out to sea for long hours, lost in his thoughts. His mother, the crusade, his dreams, all these things passed through his mind in a continuous loop. When so much thinking had exhausted Godfrey, he just stared. The occasional conversation with Walaric or Turpin helped break the monotony, but they quickly ran out of things to say as the days wore on.

On the fourth day at sea, an island appeared on the northern horizon. A large lighthouse set behind crenelated stone walls dominated the highest point of the island on its eastern side, which dropped off to a sheer cliff. The fortress overlooked a few small farms covering the western side of the island, which descended more gradually into the sea. Godfrey and Walaric watched some sheep grazing in the fields closest to the lighthouse from the ship's forecastle as the island grew nearer.

"Is that Kalscony?" Walaric asked Godfrey.

"It's certainly a mighty fortress, wherever we are," Godfrey said.

The crusading fleet drew nearer to the coast, leaving little room in Godfrey's mind for him to doubt that this was Kalscony. As they circled the island towards its eastern coast, a harbor appeared directly in front of the lighthouse. A road had been carved through the cliff from the harbor up to the fortress gate. The road was lined with small stone defensive towers on either side of it.

"No unwelcome guests getting in that way." Godfrey pointed to the road's defenses.

"Apparently not," Walaric agreed.

The ships began to dock at the port, and men began disembarking from the vessels as soon as they were able. The port quickly became crowded with the knights and men-at-arms. There was laughing and joking, loud boisterous conversations. People were clearly glad to be off the ships.

As the ship Godfrey was on docked, he impatiently stood by the gangplank, even while the crew was lowering it. Though generally patient and kind, Godfrey shoved his way through the press of knights down the gangplank to the pier. His patience with ships had run out, and he was the first off. No more ships. No more fish. Never again. He swore to himself he would have to find some other way home after all of this was over.

A man descended from the road to the port with a small retinue of footmen flanking him. He was stocky, blonde, and beginning to bald. After questioning a few crusaders, the man was eventually pointed in the direction of Godfrey's party.

"Godfrey de Bastogne," the man addressed Turpin. "I am Oksar, Baron of Kalscony. Welcome to my home."

Turpin coughed, indicating Godfrey. Looking Godfrey over, Oksar frowned and furrowed his brow. The Baron looked back to Turpin as if this were a bad joke. Turpin shook his head.

"But he is too young," Oksar protested, looking to Godfrey and Walaric again. "Boys! Bastogne sends boys to lead the crusade!"

"I may be young but I have experience," Godfrey cut in as his hand began to twitch. "I have been in battles and sieges as a squire. I have even killed a vampire."

"Individual combat prowess says nothing of your ability to prosecute a war," Oksar snorted as he waved his hand contemptuously.

"I have seen him in command," Turpin interjected. "Godfrey destroyed a whole orc camp this last winter. He will not disappoint Azgald."

"We shall see," Oksar muttered, looking out to the contingent from Errans. "Is Conrad the Wolf just a boy too? Boys, too many boys."

Godfrey's anger simmered. It was not unheard of for sixteen- or seventeen-year-olds to lead armies. Oksar's disappointment was unfounded. Godfrey could do this. The men would follow him. So what if he was not the eldest or most experienced knight in Bastogne?

Godfrey was about to say something, but Turpin shook his head. The Baron turned back to Godfrey. Fighting back a retort, Godfrey met Oksar's gaze.

"Your men are free to buy what they need at the market," Oksar grumbled. "You and your knights will be staying at the keep until the rest of the crusaders arrive."

"Thank you," Godfrey curtly replied, biting back the venom which threatened to fling from his tongue.

The Baron and his guards went off to greet Conrad and the men from Errans. Huffing, Godfrey began marching up the road to the fortress with Walaric and Turpin close behind. Most of the other crusaders were already on their way to the fortress, seeing little reason to stay at the port with the ships. The road was necessarily steep, given how sheer the cliff was. It did not take long for Godfrey to lose his breath.

"Too young," Godfrey spat contemptuously as his pace began to slow.

Walaric had remained silent the whole time. Stopping in his tracks, Godfrey gave the acolyte an accusing look. Walaric and Turpin immediately stopped, almost stumbling into Godfrey. Raising an eyebrow, Godfrey awaited their reply.

"Well aren't we?" Walaric asked doubtfully.

"You don't think we can do this?" Godfrey threw out his hands in exasperation. "What happened to all that stuff you were saying about signs and faith back on the ship?"

"Well," Walaric murmured. "The Baron has a point…"

"Do not worry about that old fool," Turpin interjected. "A castle siege requires perseverance more than any tactical brilliance. In addition to that, I am here to advise you, and this is far from my first campaign."

"See?" Godfrey stuck his thumb out at Turpin, scowling at Walaric. "I have a campaign advisor. What could go wrong?"

Not quite satisfied, Godfrey turned back up the road.

Kalscony's market consisted of few vendors, though they had stockpiled large quantities of various supplies in anticipation of the crusaders' arrival. Already some of the knights from Bastogne were purchasing food for themselves or feed for their horses. Armorers replaced missing links from some of the crusaders' chainmail while others sharpened blades. Some merchants were showing off newly forged weapons in the hopes that they would catch the attention of some knight willing to part with his money.

"Could you get something for Baruch please?" Godfrey asked Turpin, handing the chaplain a coin.

Taking the money, Turpin nodded and went off to one of the vendors' stalls. Though a few of Oksar's soldiers wandered through the market, most of the men here were the crusaders. After a few moments of aimlessly wandering, Godfrey spotted Conrad the Wolf. This time, the young duke was much closer. Godfrey guessed Conrad to be in his early twenties. Conrad was both taller and bulkier than Godfrey, had dark curly hair, and bore a vertical facial scar that left a deep gash running across his lips.

Godfrey and Walaric approached Conrad. Walaric gestured to Conrad in a sign of peace, but Conrad only glared at the acolyte. Godfrey gritted his teeth, and his hand began to shake as his blood boiled. He took a deep breath, and the trembling subsided.

"Conrad the Wolf I presume?" Godfrey extended his hand. "I am Godfrey de Bastogne. It will be an honor to fight beside you."

Conrad left Godfrey's hand hanging in the air. The bigger man took a step closer, leering down at Godfrey. Walaric took a step towards Conrad in response, but Godfrey shook his head.

"You will not lead this crusade just because you brought the most men," Conrad breathed with barely suppressed rage. "I am an actual duke. You are just the son of a duke. You have no title of your own, understand?"

"I was unaware that I had the largest company of crusaders," Godfrey assured Conrad smoothly. "You think I want to lead all thirty thousand crusaders? I'm more than happy being trusted to lead my own men."

"Don't take me for a fool," Conrad spat. "Whoever leads this crusade to victory will gain much glory and treasure."

"Take it," Godfrey replied. "I have everything I need in Bastogne."

"Then why did you come?" Conrad asked suspiciously.

"Duty to the gods." Godfrey turned and began walking away. "Same as you, right?"

Conrad stammered something indiscernible. Grinning broadly at Conrad, Walaric chased after Godfrey. A sour thought clouded Godfrey's mind. Frowning, Walaric tugged at Godfrey's cloak after they had put some distance between themselves and Conrad. Godfrey stopped and smiled humorlessly. Biting his thumb, Walaric looked his friend over carefully.

"What's wrong?" Walaric asked.

"This isn't what I thought it was going to be," Godfrey confessed. "Aren't they supposed to be our allies?"

"Don't let that stupid brute get under your skin." Walaric shoved Godfrey's shoulder. "He's just jealous that you brought more men."

"What about this Baron Oksar?" Godfrey gestured to the lighthouse.

"Who cares?" Walaric countered. "Not everyone is going to think of you as the hero of Harv or the people's champion or whatever they call you. We're here for the gods, not petty barons or the likes of Conrad the Wolf, remember?"

"Right." Godfrey nodded, biting his lip.

Turpin reemerged from the crowd. He held three large carrots in his hand. Giving one to Godfrey and another to Walaric, Turpin took a bite out of his own carrot. Godfrey bit into the root with a satisfying crunch. Walaric stared at his carrot with a look of disgust on his face.

"At least it's fresh." Godfrey shrugged, crunching on the orange vegetable. "We couldn't say that of the fish on the boat."

"Fair enough," Walaric sighed as he bit into his carrot. "It's better than hard bread at least."

"I've ordered the men to make camp by the western gate," Turpin said in between mouthfuls of carrot. "Oksar has given us first choice of camping grounds since we are the first group to arrive."

"How many more groups are expected?" Walaric asked.

"Baldwin de Ghend and Phillip d'Artois will be bringing the last of the crusaders from Lortharain," Godfrey answered. "I don't know about the others."

"There should be several thousand coming from Gothia," Turpin explained. "I hear there were quite a few who made their vows in Ogledd as well."

"Where's Ogledd?" Godfrey inquired.

"It's a kingdom on the island of Cardigal out in the Western Sea," Turpin said. "Ogledd is the northern kingdom and the Kingdom of Dyfred is the southern half."

"No crusaders are coming from Dyfred?" Godfrey asked.

"Oh yes," Turpin corrected himself. "Last I heard, Gunthar the Red, one of their dukes, pledged four thousand men from Dyfred."

"This whole island will be filled with crusaders before long." Walaric whistled.

"They should all be arriving over the next few days," Turpin added. "If our luck is any indication, there will be fewer crusaders than anticipated."

"You're always such an optimist," Walaric snorted. "I can see where Godfrey is starting to get it from."

Turpin scowled but said nothing.

"Turpin…" Godfrey looked at the chaplain in disapproval. "Why are you always so negative?"

Turpin looked Godfrey over for a moment, contemplating something. Godfrey was unsure what it was Turpin saw in that brief sad glance he gave Godfrey. Whatever it was, Turpin quickly decided against sharing it.

"Respectfully," Turpin raised a hand defensively. "That's a discussion for another day."

<u>Chapter Twelve</u>

Despite Oksar's offer to house Godfrey, Walaric, and Turpin in the fortress keep, Godfrey decided to camp outside the walls with the crusaders from Bastogne. He did it not so much to slight Baron Oksar, but to please the common soldiers under his command. Godfrey managed to do both in the same stroke. Oksar did not bother to visit Godfrey in camp, and only paid minimal respect to Godfrey when he did venture into the fortress.

Contemplating Oksar's behavior, Godfrey was beginning to doubt his choice. Having the loyalty of the soldiers was important, but having the support of the local aristocracy was more important. Besides, it seemed the only type of weather at Kalscony was a combination of cold, cloudy, and rainy. Godfrey was sure he had not seen the Sun once on the island yet. What he would give for a warm bed.

"Don't let it bother you." Varin stirred at his campfire with a long stick.

"Excuse me?" Godfrey turned to the ranger sitting by his tent.

Godfrey was unsure if Varin had actually spoken to him. He had been wandering through the crusader camp, seemingly lost in his own thoughts. Varin still had the unsettling habit of not looking directly at the people he spoke with, and that further added to Godfrey's confusion.

"Something is bothering you." Varin's eyes remained fixed on the flames consuming the wood in the fire pit. "Don't let it."

"I'm worried that there are going to be divisions between the crusaders and some of the lords we meet." Godfrey sat on a log across from Varin.

"That's likely." Varin nodded in agreement. "But you have the loyalty of your father's men. That makes you a force to be reckoned with."

"Why can't they just accept our help?" Godfrey threw out his hands in exasperation.

"The nobles leading this crusade have not agreed upon our ultimate goal yet," the ranger pointed out. "We don't really even know how we want to help yet."

"High King Alvir seems to be the source of the problem," Godfrey thought aloud. "If we defeat him at the head of his army in battle, he'll lose support from the Nordsmen. Or if he were killed, the Clans would start fighting among themselves again. Azgald would not face a unified enemy then."

"Sounds like that's what you need to convince everyone else of." Varin threw his stick in the flames, visibly reveling in its fiery demise.

Conrad the Wolf made no further contact with Godfrey over the next few days. The crusaders from Errans were encamped outside the fortress' northern gate, and kept to themselves for the most part. The tension was soon forgotten, however, as more crusaders began to arrive.

First the Gothians came, who camped on the southern edge of the fortress wall. They were a somber, pale lot from what Godfrey had seen. Then Baldwin de Ghend and Phillip d'Artois, fellow Lortharainians, came, and set up their tents in between Godfrey's and Conrad's groups. Almost a week after Godfrey's arrival at Kalscony, the crusaders from the two kingdoms of Cardigal disembarked from their transports with Morgan the Bloodied at their head.

"Rumor has it the only way either the Ogledd or Dyfred crusaders would actually come was if the Silver Suns ensured that both groups left at the same time," Walaric commented as he and Godfrey watched the last group of crusaders coming up the road to the fortress. "Such is the jealousy between the two kingdoms."

"Great," Godfrey sighed. "Well, at least now we can get things moving."

The council chamber in the keep of Kalscony's lighthouse fortress was dark and damp. Oil lanterns burned, giving off a thick sweet scent. The cold humidity clung to Godfrey. He shivered. How did people live here? This was supposed to be spring.

Godfrey shook the thought. Now was the time to be focused. He was a crusader, and all the crusade's leaders were here in this chamber. This was the first time Godfrey had seen all the crusade's leadership together at once. Studying the others across the table they sat at, Godfrey quickly realized he was easily the youngest present aside from Walaric, who stood at his side. Even Baldwin de Ghend was at least a year or two older than Godfrey.

"So what are the total forces at our disposal?" Morgan the Bloodied asked after everyone had made their introductions.

"I have six thousand infantry and five hundred knights," Godfrey eagerly answered.

The others nodded appreciatively. Phillip d'Artois cleared his throat. He was easily the oldest of all the crusaders. Wrinkles lined his face and his hair was thinning and white, but he was also easily the tallest of the crusaders, and his height gave him a commanding presence.

"The Duchy of Artois has brought seven thousand infantry and four hundred knights," Phillip replied, barely containing a smile.

Walaric gave a low whistle. Turpin rounded on him, and Walaric instantly quieted down. Taking a sudden interest in his own feet, Walaric moved to the back of the room.

"Three thousand infantry and two hundred knights," Baldwin said as he ran his fingers through his sandy blonde hair. "Sorry to disappoint all of you."

A couple of the other crusaders laughed, while Conrad and his retinue snorted. Godfrey was not sure if Baldwin was joking or not, so he hedged his bets, giving a bemused smile in reply. Conrad slammed his flagon of ale on the table with a heavy clank of metal on wood.

"Five thousand infantry and three hundred knights," Conrad sneered as all eyes turned to the young duke. "They are veterans all."

Godfrey rolled his eyes at Conrad. Phillip had brought more men than either he or Conrad had, so Phillip would naturally lead the crusade from here. At least that was what Godfrey reasoned within himself. He did not know how many crusaders the Gothians or the Cardigalians had brought yet, but he guessed it would be fewer given how many transports they brought to port.

"I have brought four thousand infantry and two hundred knights," Henry the Pilgrim, one of the two Gothian dukes, said.

Henry was almost as old as Phillip but had brought a little more than half of the forces the Duke of Artois had. Godfrey was sure Phillip would be elected to lead the crusade. Then again, Henry had gained his moniker from going on three previous crusades during his long life. Two of those crusades were to the Nordslands, too. That experience was more valuable than age alone.

"I have just over one thousand infantry and a hundred knights," Raymond of Wrehst, the other Gothian Duke, replied as he scratched his brow.

"I have about two thousand infantry and three hundred knights," Torcul of Cumbria hastily added in his thick melodious Ogleddish accent. "And my esteemed colleague here, Gunthar the Red, has brought almost as many as I have. That gives us a grand total of a little more than thirty-two thousand crusaders, if no one else but me was keeping track. Can we get on with this now?"

Glowering at Torcul, Gunthar the Red said nothing, but crossed his arms in agitation. Godfrey could not help but smile at the blunt, fiery-haired man from Ogledd. Discussing logistics was quickly growing tedious anyway.

"Very well." Phillip d'Artois cleared his throat again. "Oksar, what is the situation in Azgald? Where might the crusade best be used?"

Henry the Pilgrim pursed his lips at Phillip's immediate presumption of command. Conrad crossed his arms in contempt. The other crusaders did not seem to care or notice, aside from Godfrey.

"We have lost many of the fortresses in the northern marches in recent years," Oksar said, deferring to Phillip. "I think it would be wise to take the crusade up to Azgald's northern borders first. A surprise attack there could gain us a lot of ground very quickly."

"Then you could conveniently restore your brother as marshal of the northern defenses," Morgan said with a smirk. "The Silver Suns' former holdings are just as important."

"We need to retake lands we can defend after the crusaders leave, Grand Master." Oksar scowled. "Retaking the Eastern Marches would be wasted effort."

"The Silver Suns can hold the East," Morgan reassured the crusaders as much as Oksar. "The Knights of Saint Pelegius now hold the island of Tisgy. Their Grand Master has promised his support. Things will be different this time."

"Where is this Tisgy Island?" Torcul asked in an insolent tone.

"It's on the eastern coast of the Nordslands," Henry the Pilgrim explained, shaking his head. "But the Blighted Lands lie between Tisgy and the former Eastern Marches. There are too many undead…"

"The Pelegians have pledged to purge the undead," Morgan started.

"They can do what two previous crusades could not?" Henry countered.

His chair scraped against the stone floor as Morgan got to his feet. Shouting filled the room all at once as several of the crusaders stood. Phillip and Oksar were demanding that the crusade push north. Henry was challenging Morgan's strategy as Morgan countered Henry's suggestions. Conrad was aligning his own arguments with Henry's, though no one appeared to be paying him particular attention. Torcul and Gunthar were embroiled in some dispute that Godfrey did not think had anything to do with the crusade. Raymond of Wrehst simply sat back in his chair and watched the exchange unfold as Baldwin buried his face in his hands.

Godfrey ground his teeth at all this infighting. How petty all these lords seemed to him. None of them saw the bigger picture. It would have to be Godfrey to set things straight. They needed to defeat High King Alvir. He was sure that was the answer.

Yet every attempt Godfrey made to add his own thoughts or ask a question was drowned out by the others. He could not get a word in. No one was listening. Clenching his fists, Godfrey felt as if he were ready to explode.

"Excuse me." Godfrey loudly cleared his throat.

The bickering died down. Everyone stared at Godfrey in silence. Surprised that his outburst had actually grabbed their attention, Godfrey almost forgot what he had wanted to say.

"This crusade was called because a new Nordsman king is uniting the Clans," he said. "If High King Alvir were killed in battle, or even if he just lost enough battles to lose the Clans' support, the threat to Azgald would be over. Shouldn't we go wherever Alvir's army is?"

"That is the first good suggestion I have heard come from this group," a voice startlingly close to the back of Godfrey's chair noted.

Swiveling his head around, Godfrey saw that another person had entered the room. It was not Godfrey but this stranger's arrival that had grabbed everyone's attention. The man was tall, in his mid-thirties, and wore a closely trimmed beard that was showing its first signs of grey amidst otherwise reddish brown hair. The man wore a white tabard with the red dragon rampant of the Azgaldian royal family emblazoned upon it. A golden crown was set atop the man's spangenhelm.

"King Lothar." Oksar immediately bowed.

The crusaders who were still sitting rose, and the whole room followed Oksar's example. Closely examining each of the crusaders, the King made his way to the head of the table. Lothar gestured for them all to rise, and they complied.

"I apologize for not coming earlier," Lothar explained in a mollifying tone. "After all, you have made great sacrifices already on Azgald's behalf journeying here. But as you know, the Nordsmen attacks have grown far bolder in recent months, and I had to see to the defenses of my more vulnerable outposts."

Lothar looked to Oksar then Morgan reprovingly. Godfrey sensed a more thorough chastisement being withheld by the King.

"Make no mistake." The King pointed to the crusaders. "We will expand this realm back to its former glory, but first we must secure what we have. Biorkon. The Silver Sun fortress of Biorkon is under siege by the enemy right now. It is less than a day's travel by sea, and as of this moment, the enemy is completely unaware of the crusade's presence in Azgald. Start by relieving that siege."

Varin stepped through the forest as silently as any human could through snow. Though his eyes darted to every shadow, tree, and rock where his prey might be hiding, the ranger's movements were slow and deliberate. The snow on the ground gave a low soft crunch with each footfall, but Varin was sure the noise was far too quiet to warn anyone of his movements. He had done this many times before, back in Bastogne.

If the Nordsman scouts monitoring the woods discovered Varin and the other rangers hunting them, they would immediately alert their army besieging Biorkon. That could not be allowed. The crusaders had to catch the Nordsmen unawares so the enemy could not escape.

Varin had no doubts concerning his own abilities to move undetected, but he only had limited experience working with the other rangers of Bastogne, and none with the rest of the hunters in the crusade. Worse, the Nordsmen were an unknown foe to Varin.

Sneaking forward, Varin spotted a pair of Nordsman scouts. He froze in place. Did they see him? No. They were generally facing the trees to Varin's left and were engaged in idle chatter. Perfect.

Slowly, Varin stalked around the Nordsmen to place himself directly behind them. He drew his short sword from its scabbard. He crept towards the Nordsmen until he could distinguish their words. He still understood little of their language, but the ranger was making efforts to correct that in his spare time. Careless sentries could give away all sorts of valuable secrets.

The Nordsmen were still talking to each other; as far as Varin could tell, they were completely oblivious to him inexorably slithering between the trees behind them. From what Varin understood of the Nordsmen's conversation, they were discussing something about a girl. The ranger cared not for such distractions. Hearth, home, and the pleasures associated with them made men soft. His home was the wilderness. His home was a place where men either grew strong or died.

Clasping his hand around the mouth of one Nordsman with ferocious speed and dexterity, Varin tilted his head back and slit the man's throat with the edge of his blade. His victim collapsed with a muffled cry before he even knew what was happening. The Nordsman's companion stood dumbfounded for a moment. It was just long enough for Varin to strike again. As Varin plunged his short sword into the Nordsman's chest, his victim let out an agonized scream before falling to the ground. The ranger cursed himself for getting sloppy.

Looking about, Varin spotted another pair of Nordsmen atop a nearby hill. One drew his bow while the second began to flee. Varin rolled out of the way as an arrow came flying down at him. He took cover behind a wide tree trunk as he drew his own bow and an arrow. Daring a glance from behind the trunk, Varin let the shaft loose at his target. The Nordsman dropped with the missile projecting from his face.

Varin nocked another arrow and scanned his surroundings for the remaining Nordsman. It was impossible to spot him through the trees from where he stood. Running hard, Varin chased the enemy scout the best he could. The pursuit proved easy enough as Varin quickly discovered his prey's tracks in the snow. As long as the ranger could catch him before he could warn others…

Disappointed, Varin stopped as he spotted another cloaked figure removing a throwing-ax from the back of the prone Nordsman he had been running after. It was another crusader scout Varin recognized as Fargu. The other scout wiped the blood from his weapon with a coarse linen cloth, nodded at Varin, and vanished back into the woods. Varin was not the only ranger in the crusade who knew what he was doing after all.

There were thousands of Nordsmen and orcs surrounding Biorkon's defenses. There were too many for Godfrey to venture even a rough estimate. They appeared to be a single dark mass crashing against the walls. Siege towers moved slowly towards the grey stone battlements. Catapults and trebuchets hurled boulders both in attack and defense. The walls held. Or they did for now at least.

Silver Sun archers desperately shot their longbows into the mass of foes from atop the crenelated parapet and towers. Some of the Nordsman siege ladders met the wall, and the enemy began ascending with surprising speed. As Nordsmen and orcs clambered over the parapet, the Silver Sun men-at-arms flung themselves at the attackers with their spears and swords, refusing to give any ground. Desperation yielded countless acts of bravery atop Biorkon's walls.

Biorkon Castle sat on the edge of a narrow snowy promontory overlooking the sea to the south. The geography only allowed for one angle of attack by land, and the Nordsmen had brought no ships to blockade the fortress by sea. The newly arrived crusaders now blocked the Nordsmen's only escape route.

Godfrey's contingent formed the left flank of the crusaders' army. Morgan the Bloodied and about two hundred Knights of the Silver Sun were with them, while Conrad the Wolf and the crusaders from Errans were on Godfrey's right. The other crusaders from Lortharain formed the center of the army while the Gothians and Cardigalians held the right flank.

Eager to join the fray, Godfrey sat atop Baruch with lance gripped tightly in hand. Turpin was beside Godfrey, and the other knights of Bastogne were behind him. Turpin carried his sword in one hand and a banner depicting Godfrey's heraldry in the other. Pride swelled in Godfrey's heart at the sight of his banner held aloft as the battle was about to be joined.

The crusaders were separated from their foes by a wide stretch of snow-covered earth. Standing between the crusaders from Bastogne and the carnage before them, Walaric raised his hands in the air. Other clergymen made similar gestures to their respective groups of crusaders farther down the line. Godfrey and the others within earshot of Walaric bowed their heads as the acolyte began his prayer.

"O gods," Walaric shouted towards the heavens over an eastern breeze that picked up from the sea. "The omens are good, and we shall join battle with these vile fiends. Grant us victory in this holy work. Reward us in life or in death for our efforts here today. Amen."

"Amen," the crusaders chorused in reply.

Walaric retreated through the midst of the cavalry to stand with Varin and the other Bastognian scouts, who now formed a contingent of archers in the rear. Though he carried a longsword on his belt just in case the need arose, Walaric had no experience in fighting. Godfrey did not fault him for this retreat. Some men were born to work, others to fight, and others to pray. That was the order of things.

The other clerics had finished their prayers at about the same time. Some followed suit with Walaric in their respective contingents, while others drew weapons and stood in the front ranks of the crusader infantry. A few mounted horses, and joined with some of the knights.

There are all types here, Godfrey mused. *Some apparently can fight and pray.*

"Now!" Godfrey shouted, spurring his mount forward.

Clods of wet dirt flew into the air as the massed cavalry churned the earth with their thundering hooves. Chainmail rattled to the rhythm of the moving horses. Whizzing over the knights' heads, the crusaders' crossbow bolts and arrows struck down hundreds of Nordsmen and orcs before the knights had even reached their foes. A second volley of the crusaders' bolts and arrows struck down almost as many Nordsmen as the first.

Up until now, Godfrey realized, the Nordsmen and orcs had been ignorant of the crusaders' approach, so focused were they upon attacking Biorkon's walls. Varin and the crusade's other scouts had been thorough in covertly silencing the Nordsmen's own scouts prior to the main army reaching the siege. This meant surrendering precious time in relieving Biorkon, but gaining the element of surprise was enough to satisfy Godfrey.

Realizing another foe was upon them, some of the Nordsmen charged to counter the crusader assault. Screaming battle-cries, the knights lowered their lances just before colliding with the enemy. A sickening crunch accompanied each impact as the cavalry rode through the infantry.

Baruch trampled several enemies before Godfrey skewered one with his lance. Pulling his weapon free from the dead man, Godfrey plunged it into the ribs of another foe. The second Nordsman gripped Godfrey's lance by the shaft, and took it to the ground with him as he fell. Immediately releasing the weapon, Godfrey drew his sword and began to hack at the foes around him.

The rest of the crusader cavalry and Knights of the Silver Sun smashed through the ranks of Nordsmen and orcs. The crusader footmen soon followed, and filled in the gaps left in the Nordsmen ranks by the cavalry. The grinding melee now began in earnest.

Panicking, some of the orcs began to scatter, but noticeably, some of their kin wearing heavier armor did not. Oath-warriors, Godfrey had been told these were called. There was nowhere for them to flee except down the cliffs of the promontory into the shoals below. That option was simply an ignominious death. The Nordsmen and the orcish oath-warriors, knowing they were trapped, preferred to make a last stand.

Plunging Uriel through the neck of an orc, Godfrey's arm was drenched in the foul creature's hot spewing blood. A Nordsman charged Godfrey, but Turpin cut him down with a slash of his sword. He nodded at Godfrey, who returned the gesture before spurring his horse on to his next victim. Turpin did not seek much praise for his work.

Godfrey continued slashing through as many foes as he could reach. Crusaders fell around him, but the orcs and Nordsmen had suffered far worse. Some of the crusaders had killed the crews of the stone-throwers, silencing the bombardment. The siege towers and ladders not already at Biorkon's walls continued to press forward, but Godfrey supposed it would be in vain at this point.

A tremor rumbled through the air. No, it was a chant. The Nordsmen and orc warriors began to clear a path through their ranks. What vile trick did they have in store?

There was a large group of Nordsmen, Godfrey guessed a couple hundred, beating their bare chests with the shafts of large two-handed axes. They were chanting. They wore no armor or tunics, just trousers and bear pelts draped over their heads and shoulders.

"Berserkers," Morgan warned as Godfrey looked to the Grand Master for an explanation.

With axes raised, the berserkers gave a bloodcurdling cry and charged at the crusaders. The crusader crossbowmen fired their weapons over the heads of the knights in reply. Dozens of the wild men were knocked off their feet from the force of the bolts striking them. Most of the berserkers kept running anyway, even with missiles protruding from deep wounds. The crossbowmen cranked the strings of their weapons back as fast as they could in preparation for another volley.

"Not enough time." Godfrey shook his head at Turpin.

Turpin grinned humorlessly.

"Knights of Bastogne…" Godfrey pointed his sword at the berserkers. "Let them know your fury!"

Morgan looked as if he were about to protest, but Baruch was already galloping ahead. Turpin and Godfrey's other knights followed him in the wedge formation they trained in. Signaling the Silver Suns forward, Morgan and his knights fell into their own wedge formation slightly behind and to the left of Godfrey's.

Screaming wildly, the berserkers flung themselves at the charging cavalry. Some of the berserkers used their large axes to cleave through armor and barding with ease just as the knights tore through the mass of berserkers. Other berserkers braced the long shafts of their weapons against the ground, impaling any knight or horse unfortunate enough to cross the berserkers. Knights fell all around Godfrey. He slashed and slashed but this mad foe ignored all but the most serious wounds.

A grizzled berserker foamed at the mouth as he flew at Godfrey with a sword in each hand. Godfrey parried one of the blades with Uriel, and stuck the Nordsman through the chest, but the berserker's other blade made its way past Godfrey's shield, and its acutely tapered tip tore into his gut. The Nordsman berserker collapsed as Godfrey dropped his sword.

His vision blurring, Godfrey pulled the berserker's sword out of his belly. Blood was spilling all over his tabard and Baruch's saddle. Godfrey did not realize it was his own blood until he fell off his steed. He hit the ground face-first with a painful thud.

The moans and screams of the dying filled Godfrey's ears. He tried to stand but his arms were too weak. He only managed to push himself onto his back before his arms gave out. His head was swimming in clouded thoughts.

"Mother," Godfrey pleaded as he began to choke on his own blood. "Mother… Help. Please…"

Godfrey only saw blackness now. His limbs were numb. He knew no more.

Chapter Thirteen

Alvir glared at the messenger before him. His fists were clenched tightly. He wanted to lash out, strike something, but the High Warlord knew such a display would accomplish nothing. The message would not change even if he killed the messenger who delivered it.

The messenger was tall, even by Nordsman standards, and nearly had to hunch entering through the door of Alvir's tent. Looking over his shoulder to Tarik, Alvir saw the messenger had at least convinced his retainer of the news. Cracking his knuckles, the orc chieftain, Urzg, gave a low growl of displeasure. That made two the messenger had convinced.

"You're sure?" Alvir pressed the Nordsman before him. "We have nearly starved Pskov out, and you say there are crusaders at Biorkon?"

"Clan Frost Lion's women are not known for birthing liars," the messenger insisted.

Alvir took a step back. Crusaders were in the Nordslands. That response came faster than Alvir would have anticipated. Urzg frowned at Alvir's hesitation. This orc despised weakness even more than Alvir did. That made Urzg a valuable tool so long as Alvir appeared strong. He needed to come up with a plan fast if he wished to maintain the loyalty of Urzg's tribe.

"Map." Alvir thrust a hand out to Tarik.

Grabbing a large sheet of parchment, Tarik unfurled the map of the Nordslands and spread it across the table in the center of the tent. Alvir consulted it, tracing his finger across its features. News took time to travel, and while news traveled, so did armies.

"By the time we get down there it will be too late to relieve the Clan Owlbear warriors." Alvir shook his head, looking to Tarik then Urzg.

"They're already dead," the messenger said with a grimace, bowing his head. "The crusaders slaughtered them to a man."

Urzg snorted, picking a speck of filth from his tattered cloak.

"My lord," Tarik interjected. "It stands to reason that the crusaders did not come to Biorkon by chance. If that's the case, Azgald's own army could be on its way here now to relieve this siege…"

"I am aware," Alvir cut in. "And believe me, I have no desire to share the fate of our brothers at Biorkon. Abandon the siege. Strike the camp immediately."

"Where are we going?" Tarik inquired.

Urzg's expression changed from contempt to intrigue. Though cowardly and vile, orcs were not stupid. They could appreciate tactical and strategic nuance, even if their own raids were more direct affairs.

"With the crusade at Biorkon, they will undoubtedly pay their devotions at Vindholm before moving on to another fortress." Alvir turned back to the map. "The Silver Suns will try to get the crusaders to march east while the

Azgaldians will wish to push against our invasion from the south."

Tarik and Urzg nodded in agreement. Alvir knew his foes well.

"But the crusaders themselves will want to strike at our heartland." Alvir pointed emphatically at the map. "They may compromise on a northeastern target, Skasgun, maybe Epsberg. Tarik, Urzg, stay in the area with a small army of your best skirmishers. Raid. Pillage. Give the Azgaldians something to chase for a while. I'll take the rest of the army to Skasgun, then Epsberg if I don't find the crusaders along the way."

Urzg balled his fist and thumped his mailed chest in salute. Tarik made to leave the tent, but Alvir grabbed him by the arm.

"And one more thing," Alvir added. "Send word to Nera. We'll need her to persuade more volunteers to reinforce you up here."

"My lord." Tarik bowed before leaving the tent.

Rubbing his temples, Alvir sat in a chair near the table with the map spread out over it. Seizing the throne had been easy enough. Maintaining it was proving much more difficult. Tarik was loyal to the end, but most Clan lords watched the balance of power shift with a keen eye, while orc and cyclops lords were sure to break their vows of allegiance the instant they believed Alvir to be losing control. Assurances, gifts, threats, all these things and more were required for Alvir to maintain his grasp on the Clans even while winning a war. How much more would be required of him should he begin to lose?

Clasping the dragon pendant around his neck, Alvir took comfort. Nera would help him maintain control. Her reputation as the Great Witch of the North gave Alvir a certain measure of authority; however, what she sought at

Olso would not only cow the Clans into permanent submission—it would ensure Alvir's victory in the war against Azgald as well.

A fire crackled in the hearth on the far side of the room. The blanket covering Godfrey was warm, and the bed was soft. He tossed in the sheets, and bit back a curse he wanted to screech as sharp pain ripped through his belly. A gentle voice shushed him as a soft feminine hand caressed his hair. Warmth washed over him, and the pain dulled.

Godfrey's eyes popped open in surprise. The light pouring from outside through the window was so bright. The bed Godfrey was lying in was set in an unfamiliar room while a damsel sat in a chair beside him, hovering near him. Seeing Godfrey's eyes flash open, she withdrew her hand as if Godfrey's head were suddenly on fire. Her dark hair cascaded around her pale face, from which her grey eyes sparkled down at Godfrey. Did those eyes really sparkle just now?

"I am dead," Godfrey declared, exhaling loudly.

"What?" the damsel asked in confusion.

"You are the girl from my dreams," Godfrey explained as he closed his eyes again. "So I must be dead, and this is one of the celestial kingdoms."

The damsel blushed and stood. She flattened the creases in her green dress with her hands. Brushing her long hair out of her face with her fingers, she huffed restlessly.

"Well you're very much alive," the damsel said with a smirk. "So stop dreaming."

Godfrey sat up as he opened his eyes again. Tears filled his vision from the pain in his gut as he shifted in bed, but he was ready for it this time. Wiping away the tears, he looked at the damsel again, and his heart almost stopped. There was no mistaking it. This *was* the girl from his dreams.

"What is your name, my lady?" Godfrey offered his hand to the damsel.

"Madeline," she replied as she returned the gesture.

Godfrey kissed her hand briefly before she withdrew it. Realizing he was wearing a tunic he did not recognize, his mind raced. He looked about the room quizzically but winced with every movement.

"Where am I if I am not dead?" He met her gaze.

"In Biorkon of course." Madeline shrugged. "You've been lying here for days. Most of us thought you were going to die."

"The battle?" Godfrey pressed.

"You did splendidly." Madeline smiled, indicating the window off in the corner of the room. "I saw you lead the charge against those berserkers. It was very brave of you. Most knights of Azgald or even Silver Suns would think twice before doing that."

"I did the only thing I could think of," Godfrey confessed. "But after what they did, I might think twice next time. Why are they so hard to kill?"

"Berserkers are devoted to the Nordsman war gods," Madeline explained. "Some say the dark gods bless them for their devotion. Others say that, because berserkers think they are invincible, it takes a very heavy blow to convince them otherwise."

"I'll remember that." Godfrey nursed the wound in his gut. "I thought this castle belonged to the Silver Suns. What is a damsel like you doing here?"

"My father is the Duke of Pavik." Madeline sat back down in the chair she had risen from. "He came here to meet the leaders of the crusade when they arrived."

"And where is Pavik?" Godfrey asked.

"It's the westernmost duchy of Azgald," Madeline sighed. "In winter, it can take more than a month to reach it from here."

"That's a long way for a duke to bring his daughter," Godfrey said. "Was your father's only intention to meet the leaders of the crusade?"

"We shall see." She gave a mischievous look and rose from her chair.

Madeline walked slowly to the door without another word. Godfrey watched her. The damsel's ornate jeweled hairpin on the back of her head reminded him of the hilt of a dagger. Then again, most things Godfrey saw tended to remind him of the tools of his own trade. He was utterly captivated by her beauty, but there was also intelligence in her grey eyes. The careful way she chose her words before speaking also suggested she had spent significant time with books.

Realizing she was about to leave, he silently stammered for something to say, but words failed him. Thought itself failed him. Had he not known better, he would have said she was enjoying watching him squirm for that brief moment. With a wink, she was out the door.

Forgetting his wound, Godfrey flopped back onto the bed with a heavy sigh. His head seemed so light that it might well fly away from his body entirely. He envisioned

Madeline's face in his mind, silently repeating her name over and over again. She did not exactly seem subtle in displaying her interest either, which excited him all the more. He tried to rise from the bed to go after her, but yelped as the puncture in his stomach argued otherwise.

Walaric knocked on the door, and cautiously entered the room. A look of relief crossed his face when he saw Godfrey was awake. Striding to his friend, Walaric plopped in the chair Madeline had occupied just a minute or so before.

"Glad to see you are up," Walaric confessed. "Turpin and I have been praying for you."

"Thanks," Godfrey acknowledged. "What happened? How did the battle end?"

"Losses were minimal," Walaric reassured him. "We took them completely by surprise. Turpin says Alvir was not here though. Word is that the Nordsman High King was fighting another battle farther up north."

"I see." Godfrey scratched his forehead.

"Well we're off to a good start anyway," Walaric beamed.

"Right." Godfrey gave a bemused smile, thinking of Madeline again.

"Duke Tancred is arguing with the Silver Suns and Phillip and Henry over where to attack next," Walaric said after a while.

"Will this be how it is the whole crusade?" Godfrey rolled his eyes. "I don't understand why we don't just take the crusade to wherever Alvir is. Defeat him, stop the Nordsmen. That objective is easy enough. Who is this Duke Tancred? Why didn't King Lothar join us here?"

"You know each of these lords has his own agenda in this," Walaric quipped sardonically. "King Lothar went north to repel the main Nordsman advance. High King Alvir is probably up there with the Clan army. As for Duke

Tancred, he is also one of Azgald's lords. I think he said he was the Duke of Pavik or something like that. He is arguing that the crusade should follow the King, and try to retake some of the northern fortresses."

"Is that what King Lothar thinks is best for the crusade?" Godfrey wondered aloud.

"Lothar hasn't sent word to give any direction," Walaric replied with a frown.

"So Tancred is siding with Oksar then," Godfrey noted, suddenly finding great wisdom in the Baron's position.

"It looks like it," Walaric agreed. "You should rest up. Another council is being called together as soon as you are able to walk again."

It took another three days for Godfrey to be able to stand on his own. Standing was almost unbearably painful up until that point. Even still, he winced with every step. Madeline had not come to visit him in his room again, though Walaric assured him she and Duke Tancred were still in Biorkon. At one point, Biorkon's castellan, a middle-aged man named Poil, came in to express the Silver Suns' gratitude, but Godfrey was only disappointed it was not Madeline who had come to visit.

"There are other maidens here too," Walaric told Godfrey as he lay in bed, complaining about Madeline's absence. "There's a few other lords from Azgald looking to find marriage prospects for their daughters by the looks of it."

"Take them," Godfrey scoffed.

"They're not bad-looking." Walaric shrugged. "Besides, I'm afraid I can't. I'm binding myself to one of the celestial gods, remember? That means complete celibacy unless I change my mind and choose a nature god for my patron."

"Right." Godfrey rolled his eyes. "With that rule, how do the celestial gods find any priests to venerate them?"

"There's more to life than just girls," Walaric chastised him, apparently trying to convince himself as much as his friend.

"I was just kidding," Godfrey quipped. "I know."

Painfully, Godfrey found himself limping down the fortress corridors by the end of the fourth day since he regained consciousness. The Sun was setting, and the Silver Sun orderlies were lighting torches and candles in the hallways. Shadows danced through the halls as the candles and torches flickered. Godfrey was hoping to find Madeline, but was disappointed at every turn. Biorkon was almost as large as Fuetoile Keep and completely unfamiliar to Godfrey.

A Silver Sun chaplain led a group of knights in plainsong from somewhere farther down the corridor. Godfrey wandered towards the melodious hymn. The sound was almost hypnotic.

Morgan the Bloodied emerged from the chapel in which the knights were singing. A scowl creased the Grand Master's face as he met Godfrey's eyes. Godfrey stopped in his tracks as his hand began to tremble. This was the last person he had hoped to find.

"Godfrey." Morgan sneered as he drew closer to him. "Glad to see you are on your feet again. Perhaps now the crusade can go back on the offensive."

"I did not ask the whole crusade to stop for me," Godfrey countered.

"The second largest group of crusaders is under your command." Morgan pointed at Godfrey's chest. "If you stop, the whole crusade stops. Try not to throw your life away for no reason."

"I did not see you doing anything about those berserkers," Godfrey snapped with a voice that shook almost as badly as his hand.

"A wise commander would have let his infantry deal with the berserkers instead of wasting the lives of his knights." Morgan glared at him.

"It seemed like the right thing to do at the time," Godfrey countered, throwing out his hands emphatically. "How could I ask the men to do something I would not?"

"This is all a moot point now, wouldn't you say, Grand Master?" Turpin cut in, approaching from behind Godfrey.

Godfrey almost jumped at Turpin's surprise entrance, but he was equally relieved that he was no longer alone with the Grand Master. Grumbling something indistinct, Morgan stormed away down the corridor. Turpin's eyes followed the Grand Master until he rounded a corner and was out of sight. Scratching his head, the chaplain turned to Godfrey.

"The Grand Master of the Silver Suns would make a terrible adversary out here," Turpin said, frowning.

"I didn't start it." Godfrey's frustration returned as quickly as it had left.

"No," Turpin concurred. "But he is a powerful man, especially here in Azgald. Try to stay on his good side."

"Right." Godfrey bit back any further retort he might have wished to say.

"The council is about to be held." Turpin indicated the direction Morgan had gone. "Make a left down the corridor there, and it should be in the first room on your right. I'll be joining you as soon as I fetch Walaric."

Turpin left in the direction he had come from. Limping down the hallway, Godfrey frowned at the thought of going into the room without Turpin or Walaric. He had no other friends among the crusaders. He slowed his pace, hoping Turpin might return with Walaric before he even reached the other lords, but that did not seem likely with how little corridor remained in front of him. Turning the corner,

Godfrey was surprised to see Baldwin de Ghend about to enter the door Turpin had indicated.

"Hello." Baldwin half-smiled.

Baldwin stepped past the door and grasped Godfrey's hand.

"Charging those berserkers during the battle was awfully brave of you," Baldwin said, releasing Godfrey's hand.

"Some people would call it foolish." Godfrey grimaced.

"Other people are green with envy at such a glorious exploit." Baldwin shrugged. "You should have seen the look on Conrad's face when he heard you survived the charge."

"There is no love lost between the two of us," Godfrey sighed.

"The same could be said of Conrad and many people," Baldwin muttered.

Godfrey paused, considering Baldwin. He was different from the other crusaders Godfrey had met thus far. This was the first outside of his own men from Bastogne Godfrey met who did not seem openly antagonistic. Baldwin's amicability was a shock. Godfrey had come to expect worse.

"Why did you come on crusade?" Godfrey asked bluntly.

"Oh…" Baldwin hesitated, taken aback. "There is more than one reason to choose from? I came because the gods called."

"As did I." Godfrey smiled. "How are affairs in Ghend?"

"Trade with the dwarves is good." Baldwin cracked his fingers. "At least it is when winter isn't bad and brigands aren't out."

"Fair enough," Godfrey conceded.

"Did you know Conrad before the crusade?" Baldwin inquired.

"No." Godfrey crossed his arms.

"Let me tell you something about him." Baldwin looked to make sure no one else was within earshot. "He is a genuine prick. As such, even when he does the right thing, it's for the wrong reason. Most of the crusaders I've met are here for the right reasons. Don't judge us all by his example."

"I'll try not to." Godfrey's voice trailed off.

A tall, broad-framed man entered the corridor. A white dragon set against a red field was emblazoned on his tabard. Godfrey's heart skipped a beat as he saw Madeline standing just behind the man. The man's hair was long and as dark as hers. The resemblance left little doubt in Godfrey's mind that this was Madeline's father. Baldwin's jaw hung open at the sight of Madeline, and Godfrey shot him a dangerous look.

"This is the boy?" Duke Tancred looked Godfrey over, apparently unimpressed.

Madeline shook her head in reply, trying to conceal a smile.

"He doesn't look like much now, does he?" Tancred scowled. "He's not very tall or strong for a knight."

"Looks can be deceiving," Madeline started. "You saw from the wall how he charged those berserkers."

"Foolish," Tancred countered. "It was the antics of a young and foolish boy."

"Brave is the word you're looking for, father," Madeline insisted more earnestly than before. "He also slew a vampire back in Lortharain."

Who told her that? Godfrey wondered.

"I killed a man-eating giant when I was his age." Tancred's tone grew disinterested.

Godfrey raised an eyebrow, impressed at Tancred's feat of arms.

The disappointment in Baldwin's face grew as he apparently realized Madeline had not even noticed him. Though Godfrey had quickly grown to like Baldwin, he willed his newfound friend to simply go away and forget about Madeline. It seemed Godfrey would have enough of a challenge from Madeline's father without competition.

"Boy," Tancred addressed Godfrey directly for the first time. "You are the son of Ulric, the Duke of Bastogne?"

"Yes, my lord," Godfrey answered in what he thought was the most polite voice he could manage.

"And how many knights can Bastogne muster?" Tancred pressed.

"Well…" Godfrey thought about this for a moment. "I brought five hundred with me on crusade and six thousand infantry."

"So Bastogne is a large and powerful duchy then," Tancred said, seeming to weigh this information against other facts. "But there are other powerful lords here too."

Baldwin's eyes lit up as he was about to say something, but Godfrey stamped his foot over Baldwin's. Baldwin silently bit back a curse, looking quizzically at Godfrey, who pretended not to notice.

"Come, Madeline," Tancred continued, gesturing for his daughter as he opened the door.

Madeline caught Godfrey's eye for just a moment as she walked through the door. Then her father whisked her to a seat at a large table between him and Conrad the Wolf in the next instant. Godfrey's blood boiled at the sight. His only consolation was that Madeline did not seem to be enjoying her time with Conrad any more than Godfrey would have.

"That's a shame," Baldwin added sourly, following Godfrey's gaze. "Looks like neither of us gets her."

"Come on." Godfrey gestured for Baldwin to follow him into the council chamber. "Let's get this over with."

Spotting Godfrey, Torcul of Cumbria pulled a seat out for him. Godfrey sat next to Torcul and Baldwin found another seat nearby. Torcul slapped Godfrey on the back endearingly.

"Aye lad," Torcul swelled. "You did a great thing out there the other day."

"Except when you cried for your mother," Conrad taunted, interrupting Torcul. "What a great, brave warrior crying for his mother as he bleeds out in the snow."

Godfrey bit his lip in embarrassment. He had forgotten about that until now. Madeline frowned at Godfrey then turned her eyes down into her lap. The others fell silent.

"Oh." Conrad smirked, now jeering at Madeline. "You did not know just how brave Godfrey de Bastogne was?"

"At least he fought them," Madeline replied meekly.

"We all did," Conrad blustered. "I killed over a dozen of the brutes myself. But the first thing Godfrey does is get himself stabbed and cry. 'Mother help… Please, mother.' How pathetic."

"Enough," Henry the Pilgrim cut in as he entered the room.

Chairs scraped against the floor as everyone turned to face Henry. The look on his face was cold. No one dared to speak.

"I have seen men do far worse in the face of death," Henry added, brushing his cloak over his back. "What I hear of your own near-death experience is hardly flattering, Conrad. Shall I tell everyone here what you did at the siege of Friegslav when you got that scar? I'm sure everyone here would want to know how brave you were when facing the wizard Thuz."

"He was a wizard…" Conrad's voice trailed off weakly.

Sulking, Conrad lowered his eyes in shame. Godfrey and several others shifted uncomfortably at the word *wizard*. The old Gothian scowled as he looked over everyone present. After a satisfied look at the other crusaders, Henry moved across the room. To Godfrey's surprise, Henry took his seat next to Morgan. The two had argued so intensely back at Kalscony that this was the last thing Godfrey had expected.

"We have made amends," Henry explained to the questioning stares Godfrey and the others gave him.

Godfrey silently bet that such amends somehow involved promises of money and or lands changing hands.

The last of the crusade's leadership entered the council chamber, as did some other Azgaldian lords Godfrey had not previously met. A few maidens attended these Azgaldian lords. Godfrey guessed these damsels were the lords' daughters and unmarried sisters. Walaric was right. They were each attractive in their own way. They traded flirtatious glances with the younger crusaders, but Godfrey only had eyes for Madeline, and she for him.

One curly-haired maiden locked eyes with Baldwin, and the two mouthed silent promises to meet up later. Godfrey smiled at this development and made a note to ask Baldwin about it later. At least his interest in Madeline was now redirected towards another beautiful young damsel.

Turpin and Walaric found their places just behind Godfrey, and he turned his attention back to war and such serious matters. Love would have to wait. The murmur of voices that had arisen as the remaining crusader lords and their attendees arrived was diffused as Morgan gestured for quiet.

"This was a great victory," Morgan exclaimed. "The Silver Suns are in your debt. However, this attack on Biorkon shows just how vulnerable Azgald's eastern borders are. If Alvir is unafraid to send forces to Biorkon, then Narlstad is vulnerable, and even the holy city of Vindholm itself could be attacked."

"Alvir attacked Biorkon without knowing about the crusade's arrival," Tancred countered. "He will be more cautious in the future."

"Agreed," Phillip d'Artois added. "We should link up with King Lothar's forces in the North and press our advantage. We can invade the Clans, force them to the defensive."

"But Vindholm is sacred," Henry argued. "We cannot let the Nordsmen defile the temples there."

"The gods would curse us all if we allowed Vindholm's sacred sites to burn," Morgan noted grimly. "The King has the North under control. The crusade's duty should be to the eastern theater of this war. It is the only sensible option."

Godfrey wanted to agree with Phillip, as his support might help him gain favor with Tancred, but the Grand Master of the Silver Suns was clearly right in this instance. Closing his eyes, Godfrey silently prayed for inspiration. Was Vindholm really under immediate threat? Godfrey knew so little of Azgald's geography. Vindholm was a sacred city with many holy sites, but he did not know its strategic value. Henry the Pilgrim knew the land. He had been here before. Should he follow Henry's sentiments? Conrad was also vocalizing his support to push north, and Godfrey knew what he must say.

"The men of Bastogne will march east," Godfrey blurted out over Conrad. "Protecting the temples of Vindholm is a sacred obligation we cannot ignore. Who is with me?"

"Aye," Baldwin and Torcul chorused.

"Aye," Raymond of Wrehst concurred a moment later.

"It seems we have a majority." Henry smirked, nodding to Godfrey.

"Excellent." Morgan clasped his hands together, eager to lay out his plan of attack. "There are four great fortresses which form the backbone of the Eastern Marches: Epsberg, Mirborg, Laht, and Odsha. If we strike all four of them at once, the Eastern Marches are as good as ours."

"That will require us to break up the crusade into significantly smaller armies," Phillip protested. "The Nordsmen could easily defeat us one at a time if we committed to this plan."

"But if we strike fast enough, we could consolidate our forces again before they can counterattack." Torcul gestured with his fist.

"There is a lot of timber here in the Nordslands." Baldwin scratched his chin. "Siege engines could be built on site to save time hauling them with us from castle to castle. We leave the stone-throwers with whatever garrisons are left behind, dismantle the towers and ladders, then start over at the next objective."

"Don't you remember what Oksar said back at Kalscony?" Conrad cut in angrily. "How are the Silver Suns going to hold onto all of these castles after we go? This will just be a waste of time."

"My men and I could hold one of the fortresses until reinforcements came for us," Raymond answered. "We could live off the land there. We could send for our wives and children if we were there long enough. It would be an honor."

Tancred and two of the other Azgaldian lords murmured to each other quickly and quietly. Some sort of agreement was reached that Godfrey felt suspicious of. Madeline, listening in on her father's conversation, winked at Godfrey from across the table when their eyes met. He let out a slow breath, trusting Madeline's judgment for what it was worth.

"Let it not be said that Pavik did not do its duty to Azgald and the gods." Tancred crossed his arms. "If the crusade moves east, my men and I will come too."

The other Azgaldian lords present assented.

Morgan nodded graciously in reply.

"It's settled then," Henry affirmed. "Tancred will accompany Godfrey and Conrad to Epsberg. Baldwin and Phillip will go to Odsha. And I will take Raymond, Torcul, and Gunthar to Laht. Morgan, can your Silver Suns take Mirborg?"

"I will send to Oksar in Kalscony." Morgan smiled maliciously. "He owes a debt to the Silver Suns that I think I would now like him to pay."

"Once each army has completed its quest, we will rendezvous at Narlstad," Henry added. "That will put us in a good position to plan our next move."

The crusaders murmured in assent and began to leave. First, Torcul and Gunthar left the room as they kept a close watch on each other. Then Phillip and the two Gothians left. Baldwin slipped out after the curly-haired maiden so quickly and quietly, Godfrey barely noticed. He silently wished them luck.

Hoping to catch a private moment with Madeline, Godfrey lingered. She gave him an apologetic look, as Tancred was trying to force her into a conversation with Conrad. The other Azgaldian lords around the table eyed Godfrey as if he had overstayed his welcome.

Turpin cleared his throat, gesturing for Godfrey to follow him and Walaric out the door.

"There will be more opportunities," Turpin consoled Godfrey as they made their way out into the corridor. "If not her, then another damsel will present herself. There have been a lot of lords coming to Biorkon over the last few days introducing their daughters to the crusade's young bachelors."

"But none like her." Walaric wistfully batted his eyes at Godfrey.

Godfrey shoved Walaric away, who only cackled madly in response.

Giving a slight cough, Phillip emerged from an alcove in the corridor. Godfrey, Turpin, and Walaric stopped in their tracks. Godfrey's eyes narrowed as they met Phillip's.

"You seem to have discovered how to exert your influence over the crusade," Phillip began diplomatically. "May I have a moment with you, Godfrey, alone?"

Godfrey shrugged to Turpin and Walaric. They exchanged glances, but the two left Godfrey with the Duke of Artois and continued down the corridor without him. Phillip looked both ways down the hall. They were alone. After a long moment, he gestured for Godfrey to join him in the alcove.

"I took you for a fool," Phillip confessed. "I was wrong. Will you accept my apology?"

"I was not offended," Godfrey cautiously replied.

"You have quickly learned the one truth of negotiating on campaign," Phillip continued smoothly. "The lord with the most soldiers under his command is always in the majority. How did you figure this out while so young?"

"It was a couple of things," Godfrey admitted. "When I first met Conrad, he was jealous of me because I brought more men than he did. Then, tonight Morgan accused me of holding up the whole crusade because of my injury."

"You are sharp." Phillip smiled. "Conrad is a fool, eager for glory and bellicose. He will align himself with me, hoping to enhance his own prestige. But together, we have almost thirteen thousand men. I cannot turn down that kind of support. If you were to support me, we would have more than half the crusade on our side. Then we could ensure that things move the way we want them to."

"You mean the way you want them to," Godfrey corrected.

"Listen…" Phillip's expression grew stern. "Artois borders Bastogne. When this crusade is over, I will not forget my friends…or my enemies. Understood?"

"Your threats don't scare me." Godfrey shook his head. "What do you have to gain from capturing the Northern Marches? I thought going east would be best for Azgald, but you want to go north regardless of how much sense it does or doesn't make."

"Think over my proposal," Phillip snorted. "Choose wisely before you say anything else that might hurt Bastogne in the future."

Without replying, Godfrey briskly walked down the hall in the direction Turpin and Walaric had gone. Retracing his steps proved difficult for Godfrey. Eventually, he found a set of spiral stairs. It was not the set he had come down earlier, but he was sure it would lead him somewhere familiar.

A cold draft followed him up the stairs. He froze in place then almost fell backwards as he saw Madeline sitting on the stairs ahead of him. Gesturing for him to be quiet, she indicated he should sit next to her.

"Father doesn't know I'm here," she whispered. "But I have ways of slipping out of sight when I need to. Still, he would be very upset if he found out you approached me like this."

Godfrey believed Madeline had reversed who had found whom, but he dismissed the thought as quickly as it came.

"Right." He frowned as he sat next to her. "I thought he would be, after what I did down there."

"You think for yourself." Madeline smiled. "I like that."

Godfrey blushed.

"Tell me about your hand." Madeline was suddenly very close to Godfrey.

"What?" Godfrey could do little to hide his surprise at the sudden request.

The smell of her perfume intoxicated Godfrey. Madeline was close, but Godfrey wanted to be even closer. The look on her face completely disarmed him. Resisting the urge to kiss her on the spot, Godfrey pretended to cough.

"I'm sorry," Godfrey said. "What was that?"

"Your hand was shaking in the council chamber when Conrad was mocking you." Madeline indicated Godfrey's right hand. "It did it again when you went against father."

"Oh," Godfrey exhaled, understanding what Madeline meant. "It started doing that a while ago. I think it was some time after my first battle."

Growing uncomfortable, Godfrey thought hard about how to change the conversation.

"Who were those other men in the council chamber?" he asked.

"The Dukes of Austlad, Gotlad, and Smalad." Madeline shook her head dismissively. "A few of the barons and counts who could make it were also there. Don't worry about them. They're loyal to father."

"Right." Godfrey scratched his ear, unsure if Madeline's comment should really inspire confidence in him.

"You have lots of nervous habits," Madeline insisted. "Tell me about your hand."

Stretching his mind, Godfrey tried to think of what caused his hand to tremble. He had not realized it was shaking in the council chamber. At other times the sensation was so overwhelming it almost paralyzed him. He thought back to the vampire's castle in the swamp. There were other times too, some more recent than that.

"I guess it has something to do with fear," Godfrey divulged guardedly. "Or anger. I don't know."

"I don't think anyone else noticed," Madeline said. "Don't worry. I don't think you're a coward."

"Thanks." Godfrey breathed freely as his thoughts and feelings suddenly came pouring out. "It's just, you don't realize until you're actually there in battle. Death doesn't distinguish between brave men and cowards. It's not until you're there that you realize the squire who fell next to you could have been you instead. During that first battle, I saw men eaten alive by shambling hordes of undead. Zombies, ghouls, it was just…awful to see."

Godfrey had to take a long breath to steady himself. He had never told anyone how he felt after his first battle. There had been no point in telling Fallard, Bruno, or Fulcher. They had all been there too. Walaric would not have understood. Yet it was so easy to confide in Madeline.

"So why do you still go out there?" Madeline asked after giving Godfrey a long, hard look. "Why do you go out to see the blood and gore and men screaming as they die?"

"Duty," Godfrey answered quietly. "This is the task the gods have given me by my birth. Maybe others could do it instead of me. Bastogne has plenty of soldiers. Someone else could have led the crusaders here in my stead. But the gods called, and I obeyed. Then that obedience led me to you."

There was a long silence. Had Godfrey said too much? Earlier, he had told Madeline she was the girl of his dreams, but that statement was born of a fleeting bravado he had only rarely felt around young women. He was not about to tell her he really had been dreaming of her well before they met. Most people's faith had limits. Did he even really believe she was the girl in his dreams now that he thought about it? Or was his mind playing tricks on him?

He had trouble reading Madeline's expression. Her eyes focused on something distant. Finally, her gaze fell on him. Her lip twitched. In a flash, she gave him a brief kiss on the cheek and flew up the stairs before he could even react. Stunned, he sat on the stair for a long while, holding his face where Madeline had kissed him.

Chapter Fourteen

The crusade set out early the next morning. Riding Baruch at the head of his knights, Godfrey smiled brightly. He was optimistic, rejuvenated, nothing could upset him now.

The crisp air invigorated him. The sun was bright. Snow crunched with each step of Baruch's hooves. His wound, which had left him bedridden for days, seemed only a minor inconvenience now.

Turpin had taken one hundred knights for the rearguard to march with the baggage train, leaving Walaric and Godfrey at the head of their group. Walaric rode beside Godfrey on the horse of a knight who had fallen during the battle a few days previous. Tancred had three thousand infantry and two hundred knights with him. They marched ahead of Godfrey and Conrad's contingents. Beyond Godfrey's field of view, Varin and the crusade's scouts tracked ahead with the Pavikian rangers. With luck, the scouts would be able to sniff out any danger before the crusaders were caught unawares.

"You seem awfully cheerful for someone who almost died a few days ago," Walaric grunted heavily.

"I am in love," Godfrey sighed.

"Good for you." Walaric rolled his eyes.

"She kissed me," Godfrey added defensively.

"I bet she did," Walaric agreed sardonically. "She would not stop asking me about you the whole time you were in that bed."

Godfrey contemplated this revelation as he and Walaric rode together silently. The only obstacle between Godfrey and Madeline was her father. If Godfrey proved himself in battle, maybe the Duke would warm up to him. Frowning, Godfrey looked to his left, where Conrad's crusaders trod across the snowy plain. Tancred favored Conrad. It was obvious. Madeline's desires were second to a duke's prerogative over his daughter.

"I still wish enough ships would have stayed for us at Biorkon," Walaric grumbled. "They could have transported us up through the gulf to Vindholm. That would have saved us a couple of days of marching."

"We needed some ships to get back to the Ostlands as quickly as possible to gather our reinforcements," Godfrey chided. "Morgan the Bloodied is hoping there will be more crusaders ready to go by the time the ships get down there. In the meantime, the ships we have need to be used where they can be used best. It would take too long for the other groups to get to Laht and Mirborg if they had to go around the gulf. Besides, Mirborg is a port city and a naval assault would be best for that."

Walaric murmured something indistinct about Lortharain's crusaders getting all the hard tasks, then he grew quiet for a bit.

"That certainly was convenient back at Biorkon," Walaric brooded aloud, indicating Tancred's red-clad soldiers ahead of them. "The Nordsmen attack Biorkon and the Duke of Pavik happens to be there in the fortress with an army of his own."

"I think it was more than convenient," Godfrey confided. "I think it was by design."

"Oh?" Walaric raised his eyebrow, urging Godfrey to share his thoughts.

"Something Madeline said earlier." Godfrey shook his head. "She said he did not come just to meet the crusade's leaders. I think he wanted to make sure the crusade went north."

"Then why is he taking us to Epsberg?" Walaric drew his cloak around him as his horse continued through the snow.

"I don't know," Godfrey confessed. "At the time, I thought Madeline was talking about something else, but you saw how quickly Tancred volunteered to bring his forces with us once he saw he couldn't persuade us to go north."

"Good point." Walaric shrugged. "Where is Madeline anyway?"

"She rode ahead to Vindholm to visit the temples," Godfrey answered. "Before we left Biorkon this morning, I overheard Tancred telling some of his retainers to escort her there."

"It's probably safer there than Biorkon." Walaric looked ahead wistfully. "Are we going to stop at Vindholm? It would be a shame to come all this way to defend those sacred places but then not see them."

"Probably not until after the crusade ends, unless we are called to defend Vindholm's walls," Godfrey admitted with a frown. "We must make all haste to Epsberg if we are to maintain the advantage of surprise."

"It would probably help morale if we did stop there," Walaric said, ignoring Godfrey's objection. "I heard a lot of the men saying they wanted to make their devotions at Vindholm before going into battle again."

"I'll bring it up with Conrad and Tancred when we make camp tonight." Godfrey nodded.

"Thanks," Walaric sighed, unconvinced.

Simmering at Walaric's sarcasm, Godfrey nearly threw an insult at his friend. Did Walaric not understand strategic necessity sometimes overruled religious considerations? Probably not, Godfrey realized. Walaric's training was in the work of the gods. The acolyte probably had little understanding of war beyond what he had personally witnessed since he had joined the crusade.

"I want to go there too you know." Godfrey scowled. "I want to see the places where the gods walked, where the saints performed miracles. I want to see the sacred springs, the temples, and all the other holy sites. But sometimes, in war, you can act too late."

"Sometimes, in devotion, you can act too late too," Walaric countered.

The two said little else as they rode for the remainder of the day. Grabbing a hard biscuit from his satchel, Godfrey recalled that he had not gotten any more food while at Biorkon. He chewed on the dry, bland cake at a measured pace.

"I hope Turpin bought some better food than this back at Biorkon," Godfrey said as he took another bite.

"We'll find out tonight." Walaric grimaced, pulling out a biscuit for himself from one of his horse's saddle packs.

Godfrey, Turpin, and Walaric set up their tents near Conrad's and Tancred's later that evening. It was a choice made from tactical necessity more than anything else. Godfrey would have preferred not to be in such proximity to them. However, if the camp were to fall under attack during the night, they would need to be close to coordinate their efforts.

Conrad only ever glowered at Godfrey when the two crossed paths in camp. This did nothing to improve Godfrey's opinion of the Duke of Errans. He would just as soon punch Conrad as talk to him. It took great effort for Godfrey to approach the fire Conrad and Tancred were sitting at after the Sun had set.

"We strike camp again at dawn tomorrow," Tancred said as Godfrey sat on a log across from him and Conrad. "There is good foraging ground ahead for the men."

"Right." Godfrey took a strip of salted venison from his satchel.

Turpin had not failed Godfrey and Walaric. The spiced meat was much better than the biscuits they had acquired on the ship while at sea, though the venison was nothing spectacular. Still, Godfrey packed several hearty bites into his mouth before swallowing.

"Might I say you have a beautiful daughter," Conrad told Tancred. "She is fairer than any damsel in all of Lortharain."

Godfrey almost choked on the venison he had just swallowed. Smirking, Conrad glanced at him from the corner of his eye. Recovering, Godfrey stared at Conrad with venom. His jaw was clenched so tight it began to hurt. Tancred, apparently flattered by Conrad's remarks, looked to the young Duke of Errans with interest. Apparently, he did not notice Godfrey's reaction.

"And you have shown great prowess at Biorkon," Tancred replied with a barely contained grin. "Such gallantry will find its reward, make no mistake."

Godfrey cleared his throat. Turning to him, Tancred's countenance fell as he was forced to acknowledge Godfrey was at the fire with them. Conrad still smirked at Godfrey, obviously content with Tancred's latest words. It took a few deep breaths for Godfrey to suppress his desire to fly at Conrad and pummel him into the snow with his fists.

"Will we be stopping at Vindholm?" Godfrey asked as he attempted to avoid Conrad's gaze.

Tancred stared into the fire without saying a word.

"I know we have to hurry to Epsberg," Godfrey acknowledged. "But think about what it will do for the men's spirits if they could visit the temples, maybe hear a sermon or receive a blessing at the altars."

"No." Conrad shook his head. "Alvir could be moving against the crusade right now. We cannot delay."

"Actually I think Godfrey may be right," Tancred conceded. "We will reach Vindholm in three days. We will spend one day there to resupply and pay our respects to the gods. Then, if we march at double time, we can reach Epsberg in another four days."

"Thank you, lord." Godfrey bowed his head.

"I am thinking of the men," Tancred said, silencing Conrad before he could object. "Crusades are all about morale. Lose morale, and you lose the crusade. Keep morale, and crusaders can do incredible things."

Conrad's face twisted in consternation. Godfrey knew the battle raging in Conrad's mind. It was written across his rival's conflicted expression. Would he let Godfrey get his way or would he risk upsetting Tancred? Godfrey wondered if the only reason Conrad acted interested in Madeline at all was to be a thorn in his side. At least Tancred could avoid antagonizing Godfrey when it suited his purposes. Godfrey supposed Madeline's father was reserving his spite for a more opportune moment. It was a victory all the same—however small.

"Well I must be turning in, then." Godfrey smirked at Conrad. "It's an early day tomorrow."

Walaric waited outside Godfrey's tent. The acolyte had his arms crossed, and was shivering in the cold night air even with his heavy cloak wrapped around him. With teeth chattering, he looked to Godfrey apprehensively.

"Spread the word among the men…" Godfrey clasped Walaric's shoulder. "We will have one day at Vindholm to make devotions and restock whatever supplies they lack."

Walaric met Godfrey with a hearty embrace. His eyes gleaming, Walaric immediately set off for the tents the Bastognian crusaders occupied. Godfrey smiled after the retreating figure of his friend. Baruch snorted, drawing Godfrey's attention away from his thoughts.

There was not much for Baruch to graze on through the snow. Godfrey went to his tent and grabbed a fistful of oats from a bag sitting in the corner. Emerging from his tent with the oats, Godfrey found Baruch's snout already moving to his hand. Godfrey proffered the oats, and Baruch greedily devoured the grain. Snorting again, Baruch gave him a sad look.

"All right." Godfrey waved his hands in defeat. "I'll give you some more. Just hold on."

Godfrey went back to the bag of oats and scooped out as many as he could with both hands cupped together. Baruch ate these just as insatiably as the first handful. The horse's mournful gaze returned, however, as if Godfrey had not fed him at all.

"I'm sorry," Godfrey explained, rubbing Baruch's nose. "I know it's not much, but we can't eat it all in one night. We need some for tomorrow."

Baruch snorted again and trotted off a few paces towards Turpin and Walaric's horses.

"Good night," Godfrey muttered, stifling a yawn.

Entering his tent, Godfrey tied the door shut for the night and began tearing himself out of his armor. The air was frigid. He quickly pulled his bedroll around himself and lay down on the tent floor. Would it ever warm up here?

Walaric's mood significantly improved the next day. The crusaders all chatted excitedly on the march, and their faces grew brighter the closer they got to Vindholm. The cold did not bite Godfrey's face so harshly. The biscuits were still bland, hard, and dry, but that was Godfrey's only complaint in the day thus far. Godfrey noted that even Conrad the Wolf was in a more pleasant mood. The foraging parties caught several deer, rabbits, and some sort of snow-white quail that day. Godfrey could think of few things that would have made the march better. Tancred was right. Morale was everything for a crusade.

The second day after the crusaders decided to stop at Vindholm proved to be much like the first. Though the foragers did not find as many deer in the woods along the way, white quail could be found in almost every thicket they searched. By sunset on the third day, the city of Vindholm was in sight.

Though Vindholm sat atop a large defensible hill, and was surrounded by a strong stone outer wall, earthworks had been dug up around the hill for added defense. The trees around the hill had been cleared for some distance so that its garrison at the wall's towers could more easily see the approach of attackers. The southern gatehouse was tall and intimidating, but the temples behind the twenty-foot walls stood even taller.

There were three temples. One was dedicated to Loxias and Luna. Another was dedicated to Saint Pelegius, a mortal man who had ascended to glory at the very site over which his temple was built. The third and largest temple was set on the highest point of the hill next to the city's keep. This domed temple was dedicated to Spes, the home of all the celestial gods. Both the keep and the Temple of Spes were behind the city's inner curtain wall.

"It is the largest city in all of Azgald," Walaric told Godfrey as they rode their horses at the head of the knights once again. "It might even be the largest city in all the Nordslands."

"How could so many people live where it is so cold all year?" Godfrey shivered. "You would think they would not have enough food to live in such a harsh realm."

"Their faith brings them here." Walaric shrugged. "Pilgrims come from all over the world to make sacrifices, petition for special blessings, or even just to say they came and walked where the gods walked."

"But the gods are everywhere," Godfrey countered.

"Well what I mean is the gods have touched these grounds," Walaric explained. "Three temples are all here in the same city, plus dozens of sacred springs and groves blessed by the saints too. Gods great and small have been here. Loxias himself even canonized Pelegius here in ancient times. This is the city of the gods because they themselves have marked this as a holy city."

"And that is exactly why the Nordsmen seek to defile it," Godfrey spat. "They know that, by desecrating so many sites at once, it will severely weaken the celestial gods."

"It may even irreversibly turn the tide of the War in Heaven to the dark gods' favor," Walaric expounded.

"But we will not let them." Godfrey clenched his fist as his heart filled with righteous indignation.

"No," Walaric agreed.

Immediately after crossing through the city gate, Godfrey, Walaric, and all the knights with them dismounted from their steeds, and offered up their prayers to the gods. Marveling at the thought of standing on sacred ground, Godfrey silently hoped the gods would bless him. Turpin joined them with the rearguard, though Godfrey was surprised to see that the chaplain remained mounted.

"Forgive me for interrupting." Turpin half-smiled to Godfrey. "But your knights are blocking the entrance for the rest of the crusaders."

"Right," Godfrey said as he and Walaric got to their feet, flushing with embarrassment.

"Go on." Turpin gestured encouragingly. "Make your devotions at the temples. The hour is not so late yet."

The knights dispersed as the rest of the crusaders flooded into the city. Spotting Conrad, Godfrey quickly led Baruch and Walaric away from the Duke of Errans down an alleyway. Walaric tugged the reins of his own horse, urging it to follow them. There were dozens of winding side streets and alleys that crisscrossed the main thoroughfares. It was easy enough to avoid Conrad without impeding their own progress too badly.

"What is your horse called again?" Godfrey asked, realizing Walaric never told him.

"I don't know what his old master called him," Walaric admitted. "But I'm calling him Moon Frost."

"Seems appropriate to the climate." Godfrey nodded, appreciating the steed's white hair.

"I thought so." Walaric grinned.

Godfrey and Walaric found a stable, and left the horses with the stable-hands. Reaching into his satchel, Godfrey produced a large silver coin. He tossed it to the master of the stable. The old man deftly caught the coin, and hastily tucked it away into his pocket. Satisfied, Godfrey and Walaric left, and began wandering through the streets. Torches and candles were being lit near doorways in the quickly fading light.

"You're going to run out of money if you're not careful," Walaric admonished Godfrey, looking back to the stable they had left.

"I had to pay the man." Godfrey frowned. "Besides, that was to take care of both of our horses."

"Okay fine," Walaric conceded the point. "Just don't spend it all at once."

"Madeline is here somewhere." Godfrey began scanning the darkening streets. "Let's try to find her."

"Do you have any idea where she would be?" Walaric crossed his arms.

"No." Godfrey frowned.

"Let's go to the Temple of Spes," Walaric suggested. "Maybe we will see her along the way."

The few commoners out in the late evening stopped Godfrey and Walaric on their way to the temple, thanking them for their sacrifice, and lauding their piety. The two humbly accepted the praises as they went. If only these people knew the frustration of the crusade's inner politics, Godfrey thought.

The two passed through the inner curtain wall without seeing Madeline. Godfrey clenched his teeth nervously. Panic struck as he thought he might somehow miss her altogether while he was at Vindholm.

"Perhaps she is at one of the inns," he suggested, scanning the street.

"At least you will get to make your devotions at the temple." Walaric frowned.

"Right," Godfrey conceded distractedly.

Godfrey could not shake the feeling that though the gods and temples would be there tomorrow, Madeline might not. Still, Godfrey's piety won out. Perhaps the gods would bless him for making them his priority.

The Temple of Spes was an impressive structure. Its ancient stone columns were massive and its frieze was cluttered with images from myth. It was hard to distinguish what events the frieze was trying to depict. Darkness had finally overcome Vindholm for the night. Yet even in the darkness, the temple was obviously in a state of disrepair, and the ice from long winters through the centuries had begun to work cracks into the pediment. A long set of wide steps cut up the podium to the temple. Ascending those steps proved arduous.

"It's to remind the pilgrims that faith requires work," Walaric said in between gasping breaths as he and Godfrey climbed the steps.

"As if we did not already have to work to get here," Godfrey muttered, huffing just behind Walaric. "Not that I am complaining."

"Oh no," Walaric panted sardonically. "Travel to the far reaches of the world with a good chance of dying in battle. What is there to complain about?"

"You two should be careful not to blaspheme." Madeline crossed her arms as she stepped out from behind one of the columns. "It's unbecoming of crusaders to complain about their trials like that."

Madeline looked down at Godfrey from the top of the steps with a mockingly imperious gaze. No matter how many times he saw her, his heart still jumped at her appearance. She was wearing a heavy wool cloak as well as gloves and fur-lined boots. Admiring her beauty, Godfrey had almost forgotten that she was chastising them.

"The gods too are fond of a joke," Walaric countered before Godfrey could say anything.

Madeline scowled at Walaric.

"You're right." Godfrey bowed his head in a penitent gesture. "We did volunteer for this after all."

The wind whipped Godfrey's cloak around, sending a chill through his spine. Walaric shuddered too. With a sigh, Madeline rolled her eyes at the two of them.

"Well I think freezing to death outside tonight would probably be a harsher penance than the gods would intend." Madeline tugged on Godfrey's tabard, drawing him up the last step. "Inside, both of you, now."

Madeline paused for a moment. She looked up into the stars. Her breath left her mouth in steamy trails as she contemplated something. Godfrey had trouble concentrating on whatever she was about to say. Her skin reminded him of polished white marble. The distraction did not last long though.

"Actually…" She looked at Walaric then Godfrey. "I think you should see something first, Godfrey."

Walaric fumed at the omission. Madeline's awkward expression made it clear that she intended Walaric to go on without them. She made a conciliatory gesture, but Walaric only rolled his eyes in contempt. With a sigh, he turned away from her.

"I get it," the acolyte snorted. "I'll just see myself into the temple."

"Sorry," Godfrey began, but Walaric was already leaving.

"It's fine," Walaric called out over his shoulder as he continued into the temple.

Godfrey doubted that.

If only there were a girl for him, Godfrey thought. Then this stuff would not be so…but there was no girl for Walaric. There never would be if he really ended up devoting himself to Luna or one of the other celestial gods or goddesses. It was the nature of his vocation. Still, Walaric had chosen this path after all, right?

Godfrey had never asked Walaric that particular question now that he thought about it. Upon further consideration, Godfrey realized that many people's paths were chosen for them. Godfrey knew serfs worked the land upon which they were born. Other commoners followed in the professions of their fathers who were, in turn, controlled by guilds. Even the liberty granted by wealth was constrained by the rival ambitions of feudal lords and ladies. For instance, Madeline standing before Godfrey now surely did not have her father's approval. This meeting, like the one on Biorkon's stairs, had to be a secret.

"What are you thinking?" Madeline gave a faint smile now that Walaric had gone inside the temple.

"I was just wondering what you wanted to show me." Godfrey's heart began to race.

The anticipation heightened his senses. It made time slow. The experience was not entirely unlike the tension he felt before combat. Only, in this instance, his hand did not tremble.

"Come with me." Madeline extended her hand.

Taking Madeline's gloved hand, Godfrey was led to a garden behind the temple. There were no flower blooms or any signs of greenery in the cold darkness, but the way the slumbering shrubs, trees, statues, and stone benches had been arranged told him that at another time of year, this spot of ground had been well cared for.

"This site is used for augury," Madeline explained. "The priests watch birds here for signs during the day. But at night, there are other marvels in the heavens to watch."

Madeline offered Godfrey no further explanation. Brushing snow off a nearby bench, she sat and offered

Godfrey a place at her side. He sat, setting his spangenhelm on the ground next to them. The icy stone soon stung him through the seat of his trousers.

"Does it ever really warm up here?" Godfrey complained.

Godfrey immediately regretted asking the question. Complaints were not the sort of thing that kept damsels interested in young knights. However, Madeline took it in stride.

"This is nothing compared to Farthest Thule," she teased. "Or at least that's what I've been told."

"I've never heard of it," Godfrey admitted.

"As the name implies," Madeline started in a lecturing tone, "it's the farthest realm beyond the known world. It's so far north men cannot live there. Only a small kingdom of elves is said to be up there. And they only survive thanks to powerful magic."

"Have you ever seen any of these elves?" he asked. "They had some great empire centuries ago, and I've seen the ruins of some of their cities down in the Ostlands."

"No," she confessed. "But my grandparents used to say they had before they passed on. An elf army helped out during one of the crusades back when they were young."

"Interesting," Godfrey noted. "How did the crusaders get the elves to help?"

"One of the crusaders found Farthest Thule," Madeline answered. "The elves agreed to help the crusader on the condition that he would never reveal the location of their city. The elves jealously guard such secrets."

Godfrey considered this for a while.

"But we are only really in the southernmost part of the Nordslands." He began to put to rest a half-formed plan in his mind. "We would have to get through most of Azgald and all the Nordsman clans before we would be anywhere near Farthest Thule, huh?"

"That's why Azgald has only sought out Farthest Thule in vain." Madeline shook her head. "With the Nordsmen, orcs, trolls, giants, cyclopes, and undead that stand between us and that realm, contact is all but impossible."

"Not for that crusader your grandparents spoke of," he countered.

"He was lucky," she said, dismissing the thought.

"Or he was blessed by the gods," Godfrey suggested as he turned his attention back to the temple behind them.

A smile cracked across her face.

The two sat and said nothing for a while. Though he made no mention of going inside, his body was almost completely numb. Even Madeline was beginning to show signs of cold. Shifting on the bench, Godfrey began to worry about whether Conrad or Tancred would unexpectedly show up.

"You never did say what you wanted me to see," Godfrey said, breaking the silence.

"Oh." Disappointment washed over Madeline's face. "I was hoping tonight…"

With a sudden flash of light, her countenance changed from dull to luminous just as much in the physical as the emotional sense. Shocked, Godfrey looked from her face to a strange shimmering green light in the sky overhead. He almost fell back at the eerie display, but steadied himself just before he could lose his balance.

"What manner of sorcery is this?" Godfrey had trouble keeping the fear out of his voice.

"It's not sorcery," Madeline reassured him. "In Azgald, we call this the northern lights."

"It's beautiful." He relaxed a bit, watching the lights dance through the sky. "How do you know it's not magic?"

"Magical beings can sense when magic is being used around them." Her answer took on a cautious tone.

"Whatever powers create the northern lights on nights like this do so naturally, even if there is no rhyme or reason as to when."

"How do you know so much about magic?" His voice had grown graver than he meant it to.

"A few days ago you entrusted me with a secret," she began. "You told me something very personal you had never told anyone before. Now I'd like to tell you something very personal about me that I have never told anyone before."

Chapter Fifteen

"Gods above," Godfrey swore. "You're a witch!"

The pain disfiguring Madeline's face immediately made him regret his outburst. That was the sort of thing that could not be unsaid. That sort of pain was not quickly forgotten. If Godfrey could have jumped off a cliff or buried himself under a rock, he would have done so a thousand times over in that moment.

"I didn't mean…" he stammered.

"What did you mean then?" Madeline shot back. "Did you mean that I'm an abomination? That I'm anathema?"

"No," he started.

"Witches are anathema." She rose to her feet and was about to walk away. "In Azgald, the witch is not suffered to live. They are killed when they are found. Are you afraid of me because now you know I'm different?"

What was it Godfrey was feeling? Was it fear? He had no trouble taking Fallard's sword to slay the vampire when he thought it was magical. Swords were inanimate though. Yet when there was intelligence behind the power, that made things different. Madeline could curse him or take control of his mind or do who knew what else. Would he even know if she tried to put him under some enchantment?

Grabbing her tightly by the arm, he rose to his feet as well. He knew better than the doubts which gnawed at the back of his mind. The embarrassment made him flush and grind his teeth.

"Forgive me," Godfrey pleaded with hot tears welling in his eyes. "I don't know what I was saying. I've just never really…"

"Met someone like me before," she finished his sentence.

Madeline brushed his arm aside and stared at him hard for a long moment. Eventually, her expression softened, and she reclaimed her seat. She gestured for him to sit beside her again, and he complied. They both stared into the dancing lights in the sky for a few moments. The sight took the edge off Godfrey's distress, and he hoped it would do the same for Madeline.

"A witch uses her powers for evil and selfish purposes," she said at last. "Witches have brought down entire kingdoms in the past. To call someone a witch is a very serious allegation if not just an insult."

"What should I call you then?" He chose his words more cautiously.

"I am still Madeline." She smirked. "And I am still a young woman. And now you know I am also a sorceress. But still call me Madeline. Most people are very afraid of things they don't understand, and magic is something most people don't understand. Simply telling someone I am a sorceress, and not a witch, isn't enough proof to calm most people."

"But your father is a duke," Godfrey countered. "Couldn't he protect you?"

"Father's enemies would say I put a spell on him." She shook her head. "They would say I have entranced him, and manipulated him, and make up all sorts of lies because they are afraid or else want to take advantage of him in some way."

Godfrey thought back on the vampire in the swamp. She had used her powers against her father to turn him into one of her thralls. The fear of such entrapment was not unfounded.

"It sounds like what my father would say back in Bastogne." Godfrey shook his head in understanding.

"There's a reason you hear a lot about witches being burned, and not much about living sorceresses," she continued. "No, it's best that most people don't know."

"Can you really play with people's minds like that?" The worry in his voice was hard to disguise.

"No," she reassured him with a chuckle. "My powers are actually quite limited. As I said before, I am good at slipping in and out of places unseen. My magic helps with that. Father doesn't know about that power."

"He does know you have magic though?" Godfrey asked.

"He does," she confirmed. "Mother knew too. They found old books, rare books or forbidden or something, when I was small, that taught me how to control my powers. They told me to keep it a secret."

"If it's so important to keep your magic a secret, why are you telling me?" he insisted. "What if the wrong person finds out?"

"Then my brave knight will just have to protect me." She gave a mocking whimper. "My other talent is conjuring fire, but not just any fire. It's the fire of the gods, a gift from Loxias. It is a fire that can heal or consume at my choosing. That power was very hard to hide when I was small. My parents knew about that one practically since I was born. You would have figured out all of this eventually, and secrets are bad for relationships."

"When we first met at Biorkon…" Godfrey was beginning to make a few connections.

"You would have died," she finished. "The Silver Sun physicians said you would die. Your wound was grave, but I was able to mostly close it after my first visit."

"Why did you save me?" he asked.

His question was genuine. He had never been the recipient of such affection before. The only tenderness that came close as far as he could tell was his mother's, and that was not fully appreciated while she was still alive. The thought pricked him, but Godfrey quickly dismissed it.

"I saw you from the tower window," Madeline explained. "You led the charge against those Nordsman berserkers. No Azgaldian lord or knight of the Silver Suns would have done that."

"Because they knew what those berserkers could do." He flinched at the memory of the battle.

"You would have charged them anyway," she countered. "Heroes shouldn't always have to die sacrificing themselves. Azgald has enough martyrs already. I wanted to see one of those heroes live, and I was in a position to do something about it."

The look in her eyes told him something he could not find the words for. His heart was racing and he knew hers was too. He closed his eyes and began to lean in for a kiss. Gods above, he hoped he would not make a fool of himself. His hand began to shake violently, but it stopped the instant her hand found his. Their lips locked, and the two embraced for a long time after.

Following Madeline through the temple's entrance, the first thing Godfrey noticed was the gilded white stone decorating the building's interior. The craftsmanship was as ornate as it was ancient. No expense had been spared in the construction of this sacred site. The atmosphere was reverent as it was in most holy places. Each of their steps echoed through the chamber.

Walaric was waiting for them just beyond the temple entrance. His arms were crossed, and he lazily slouched against a tall pillar. His expression changed from boredom to mild annoyance as he saw the two approaching.

"How was it?" Walaric sardonically raised an eyebrow.

Madeline blushed, and Godfrey looked to his feet.

"The northern lights are something else," Godfrey managed after a moment.

"The what?" Walaric seemed unsure if there was a euphemism he was missing. "Never mind. Come see this."

Following Walaric's lead, Godfrey gawked at the two massive statues standing between the altar in the center of the main sanctum. Wafting smoke rose between the statues' large outstretched angelic wings from the altar as priests burned the evening sacrifice. The two statues were cast in silver. Though the lighting was poor, it was obvious the statues shared all the similarities of a brother and sister. The angelic statues wore tall plumed helmets, scale mail, and each held a spear in one hand while holding a large, round shield in the other. The style was ancient, and the detail put into the statues was beyond the ability of any living sculptor, as far as Godfrey was concerned.

"Tzuk and Lihi." Madeline indicated the male and female statue in turn. "They are the twins that guard the gates to Spes."

"I know," Godfrey reverently whispered.

So many frustrations filled his mind. Conrad, Phillip, Tancred; these men were only seeking their own ends. Godfrey wanted what was best for the crusade. His motives were pure. However, glancing at Madeline, he realized he probably wanted something for himself out of this too. Praying to the gods could bring him peace and guidance though. It had in the past.

"I'll offer sacrifices and prayers," he resolved.

Madeline and Walaric nodded in approval.

As he stepped forward, the spangenhelm slipped from Godfrey's hand and hit the polished stone floor with a clatter. Madeline and Walaric turned, but Godfrey had already collapsed on the floor. Panicking, Walaric and Madeline knelt over him. Godfrey's vision blurred to blackness. His breathing was shallow, and his senses dulled. He was only vaguely aware of Madeline and Walaric attempting to rouse him. The last thing Godfrey heard was the priests stepping away from their sacrificial rituals at the altar, chastising these rowdy young pilgrims who had come in so late.

Godfrey found himself atop a high mountain. It was disorienting. He vaguely remembered being somewhere else. There were people he was with whom he had cared about, but he could no longer recall their names or faces. They must not have been important.

Godfrey did not recognize where he stood or the surrounding peaks. The Sun radiated high above him. For all of the Sun's warmth, he was still standing knee-deep in the snow. Already the cold was beginning to bite at his toes through his boots. He was starting to hate winter and Azgald and Azgald in winter.

He had to get back to the crusade. That much was important. But which way should he go? No direction seemed right. At last, he decided going somewhere was better than going nowhere. Perhaps a path would reveal itself.

Drawing his cloak around him, Godfrey wandered aimlessly. The silence was absolute. Hours passed without purpose. It became mind-numbing well before he began to lose the feeling in his fingers and toes. Still, no direction seemed right.

Eventually, he came across a path leading down the mountain, and he began to descend the steep slope. Down off the mountain appeared to be as good a choice as any. Why not?

His foot slipped out from under him more than once, despite how carefully he tried to keep his balance. Each near-fall caused Godfrey's heart to pound. One wrong move could be his death.

Then he fell.

Slipping down the side of the mountain, he tried desperately to grab hold of something. All there was to grab was snow- and ice-covered rocks. He stopped momentarily as he caught a rock just long enough for it to cut through his glove. Searing pain forced him to release the rock as it tore across the palm of his hand. With warm blood gushing out of the wound, Godfrey's descent picked up speed again. He knew it. He knew it since before the vampire's castle back in the swamp. He was going to die falling. It was the one thought that filled his mind.

Godfrey approached a sheer cliff with alarming speed. He tried to grab another rock with his uninjured hand, but he could not get a grip on any surface. He was tumbling now. Pleading to the gods for a quick death, he closed his eyes and clenched his teeth as he flew over the cliff. The impact on the ground below never came.

Something large gripped Godfrey around the waist tighter than any human could. Opening his eyes, he almost vomited at the sight of the mountains rushing past him below. A pair of white-feathered talons held him suspended in the air. The talons belonged to a griffin with the complexion of a snowy owl.

"Loxias' chariot," Godfrey gasped.

The griffin glided to the top of another mountain. It delicately set Godfrey down on his side and sat next to him on all four legs. Choking on bile that had escaped into his mouth, Godfrey sucked in several gasps of frigid air. After a moment, he slowly rose to his feet.

"My thanks, noble griffin," he coughed.

The griffin cocked its head, indicating some point farther down the slope. Godfrey took a few steps to get a better view. Nestled in the crook of a pass below, a black dragon lay curled with steam rising from its nostrils. It began to stir. The griffin screeched, stretching its wings in challenge to the dragon as the monster uncurled. A plume of smoke billowed from the dragon's snout, and it stared greedily up at Godfrey and the griffin. Looking to Godfrey, the griffin cried again. As he stared into the griffin's amber eyes, everything became clear to him.

"I know." Godfrey drew his sword as he mounted the griffin.

A blinding light forced him to shield his eyes. Everything moved slowly as he felt something pulling at him from the back of his mind. What was happening? It was unfair. He had to kill the dragon. The crusade depended on it.

"The crusade is for naught if the dragon now is slain not," Godfrey blurted out, lying on the polished temple floor.

His sword was drawn but lying inches from his hand. His other hand was no longer cut. It was only then that Godfrey realized he had never left the temple. Madeline and Walaric were kneeling over him with confused expressions. A group of intrigued priests hovered just a step or two behind Madeline and Walaric.

"What did you say, boy?" one of the priests asked, stepping closer.

"What did I say?" Godfrey repeated blearily.

"You just made a prophecy." Madeline shivered.

"You said it in dactylic hexameter." Walaric was clearly impressed.

Madeline and Godfrey stared back at Walaric, not comprehending what he just said.

"It's the epic meter," Walaric explained in a flustered tone. "Oracles use it. Prophecies are written down in it… Never mind."

"How long was I out?" Godfrey tried to stand.

"Just for a moment," Madeline reassured him, helping him to his feet.

"The gods took you," Walaric said in astonishment as he arose. "What did they say? What did they show you?"

"I think you need to come with us," one of the priests interrupted.

The second and third priest flanked him and took Godfrey from Madeline's grip before he was fully aware of what was happening. The first priest began leading him to the back of the sanctum, and the other priests practically dragged him along.

"Wait." Walaric stretched out his hand. "I can vouch for him. I'm an acolyte."

"He's a crusader." Madeline tugged at Godfrey's cloak. "Don't take him."

A pair of menacing spear-armed temple guards emerged from the shadows to block Madeline and Walaric from following Godfrey. It was only as Madeline and Walaric's protests reached a crescendo that Godfrey shook himself out of his daze. The priests gripped his arms tightly on either side of him as they walked, preventing him from going any direction but to the stairs at the back of the sanctum. The lead priest descended the stairs, and with a shove, Godfrey followed.

"What is going on?" He looked to his captors for an explanation. "I don't understand any of this. Where are we going?"

The priests did not answer him as they forced him down the stairs. His strength had returned, and his wits were fully about him now. Should he resist? He had never been on the wrong side of the church before. He was not even sure why he was being taken, much less where.

At the bottom of the stairs was a cold, damp chamber. The few torches in this area cast eerie shadows against the slick stone walls. While the sanctum filled Godfrey with awe, this place filled him with dread. The iron bars forming cell doors along one of the walls told him this area's purpose.

"Why would a temple need a dungeon?" Godfrey made no effort to hide his confusion.

The first priest unlocked one of the cell doors with a heavy brass key, and the other two clerics shoved Godfrey inside. Shutting the door behind him, the first priest examined him with a look of cold aversion. Godfrey's hand began to tremble at the sight.

"Sit," the first priest commanded, indicating the only chair in the cell.

Godfrey obeyed, but the other two priests immediately shackled him to the chair with iron chains. Then, with a chill running down his spine, he realized this was an interrogation.

"I'm not an apostate," he pleaded. "I've committed no heresy."

"We'll see," the first priest answered ominously.

Godfrey quickly ran the events since entering the temple through his mind. He had done nothing wrong. He was granted a vision from the gods. Why were these priests treating him as if he had desecrated the altar?

"To which gods do you pray?" asked the second priest as he moved in front of Godfrey.

"Loxias," he began. "I venerate the nature gods too when their blessings are needed."

"What do you know of Yoan?" the third priest demanded.

"What?" Godfrey's head began to spin. "Nothing I guess."

The questions continued to bombard him one after the other with little time for him to answer.

"Yoan," the first priest cut in. "The dark goddess of war and cunning is not your mistress?"

"I've never heard that name before." Godfrey turned his head to answer, but the third priest was breathing down his neck again.

"Have you been consorting with witches?" the third priest asked.

"I…" Godfrey stammered.

"Where did you meet the witches?" The first priest's face was mere inches in front of Godfrey's. "Did they summon demons or put you under a spell?"

"How many witches were there?" the second priest interrupted before Godfrey could answer. "What did they promise you?"

Madeline had convinced Godfrey that she was not a witch, but she still had magical powers. These priests were relentless in their questioning, and Godfrey doubted they were the understanding sort. He still did not fathom how the priests could be so hostile towards him. He had rarely had anything but positive experiences with the clergy before. These men were certainly a far cry from the likes of Bishop Clovis. The only thing Godfrey was certain of at this moment was that betraying Madeline's secret would spell her doom and maybe his.

"I didn't meet any witches." He shook his head. "None."

"It's written on your face, boy," the first priest spat.

"Lying won't help you," the third priest chided, crossing his arms as he took a step back.

"I don't know what any of this is about." Godfrey's exasperation came out like a wave. "Why am I here? I didn't do anything wrong."

"You uttered a prophecy," the first priest muttered, stabbing a finger at Godfrey's chest. "We must be sure it was not made under the influence of one of the dark gods as a means of deceiving us."

The third priest grabbed a barbed metal hook off a corner table Godfrey only now noticed for the first time. An assortment of other sharp metal objects with short handles lay scattered across the table. Such tools only had one purpose.

The priest with the hook approached. Godfrey rocked back and forth in his chair as hard as he could, hoping to loosen his bonds. The other priests held him down so he could not knock his chair over. Was there anything else he could try to escape? Desperation made sweat prickle on his brow.

Not a moment too soon, the priests froze in place at the sound of heavy footfalls coming down the stairs. Clearing his throat, Turpin peered through the cell door. He was holding Godfrey's sword. Dark circles hung under Turpin's eyes, but his face was set. The priests looked from Godfrey to Turpin, unsure how to respond. Without a word, Turpin let himself in through the creaking cell door. Holding the sword aloft, Turpin showed Godfrey and the priests the flat of the blade. A new inscription ran across the blade in an elegant script: *Uriel.*

"What does it mean?" Turpin asked Godfrey. "This inscription was not here before."

"I named it that." Godfrey began to shake as he recognized the word etched across the flat of the blade. "At Fuetoile Keep, I called the blade that in my mind the morning I was knighted."

"It means *light of the gods,*" the first priest answered reverently.

The priest who had spoken reached out for the blade. Turpin obliged the priest with a grimace. Conferring among themselves, the priests examined Godfrey's sword. Their voices were hushed and indistinct to Godfrey's ears. Turpin gazed sternly at the clergymen as if preparing for the worst response possible. His hand rested on the hilt of his own sword. Having killed his share of both men and monsters, Godfrey was not averse to fighting, but before now he had never once thought he might need to fight the clergy in order to save himself. Godfrey silently prayed it would not come to what Turpin was preparing for.

"It is the work of the gods," the second priest announced after they had finished deliberating. "The prophecy shall be recorded. Release the prisoner."

Turpin stood at ease as the first and third priest unshackled Godfrey. The second priest gave the sword back to Turpin, who handed it to Godfrey. Rubbing his wrists, Godfrey ached as he stood. The priests had not tried to make Godfrey comfortable during the questioning. He doubted he was about to get an apology either.

Looking the blade over, Godfrey examined the inscription more closely. The lettering was filled in pure gold. The blade itself seemed to shine more brilliantly than before. Was this what a magic weapon looked like?

"Your sword has been blessed by the gods," the second priest answered Godfrey's unspoken question.

"Then that means the gods have chosen me as their instrument above all the other crusaders?" Godfrey pressed.

Hesitantly, the priests nodded in agreement.

"You have to understand..." The first priest's tone had grown contrite. "There are heretics, spies; agents of the dark gods constantly seek to overthrow us through subterfuge. We had to be sure."

"Then I think supplying my men from the temple's food stores will serve as an adequate apology for locking me up here like this," Godfrey censured the priests.

The priests looked at each other with reservation.

"Or do you want to be remembered as the insolent priests who almost tortured the gods' chosen vassal?" Godfrey's agitation was barely held in check.

Chapter Sixteen

Varin leaned against the wall inside an old musty inn near the outskirts of Vindholm. The hour had grown late, yet the dining area was alive with the chatter of crusaders. News of Godfrey's vision had spread quickly from the Temple of Spes all the way to the far corners of the city. Gossip traveled faster than anything else Varin could think of.

Mildly amused, Varin watched two knights sitting at a table in a heated debate concerning the prophecy. Wild speculation was what most of their opinions boiled down to. Normally, Varin would hold his tongue, content to listen, but his desire to correct the two knights was quickly proving stronger than his natural inclination to remain aloof.

"What do you think it means?" the knight named Euric asked another knight named Rodair.

"It can't be a real dragon." Rodair shook his head. "Such monsters are all but extinct."

"Is it a fortress to be taken?" Euric's imagination seemed to run wild. "Perhaps it's an enemy to be assassinated?"

"Prophecies are such amusing things," Varin interrupted the two knights, tilting his head slightly in their direction. "We can never know their true meanings until they have already come to pass."

Startled by the sudden disturbance, the knights exchanged a quick glance before tacitly agreeing to include the peculiar ranger in their conversation. Varin did not care what they thought of him. His own contempt for most people was enough to insulate him from most of the strange looks and half-muttered insults people tended to exchange when they thought he could not hear or see them. His rare efforts to join in any sort of social contact would usually only reinforce Varin's opinions concerning why he did not like people in the first place. He doubted this conversation would prove any different.

"Well," Sir Rodair began. "We know the gods must not be happy with the direction of the crusade."

"They would not send us a prophecy like this one if they wanted us to stay the course," Sir Euric agreed, taking a sip of ale from his flagon.

"And what direction is this crusade going?" Varin asked, raising an eyebrow. "What course are we following?"

The knights' expressions contorted in consternation.

"We relieved the siege at Biorkon," Euric offered. "And now we are going to Epsberg."

"But was going to Epsberg the right choice?" Rodair countered. "Some of the lords wanted to push north."

"And east is not where the Clans' high king is," Varin explained. "Word is that the Nordsman high king is from Clan Black Dragon. I think we should be seeking him out, vanquish him in battle."

Rodair and Euric appeared unable to refute Varin's reasoning. Now that the seed of doubt had been planted, going to Epsberg seemed like a very bad idea. Varin wondered if this was this how Godfrey would interpret his prophecy? Could this young noble barely coming into manhood be trusted with such a critical task?

"I don't believe you." Conrad shook his head bluntly. "You are just making this up to gain popularity."

Conrad, Tancred, Godfrey, and their entourages had gathered at the Temple of Spes in response to news of the prophecy. They were in the chambers of the high priest on the upper level. Each wall was lined by bookcases filled with copies of sacred texts Godfrey had grown accustomed to seeing in similar settings.

Madeline was there too. She stood defiantly next to Godfrey as if daring her father to forbid it. Tancred gave his daughter a disapproving glance, but said nothing about her proximity to Godfrey. He would reprimand her later, Godfrey was sure.

The group stood in an uncomfortably close circle while the high priest himself was busy consulting the augers in the temple's main sanctum for further clarification on the vision. Godfrey was not entirely sure the high priest was doing anything but wasting his time consulting bird-watchers at this hour.

"Why would I make this up when the crusade is already going to the Eastern Marches as I argued it should?" Godfrey countered.

"He has a point." Tancred rounded on Conrad. "Besides, it doesn't matter what you believe. What matters is containing this information."

"That's going to be hard." Godfrey scowled. "All of Vindholm already knows about the prophecy by now."

Godfrey was still grappling with the prophecy's meaning. He did not like any of the answers he came up with. Nobody wanted to hear that they were going on the wrong path. Nobody wanted to hear that the crusade's true objective would be as hard to accomplish as slaying a dragon.

"But the crusaders outside the city have not heard yet," Turpin noted.

"Wait," Walaric cut in. "If this is a true prophecy from the gods, shouldn't we act upon it? Even if we could keep it a secret, I don't think we should. Besides, you can't swear the whole city to secrecy on this. Someone will tell."

Turpin turned to Walaric. "How would you suggest we act upon it?"

Walaric stammered for an answer but came up with nothing.

"My point exactly," Turpin replied to Walaric's lack of response. "Godfrey, what do you think we should do?"

Godfrey's eyes were drawn to Tancred's tabard. His stomach sank. The tabard's heraldic device was a dragon rampant. He had noticed this when they first met, but now it took on a completely different meaning. So much doubt clouded his mind. He bit his lip, putting the thought away.

"We press on," Godfrey answered. "There's no point in trying to keep this a secret. The gods are with us. Perhaps their desires will become clearer in time."

"You should address the men as soon as possible," Tancred suggested. "Arrest their fears, keep them in good spirits. We need to focus on reaching and capturing Epsberg until we can rejoin the other crusaders."

The others nodded in agreement.

"Summon the men," Godfrey said. "Do it first thing in the morning."

He met Tancred's eyes.

"I want to speak to all of the crusaders." Godfrey frowned. "And I want the soldiers of Pavik there too."

The next morning was warmer than the previous day. Godfrey supposed the weather was going to go back and forth like this for a little while before it finally decided to be spring in the Nordslands. Glancing behind him, Godfrey better appreciated the grandeur of the Temple of Spes in the full light of day. It was a magnificent structure, though it was old, and falling into disrepair. It was a relic from another era.

Below Godfrey, at the base of the steps leading up to the temple, all the crusaders in Vindholm had gathered together. Madeline, her father, and a number of other Azgaldians both common and noble were also present. Many in the crowd were murmuring. Godfrey had wrestled all night with what to say. He still had no idea. All eyes had turned to him. The time was now.

"Men of Bastogne," Godfrey said, clearing his throat. "Men of Errans, Pavik, and Vindholm, hear me. There is a rumor that I was touched by the gods and made a prophecy. I will not deny it."

An uneasy murmur surged through the crowd. Tancred covered his face with his hands, and Walaric clenched his fists apprehensively. Madeline's and Turpin's reactions were lost in the crowd. Godfrey did not care how Conrad reacted, and did not bother to look in the direction of the Duke of Errans.

"I have wrestled with the prophecy's meaning." Godfrey gestured down into the audience. "And I do not believe that any of the possibilities promise an easy victory. Then again, easy victories are not why anyone goes on crusade."

The muttering subsided again.

"Many mortals have doomed themselves when acting too rashly upon a prophecy," Godfrey continued. "I do not know what the words I spoke last night mean, but I think the gods will reveal more in time. For now, this is what I do know: there is but one omen—that a man must fight against evil."

Godfrey drew his sword, flashing the blade high over his head.

"A new inscription was written upon this blade by the finger of Loxias," Godfrey explained. "It is now a holy blade. Take comfort, crusaders. The gods are still on our side. Make your devotions, take what provisions you need from the temple stores, we strike out for Epsberg at first light tomorrow."

With a swish of his cloak, Godfrey turned towards the temple and made his way back inside. He sheathed his sword as he paused just in front of the temple's solid wooden doors. One of the priests from the previous night pulled Godfrey aside. He gave Godfrey a long, hard stare as he gripped Godfrey's tabard in a balled fist. Meeting his gaze, Godfrey deliberately pulled the priest's hand off his tabard.

"We agreed to provision your men, not all the crusaders in Vindholm," the priest spat as Godfrey released his hand.

"Did you want half the men to desert?" Godfrey countered. "An empty cellar is better than not having an army to protect it at all. Find a way to make it happen."

Grinding his teeth, the priest stormed away. The temple doors opened with a heavy creak for Godfrey. Solemnly entering the Temple of Spes, Godfrey knelt at the altar between the statues of the twin angels. He produced a small golden coin from his satchel, and handed it to one of the acolytes nearby. The acolyte left and returned with one of the white quails for sacrifice.

Godfrey knelt in silent prayer as the priests and acolytes burned the sacrifice. The aroma of burning quail meat intoxicated Godfrey's senses. Wrestling between the distraction of the savory meat and the fatigue from his lack of sleep the previous night made concentrating on prayer all the harder. The clergy's chanting was supposed to help direct the supplicant's thoughts towards the divine. Yet once again the divine provided no answers for Godfrey when he wanted guidance the most as far as he was concerned. Obediently, he continued to kneel until the end of the ritual, though Godfrey had given up hope of further divine manifestations well before.

When Godfrey arose from the ritual, he found a queue of crusaders standing behind him. They were staring at him. Godfrey shifted uncomfortably. One of the crusaders stepped forward. Godfrey immediately recognized him as Sir Euric, one of the knights from Bastogne.

"Do you really have a sword blessed by the gods?" he asked, proffering his hand.

"See for yourself." Godfrey unsheathed Uriel.

Handing the blade to Euric, Godfrey watched the knight study it carefully. The knight frowned, then Godfrey frowned. What was Euric looking for?

The knight held the blade close to his eyes as he tried to take in every detail of the inscription. Euric held the blade for a long time before returning it.

"It's true," Sir Euric announced as tears streamed down his face.

No sooner had Uriel returned to Godfrey's hand than other knights and footmen were crowding around to examine the sword for themselves. Some had reactions similar to Euric's. Others walked away disappointed. Finally, Turpin and Walaric came in to disperse the crowd surrounding Godfrey.

"You know who wears the dragon rampant on his heraldry, don't you?" Walaric asked as soon as the last of the crusaders had dispersed.

"The Duke of Pavik." Godfrey grimaced.

"And the King of Azgald," Turpin added darkly. "Both families claim dragon-slayers as ancestors. The Wyrmwind Peaks were filled with dragons long ago."

"No." Godfrey shook his head. "It's not King Lothar."

"Then you think Duke Tancred is trying to sabotage the crusade?" Walaric asked.

"The thought has crossed my mind," Godfrey admitted.

"Well that will spoil things between you and Madeline, won't it?" Walaric furrowed his brow. "Killing her father might complicate a marriage."

"No one said anything about killing the Duke of Pavik." Turpin raised his finger at Walaric in a silencing gesture. "Nor did they say anything about a wedding of Godfrey and Madeline."

Godfrey ground his teeth at that last statement. Who was Turpin to say such things? He did not know of Godfrey and

Madeline's meeting the night before, the secrets they shared, their kiss. Godfrey bit back a retort as Turpin started to speak again.

"Focus on what we know," Turpin continued. "Godfrey is right. We need to wait before we act on the prophecy. We can only press on as we initially intended until we learn more."

Godfrey wandered through Vindholm in search of Madeline. The rest of the day, he was unable to find her. He was sure her father had everything to do with her absence. Godfrey almost wished the gods would identify Tancred as the dragon to be slain.

Finally, Godfrey found himself back at the Temple of Spes. There was still a crowd of crusaders gathered around the structure. Some were walking away with sacks or barrels filled with food. Most of those present buzzed in agitation at the high priest at the top of the stairs.

"I'm telling you there is no more." The high priest waved his arms in exacerbation. "We have no more provisions. Your friends already took everything."

"Let's go in and see for ourselves," a particularly vexed crusader suggested.

The color in the high priest's face drained. Menacingly, the crowd of crusaders began to ascend the stairs. The high priest's eye caught Godfrey and shot him a pleading look. Could Godfrey just stand by and watch this happen?

The priests of the temple had held Godfrey captive the previous night. They had threatened him with torture. How far would they have gone before they were satisfied that Godfrey was not an enemy agent? Were these angry crusaders not exactly what those priests deserved?

"Stop," Godfrey shouted over the crowd.

The crusaders halted, and looked down at Godfrey.

"Looting the Temple of Spes would not reflect well on this crusade," Godfrey continued once the angry shouts subsided. "The church has given what it can, and the gods will provide the rest. Go rest now. There is a long way ahead of us still."

Godfrey was surprised at how easily the crowd dispersed at his word. If being the son of a duke and one of the crusade's leaders did not lend him a certain amount of authority, possessing a magic sword certainly did. The high priest let out a sigh as the last of the crusaders left the temple. Godfrey moved on without hearing the old man's thanks.

There were several well-kept inns near the temples in the high city. Without giving it much thought, Godfrey simply chose the closest to where he was standing as dusk approached. Entering the inn through its creaking door, he was overwhelmed by the noise of performing jongleurs and the boisterous conversation that came with heavy drinking. The inn was warm, and the fire from the hearth inviting. There was a large group of crusaders Godfrey recognized sitting at the tables eating, drinking, and singing songs slurred by ale. Spotting the innkeeper passing out a tray of drinks to a table of knights, Godfrey waved at the portly man wearing a stained apron.

"Godfrey de Bastogne." The innkeeper's surprise was ill-contained. "Would you like to stay here tonight? I will offer you my finest room at a great discount, only one gold piece."

Godfrey was unsure how much of a discount that really was. Searching for an appropriate coin in his pouch, he realized his share of gold pieces was beginning to diminish. Spending so much time in the high city was proving expensive. Little wonder it was only the wealthier knights he saw at inns like this.

Handing the gold to the innkeeper, Godfrey was led up the stairs to his room. The furnishings were lavish, far more so than what he required. A bottle of fine wine and a tray of rich cheese were brought up by the innkeeper's son. Now Godfrey understood why the room had cost him so much. He promised himself he would be more frugal at the next city he stopped at.

Tancred's soldiers led the crusaders out of Vindholm at dawn as planned. A crowd had gathered to see them off with cheers and the singing of hymns. In vain, Godfrey searched for Madeline in the crowd as he rode Baruch through the procession. The terrible thought crossed Godfrey's mind that he might never see her again if Duke Tancred had anything to do with it.

Though the crusaders marched to Epsberg with all the speed they could muster, Godfrey had plenty of time to brood about Tancred preventing Madeline from seeing his departure from Vindholm. Godfrey just knew this was Tancred's fault. Tancred, likewise, seemed aloof to Godfrey. This only confirmed Godfrey's suspicions. It was in this dark mood that he first caught sight of Epsberg Castle.

The castle was a tall, daunting fortress made from dark stone. A moat partially surrounded the wall by its imposing southern gate, where the ground was flat. The northern end of the castle wall was instead protected by a steep rock face.

Godfrey, Tancred, and Conrad surveyed the Nordsman castle atop their steeds from the relative safety of a distant hill to the southwest. The majority of the crusaders and Tancred's men waited at the base of the hill out of view from Epsberg's defenders. Even from this distance, Godfrey was sure this was going to be a tough siege.

"The eastern and western slopes are going to be hard but manageable," Tancred observed. "But the northern side is going to be impossible to scale."

"Leaving us three angles of attack," Conrad finished Tancred's thought.

"There is an upper, lower, and middle bailey." Tancred noted the walls trisecting the castle's courtyard. "We should assault from all three directions at once, taking the three courtyards simultaneously. That should minimize resistance once we take the walls."

Shivering, Godfrey noted the thin layer of ice only partially covering the water that filled the moat by the southern gate. The only plausible path to the gate was a narrow causeway. It was designed to only let a small number of people across at once, to minimize the number of attackers in the event of a siege. Godfrey pitied whoever was going to have to assault the gate.

"Who is getting stuck with the gate?" Godfrey crossed his arms.

"You of course," Tancred sneered without hesitation. "Loxias blessed your sword after all, did he not?"

"So he did," Godfrey replied curtly after a moment's pause.

"Then it is settled." Conrad smirked. "I will take the western wall, Godfrey has the gate, and you will take the eastern wall, Tancred?"

"Yes," Tancred agreed. "I can reach the middle bailey easiest from the eastern side if our catapults can knock out the towers watching the approach."

Godfrey's hand trembled. He was being given the toughest part of what was already going to be a hard siege, and he had no say in it. As long as Conrad and Tancred were in agreement, Godfrey could do little to protest.

Shaking his head ruefully, he slowed his breathing. He remembered Cheldric's unenviable task in the childhood tale. So too would the bards remember Godfrey in this siege. His hand stopped trembling. He would do his part and trust the gods to deliver him. If they did not, glory was his anyway.

"One last thing," Godfrey added. "We should not leave the northern wall unguarded. Both of you should extend your forces to cover the northern wall as well."

"You see that rock face?" Conrad pointed at the distant castle. "No one is scaling that."

"Forgive me, Conrad," Godfrey sardonically replied. "But we can't even see most of the northern wall or the rock face from here. Besides, I'm not talking about attacking the northern side. I'm talking about preventing any of the Nordsmen from getting out. There could be footpaths leading down from the wall."

"Even with fifteen thousand men," Tancred cut in smoothly, "I am not sure we can spare the manpower to completely surround the castle. We want to take Epsberg as swiftly as possible after all."

"What if a Nordsman gets out and calls for reinforcements?" Godfrey objected. "We don't want to get caught in between the castle walls and an enemy relief army. We were all at Biorkon, remember?"

"No messenger will get out," Tancred insisted. "I will have my knights patrol the northern side."

"That might not be enough under cover of darkness," Godfrey protested.

"We will take Epsberg so quickly, it will not matter if a messenger slips through our patrols," Conrad spat.

Seeing the argument lost, Godfrey glowered without another word.

The crusader contingents and Tancred's men positioned themselves around the castle at the agreed-upon locations. Immediately, craftsmen began constructing siege engines out of timber gathered from the nearby forest. The first siege towers and ladders were constructed almost overnight. Baldwin was right. There was no shortage of wood in the Nordslands.

Godfrey was overseeing the construction of a large battering ram in his part of the crusaders' camp. He did not know much about woodworking. In truth, his overseeing was mostly helping to fetch timber or nails as the occasion required. Fortunately, there were artisans among the camp followers who actually did know how to construct such devices. More than one bemused craftsman saw the humor in the son of a duke following their instructions for a change.

"If you're not careful," Walaric teased Godfrey, "the moniker 'champion of the common folk' is going to stick."

"That might not be so bad," Godfrey thought aloud, trying to avoid hitting his thumb with the hammer he was using.

What started out as simply a large, rough-cut tree trunk was quickly smoothed out and suspended in a wheeled frame by ropes. Next, a steep, angular roof covered the frame. By the middle of the second day of the siege, a large, metal spike was fashioned to the end of the ram.

Elsewhere in the Bastognian section of the camp, a pair of trebuchets were nearing completion. Conrad's men, likewise, had finished a trio of siege towers and several ladders. Tancred's men also built a pair of siege towers and a few catapults were almost complete. After a week of nonstop construction, the crusaders had amassed a large arsenal of siege engines. The assault was almost ready.

Epsberg's Nordsman defenders incessantly jeered at the crusaders from the castle walls during these preparations. Their speech was meaningless babble to Godfrey, though he could sense the Nordsmen's contempt for the crusaders. He did not care. Soon they would be dead.

"Perhaps we should try to parley with them," Walaric suggested, running his hand across the battering ram.

Godfrey and Turpin both laughed in reply.

"I'm serious." Walaric's annoyance was written across his face.

Whatever humor Godfrey felt quickly deflated. His feet squished the mud in the melting snow as he shifted his posture. Walaric had a point.

"It could save us both time and blood if we could negotiate Epsberg's peaceful surrender," Godfrey admitted.

Pausing for a long moment, Turpin eventually nodded in agreement.

"Let's bring it up with Tancred and Conrad." Walaric began walking toward the Duke of Pavik's part of the camp.

Godfrey frowned, hesitating.

"Acting independently of those two could breed further hostility," Turpin warned Godfrey. "That is the absolute last thing we want. We need them to know what we are doing, and we need them to be on our side."

"You're right," Godfrey conceded. "Let's go."

Throughout the camp, all manner of preparations were still being made. Blades were being sharpened. Armor was under repair. More siege engines were being constructed. Priests took confessions or led the crusaders in song and prayer.

Walking through the midst of this, Godfrey still marveled at how many knights and footmen had flocked to his banner for the crusade. Did these men of Bastogne really trust him to lead them to victory, even with visions and magic weapons following him?

In Tancred's section of the camp, the men of Pavik behaved much as the Bastognians did. Godfrey half-smiled at the sight. At least Tancred's men did not seem as bad as their lord.

Finding Duke Tancred proved easy enough for Godfrey. Tancred's tent was larger than many of his knights', and it proudly displayed his heraldry. The Duke of Pavik was speaking with Conrad and one of his artisans as Godfrey's party approached.

"Good news," Tancred started as Godfrey came within earshot. "My artisans have secured a large supply of stones from nearby. We should have plenty of ammunition for the catapults."

"Excellent," Godfrey agreed. "However, I wonder if there is not a faster way to take Epsberg for the Silver Suns."

"Get to the point," Conrad huffed.

"Do you think it's possible we could force a surrender?" Godfrey looked Tancred sternly in the eye. "We do have a superior force."

"It's possible." Tancred stroked his beard. "Nordsmen are stubborn but not stupid. If we can convince them that they don't stand a chance, promise safe passage out of the Eastern Marches, they may yield without a fight."

"Or they could stall us out in negotiations while they await a relief force," Conrad countered. "Besides, they know a siege will cost us a lot of men. No, we should storm the castle as soon as we are able."

"We should send an envoy to parley," Turpin insisted. "If they do not agree to our terms within a day, we attack immediately."

"I agree." Tancred nodded. "But we have to be in the strongest position possible. Wait a few more days, construct a few more siege engines, show them we have the means to topple them without question."

"Fair enough," Godfrey conceded.

"In three days we send an envoy," Tancred reassured him, putting a hand on Godfrey's shoulder. "It will give them plenty of time to think about their mortality."

Returning to the Bastognian section of the camp, Godfrey observed two more catapults being constructed. Walaric gave the siege engines a questioning look. Sensing Walaric's confusion, Godfrey pivoted the acolyte from the siege engines to the gate.

"Since we have that large moat and only a narrow causeway to the gate," Godfrey explained to Walaric, "I think trying to knock out a nearby section of wall would be best if the battering ram cannot breach it."

"Good thinking," Walaric agreed.

Looking at Godfrey's sword, Walaric stopped himself short of whatever it was he was going to say next. Godfrey gripped Uriel's hilt as it sat secure in its sheath.

"What is it?" Godfrey asked.

"What do you think your sword will do now that it's been blessed?" Walaric asked.

"What do you mean?" Godfrey furrowed his brow.

"Well, swords that have been blessed by the gods get some sort of magical properties," Walaric continued. "Some of them can cut through solid rock, glow when enemies are near, or set fire to the people they strike. At least that's what the legends and stories say."

"I guess we'll find out the next time I have to use it," Godfrey replied with a shrug. "I don't want to tempt Loxias by swinging it around just to see what it will do."

"I see." Walaric rubbed his nose. "That's a good point. I just thought you might have been given a clue in your vision or something."

"No." Godfrey shook his head.

"Then how do you know it was even Loxias who blessed your sword?" Walaric crossed his arms. "We were in the Temple of Spes. It could have been any of the celestial gods, demigods, or saints."

"Loxias is the only god I pray to by name when not propitiating nature deities." Godfrey cracked his knuckles. "Who else would bless my blade?"

The next morning, Godfrey was stirred from his sleep early. Walaric was shaking him.

"Enough." Godfrey stretched groggily. "I'm awake."

Walaric stopped and stood over him. Sitting up, Godfrey rubbed the sleep from his eyes. The acolyte's expression was apprehensive. Whatever sleep remained in Godfrey's eyes instantly vanished. Something had gone wrong. Very wrong.

"Well," Godfrey said, rising to his feet. "What is it?"

"I'm not sure." Walaric frowned. "But it's trouble. You need to come out and see."

Godfrey huffed in agitation. He hated it when people would not just tell him what was going on. He pulled on his armor as quickly as he could, and left his tent with Walaric.

The air was crisp outside. Several knights and men-at-arms stood, staring at Epsberg's gates. Walaric directed Godfrey's gaze to what the others were staring at.

A body hung from a rope in front of the gate. The corpse was armored and wore a blood-stained tabard. It was one of Tancred's knights.

"I don't understand," Godfrey started.

"Tancred tried to negotiate with Epsberg's defenders in secret last night," Turpin explained as he approached Godfrey and Walaric from his own tent.

"But he said to wait a few more days," Walaric spat. "He must have thought he could leverage a better deal for himself."

"Well..." Godfrey grimaced. "I guess Epsberg isn't surrendering today."

A horn blew from Conrad's part of the camp. It was the signal to begin the attack.

In confusion, the Bastognian crusaders looked to Godfrey for orders. Tancred had acted in direct contradiction of his own counsel to Godfrey, and now Conrad was signaling the attack without any consultation. Godfrey's frustration would have to wait, though. Now was the time for action and unity.

"You heard it," Godfrey shouted to the soldiers around him. "To the siege engines. For Bastogne. For the gods!"

__Chapter Seventeen__

Crossbowmen surrounded the battering ram as other crusaders pushed it across the causeway. The crossbowmen shot up at the Nordsmen, trying to deter the enemy archers while the battering ram moved into position. Their boots sloshed through the mud as the wooden construct trudged along its creaking wheels. Epsberg's defenders, however, threw rocks and fired other missiles down on the crusaders from the castle walls and gatehouse without faltering. An occasional Nordsman fell from the wall with a bolt sticking from his head or neck, but the crenelated parapet protected Epsberg's defenders from most of the shots.

Godfrey grimaced at the sight from his position just behind the battering ram. This was going to be tough. The corpse of Tancred's rejected ambassador still hung from its rope in front of the gate as if mocking the approaching crusaders. How many scores of crusaders were already dead? How many more would join the knight hanging from the rope? Godfrey did not care to guess.

The missiles came down like an incessant hail. Screams pierced the air as men died. A rock crushed a crossbowman's head as it fell on him. A footman doubled over as an arrow struck his chest. A crusader fell into the moat as a pair of arrows punctured him. Briefly thrashing on the surface of the frigid water, the unfortunate crusader choked on the murky liquid and sank to the bottom, never to rise again.

Larger projectiles from the crusaders' catapults and trebuchets thunderously resounded off the castle walls as stone struck stone. Cracks formed across a section of the wall near the gate where the siege engines tried to concentrate their fire. The process was still far too slow for Godfrey's liking.

The battering rams' wheels cut deep grooves through the mud. Godfrey and twenty or so chosen knights followed the siege engine with their shields raised over their heads while Turpin held Godfrey's banner aloft beside him. Godfrey had personally selected each knight in his retinue before the assault began in earnest. It was a mark of honor to be selected for such a task.

Behind Godfrey's retinue were as many Bastognian footmen and knights as could reasonably fit on the causeway. With so little firm ground between the wall, moat, and gatehouse, he decided to leave the siege ladders at the rear of the attacking force. All hopes for the assault on the southern wall rested in either the battering ram or the stone-throwers. The ladders could not be used until the crusaders tried to cross the wall dividing the lower and middle bailey. If the crusaders made it that far; they still had to breach the outer defenses first. Godfrey clenched his teeth at the thought.

Godfrey and his knights were dismounted. Their horses would have been too tempting a target for the Clan archers, given how slowly the siege engine progressed across the causeway.

"I feel naked without Baruch," Godfrey told Sir Rodair as the knight marched next to him.

The pace was agonizingly slow. The crusaders could only move as fast as the battering ram could be pushed through the mud.

An arrow pierced Sir Rodair's shield, lodging itself in the wood.

"I know what you mean," the knight gruffly replied, examining the arrow stuck in his shield.

Breaking the arrow shaft with a loud crack, Rodair pulled the fragments out of his shield. With a look of disdain on his face, he discarded the arrow fragments. The broken shaft was soon lost in the mud as crusaders plodded over the shards.

The melting snow softened the ground so much that Godfrey sank a little with each step he took. Stinking muddy water filled every footprint Godfrey left in his wake as he laboriously lifted his feet out of the mire. He silently prayed this assault would not grind to a halt.

The stink of burning pitch caught the air as the Nordsmen began firing flaming arrows at the battering ram. Godfrey's heart skipped a beat. Not this. Not now.

The fiery darts flew lazily and inaccurately. Most sizzled and died in the muddy causeway or moat. A few bounced harmlessly off the ram's roof before they could cause any real damage. This did not put Godfrey's fears to rest, though.

The battering ram was close to the gate now. A few flaming arrows burned weakly on its roof. The causeway widened out to firmer ground for the last few yards in front of the gate. The crusaders were so close that the Nordsmen began dumping buckets of boiling tar down on them. If Godfrey's muscles tensed any more than they already had, he would be unable to move.

"Loxias please," he murmured under his breath. "Protect the ram."

A crusader, Sir Karst, fell screaming as a fiery arrow immolated his tar-spattered body. The knight's burning flesh left a terrible odor in the air. Swallowing hard, Godfrey ignored the stench and kept pressing on as Sir Karst's screams died out.

Now with the battering ram's frame squared directly against the gate, the crusaders drew the ram back and heaved it with all their might. Sir Euric, the knight who had spent so much time examining Godfrey's sword at the temple, drew his ax and cut down the body of Tancred's deceased knight from the rope in front of the gate. It was the least he could do for the dead, but he did not dare do more than that for now.

"Keep at it, men," Godfrey encouraged the crusaders operating the ram from a few paces back, where the causeway ended. "Crossbows, keep it covered."

The ram's thunderous impact was the only reply Godfrey needed. The crusader crossbowmen continued to exchange fire with the Nordsmen, but the real danger was the amount of tar accumulating on the battering ram's roof.

After several impacts, the crack of splintering wood resonated in Godfrey's ears. The ram had penetrated the gate, but just as it did, the siege engine's roof burst into flame. The crusaders manning the ram scrambled away from the blaze, and were met by a hail of enemy arrows. Some retreated to the causeway. Others were cut down by the missiles. A few cowered under the gatehouse, frozen with fear.

"No," Godfrey yelled, rushing towards the burning siege engine.

He was unsure of how he was going to put out the fire, but he ran all the same. He could not let it end like this. So many men had already died to come this far.

Someone unexpectedly tackled him to the ground. Turpin had him pinned.

"You can't save it." Turpin shook his head at the bewildered Godfrey. "We have to fall back. Wait for the stone-throwers to breach the wall."

"And cross the causeway again, losing how many more men?" Godfrey countered, his bile rising. "I won't let all this come to nothing!"

His hand was shaking. Why did the gods allow this? Suppressing his anger, Godfrey reasoned rage would not win the day.

"I'm sorry," Turpin insisted. "But you knew this might happen."

Turpin got to his feet. He seemed oblivious to the deadly missiles falling around him. Using Godfrey's banner to steady himself, the chaplain offered his other hand to Godfrey.

"Right," Godfrey agreed, taking Turpin's proffered hand.

With Turpin's help, Godfrey rose to his feet.

"Fall back," he said and gestured to the crusaders.

"But my lord…" Euric pointed back to the gate.

The fire had spread so that it not only covered the siege engine, but the gate itself also began to burn where the ram was lodged in it. It did not take much effort for Godfrey to realize how this could be used to the crusaders' advantage. By the panic-struck expressions of the Nordsmen on the wall, Godfrey guessed Epsberg's defenders were quickly coming to the same realization.

"Praise the gods," Godfrey exclaimed. "Keep that blaze going."

Godfrey, Turpin, the fifteen or so remaining chosen knights, and a handful of other crusaders rushed up to the gate. An arrow knocked the crusader next to Godfrey off his feet. A large rock narrowly missed Turpin.

Next to the burning siege engine, Turpin tore off his cloak and stuffed it into the flaming hole created by the ram. Others followed suit with their own cloaks, placing them wherever they could best help the fire spread.

Water poured down on Godfrey from above. Confused, Godfrey thought it was rain at first. Though the sky was grey with clouds, the water only came down from directly overhead in short bursts. The Nordsmen were dumping buckets of water onto the ram in an attempt to put out the fire. Godfrey would have laughed at this strange reversal had his life not been at stake.

"Crossbows," Godfrey shouted to the crusaders still on the causeway. "Aim at the men on the gatehouse. Don't let them put out the flames."

Godfrey had to repeat himself even louder and gesticulate above his head, but the crossbowmen began concentrating their shots up at the gatehouse. Raising his shield, Godfrey narrowly deflected a rock which might have otherwise broken his neck, but the crossbows lessened the intensity of the Nordsmen counterattack on the ram.

The fire had done its work, and both the gate and ram were quickly becoming smoldering wrecks. Signaling for the rest of the crusaders on the causeway to close the gap, Godfrey looked to his selected knights.

"You know why I chose you?" Godfrey addressed the knights around him. "Though you are all strong and brave, that is not why you are to be first through the gates with me."

The crusaders looked to him expectantly.

"You are here because of your faith," Godfrey confided. "Not just the faith with which you served my father."

He looked directly into Euric's eyes, remembering how the knight reacted to his encounter with Uriel. He smiled at Euric, Rodair, and the other chosen knights in turn.

"You put your faith in me," Godfrey continued. "You were some of the first to join me on this crusade. You put your faith in me, and believed me when you heard about my vision. And you believed me when I said the gods blessed my sword. I don't doubt the faith of any one of you."

He drew Uriel from its sheath, and Godfrey's blade sparkled despite the layer of clouds hanging low in the sky.

"Now let's see what the gods have in store for us!" Godfrey brandished Uriel overhead.

Storming through the open gate as the broken charred remains of the door fell off its hinges, he and the other crusaders bellowed as they entered Epsberg's lower bailey. Nordsman archers and axmen were waiting for him and his knights as the crusaders began pouring through the gate. The archers let off a volley of arrows, killing five more of the knights on the spot. Somehow not a single arrow so much as grazed Godfrey, though he was at the front of the crusaders' charge.

Counidercharging with chilling war cries, the Nordsman axmen got between the crusaders and archers. The collision with the crusaders almost knocked Godfrey off his feet. They appeared even bigger to him now that he was fighting them on foot. With an upward slice, Uriel bit deep into the torso of the Nordsman in front of him. A second slash from Godfrey sent another Nordsman tumbling backwards. Every one of his strikes easily landed a killing blow.

Despite Godfrey's amazing newfound prowess, the Nordsmen had little trouble keeping the rest of the crusaders from gaining much ground inside the castle's lower bailey.

"Godfrey!" Turpin shouted from several paces back.

Looking about, Godfrey realized he was almost completely surrounded by the enemy. He was too far ahead of his men. Slowly giving ground, he parried a blow then another. He hoped he had not realized his mistake too late. This was not good.

"To me!" Godfrey tried to rally the crusaders forward. "For Bastogne! For Azgald!"

Blocking an ax with his shield, Godfrey struck his attacker with the pommel of his sword. The assailant fell back, clutching his bleeding face. Two more Nordsmen rushed Godfrey at once. Godfrey cut into the belly of one of the attackers, but the other Nordsman knocked him into the mud with the boss of his shield. Just as the enemy was about to sink his ax into Godfrey's chest, one of the crusaders threw himself in front of Godfrey. It was Sir Euric.

Euric blocked several blows from the Nordsman, allowing Godfrey to get to his feet again. Euric struck down the Nordsman with his ax, but another Nordsman came in on his right and hacked through the crusader.

Howling with fury, Godfrey cut the Nordsman down in an instant. The other crusaders were pushing the Nordsmen back. The lower bailey would soon be theirs.

Godfrey knelt over the broken form of Sir Euric. They were both caked in mud. His chest rising and falling sporadically, the knight wheezed as he lay on his side. Dark blood seeped from the wound, soaking his tabard. As he turned Euric over on his back, Godfrey's eyes met his.

"You saved me," Godfrey stammered.

"I saved the gods' chosen servant," Euric rasped with a weak smile. "More importantly, I saved my lord's son. I suppose that will get me a fine mansion in the heavens."

Euric coughed up blood and was dead a moment later.

"So be it, son of Bastogne," Godfrey murmured, turning back to the enemy.

With a loud crack, part of the southern wall came crashing down. More of Godfrey's crusaders began pouring through the breach in the wall. Overwhelmed by the sudden influx of Bastognians, the Nordsmen in the lower bailey began falling back to the middle bailey. The stone-throwers had done their work.

"Some of you take the gatehouse." Turpin pointed back to the crusaders behind him. "Get those archers up on the wall. Kill them all."

A group of footmen found a solid wooden door at the base of one of the gatehouse towers. Hacking it down with their axes, they surged up into the tower. Others began climbing a set of stairs leading up to the wall's parapet. Satisfied with Turpin's call, Godfrey turned his attention back to the retreating Nordsmen.

"Charge!" Godfrey yelled, rushing into the midst of the withdrawing Nordsmen.

Shouting, the crusaders followed Godfrey as fast as their legs would carry them. The enemy's retreat broke into a rout. Trampling over the dead and dying, the Nordsmen raced through the gate to the middle bailey in a panic. Godfrey and the other crusaders cut down as many as their weapons could reach in the attempt to overtake them. If the crusaders were lucky, they might even penetrate into the middle bailey.

As if in response to Godfrey's very thought, a heavy iron portcullis slammed the gate shut, dividing the lower and middle baileys. At least a few dozen Nordsmen were still trapped in the lower bailey. The Nordsman archers on the wall fired down on the crusaders, despite their own men still in the midst of them.

With no other option, the Nordsmen caught between the wall and the crusaders flung themselves at the Bastognians one last time. They sold their lives dearly. Yet Godfrey wondered if the Nordsmen just out of reach could appreciate the sacrifice of their fellows.

Godfrey was about to cut down the Nordsman in front of him, but an arrow took the enemy out from behind. He cursed, shaking his head in disgust. The Nordsman archers were killing more of their own this way than crusaders. Unable to block their own archers' fire from behind, the last of the Nordsmen in the lower bailey died with arrows in their backs.

Holding his shield over his head to deflect the rain of missiles, Godfrey looked up at the wall. It was just as high as the outer wall, and seemed to have almost as many archers defending it. Turpin finally caught up to Godfrey. The chaplain was panting. Sweat dripped down his brow.

"Siege ladders are coming from the causeway now," Turpin reassured Godfrey.

"Ladders to the wall," Godfrey ordered. "Everyone else hold here."

Godfrey and the crusaders covered their heads and bodies with their shields the best they could. The Nordsman arrows deflected off helmets and shields. Still an occasional missile hit its mark. The constant hail of arrows and screams of sudden pain and terror emanating from crusaders all around him let Godfrey know the Nordsmen still had plenty of fight left in them.

Only now did Godfrey recognize that there were no berserkers among Epsberg's defenders. Perhaps they were a rare breed of warrior, or they only committed themselves to the attack rather than defense. Godfrey would have to ask Madeline about that when he had the chance. There were more pressing matters now.

Not a moment too soon, the crusaders began to clear a path for their fellows carrying the siege ladders. There were five of the heavy wooden devices. Godfrey was at the first ladder as soon as it was placed against the wall. Turpin was at the next ladder almost immediately afterward. Godfrey slung his shield over his back as Turpin sheathed his sword. Putting a foot on the first rung of the ladder, the chaplain gave Godfrey the briefest nod.

"The castle is almost ours." Godfrey pointed Uriel to the top of the wall, addressing the crusaders around him. "Victory awaits us up there. That or death and glory with me."

With heavy steps, Godfrey ascended the ladder as quickly as his tiring legs would allow. Turpin was half a pace behind him on the ladder to his left. Sir Rodair led the crusaders up the ladder to Godfrey's right.

Halfway up the ladder, Turpin took an arrow to the shoulder. Godfrey stopped in his ascent as Turpin let out a cry of pain. The banner in Turpin's hand dropped. Seizing up, the chaplain fell from the ladder and plummeted to the ground hard.

Godfrey's stomach sank to somewhere deep within his bowels. He stared at Turpin's contorted form lying on top of the banner. The chaplain did not move.

"My lord," Rodair called to Godfrey. "You have to keep moving, my lord."

There was urgency in Rodair's call. The man clearly feared Godfrey would refuse to go any farther. With that thought, Godfrey shook the numbness from his mind. Rodair was right. The knight was farther up his ladder than Godfrey. There was a queue of crusaders building up beneath Godfrey on his ladder. He could not mourn now.

Blinking away the tears, he continued up the ladder with grim resolve. He stomped up as quickly as he could, closing the distance Rodair had gained over him. Arrows narrowly missed Godfrey. A rock grazed his spangenhelm, but it only dazed him for a moment.

Jumping over the parapet as soon as he reached the top of the ladder, Godfrey launched himself at the nearest Nordsman. The enemy archer had a sword drawn, but was caught off guard by Godfrey's reckless abandon. Godfrey slashed through him, then bashed another off the wall with his shield. Rodair and the other crusaders joined Godfrey atop the parapet, cutting down all resistance. More crusaders fell, but the wall was nearly theirs now.

Godfrey surveyed the scene of battle from atop the parapet. Conrad's contingent had three siege towers against the western wall with crusaders spilling out onto the defenses. The fighting was intense and Conrad was in the thick of it. Godfrey had to give the Wolf credit for that at least.

Tancred's soldiers were fighting it out with Epsberg's defenders in the middle bailey. The eastern wall was completely overrun by the knights of Pavik. Some of them had even broken into Epsberg's keep.

Godfrey's jaw dropped. There was Tancred with a trio of footmen on the keep's roof. They were raising not the banner of the Knights of the Silver Sun over the keep as they should have, but Tancred's own standard. Falling to his knees, Godfrey cursed Tancred's vanity. The battle was won, but not for the crusade.

Chapter Eighteen

Turpin's eyes followed Godfrey as he paced back and forth. The chaplain's shoulder was bandaged where the arrow had pierced him, and he wore a simple tunic instead of his armor. He sat on a stool in Godfrey's tent awkwardly, still sore from his fall off the ladder. Grimacing, Walaric stood with his arms crossed.

"How could he do this?" Godfrey blustered for the seventh time in an hour. "He tricked us. He used us to take Epsberg for himself."

"What are you going to do?" Turpin shot back. "Besiege the castle again?"

"What if Tancred was the dragon from the vision?" Godfrey protested. "Is this not proof enough that I have to slay him? It's for the crusade!"

Walaric and Turpin exchanged glances. Sensing their unease, Godfrey wondered if maybe he was wrong. He blushed with embarrassment as he realized his last remark had gone too far. None of this was going the way he thought it should. Why did everything have to be so complicated?

"You're not making sense, Godfrey," Walaric countered. "We should kill Azgaldians and other crusaders to help the crusade? That's madness. Besides, Conrad and Tancred outnumber us anyway. We would all die for nothing."

"But I have a magic sword," Godfrey continued despite knowing he was wrong. "Does Uriel not signal the gods' favor?"

"Even still," Turpin interrupted, rubbing his brow. "One magic sword can help you, but it's not enough to win a battle. Aside from that, do you think our men would be willing to fight against their fellow crusaders over a castle they had just won from the Nordsmen?"

"At least Epsberg is no longer in the Clans' possession," Walaric added.

"You're right," Godfrey relented. "But I won't march with them again. I'm not helping those two anymore. We're marching to Narlstad without Conrad and Tancred."

"We'd be too few." Turpin shook his head. "It was a gamble breaking the crusade up into these smaller armies to begin with."

"Narlstad is only a couple of days southwest of us," Godfrey persisted.

"A couple of days is plenty of time for a small army to get ambushed." Walaric frowned.

"Tancred is offering our men their share of the loot," Turpin cut in, changing the topic. "Let them have it, even if this whole situation is not exactly to your liking."

"I didn't come on crusade to get stuck in the middle of these power games," Godfrey spat, stopping his pacing for the first time since they began talking. "There was already plenty of that back at home. Taking Epsberg's treasures would make it look like I'm supporting Tancred's claim."

"If you don't let the men have their loot, they may not be able to afford staying out here on campaign." Walaric gestured out the tent door. "We have practical concerns to worry about. We need to buy food, repair armor and weapons, and so on. Let Tancred and Morgan argue about who will keep Epsberg."

Godfrey paused, biting his lip.

"We don't want desertions," Godfrey conceded. "But Tancred and Conrad can defend their prize without me. We're leaving at first light tomorrow."

"I'll let the men know to prepare to leave," Turpin said.

"I'll let Tancred know we'll take the money." Walaric gave Godfrey an earnest look.

Walaric and Turpin left the tent. Godfrey was still fuming, partly due to his anger at Tancred's betrayal, but also because of his own overreaction to it. Or had he overreacted? Walaric and Turpin seemed to think so, but Godfrey was certain Tancred's deception warranted a stronger reaction than a dismayed shrug.

Godfrey lit a candle as the Sun began to set. Pulling out a quill and ink bottle, he began searching for parchment. He was not good at writing. His script was poor, and the effort often cramped his hand on the few occasions he needed to write. But he needed advice from his father, and writing a letter was the only way to get that advice so far from home.

At last he found the parchment, sat at the small table he had taken from his room back at Fuetoile Keep, and went through the excruciating effort to write what was on his mind. The words were as difficult to find in his head as they were to put in ink. There were so many thoughts, so many conflicting feelings. It was well after dark, and several sheets of parchment had been crumpled or shredded before Godfrey finally finished his letter. Sealing it with hot wax from the candle, Godfrey then blew out the flame. He slept uneasily that night.

It was not quite dawn when Conrad came crunching across the frosty ground. Godfrey's tent and the few personal belongings that accompanied it had already been packed with the baggage train, leaving him with Baruch. Godfrey gritted his teeth as he spotted Conrad moving towards him from among the crusaders preparing for the march.

"Heading to Narlstad already then?" Conrad sneered.

"You're quick aren't you?" Godfrey rolled his eyes.

"My men are ready to go when you are, o chosen one," Conrad replied with a mocking bow. "Just give the command."

"I thought you would have wanted to stay with your prize," Godfrey snorted, mounting Baruch. "Didn't you come here for land and treasure?"

"Bastogne took its share of treasure from Epsberg." Conrad's smirk was razor-thin. "There is plenty more to get still."

His rage boiling, Godfrey made no reply.

"I'll see you on the road," Conrad said, then turned and left.

The crusaders were ready to depart just as the Sun rose. Godfrey had not spoken directly with Tancred since before the assault on Epsberg. There was nothing to say. With the crusaders on the march and Godfrey riding at the head of his knights, part of him hoped this would be the last he would have to see of the Duke of Pavik.

Then there was also that part of Godfrey which longed for Madeline. Their encounters had been few and brief, but he knew she burned for him as he did for her. Of course her father would stand between them. That was how it worked in all those silly romantic poems. Godfrey gritted his teeth at the thought. That obstruction was bad enough. Why did Tancred have to foil his efforts in the crusade too?

The men of Pavik were hard at work repairing the breaches in the wall. The damage was obviously significant from Godfrey's vantage point, but not beyond a few days' labor by a handful of skilled artisans. Tancred would soon be secure in his new fortress.

"Let him rot in his prize," Godfrey muttered to himself, taking a final look back at Epsberg.

"It's almost as if he's expecting someone to contest his claim," Turpin noted from beside him.

The chaplain was wearing his armor again, but he winced as he moved.

"You entrust Conrad with the rearguard?" Walaric frowned from the other side of Godfrey.

"No," Turpin admitted. "But if we don't act like we do, this whole expedition is over."

"Right." Godfrey gave a humorless smile.

"At least he's downwind of us." Walaric gestured behind him. "We don't have to smell the likes of him anyway."

The men had only been marching for a few hours when Godfrey spotted one of the crusade's scouts emerging from the woods down the road. He was a small, pale man wrapped in a dark cloak. Godfrey instantly recognized him as Varin. Despite his eccentricities, Varin was an accomplished ranger, the sort of man who was only seen when he wanted to be seen. He was bounding to Godfrey as quickly as his legs would carry him. He would not overtly display such urgency unless something was awry.

"My lord," Varin rasped, clutching his longbow with white knuckles. "Nordsmen are approaching Epsberg."

"Have they discovered us?" Godfrey asked, gesturing for the crusaders to stop.

"No, sire." The ranger locked eyes with Godfrey, another unusual behavior for the strange man. "They are taking a different path."

"We could intercept them," Walaric cut in enthusiastically. "We could ambush them before they reach Epsberg."

"How many?" Turpin inquired.

"Many thousands." Varin began to catch his breath. "They are more than us at any rate. They have cyclopes too."

Godfrey swallowed hard at that last bit of information. Cyclopes were dumb brutes but no less deadly for their lack of wit. Encountering a single cyclops could be the death of many men. Encountering cyclopes could be the death of an army.

"We could wait until they reach Epsberg," Turpin suggested. "Crush them between the castle and ourselves like at Biorkon."

The plan made sense to Godfrey, but he had only just vowed the night before not to help Tancred anymore. The gods must have a sense of humor, Godfrey decided. Part of him really wished he could just keep marching to Narlstad, but he knew he was better than that. He would do the right thing, even if reluctantly.

"It's too good of an opportunity to miss," Turpin admonished, reading Godfrey's expression. "Don't let your pride get in the way."

"Rodair," Godfrey called back to the retinue. "Send word to the rearguard. We're going to follow these Nordsmen back to Epsberg and strike them once they lay siege to the castle."

"Yes, my lord." Sir Rodair spurred his mount back to the rearguard marching behind them somewhere along the twisting road beyond the baggage train.

"Varin," Godfrey addressed the ranger. "Let's follow the Nordsmen from a safe distance. I don't want them to know we're on to them."

"I'll pass the word to the other scouts." Varin bowed and hurried off into the woods.

Leaving the baggage train behind, the crusaders departed from the road and began marching through the trees. The frost had melted, leaving the ground soft and muddy. The smell of pine needles mixed with the sweat and grime of the men and horses. Rodair galloped back to the knights several minutes later.

"Conrad is taking his men back to Epsberg the way they came," Rodair reported as his horse slowed to a trot, matching Baruch's stride. "He says that if you will attack them from the south, he will strike them from the west."

"That will be the same positions we attacked Epsberg from during the siege," Godfrey noted. "Fair enough. Hitting the Nordsmen from two directions at once will add to their confusion."

"But it will be more difficult to pull off," Turpin murmured.

"Right." Godfrey tensed in frustration. "But we don't have time to deliberate. Conrad is already moving into position."

Yielding, Turpin fell silent. Somewhere up in the branches, a raven crowed. It swooped down, passing just over Godfrey's head. The color flushed from Rodair's face as he saw it happen. Other crusaders saw it too. They began muttering uneasily. It was a sign, an omen. All eyes turned to Walaric. At first, the acolyte's skin was pale, and his mouth hung open. After a moment, however, the trance was broken though his expression remained pensive. Considering what he had just witnessed, the acolyte pursed his lips thoughtfully.

"It's not strictly a bad omen," Walaric noted. "We had already committed to going along with Conrad's plan."

Some of the color returned to Rodair's face, though he still appeared uncomfortable. The other knights stared, waiting for further explanation. Though not a fully trained priest, Walaric commanded the respect of the crusaders by nature of his chosen vocation. Even an acolyte's words were to be taken seriously when he spoke on behalf of the gods. That is what Godfrey had come to see at least.

"If it were a bad omen," Walaric explained, "it would have come before we decided. But since it came after, it means the raven will pass over our enemies' corpses, not ours."

Satisfied with Walaric's analysis, Godfrey and the crusaders relaxed. The interpretation seemed sound. Time would tell if the omen was interpreted correctly. The march resumed.

"Did you just make that up?" Godfrey whispered to Walaric once he was close enough for only the acolyte to hear.

"It's my prerogative to interpret omens how I see them," Walaric huffed. "The raven is generally an ominous sign, but I stand by what I said."

Turpin grunted but said nothing. Apparently Walaric was not the only one within earshot of what Godfrey was saying. Godfrey was about to say something else in response to Turpin's reaction. With a frown, Turpin raised his hand, cutting off his query.

"Don't tempt the gods." Turpin shook his head. "You got your answer."

"But you see it differently?" Godfrey asked. "You can interpret omens too. You're a chaplain after all."

"A servant of the gods has interpreted the omen," Turpin insisted. "You got your answer. Don't let the men see you fretting over it."

"Right." Godfrey glanced over his shoulder at the knights behind him.

The crusaders appeared oblivious to the exchange. Fair enough. He would let it go. The gods were with Godfrey, and that was what mattered. Letting go of what else the omen might mean, Godfrey turned his thoughts to more pressing matters.

Varin or another ranger occasionally appeared out of the trees, instructing the army to adjust the direction of their march, to wait a few minutes until another scout came back with intelligence, to describe the enemy's movements, or to report on hazards they had dealt with.

"Thank the gods for good scouts," Godfrey exclaimed, pointing out one such neutralized hazard Varin had dealt with.

It was a group of about half a dozen giant spiders lying on their backs a few yards away. Each was roughly the size of a large horse. With sickly ichor weeping from punctures and slashes across their bodies, each spider was quite certainly dead. Walaric gave a low whistle in response.

As the army continued through the woods, Godfrey spotted a few other monsters or beasts similarly slain. Walaric was quick to point out the ones Godfrey did not see or failed to comment on. There were more giant spiders of the same brownish red hue as the first set. Some hideous grey-furred beasts in the shape of men lay sprawled in a stony creek, pale from the loss of blood. An eviscerated dire bear lay half concealed in a bush to Godfrey's left. It was Turpin's turn to whistle in amazement at this last feat. Godfrey would have to remember to reward Varin somehow for that one.

At last, the crusaders came to a clearing in the woods. Epsberg was in sight for the second time that day, far sooner than Godfrey would have wished to see it otherwise.

Varin was right. The Nordsman host had gathered around the southern side of the castle. They outnumbered Godfrey's crusaders at least three to one. However, the Nordsmen had also just arrived. They had not yet begun to cross the causeway to the breach in the wall Godfrey's crusaders had made the day before.

The Nordsmen had cyclopes too, just as Varin had said. The orcs in the Nordsman army were roughly the size of a man and were almost indistinguishable from men at this distance, but the cyclopes were nine feet tall and much broader. There were dozens of them. Godfrey unwillingly thought back to what he had seen cyclopes do to men. He clenched his teeth but shook the memory after a moment.

"Advance," Godfrey ordered. "Go nice and steady. Crossbows to the rear. Stay well behind the spearmen, and fire over their heads. Knights come with me to the right flank."

"Wait." Walaric pointed to the Clan army.

Part of the enemy force had turned to face the crusaders, but it was the cavalier carrying a white flag of truce coming from their midst that caught Godfrey's attention. Another Nordsman rider followed the first, and a pair of cyclopes flanked either side of the two horse-mounted warriors. Four such monstrous brutes seemed excessive for the occasion. Two would have been plenty.

"*Now* they want to parley," Godfrey sighed. "Where is Conrad?"

"I don't see him." Turpin frowned, scanning the trees from which the crusaders of Errans were supposed to emerge.

"Maybe this will buy us some time for him to get in position at least," Godfrey said.

"If he comes at all," Turpin muttered.

Godfrey had not wanted to consider that possibility. Yet it had pressed at him from the back of his mind since Rodair first told him of Conrad's plan to attack from another direction. Grimacing, Godfrey could not deny the possibility that Conrad's arrival might be too late, whether it was intentional or circumstantial.

"Conrad is selfish and foul but he would not abandon some five thousand crusaders just because of our personal differences." Godfrey tried to reassure Turpin as much as himself, "Weren't you the one just saying we all had to act like we were in this together?"

Turpin's expression appeared to be caught between conflicting emotions. Those were the words he said, but those same words went against his general pessimism. Godfrey could hardly blame the chaplain for doubting Conrad's loyalty. Just a short while ago, Godfrey himself was musing over the idea of leaving Tancred to his fate. Godfrey hoped that if the honor that compelled him to come to Tancred's aid failed Conrad, strategic opportunity would not. Visibly conflicted, Turpin said nothing for a moment. Finally, the chaplain's gaze turned towards the sky. As if remembering something from long ago, he smiled.

"Here's to putting our faith in the gods." Turpin raised his own white flag of truce before spurring his mount out to meet the Clan envoy.

Godfrey and Walaric spurred their mounts forward to catch up with Turpin. Upon closer examination, Godfrey noticed the cyclopes guarding the envoy differed from the ones he had seen back in Lortharain. These cyclopes were bluish-grey in color and carried large spears and shields, unlike the greenish-brown cyclopes that preferred to carry clubs or oversized hammers back home.

The lead rider from the Nordsman envoy planted his flag in the ground as they stopped. The muddy ground gave a short, soft gurgle as Turpin likewise planted his flag a few paces away. Godfrey nudged Baruch past Turpin a pace and dismounted. The second Nordsman rider met Godfrey and also dismounted his horse. The wind picked up, flapping flags and cloaks about noisily.

"This seems like an excessive retinue for a parley," Godfrey said, indicating the cyclopes. "Or is it the Clan way to have their opposition smashed to a pulp if negotiations do not go to their liking?"

"I am negotiating from a position of strength." The Nordsman mimicked Godfrey's gesture towards the cyclopes. "These loyal bodyguards are a symbol of the strength I command."

"High King Alvir," Godfrey ventured a guess.

"High Warlord Alvir in your tongue," Alvir corrected. "Not just anyone can be born to the throne in the Nordslands. Clansmen have to fight to win and keep their titles and lands."

"That's not too different from how things work in Lortharain," Godfrey snorted.

"And you are?" Alvir inquired.

"Godfrey de Bastogne."

"You are the leader of the crusade?" Alvir looked the Bastognian crusaders over. "I thought there would be more of you."

"There are more crusaders," Godfrey reassured him. "Some are taking other lands from you as we speak. Some are closer than you think."

Alvir frantically twisted on the spot, scanning the tree line. In that brief moment, Godfrey caught a glimpse of a dark dragon-shaped pendant hanging from a chain around Alvir's neck. The dragon certainly was a popular heraldic device in these lands, even among opposing peoples.

Alvir's momentary nervousness quickly subsided, though. He turned more slowly in the opposite direction, attempting to catch any sign of an approaching army. Silently, Godfrey cursed as Alvir's eyes narrowed on him. Godfrey had given away too much too soon. Conrad had better hurry.

"A bluff." Alvir waved his hand dismissively. "You think you can make me surrender with empty threats?"

"Perhaps I am stalling you until Conrad the Wolf appears on your flank with another five thousand men," Godfrey suggested with a shrug.

"Conrad the Wolf is on crusade?" Alvir huffed. "Now I know you are lying. I've heard of his exploits, his selfish nature. He would not come on such a venture without something to gain."

"Even if I were lying," Godfrey slowly deliberated, "you are in a bad position, and you know it. More than five thousand crusaders stand before you here. Inside Epsberg is the Duke of Pavik with almost another three thousand men. You would not come out well even if you survived the attack from just my men and Tancred's."

"My cyclopes would also cost you dearly," Alvir noted. "They aren't just strong, but also too stupid to know when to retreat from a fight. Their stupidity grants them bravery beyond any of your knights. You may bloody my army on this field, but you would be annihilated to a man. I would make sure of it."

Godfrey stared Alvir down, contemplating the risks. By the gods, where was Conrad? Alvir looked around with a disappointed expression. Shifting his weight from one foot to the other, the Nordsman released a heavy sigh after a moment.

"Well it seems your friend is not coming," Alvir said with a smirk.

Damn his soul to the darkest abyss, Godfrey silently cursed. *Damn you, Conrad. Damn you to the lowest hell.*

"Apparently not," Godfrey conceded. "But I do have this."

As Godfrey unsheathed Uriel, Alvir took a step back in surprise. The sparkling blade caused the cyclopes to wince. The High Warlord's and his bodyguards' shock was greater than Godfrey had anticipated. Godfrey extended the sword towards Alvir for him to examine. Squinting, Alvir studied it.

"You have the blessing of your gods," Alvir grumbled.

The High Warlord brooded. His expression was stern. Now Godfrey felt he had an advantage over the man.

"What are your terms?" Alvir demanded.

"Withdraw from the Eastern Marches immediately," Godfrey proclaimed without hesitation.

"That's it?" Alvir asked after a moment. "You don't want me to agree to cease hostilities, pay a ransom, or cede more land to you?"

"No." Godfrey shook his head. "I don't think you would honor that sort of treaty after the crusade disperses. We need to kill enough of your soldiers to ensure that any treaties we make with the Clans can be enforced by Azgald after we return home."

"That's a rather insolent position," Alvir hissed.

"I am negotiating from a position of strength." Godfrey sheathed his sword emphatically. "And next we meet, I will be negotiating from a position of *greater* strength."

"We shall see." Alvir's lips curled darkly. "My gods are also with me."

"So it is with the War in Heaven," Godfrey retorted.

Alvir turned, taking a few steps back to his horse. He paused. The wind died down. Alvir's retainer glanced at the High Warlord curiously from atop his steed, but said nothing.

"You'll come to regret not settling this now." Alvir shot a glance back at Godfrey.

As the High Warlord, his retainer, and the cyclopes made their way back to the Nordsman army, Godfrey wondered if letting Alvir go was the right decision. The magic sword seemed to frighten the Nordsman enough, but Godfrey had deliberately chosen not to reveal the exact nature of its powers, instead letting the High Warlord's imagination run wild. No, Godfrey needed more men than he had now to win a battle like this.

Godfrey mounted Baruch, and turned back to Walaric and Turpin. The chaplain nodded his approval, as did Walaric when their eyes met.

"Withdraw fifty paces," Godfrey ordered his crusaders.

With the clanking of spears, shields, and chainmail, the men complied. Alvir's forces withdrew past the crusaders as the men of Pavik cautiously watched from Epsberg's walls. When the Nordsmen were out of sight, the crusaders and Azgaldians cheered. Duke Tancred rode out from the gate with a few of his knights.

"That was High Warlord Alvir." Tancred pointed in the direction the Nordsmen had gone.

"So I have learned," Godfrey muttered.

"What were the terms of your parley?" Tancred pressed.

"A small respite," Godfrey gestured dismissively. "He is withdrawing his army from the Eastern Marches."

"Surely he knows there must be other crusaders in the Eastern Marches," Tancred mused. "I am surprised you convinced him to retreat so easily."

"Were Conrad here we could have killed—" Godfrey stopped mid-sentence.

Conrad approached Godfrey atop his steed. The crusaders from Errans were emerging from the surrounding trees. The closer Conrad got, the tighter Godfrey's jaw grew.

"We could have killed the whole Nordsman army," Godfrey spat, finishing his sentence just as Conrad arrived with his retainers behind him.

Conrad opened his mouth to speak, but Godfrey struck him in the jaw with his fist. The Duke of Errans fell off his horse, plopping into the mud at the unexpected blow. Astonished gasps escaped the knights around the gathered lords.

"You waited." Godfrey pointed an accusing finger down at Conrad. "You held your men back, hoping I would attack the Nordsmen without you."

Conrad's eyes flashed in anger up at Godfrey, but he said nothing.

"Deny it," Godfrey dared.

One of Conrad's knights helped him off the ground. Conrad wiped the mud from his tabard but still did not answer. His eyes burned with hate, telling Godfrey everything he needed to know.

"That was their High Warlord there," Godfrey shouted. "We could have defeated his army, and ended the crusade here today!"

"You are the one with the sacred blade." Conrad spat blood into the mud. "But it's hard to imagine how you won the gods' favor with such cowardice."

"There is a difference between cowardice and prudence," Tancred said, speaking up for the first time in Godfrey's defense.

"I've had it with you too," Godfrey shouted back at Tancred, too angry to understand what the Duke of Pavik had actually said. "Were it not for you, none of this would have happened. Keep your new castle, but don't expect me to come back again."

<u>Chapter Nineteen</u>

Varin scampered through the woods as fast as his legs would carry him. His breathing was heavy, and sweat covered every inch of him. Arrows whizzed past him as shouts called out from behind him. It was some sort of orcish dialect. Varin knew the common orc languages back in the Ostlands, but not those used in the Nordslands. He did not need to know their language though. Commands such as *stop him* and *kill him* were easy enough to understand in any language. The baying and howling of wargs were also universally understood. They wanted meat. He only hoped he could make it back to the army in time.

Ducking behind a tree, Varin dared to look behind him as he drew an arrow from his quiver. Nearly a dozen Nordsmen and orcs were pursuing him. One Nordsman barely kept a pair of thick-built wargs restrained on chained collars in their pursuit. Nocking the arrow back on his bowstring, Varin took aim at one of the beasts. His breathing from his flight was so labored that he could hardly manage the task. He let loose the missile. With a squeal, the warg was down, his arrow protruding from its dark matted fur. That was luck more than anything.

The Nordsman beast-handler dropped his chains, and the remaining warg rushed Varin at a full gallop. Drawing another arrow, Varin fired it faster than he thought possible. Aiming was hardly necessary, the beast was so close. The warg skidded across the muddy earth with the arrow piercing its wide jaw. Its foul breath washed over Varin as the warg came to rest at his feet. The creature whimpered and died.

Hoping that had bought him some time, Varin sprinted forward again. Hurled javelins and more angry shouting followed him. There was no chance to hide. The pursuit was too close.

Something ran very closely behind Varin, and was gaining on him. It was almost on top of him. Drawing another arrow as he ran, Varin turned and fired. The arrow burrowed itself in the gut of the Nordsman beast-handler less than two yards behind him. The Nordsman cursed and fell. Though he had killed another pursuer, Varin was also robbed of the precious little distance he had over the enemy. How much longer could he do this?

Two ax-wielding orcs rushed Varin. He dodged the first orc's blow, dropping his bow. Varin drew his sword as the second orc swung his ax, and he barely parried it. He shoved the brute into the path of the first orc's ax just as it was about to come down on the ranger. Shock and rage filled the orc, but it was short-lived. Plunging his sword into the monster's face, Varin ended the creature.

Picking up his bow, Varin ran again. His muscles screamed in protest. He could barely control his breathing. Just a little farther.

Varin stumbled out onto a wide dirt road. There was Godfrey mounted atop his steed at the head of the crusaders with his knights. Godfrey signaled the men to halt at the sight of the ranger, concern etched across his face.

"My lord," Varin began between gasping breaths.

"Ambush!" someone shouted from farther down the column of marching soldiers.

Orcs, Nordsmen, and cyclopes ripped through the trees on either side of the road. Their weapons clanged against armor and shields as they tore into the crusaders in the middle of the column. Men fell in the confusion before they could even understand what was happening.

"Gods above," Godfrey pleaded. "Not cyclopes!"

Catching his breath, Varin withdrew into the midst of the crusaders. The ranger was spent. Godfrey did not fault him for it.

Screaming, shouting, dying, the noises of battle cleared Godfrey's head of the simmering anger which had gnawed at him for the last few days. There would be more time later to reminisce over striking Conrad off his horse. Now his fury was turned against Alvir. He was sure the High Warlord had arranged this attack.

"It would sure be nice if we had the others with us," Walaric moaned. "We're only just now out of the Eastern Marches."

"Stay close," Godfrey warned. "Knights, drive them back!"

Godfrey turned Baruch around, and the knights charged at the enemy. Walaric followed close behind on his steed, but Godfrey quickly lost track of the acolyte. Ahead of Godfrey, the cyclopes impaled crusaders with their oversized spears. Pitching their unfortunate victims over their heads or flinging their broken forms from their weapons, the cyclopes certainly did not lack in strength.

Drawing Uriel, Godfrey shouted as Baruch raced to the nearest monster. The shining blade easily sliced through the cyclops's thick hide. Godfrey was almost as surprised at this feat as the dumbfounded cyclops was. Still uncomprehending, the cyclops clutched at the gaping wound across its belly as it fell.

Others found it far more difficult to slay the cyclopes. The cyclopes' long reach prevented most crusaders from getting too close to their larger foes, and the orcs and Nordsmen guarded the cyclopes' blind spots. Arrows and crossbow bolts bounced harmlessly off the cyclopes' skins, except where it was softer around the joints and neck. One cyclops roared in anguish as Varin managed to place a shot in the creature's eye with his bow. The monster feverishly swatted at its ridged forehead in its efforts to dislodge the missile from its eye. Godfrey really needed to think of a good reward for the ranger after the crusade was over.

A dismounted knight slashed at the cyclops blinded by Varin, cutting across its thigh. The creature bellowed again, and lashed out. Catching the knight in its meaty paws, the cyclops hurled the screaming man as hard as it could. Another crusader chopped into the monster's knee with his battle-ax, finally felling the creature. Two more crusaders finished off the cyclops with their spears. It had taken five men to kill one cyclops. That was not a good ratio.

Another cyclops swung its two-handed maul indiscriminately as it charged into the midst of the crusaders. Men fell right and left. One lucky crusader somehow managed to lodge his spear into the cyclops' neck from directly in front of it. Sputtering blood from its mouth, the creature fell.

"The gods love you today." Godfrey gestured down to the crusader on foot.

"It's the one eye." The crusader pointed to his forehead. "The cyclopes have trouble with depth perception."

"Oh." Godfrey could hardly contain his amazement.

Their defense tightening, the crusaders began to drive Alvir's forces back to the trees. Turpin's rearguard had joined up with the main force, and was pushing into the enemy's flank. The tide was turning, and Godfrey breathed a sigh of relief.

Godfrey charged a cyclops, sundering its spear shaft with a blow from Uriel. The monster dropped its broken weapon, and reached for Godfrey. He spurred Baruch forward, narrowly avoiding the cyclops's grasp. Uriel still shimmered as he drove his blade deep into the monster's bare chest. The howl it let out nearly deafened Godfrey.

Dazed, Godfrey only recognized that the cyclops had its hands around him as it lifted him out of Baruch's saddle. Drawing his sword out of the cyclops's chest as it lifted him over its head, he silently prayed it would not toss him. He slashed down at the monster before it could throw him into the trees. With a deep gash running across the top of the cyclops's head, the creature collapsed in a heap.

Landing on top of the dead cyclops, Godfrey had no time to remount Baruch as he was surrounded by orcs and Nordsmen. He blocked a blow from an orc's club, and parried a Nordsman's sword. Godfrey struck out once, twice, and a third time, killing as many foes. His blade ignored all armor.

Finally arriving, Turpin and the knights of the rearguard trampled the enemies between them and Godfrey beneath their steeds' thunderous hooves. Lances, swords, and axes struck down all within reach. Godfrey nodded in thanks to Turpin, then he made a gesture of gratitude to the gods.

Fear gripped the remaining Nordsmen and orcs; Godfrey saw it written on their faces. The enemy began to retreat into the trees. Looking about in confusion, the few remaining cyclopes decided to follow their allies back into the woods. Godfrey suspected the larger brutes withdrew not out of fear like the others, but simply because they were following their fellows.

"Hold," Godfrey ordered.

An injured orc whimpered on the ground next to Godfrey. A deep cut ran across its leg. Absolute terror gripped the creature as Godfrey stared down at it impassively. The orc tried to rise and flee but could not because of its wound. Godfrey stabbed it without a second thought, ending the orc's life.

The crusaders maintained a defensive formation, facing out to the woods as their enemies vanished back into the trees. Wiping slick blood from his sword, Godfrey surveyed the scene of carnage. There were dead and wounded all around him. Baruch stood idly nearby. Stepping over the dismembered limbs of a dead orc, Godfrey patted his steed. After scanning the trees for a minute, Godfrey caught Varin's eye. The scout, covered in orcish blood, nodded in return.

"All clear," Godfrey called out. "Stand down."

The tension eased as the crusaders lowered their weapons. They began talking, treating their wounded, rendering mercy killings to the enemy wounded. Sir Rodair's squire helped the knight to his feet, a cut leaking blood down his forehead. The squire pressed a rag to the wound, stopping the bleeding.

Turpin had dismounted. He was hunched, checking over Walaric, who was lying on his back. Walaric had been wounded in the battle. Panic causing his heart to race again, Godfrey rushed over to his friend.

"I can't feel my legs." Walaric struggled to lift himself, but failed in the attempt.

"Don't move." Turpin shook his head. "You'll only make it worse."

"What happened?" Godfrey examined Walaric.

"Cyclops." Walaric pointed back to the woods. "It knocked me off my horse. Where's Moon Frost?"

"The horse is fine," Turpin reassured Walaric with a quick glance towards the steed standing just out of Walaric's field of vision. "Don't worry about that. We'll need to lift you on a litter. Then you'll have to ride in a cart back in the baggage train."

"Great." Walaric rolled his eyes.

"You could be dead," Godfrey noted.

"I'm paralyzed." Walaric's exacerbation reached a crescendo.

"That's still better than being dead," Turpin said.

"Speaking of the dead…" Godfrey turned to Sir Rodair as the knight approached. "Have them buried on the side of the road, but put their weapons and armor in the baggage train."

"That would dishonor the dead," Rodair protested. "The fallen must be buried with their arms and armor."

"We're running out of money, even after Epsberg." Godfrey bit his lip. "We need to reuse what we can, and sell anything extra once we are at Narlstad. I think the dead would feel it a greater honor to continue to aid the crusade than to let steel rust in the ground."

The dead were buried as instructed. Walaric and Rodair withheld any criticism they might have wished to share with Godfrey over stripping the dead of their arms and armor. Practical concerns weighed more heavily than ritual in this case. Once that was completed and the crusaders resumed their march, Narlstad only took a few more hours to reach. At least Walaric did not have to ride with the baggage train for long.

"The way I see it," Sir Rodair confided once Narlstad was in sight, "this is Conrad's fault."

"Of course it is." Godfrey stared hard at the road as Baruch's hooves clopped across the dirt. "If it were not for his stunt back at Epsberg, this whole crusade might be over already."

"I can't understand the man's motivation." Rodair shook his head, gripping the reins to his horse tightly. "Why would he jeopardize the whole crusade over personal jealousy?"

"This whole crusade could have been over by now," Godfrey spat. "Victory was there. It was right there."

His hand was shaking.

"Now this instead…" His voice trailed off.

As the crusaders approached Narlstad's imposing stone gates, a pair of Silver Sun sentinels peered down at them from atop one of the gatehouse towers. One of the sentinels shouted something as he recognized the approaching army. A herald blew his trumpet in response.

The gates creaked open. Dismounting Baruch, Godfrey spotted the Silver Sun castellan approaching from the courtyard. The castellan was tall and broad, his cloak hanging loosely over his shoulders.

"Godfrey de Bastogne I presume?" the castellan asked. "I am Marshal Horvath."

"A pleasure." Godfrey led Baruch by the reins up to the marshal.

"You have retaken Epsberg?" Horvath inquired.

"In a manner of speaking." Godfrey gritted his teeth.

Marshal Horvath considered Godfrey's cryptic reply. He frowned as he looked over the army behind Godfrey. Godfrey tried to steady his breathing. He would not let his emotions get the better of him here.

"I thought there would be more crusaders with you." Horvath met Godfrey's eye. "Where is the Duke of Pavik?"

"They are still at Epsberg." Godfrey tried to keep his tone measured. "Tancred has claimed the fortress for himself, and Conrad the Wolf is supporting him."

"I see." Horvath's face was set. "And how do you feel about this, crusader?"

"I didn't come here to help the Duke of Pavik in his personal conquests." Godfrey's voice began to shake. "I came here to stop the Five Clans."

"Strange that Tancred would do such a thing and leave his daughter here with us," Horvath said.

"Madeline is here?" Godfrey's heart raced.

"She was," the castellan corrected. "Her party left for Helsirki earlier today. Had we learned of Tancred's treachery any sooner, we would have kept her as a hostage."

"Which way is Helsirki?" Godfrey's eyes narrowed.

"Follow the road west." Horvath pointed the way. "Do you intend to bring her back so we can secure Epsberg from Tancred?"

"Alvir's army is out there." Godfrey gestured to the surrounding countryside. "He has cyclopes under his banner now. If they find her…"

Remounting Baruch, Godfrey turned to Sir Rodair.

"When the rearguard gets here with the baggage train," Godfrey instructed, "tell Turpin to wait here with the army. I'll be back by morning."

Spurring Baruch onward, Godfrey barely heard Rodair's protests. The sounds of galloping hooves and rushing wind drowned out everything else for Godfrey. Heading back east, the road would have taken Godfrey back to Epsberg, but going west, Godfrey was going into unfamiliar territory. Varin and the other scouts had rejoined the crusaders upon reaching Narlstad. Godfrey had no support. Traveling alone was more dangerous but faster.

The thought of Madeline in danger was almost too much for Godfrey to bear. He could think of little else as Baruch galloped down the road. He would not let anything happen to her.

The Sun was setting, and the freezing air bit Godfrey's face. Baruch had ridden hard for too long. The steed panted in exhaustion, and Godfrey was sore. Their gallop had slowed to a steady trot despite the urgency that compelled Godfrey forward. Both rider and steed had reached their limits.

The trees on either side of the road were dark, and it was getting hard for Godfrey to see in the fading light. The road twisted and turned through the woods, decreasing his field of vision even further. Godfrey was starting to feel foolish, rushing out to chase Madeline without any evidence she was in danger. She was probably several hours ahead of him still. He may not ever catch up to her, and she was probably perfectly fine anyway.

"Do you smell that?" he asked Baruch as the hint of smoke cut through the trees.

The smell grew stronger. The smoke carried the scent of wood and cooked meat. Scanning ahead for signs of a camp, Godfrey found none. With the Sun almost set entirely, he rounded another bend in the road. Faint embers glimmered a little farther down the road. There had been a fire.

Drawing closer, he saw that the embers covered a much wider area of forest than a campfire. Several lumped masses were scattered across the road. They were corpses. Godfrey dismounted Baruch. He drew Uriel, its glowing blade radiating a dull white-blue. Using his sword as a torch, he examined the nearest corpse. It was the charred remains of an orc. The next two bodies were likewise the burned husks of orcs. Farther down was a Nordsman with a battle-ax's head stuck in his chest. Next to the Nordsman was what appeared to Godfrey to be the pulverized remains of an Azgaldian knight.

"Madeline!" Godfrey shouted, pressing forward on foot. "Madeline!"

Stumbling over more bodies and weapons, he realized there had been a battle here. There were about a dozen Azgaldian corpses wearing tabards and surcoats with Pavik's heraldry. Their steeds were all dead too from what Godfrey could tell. There were roughly twice as many Nordsmen and orcish corpses, and one large cyclops burnt to a crisp.

"Godfrey?" Madeline called out from the woods.

Turning in her direction, Godfrey saw her emerge from behind a tree. Her clothes were ripped and stained with blood, but she appeared uninjured. Sheathing his sword, he embraced her. She was safe. That was all that mattered.

"You were ambushed?" he asked.

She nodded in reply.

"We were too just today," he added. "High Warlord Alvir marched on Epsberg after we had captured it."

"His beasts tried to capture me," Madeline explained as Godfrey released her from his embrace. "They killed everyone else."

"How did you escape?" He looked at the carnage around him.

"My fire," Madeline said, indicating the burnt cyclops.

"Right," he hissed, still uneasy with the full implications of Madeline's powers. "Why would Alvir want to capture you?"

"To ransom me back to father," she guessed. "Pavik is separated from the Five Clans by the Hydra Gulf. He may have wanted to take me hostage to gain Mendelpav Citadel or some other foothold in our duchy."

"That makes sense," Godfrey agreed. "I'm glad you're safe."

"I'm glad you came for me," Madeline added, gesturing to Baruch. "Walking back to Narlstad alone would have taken a lot longer."

With the danger past, Godfrey's heart sank as he remembered something he had forgotten. He looked out at something distant. He did not want to tell her.

"What's wrong?" She touched his arm.

"Your father…" Godfrey choked on the words as emotion filled his voice, and he pulled away from Madeline. "Your father, he didn't help us retake Epsberg for the Silver Suns. He claimed it for himself."

Madeline frowned, visibly struggling to find something to say.

"Conrad is supporting his claim," Godfrey added.

"To what end?" She bit her lip.

"I think it's in exchange for your hand in marriage," Godfrey admitted.

Madeline buried her face in her hands, as if willing it not to be true. But Godfrey saw it in her expression the instant before she pulled into his bosom. Godfrey knew that she knew he was right. Whatever their desires were did not matter. It was up to the Duke to decide whom his daughter would marry.

<u>Chapter Twenty</u>

It was early morning when Godfrey and Madeline returned to Narlstad. Godfrey's bones ached from the cold. They had ridden all night, and he did not feel like saying anything anymore. He was glad Madeline was safe, but he was just too tired to engage in conversation at this point.

Horvath and Turpin approached them from just outside the heavy wooden gate when they ascended the hill. Horvath mimicked Turpin's grim expression, though Godfrey was unsure if Horvath normally expressed himself this way. Godfrey's only interaction with the castellan left him with bad news, so Godfrey had seen Marshal Horvath wear few other expressions.

Feeling Madeline beginning to dismount Baruch from behind him, Godfrey stopped her with a gesture. He remembered what Horvath had said about holding her hostage. Despite her father clearly having wronged the Silver Suns, Godfrey was not about to jeopardize her safety, even for justice's sake.

"Not yet," he whispered.

"But," she began.

"We don't know if this is a safe place yet," he explained.

She resumed her spot on Baruch without further argument. Godfrey urged Baruch forward a few more paces. Horvath and Turpin were now within earshot. Examining Turpin for any clues that might reveal what he and Madeline might expect from the Silver Suns Marshal, Godfrey was disappointed to find none.

"You're safe, my lady," Turpin said, giving a slight bow.

"We are glad you brought her back," Horvath added, acknowledging Godfrey.

"Godfrey saved me," she cut in before Godfrey could say anything. "The others were killed by the enemy."

This was not strictly a lie, but the slightest resentment simmered in Godfrey. Did she not trust him? Did she think he had forgotten to keep her secret? He remembered all the trouble he had gotten into with the priests back at the Temple of Spes. He was not about to say anything that might arouse fear or suspicion.

"Come with me, my lady." Horvath proffered his hand. "You must be tired."

"If it's all the same," Godfrey interjected, "I'll be watching after Lady Madeline."

She huffed in apparent protest, but Godfrey could not tell for certain. Right now he did not care. Horvath paused for a moment, calculating something before lowering his hand. The castellan glanced at Turpin. Then he looked back to Madeline. Meeting Godfrey's eyes, Horvath's expression was unreadable.

"As you wish, my lord." Marshal Horvath gestured to the open fortress gates.

Turpin gave a discreet nod, and Godfrey urged Baruch through the gates. Turpin and Horvath followed. Once they were in the outer courtyard, a Silver Suns servant offered to take Baruch's reins. Godfrey and Madeline dismounted, and the servant led Baruch to the stables. The crusaders from Bastogne were mingling with the Silver Suns, repairing arms and armor, mending clothes, eating, drinking, and gossiping.

"Any word from the others?" Godfrey asked no one in particular.

"We just received word that Mirborg is back in Silver Sun hands," Horvath answered as they continued to the inner gate. "One of the garrison's captains betrayed his section of the wall to our forces in the night. The defenses crumbled after that."

"That's encouraging," Madeline chimed in.

"Word is the siege at Laht is also going well," Horvath added. "But they are having trouble at Odsha."

"We should go and help them," Godfrey suggested.

"Grand Master Morgan is already on his way to Odsha," Horvath countered. "The fortress will have fallen before you get there."

"Fine," Godfrey conceded as they passed through the gate to the inner courtyard.

"Your men should rest here for at least a few days," Horvath advised. "That was a bold move your crusaders made, attacking four castles at once, but my spies say Alvir is moving his own forces into this region to counter the crusade. Rest, regroup, then plan your next move."

"That sounds like a good idea," Godfrey acknowledged.

"Where are the rest of *your* men?" Madeline asked Horvath.

"Excuse me?" Horvath was caught off guard by the question.

"There were a lot more Silver Suns here before I left." Madeline looked about the courtyard seeming to count the soldiers present.

"They are joining the Grand Master at Odsha." The irritation in Horvath's voice was unmistakable.

"Is that the Grand Master's only destination?" Madeline raised an eyebrow.

"Once Odsha has our standard raised over it," Horvath said, "they are going to Epsberg to persuade your father and Conrad the Wolf to yield the castle."

Scandalized, Madeline stopped and turned to Godfrey.

"It was the Silver Suns' castle before the Clans took it," Godfrey reasoned, stopping in his tracks. "And the crusade offered to reclaim it for the Silver Suns."

Her expression was hard. Clenching her fists, she glared at Godfrey as if he had betrayed her at the deepest level. Godfrey gritted his teeth. How did she expect him to react? Tancred was wrong. Did Madeline not understand that?

As if sensing Godfrey's frustration, Turpin stepped to his side.

"Your father acted in bad faith," Turpin clarified. "He took advantage of us."

Madeline was about to say something more, but apparently thought better of it. She looked from Turpin to Horvath to Godfrey. Unclenching her fists, she sighed.

"You're right." She lowered her gaze. "What is going to happen to father?"

"As I said," Horvath reaffirmed, "the Grand Master hopes to persuade your father and Conrad the Wolf to yield Epsberg to the Silver Suns. He won't use any unnecessary force."

"It would not be wise for Azgald and the Silver Suns to be at each other's throats with the Clans on the offensive," Godfrey said, turning to Horvath.

"Agreed," Horvath concurred. "But the Duke of Pavik's actions are unacceptable. We will just have to see what terms he and the Grand Master come to."

With that, Horvath showed Godfrey, Turpin, and Madeline into the citadel. The interior of Narlstad's keep reminded Godfrey of Biorkon. The castle was as much a monastery as a fortress, the Silver Suns within the keep constantly singing hymns, praying, and burning that incense Godfrey despised.

Horvath led Godfrey, Turpin, and Madeline up a set of spiral stairs. They ascended four or five levels up the keep's southeastern tower before stopping. Godfrey silently hoped he would not need to climb too many more stairs today.

"This will be your room, Lord Godfrey." Horvath indicated a plain door as they stepped out onto the landing. "Lady Madeline's room is at the top of the tower on the next level."

"I'll escort Madeline the rest of the way," Godfrey said, half-wishing he could stop here. "Thank you, castellan."

"Very well." Horvath's indifferent reply surprised Godfrey, who expected some sort of resistance from either Horvath or Turpin.

He saw none in either of them. He had grown accustomed to someone somewhere always telling him that he should not do what he intended, for some reason. More surprisingly, Turpin did not seem to have a rebuke for Godfrey after he ran off after Madeline by himself.

With a bow, Horvath excused himself back down the stairs. Turpin followed the castellan without a word. It was just Madeline and Godfrey again.

"Lead the way, my gallant knight." She gestured toward the stairs.

After reaching the highest level, Godfrey recognized the door to the room at the top of the tower was identical to all the others he had seen as they walked up the stairs. He opened it without so much as glancing inside, and gestured for Madeline to enter. She complied with a curtsey. It was only as she passed him that Godfrey realized they both smelled like they had been out in the woods for far too long.

Following her in, he closed the door behind him. The room was a semi-circle, the wall dividing it from the stairwell and anteroom on the other side. It was austere, with little adornment aside from a few candles and a prayer book set on a small desk, a hard wooden chair, and a small brass four-pointed star hanging from the wall. Madeline reclined on the bed occupying the center of the room, and invited him to sit in the chair with a wave of her hand.

"This reminds me of the shrine at Harv," he noted with a touch of sadness as he took his seat. "It's where I first met Walaric."

"Where is he?" she asked.

"He was hurt pretty badly in the ambush." Godfrey frowned. "He couldn't walk. They must have taken him to the infirmary."

"Maybe I can help," she suggested.

"Good idea," he agreed. "Let's find him after we've rested a bit."

His eyelids growing heavy, Godfrey stifled a yawn. The temptation to curl up in the bed next to Madeline grew stronger, and the thought chased away his desire for sleep. She was a very beautiful young woman. And she had feelings for him too.

"Go get some sleep," she advised, a touch of sobriety crossing her face. "We will talk more later."

"Later," Godfrey repeated blearily, scraping the chair against the floor as he stood. "That will be good."

"Oh," she added. "And if you ever think about trying to do anything unchivalrous with me, I'll burn you to a crisp."

Madeline snapped her fingers, and a few small sparks sputtered away from her hand. Whatever fantasies he had begun to entertain concerning Madeline vanished as his feet found purpose in walking out of the room. Once he left, he let out a long yawn. His thinking was becoming muddied and his movements slow as he descended the stairs.

Godfrey's room was much like Madeline's with few differences he could notice upon entering. He turned to the brass four-pointed star hanging from the wall in his room. He realized he should give thanks. He muttered a prayer of gratitude to Loxias that was probably too brief. But fatigue was overcoming him. Flopping onto the bed, he did not even bother undressing before falling asleep.

The next day started relatively uneventfully. Godfrey made sure to bathe at the first opportunity. He also spoiled himself on the first hot meal he had eaten in a while. It seemed surreal just waiting in one place after so much constant travel.

"I will let you know the instant I hear anything about the other crusaders," Turpin reassured him as the two ate porridge at a table in the great hall. "Don't worry about them for now."

"Besides," Madeline cut in as she joined Godfrey and Turpin at the table, "we have Walaric to worry about."

"He's in the infirmary?" Godfrey asked.

Turpin nodded in reply as he slurped down the rest of his porridge. Godfrey hastily tilted his own bowl, letting the warm contents slide down his throat. Having finished his meal, he set the bowl down on the table, and pushed his chair out with a scrape.

"I know the way," Madeline said in response to his questioning look.

"Let's go," he replied, waving farewell to Turpin.

As Madeline led Godfrey through a series of narrow corridors, he could not help but be reminded of Biorkon. Both fortresses lacked adornment, and the Silver Sun inhabitants lived like monks when not actively training for combat. As a crusader and a traveling squire not long before that, Godfrey had grown used to a lack of material comforts, but he had difficulty imagining forgoing such things indefinitely. There was a simple beauty to their chants, prayers, and hymns. He just also wanted to make time for feasts, jongleurs, and jousts too.

"The Silver Suns have jousts on the field," Madeline said when Godfrey made these complaints known.

"Right," Godfrey conceded. "But the Silver Suns don't keep score. They don't give out accolades. It's not a sport for them."

"I thought jousts were meant to keep a knight's skills sharp," Madeline jibed.

"Well yes." Godfrey was slightly flustered by this intentional misdirection. "But that doesn't mean we can't all watch and enjoy it. Jousts and tournaments can be pretty large events back in Lortharain."

"Did you have a favorite back home?" Madeline asked.

"Karl the Hammer from my father's court," Godfrey answered. "He was just as good with a lance in a joust as he was with his maul in a battle. He always managed to do something unexpected to throw off his opponents on the field, a real crowd-pleaser."

"I guess we Azgaldians just take life a little more seriously up here," she said with a shrug. "But I don't think anyone would mind if you wanted to watch a joust, keep score, and give prizes to the Silver Suns."

"Maybe I will," Godfrey muttered as he became lost in his thoughts.

Entering the infirmary, he and Madeline approached Walaric as he lay sleeping in one of the beds lining the chamber walls. A few other patients lay in some of the remaining beds. Some were awake, chatting with visitors. Others slept like Walaric. All were wounded crusaders Godfrey recognized from his own forces.

"I'm going to try laying my hands on him like I did for you back at Biorkon," Madeline explained to Godfrey. "But let's wait a little while for some of these other visitors to clear out. I don't want them to see my magic."

"The day is still very young," he countered. "Do you think there will be less activity as the day goes on?"

"You have a point," she conceded.

"Is your healing magic flashy?" He subtly gesticulated to emphasize the last word.

"Not as much as the other fire," she said.

"Just try to be casual about it," he suggested. "Make it look like you're praying over him or something. I'll keep a watch out for you."

Madeline nodded in agreement. She knelt over Walaric, laying her hands on his head. Glancing around them, Godfrey did not think anyone was paying them particular attention. He looked at Madeline, then tipped his head to Walaric. Taking a deep breath, she closed her eyes. A soft glow emanated from her hands. Godfrey gritted his teeth nervously. The light was not so bright that it drew anyone's attention, but it was not as subtle as she had suggested.

After a moment, she stopped. The glow disappeared. Walaric's eyes flashed open. Confusion struck his face as he tried to make sense of Madeline's hands resting on his head. She quickly withdrew her touch, but an impish smirk crossed Walaric's face.

"Oh ho ho!" Walaric exclaimed.

"It's not what you think." She shook her head reprovingly.

"We were praying over you." Godfrey crossed his arms.

"Oh," Walaric huffed, noticing Godfrey for the first time.

Jealousy aside, it was not until that moment that Godfrey fully appreciated the sacrifice the clergy made by vowing to never enter a romantic relationship with another person. For just a few seconds, Godfrey saw Walaric's eyes light up with the possibilities afforded by the thought that Madeline had come to visit him by herself. The disappointment in Walaric's expression was unmistakable as he realized things were not as they first appeared. Godfrey could not help but give a sad smile at the thought.

"Try to stand," Madeline urged.

Walaric shifted in bed, straining his arms.

He struggled but without success.

"I still can't feel my legs." He gave up, lying back down.

"I thought it would work." Madeline frowned.

"You thought *what* would work?" Walaric eyed her suspiciously.

"The prayer," Godfrey covered for Madeline's momentary lapse. "The gods gave me a gift without my asking. I am set apart as one of their champions. Why should they not hear my prayer?"

"The gods answer all prayers," Walaric reassured Godfrey. "But sometimes the answer isn't always what we think is best."

"Maybe this prayer wasn't strong enough." Madeline looked at Godfrey. "Maybe we need to try again later or do it longer."

"Right." Godfrey was unsure he was still able to follow the metaphor for magic.

Walaric did not know about Madeline's abilities yet, and Godfrey supposed that talking about what went wrong with the spell in front of him was not something they should do. He was sure Madeline would trust Walaric enough with the secret, but others were in the infirmary too. If Godfrey understood correctly, Madeline was saying she did not know why the spell did not work either. They might have to try again later, as she suggested.

"At any rate," Walaric continued, "the doctors say this paralysis may only be temporary. We'll know in a few weeks whether I'll ever really be able to walk again."

"Well there's some hope." Godfrey patted Walaric's shoulder.

"I guess you should just try to get some rest in the meantime," Madeline added.

"You're leaving us?" Walaric scowled. "Where are you going?"

"This castle has a pretty large library." She gestured around her. "There may be some secrets hidden away in an obscure tome that could help us."

"What kind of secrets?" Walaric pressed.

"If the crusaders get divided between supporting the Silver Suns and my father, we may need some extra help." She pursed her lips, then left without another word.

"Well that was cryptic," he snorted.

"I think I have an idea what she may be looking for." Godfrey's voice trailed off as he watched her walk out of the infirmary. "I'm going to go help her if I can."

"Now *you're* leaving me?" Walaric's scowl grew deeper.

"I'll be back," Godfrey insisted. "Maybe Madeline will have some books at the library we could have you look through."

"She didn't even say what she was looking for," he pointed out.

"Like I said," Godfrey replied, "I think I know. Let me catch up with her, and we'll see if there's something we can all do to help."

"Don't be long." Walaric tugged at Godfrey's sleeve. "This place gets boring pretty fast."

Staring up at the ceiling, Walaric quietly began muttering one of his poems. Godfrey could not make out the words his friend was chanting, but it had a slow sad meter. With an awkward nod, Godfrey left Walaric and chased after Madeline.

Exiting the infirmary, Godfrey frowned as he thought of Walaric's plight. If the acolyte were paralyzed permanently, he certainly could not continue on the crusade. Bishop Clovis would have to come for Walaric and take him back to Bastogne. But then what would happen to Walaric? Did he have family to take care of him, could he still become a priest, or would he be forced to beg at the footsteps of some shrine? It was only then that Godfrey realized how little he knew about his friend's family and home life. Walaric mentioned something about an orphanage a while ago. Maybe Clovis was the closest thing Walaric had to family.

Godfrey dwelt on these thoughts for a long time before realizing he no longer recognized where he was going. The corridor was completely unfamiliar to him. Retracing his steps proved futile. He had mostly been following Madeline without thinking too much about where he was going. After a while, he ran into a Silver Sun orderly, who pointed him in the right direction.

Entering a large, dusty room at the top level of the main keep, he found her sitting at a table with nearly a dozen books stacked up beside the one she was reading. The lighting was dim, and she read with the aid of a large oil lamp sitting on the edge of her table. There were shelves lined up in several rows and columns going from one end of the room to the other. Tables like Madeline's were set at intervals in the aisles between the shelves, but only a couple of monks and Silver Sun orderlies occupied the chamber, aside from Godfrey and Madeline. Silence covered the chamber as thickly as the dust did.

"So this is Narlstad's library." Godfrey's hushed whisper took on a venerating tone.

"There are only a couple other such libraries in all of Azgald," Madeline whispered back, turning to Godfrey with a creak of her chair. "Vindholm has one, and the third library is at Sudvall in the Duchy of Smalad."

Godfrey turned his attention to a solitary monk a few tables down. He was scribbling into an open tome with a large quill while consulting an old, tattered codex. Godfrey frowned at this. The monk looked tired, and his movements were sluggish as if he had been reading and writing for some time.

"What is he doing?" Godfrey indicated the monk.

"Copying the manuscript," Madeline said, shrugging.

"I know but why?" Godfrey's frustration began to show.

"The Silver Suns don't just fight and pray." She gestured to the countless volumes around them. "They use their wealth to support scholars as well. Without monks and nuns copying down these books, we would eventually lose all this knowledge."

"Right." Godfrey looked over her shoulder, satisfied with her answer.

Madeline's hair smelled of some sweet fragrance he could not identify. It was good to know they had both bathed today. Trying to read the page of the book she had open, he squinted. After a moment, he realized the script was written in characters he did not even recognize.

"And what language is this?" He reached over her shoulder, pointing down at the page.

"It's elvish." Madeline's own annoyance was beginning to grow. "Back in the Imperial Age, all important books were written either in elvish or celestial."

"That makes sense." He nodded. "What are you reading about?"

"Some things we were talking about back in Vindholm have given me an idea." Her voice took on an evasive tone.

Godfrey furrowed his brow but said nothing.

"Let me read more into this before we get too far into it." Madeline pointed to her stack of books. "My plan may not be feasible."

"I thought maybe Walaric and I could help." Godfrey rolled his eyes. "If you told us what you were looking for, we could make this go a bit faster."

"I appreciate it." She smiled, diffusing the tension. "But neither of you reads elvish, so I don't think there's much you can do."

Godfrey made no effort to hide his annoyance at this answer.

"I am looking for Farthest Thule," she said with a huff. "I believe I may be able to find some clues in the elves' writings that might lead us there."

"I thought so." Godfrey looked at her skeptically. "You want to ask them for help? The elves' power has all but vanished, and they have gone to great lengths to isolate themselves from the rest of us. Why would they help us?"

"The elves helped out some crusaders in the past," she reminded him. "Aside from that, the state of the crusade is pretty dire. Conrad tried to get you killed. Some crusaders have deserted. We need the help."

"Who says they simply won't try to advance their own interests even if we do persuade them to join us?" He sighed, turning away.

"Defeating Alvir is in their interest." She stood, grabbing Godfrey's face and forcing his gaze to meet hers. "This High Warlord has united the forces of darkness in a way that few others have before. Imagine if he united all the Nordsmen Clans, the trolls, the orcs, the cyclopes. Azgald already stands on the brink of destruction. Imagine if he got the necromancers on his side. Farthest Thule would not be out of Alvir's reach."

Releasing Godfrey's face, she sat again. She stared at him long and hard. He softened his expression after a moment, putting his doubts aside, despite the nagging realization that her own father had indeed pursued selfish desires in the face of Alvir's dark threat.

"Have faith," she said, noting the change in Godfrey's expression. "The gods have set you apart for something great. Who is to say this is not it?"

"If one crusader can find Farthest Thule," he agreed, "then there's no reason a crusader with a holy blade cannot."

"The Nordsmen would not spare Farthest Thule once they find it," she added. "The Clans would enslave the elves just as they have already done with the dwarves and men they have conquered."

"The elves just need to be brought to see it," Godfrey concluded. "You're right. Walaric and I don't speak elvish, but he speaks celestial. Let us help you find those clues."

"Give Walaric these." She handed Godfrey a few of the tomes on her desk. "See if he can find any reference to Farthest Thule in them."

"It will keep him from getting too bored in that infirmary anyway." Godfrey tucked the volumes under his arm.

Madeline shushed him for getting too loud, and he cringed in embarrassment.

"I'll have a look around before I go," he said.

"Have fun." She buried her face in one of the open books at her table.

Turning to the nearest shelf, Godfrey picked up a scroll at random. He unrolled the parchment, and saw that it was written in elvish too. Disappointed, he put it back, and grabbed the scroll next to it. More elvish script. The third scroll was written in celestial. He recognized the letters at least, but the words did not make any sense to him. Walking down a few aisles, he selected a very large codex with the words *Nature of the Planes* written on its spine. At least he could read the title of this one.

He hefted the codex off the shelf and set it and the books Madeline had given him on the nearest table. The covers of all of these works were old and worn. The pages were yellowed and musty. He opened the last book he had grabbed, and a few pages in the middle immediately came loose from the binding. Carefully, he turned to the first page. Though the script was miniscule, he could read the words on the first page. However, the author's introduction immediately jumped into a dense topic Godfrey was entirely unfamiliar with. There were a lot of terms he did not recognize, and trying to figure out what they were from context was proving quite tedious. Frustrated, he closed the volume and placed it back on the shelf. He gathered up the books Madeline had given him, resolving to give them to Walaric then spend the rest of his free time on less-strenuous mental activities. That was enough time with books for now.

Since Madeline insisted on solitary confinement in the library, and Walaric was still bedridden, Godfrey took up patrolling Narlstad's walls. The outer wall gave him a longer route to meander across, but the inner wall gave him a better view of the surrounding countryside from its higher vantage point. He switched between the two routes at first, but after a few days he grew tired of making idle chatter with the Silver Sun guards who were stationed along the walls.

He visited Walaric in the infirmary on occasion, but the acolyte was growing more pessimistic the longer he went without the use of his legs. Madeline did not know why her healing magic would not work, though she admitted she had never tried to use it for much more than closing her own minor cuts before. Godfrey's injuries were the most severe she had ever successfully treated. Walaric's injury was severe but not life-threatening like Godfrey's had been. It stood to reason that she should have been able to heal him if she could heal Godfrey. There was still so much Madeline did not understand about her own abilities and the limits thereof.

Godfrey eventually found himself mostly staring off into the distance from atop one of the keep's four towers. The towers had the best view, and he discovered there was only ever one tower occupied by sentries at a time. From atop the windswept tower, Godfrey spent days gazing off into the horizon. He was growing tired of dealing with people. The isolation was comforting.

The creak of the opening trapdoor made him jump in surprise. A moment before, he was leaning over the parapet, brooding over the state of the crusade. Thoughts of Tancred's treachery and punching Conrad the Wolf faded to the back of his mind as he saw Turpin emerging through the open trapdoor. The chaplain did not comment as Godfrey took a second to regain his composure.

"Some of the men are running out of money," Turpin said and grimaced, leaning against the parapet as Godfrey had been a moment before.

"So the loot from Epsberg is running out?" He resumed his spot by Turpin.

"I think Tancred reserved a larger portion for himself than he will admit," Turpin mused.

Godfrey wiped his face with his mailed gauntlet.

"If we could get moving again, the men could forage." Godfrey scanned the horizon. "They would not need to keep spending their money on the Silver Suns' food."

"Aye," Turpin agreed. "But that is not the present situation."

Godfrey felt the satchel slung on his belt. It was much lighter than when he had started the crusade. A twinge of regret streaked across his conscience. If only he had been more frugal before now. He unclasped the satchel. Reaching inside, he found he had only a few silver coins left, but there were more of the larger gold coins still.

"Divide these among the poorest of our crusaders." Godfrey handed all the gold coins to Turpin. "Discreetly, please."

Turpin counted out the gold.

"This should help." Turpin produced a few gold coins from his own bag. "But we will need to take more loot from the next battle if we want to stay on crusade any longer than that."

"I'll write father again," Godfrey added. "Maybe he can send more money."

Moving towards the trapdoor to leave, Turpin suddenly froze in place. Following the chaplain's gaze, Godfrey saw an army approaching from the east.

"The Clans?" Godfrey asked.

"No." Turpin squinted. "Look at the banners."

"Crusaders," Godfrey exclaimed. "It's Phillip!"

Phillip, Baldwin, and Torcul met Godfrey, Turpin, and Horvath in Narlstad's great hall. Many of the other crusaders and Silver Suns also filled the great hall. Godfrey caught warm greetings and rude jokes being exchanged among the reunited crusaders. It reminded him of when he was young back in Fuetoile Keep. Was Godfrey growing homesick?

"Where is your acolyte friend?" Torcul asked him, searching the noisy crowd.

"He's hurt." Godfrey frowned. "He may be crippled for the rest of his life."

"Damned shame," Torcul cursed.

"Where is Gunthar?" Godfrey changed the subject.

"He went with Oksar back to Kalscony," Torcul spat. "Gunthar the Red says that, by taking Laht, his crusading vows are fulfilled. He's going back home to Dyfred."

Godfrey shot the man a quizzical look.

"In truth," Torcul corrected, "Gunthar is abandoning us because he lost a lot of men at Laht. The coward doesn't have the stomach for this business."

"Aren't you worried about what Gunthar might do back in Cardigal while you're still here?" Godfrey remembered what he was told about the rivalry between the kingdoms of Dyfred and Ogledd.

"Aye," Torcul confessed. "But the gods watch over crusaders. Cumbria will still be there when I get back."

Phillip d'Artois cleared his throat loudly, and Godfrey and Torcul broke from their conversation. The room quieted down as all eyes turned to Phillip. The old man certainly looked the worse for wear as far as Godfrey was concerned.

"The Eastern Marches are back in our hands," Phillip announced.

Godfrey noted that the Duke of Artois did not say *Silver Suns* hands.

"I have also received news from the Ostlands," Phillip continued. "More of our Gothian brothers will be joining

Henry the Pilgrim and Raymond of Wrehst, and they will continue to aid the Silver Suns in holding that realm."

"That will leave us free to take the offensive up into Clan territory," Baldwin added.

"Precisely," Phillip agreed.

"Shouldn't we wait for Conrad the Wolf to rejoin us?" Godfrey had difficulty containing the venom in his words. "He still has a sizeable army. We were lucky and caught the Nordsmen off guard. But with Gunthar the Red returning to Cardigal, don't you think it would be wise for us to wait until Conrad is back?"

"Why would you want to wait for him?" Phillip asked. "It's no secret what happened between you and Conrad at Epsberg."

Godfrey flushed with anger and embarrassment. He only wanted to shame Conrad and Gunthar by noting their absence. He had not really thought the comment through.

"I think Conrad will be back with us soon enough," Phillip reassured Godfrey. "Morgan the Bloodied can be very persuasive."

Averting his eyes, Godfrey crossed his arms.

"By going to the Northern Marches we can draw Alvir to us," Phillip continued. "If we kill him in open battle, the Clans will be divided again."

"We almost did that already at Epsberg," Godfrey muttered.

Phillip ignored Godfrey. Baldwin and Torcul, however, gave him a concerned look. Shaking his head, Turpin gestured for Godfrey to hold his tongue.

"The Silver Suns are eternally grateful for the crusade's support," Horvath cut in. "Once our position out in the Eastern Marches has been consolidated, I am sure the Grand Master will send men to join you."

"Pskov will be our next destination," Phillip declared. "From there we could take Fhunlan or Brismarik if the gods will it."

The Duke of Artois looked into Godfrey's eyes as if daring him to challenge the decision. Godfrey only frowned, and stared at the floor. He was growing tired of this constant contest of wills. He missed home.

Chapter Twenty-One

A week later, Godfrey spotted Conrad the Wolf and Duke Tancred's armies approaching Narlstad with Morgan the Bloodied and his Silver Suns. Madeline stood atop the southeastern tower with him. She held his hand. Though right now, it was little comfort to Godfrey.

"You still haven't finished reading those books in the library?" Godfrey asked more to divert his attention from the sight of Conrad and Tancred's approach than anything else.

"Translating elvish is a difficult task," Madeline admitted. "The verb stems can change pretty radically depending on the form, and elvish writers are known for using some rather poetic expressions even on mundane topics."

"Sounds tough," Godfrey agreed, only partly understanding her explanation. "Walaric hasn't found anything helpful in the books you gave him, either."

"I didn't say I haven't found anything helpful," she corrected.

"So where do you think Farthest Thule is?" Godfrey's full attention was now on her. "What did you find?"

"Some elvish poetry makes mention of a 'home with the dragons high and cold'." Madeline looked out past the horizon. "Other poems talk of 'silver halls'."

"Well that's obviously the Wyrmwind Peaks," Godfrey hissed. "How has no one figured this out before now?"

"Elvish is a hard language to translate." Madeline emphasized this point with a gesture. "For instance, 'dragon' could be a metaphor for something hard or dangerous. Depending on the context, it could mean just about anything really. 'Silver' can also be an insult if contrasted with 'gold', but it just means 'wealth' a lot of the time. It's not very direct, and there's a lot of symbolism, idiomatic expressions, that sort of thing. Others have translated those phrases to mean entirely different things."

"Then how are you sure?" he pressed.

"I'm not entirely sure actually," she admitted. "It's a hunch, a starting point. I still have more to read through."

Godfrey's attention was back on the approaching host. They were almost at the open fortress gates. Madeline gripped his hand again and squeezed it tightly. She looked at Godfrey with all the intensity a young woman could ever feel. The two exchanged a long kiss.

"I won't marry Conrad." Madeline's expression was resolute. "Father can't make me."

"Refusing a duke can be difficult," Godfrey countered.

"You're also the son of a duke," Madeline said. "Have your father write my father."

"Okay." Godfrey bit his lip, thinking of his father for the first time in too long.

Godfrey felt the slightest twinge of guilt. He had written the letter asking his father for more money, but he had not written any other letters back home for any other reason since then. Then again, no one back home had bothered writing him in all this time, either. Godfrey should have received a response to his first letter by now.

"Would you be all right leaving Azgald?" he asked. "Lortharain is pretty far."

"A lady's place is always uncertain until she is married." Madeline shrugged. "Often her home in adult life is determined by which lord can best negotiate with her father."

Godfrey was about to say something, but she put her finger to his lips.

"Just make sure your father negotiates better than Conrad," she reassured him. "He's a brute I really don't want to spend the rest of my life with."

"You will like Bastogne," Godfrey promised. "It's not so cold there, and it's a wealthy duchy. King Wilhelm is not the greatest lord we have ever had, but he hardly ever visits Bastogne. He won't stick his nose into things too often."

"I'm sure there will be much to love about that land." She smiled.

Madeline gestured to the trapdoor on the tower roof, and Godfrey opened it for her. She descended the ladder, and he followed her. For how cold and drafty he generally found the tower, it was certainly much warmer than outside.

"Where are we going?" he asked once they had reached the bottom of the ladder.

"We're going to see father, of course," Madeline answered, descending the stairs.

Conrad and Tancred had gathered in the great hall with Horvath, Morgan, and their retainers. They did not seem to notice Godfrey and Madeline enter the chamber at first, as they were caught up in a heated discussion. Madeline gestured for Godfrey to join her in a corner of the room away from the discussion. Hoping to remain unnoticed, he complied.

"No." Tancred gestured to Horvath. "I'll take the hundred talents of gold now, thanks."

"All treaties negotiated with the Grand Master must be ratified by a quorum of three lesser marshals before they are official." Horvath shrugged unhelpfully. "You know this is our order's law."

"You agreed to pay one hundred gold talents for our services in reclaiming Epsberg for the Silver Suns." Conrad pointed an accusing finger at Morgan. "Pay up."

"Are you a crusader or a mercenary?" Morgan waved away Conrad's finger before turning to Tancred. "I agreed to pay the hundred talents as a ransom to get you out of Epsberg, you traitor. Since I did not say when I would pay it, you will have to be patient while I procure the funds."

Torcul, Baldwin, and some of the other crusaders entered the great hall, initially attracted by Conrad and Tancred's arrival. The argument attracted more crusaders and Silver Suns. Godfrey spotted Turpin and some of the other Bastognians among them.

"You and I both know Epsberg is worth far more than the hundred talents," Tancred said in dismissal of Morgan's accusation.

Morgan's face twitched in agitation.

"You said you needed a quorum of three to ratify this treaty?" Tancred continued, indicating Conrad. "Well, how about our quorum of almost eight thousand soldiers already inside Narlstad's walls? We'll take the gold by force."

"This is outrageous," Morgan spat.

"I won't stand for it," Godfrey interjected, pushing forward. "Your greed will be your undoing, Duke of Pavik."

Tancred's ire now found its focus on Godfrey. Standing right in front of the Duke of Pavik, Godfrey took a deep breath. He puffed out his chest, hoping to appear confident.

"Earlier I prophesied that this crusade will fail unless a dragon is slain." Godfrey pointed to the heraldic device on Tancred's tabard. "Maybe that dragon is you."

"Ah yes." Tancred gave a bemused smirk. "Godfrey de Bastogne."

"But no longer heir to Bastogne." Malice dripped from Conrad's words.

"What do you mean?" Godfrey narrowed his eyes in suspicion.

"We came across a couple of friends of yours on the way over here." Conrad stepped to the side, gesturing back to the hall's entrance.

Godfrey blinked in disbelief. Bishop Clovis and one of Godfrey's father's knights, Karl the Hammer, stood in front of him. The Bishop's face was creased with a frown. He had aged a lot. What had brought these two all the way up here?

"We need to confer in private, Godfrey," Clovis advised.

"There's no need for privacy," Conrad boorishly insisted. "You already told us. By now, all the crusaders in Narlstad know. Please tell everyone here!"

"It's all right." Godfrey gave the Bishop an uncertain smile. "Go ahead and say it."

"Your father has not been able to respond to your letter because he died shortly before it arrived," Clovis explained. "Sir Karl and I came up to tell you personally because King Wilhelm has installed his own nephew as the new Duke of Bastogne."

Clovis and Karl whisked Godfrey and Turpin away and huddled in a corner of the great hall out of earshot of Tancred and Conrad. The Bishop put a finger to his lips, indicating they should whisper. Turpin nodded in agreement, and Godfrey swallowed hard in an attempt to control his emotions.

"Father's dead," Godfrey began, his hand trembling with shock and anger. "But my birthright…"

"King Wilhelm argues that all dukes derive their authority from the King," Karl spat. "So it is ultimately his right to choose who the dukes are."

"That just slaps hundreds of years of tradition in the face." Turpin gritted his teeth, enraged.

"I don't agree with this decision." Clovis shook his head. "But it is not without precedent. King Wilhelm has his supporters back in Lortharain."

"Well so do we," Turpin countered, his nostrils flaring and his eyes wild. "A crusader's lands are inviolate while he is away. How is a crusader's inheritance any different?"

Godfrey had never seen Turpin so visibly angry before. Even when the chaplain struck Godfrey back at Fuetoile Keep, he did so with the restraint of a parent disciplining a child. Now Turpin was uncontrolled and furious. He paced back and forth for a moment, allowing his rage to subside.

"Godfrey." Turpin regained a measure of control in his voice. "Harv will support your claim to Bastogne. Your cousin, Fallard, will aid you in battle. We have thousands of Bastognian men right here battle-hardened and loyal to you. We can be back in Lortharain in just a few weeks, and restore the Duchy to you with six months of hard fighting at most."

Tancred and Conrad now stood with crossed arms in front of Godfrey and his allies. Their conversation could no longer be private. Karl gave Godfrey a reassuring wink before they turned out of their huddle to face Conrad and Tancred.

"I was able to secure a score of gold talents from Fuetoile Keep before leaving," Karl the Hammer added loudly enough for everyone in the great hall to hear. "The Bishop and I brought them with us for you to keep your army in the field long enough to retake Bastogne."

Tancred shot Bishop Clovis a surprised look. Obviously, neither he nor Conrad had known about the gold Karl had taken from Bastogne.

"More correctly," the Bishop explained, catching Tancred's eye, "we left the gold under guard at Vindholm until we could make contact with you, Godfrey."

Looking from Turpin to Morgan and Tancred, Godfrey felt the weight of the whole crusade upon his shoulders. All eyes were upon him. He still had five thousand infantry and four hundred knights with him. With twenty gold talents added, Godfrey could do something with that for at least a little while longer.

"Ghend will also support you," Baldwin added, cursing. "If that's how Wilhelm treats his vassals, we'll put him in his place."

The crusaders began to murmur as Tancred and Conrad exchanged uneasy glances. They obviously had underestimated Godfrey's popularity. This was not the reaction either had foreseen. Godfrey supposed that Tancred and Conrad had been hoping this news would simply force him out of the crusade landless and destitute. Comprehension dawned on their faces as they realized that was not going to happen.

"I appreciate the thought, Baldwin." Godfrey took on a mollifying tone. "But my crusading vows have not yet been fulfilled. I'll not draw half of the crusade back to Lortharain with me for my own benefit. As Torcul said earlier, home will still be there when we get back."

Godfrey turned to the room at large. Phillip had also entered the great hall at some point, without his knowledge until now. Godfrey's reaction had stunned them all into silence.

"Some have already abandoned the crusade." Godfrey gestured to the room. "Constant bickering and infighting have already robbed us of victory at least once. How many more crusaders need to desert or be killed before we stop trying to stab each other in the back?"

He turned to Tancred. Fire still burned in the Duke's eyes. If there was ever a time to be bold, it was now.

"The Duke of Pavik used the good faith of the crusade to steal a ransom from the Silver Suns," Godfrey declared. "I decree that any contract made between the Silver Suns and the Duchy of Pavik regarding Epsberg is void."

"By what authority can you make such a claim?" Tancred sneered. "You have no lands or titles to support you."

"I am the champion of the gods." Godfrey unsheathed Uriel, flashing the blade in Tancred's face. "If my word does not mean anything, then what does?"

Cold fury emanated from Tancred as he stared Godfrey down. Godfrey did not flinch. Tancred looked to Conrad, but the Duke of Errans appeared uncertain. Seeing no support, Tancred snorted in disgust.

"I'll not forget this." Tancred pointed to Godfrey. "My men and I will leave immediately. Do not expect further help from us."

Thinking better of it, Godfrey held back a retort about not wanting such help in the first place.

With that, Tancred stormed off. Godfrey sheathed his sword, breathing a sigh of relief. Conrad hesitated as if unsure whether he should follow Tancred or remain in the great hall. Conrad's gaze met Godfrey's, and the Duke of Errans turned away angrily. Yet Conrad still did not leave.

"Don't think for one moment that we are friends," he muttered as Godfrey approached him.

"I wouldn't dream of it." Godfrey shook his head. "But can I count on you to work with me for the crusade?"

"I'm here aren't I?" Conrad stared at the floor.

"Let's take another day or two before leaving Narlstad," Godfrey suggested, looking to Phillip. "Give the men of Errans time to rest from their march."

Phillip nodded in agreement. Godfrey hoped the Duke of Artois appreciated his effort to defer to his leadership. Morgan and Horvath approached Godfrey as the room began to buzz with activity.

"I was wrong about you," Morgan apologized. "You have made a friend of the Silver Suns this day."

"I'm just trying to do what's right," Godfrey answered.

Morgan nodded, and Godfrey bowed in return.

Godfrey turned to Bishop Clovis and Karl the Hammer. "Welcome to Azgald. Thank you both for coming so far."

"Certainly," the Bishop agreed.

"Walaric was gravely injured." Godfrey frowned. "He lost the use of his legs in battle on the way here. He's in the infirmary."

"I'll see to him," the Bishop reassured Godfrey, though he winced at this news.

"I fear my presence back in Lortharain will not be welcome given the circumstances under which I had to bring you your father's gold," Karl admitted, clearing his throat. "But it was your father's dying wish that I bring you as much of your inheritance as I could."

"Twenty talents is a lot," Godfrey said.

"We had help," Karl added. "But even with help, the transfer did not go unnoticed. There was blood spilt in

Fuetoile Keep. Only Bishop Clovis's protection saw us the rest of the way."

"I see." Godfrey grimaced, imagining the gold-laden carts under attack. "You were always a loyal knight in my father's household, and you have shown me loyalty through your actions here today. House Cretus will honor your loyalty."

"Thank you, sire." Karl bowed.

"You've seen my father's chaplain, Turpin, still in our company," Godfrey added. "Sir Rodair is here too. I think there are others here you should know as well."

Leaning on the shaft of his heavy two-handed maul, Karl knelt in front of Godfrey.

"In this moment I swear fealty to you as I did to your father in past years." Karl kept his eyes to the floor. "In this same moment I also vow to join the crusade until its successful completion. May the gods witness my vows."

"I accept your oath of fealty." Godfrey offered his hand to Karl, bidding him to rise.

"And the celestial gods accept your crusading vow as well," Bishop Clovis acknowledged with a gesture to the heavens.

Standing, Karl the Hammer embraced Godfrey as tradition demanded. What a rare thing, Godfrey thought. How many men had he met on crusade who acted out of pure self-interest? Yet Karl the Hammer acted out of pure loyalty to Godfrey's now-dead father.

After Godfrey released Karl from the embrace, Turpin slapped the knight on the back. Karl turned and smirked at the grizzled chaplain. There was a knowing gleam in both men's eyes; something that came from years of hard trials endured together.

"Your maul is greatly needed up here," Turpin said.

"To outdo Rodair's sword and Euric's ax once again," Karl reminisced aloud on days past.

"Rodair's sword yes," Turpin agreed with a frown. "But not Sir Euric's ax."

"He died saving me at Epsberg," Godfrey added solemnly.

"Then it was a good death." Karl nodded in understanding. "That's not the sword you came on crusade with, is it, Godfrey?"

"Yes actually," Godfrey said, drawing the blade from its sheath for Karl and Clovis to examine. "The gods blessed it at the Temple of Spes back in Vindholm."

"That is a rare honor," the Bishop noted. "Even the most holy paladins are considered fortunate to be granted such favors."

"But why?" Godfrey asked. "This sword has caused as much resentment among my fellow crusaders as it has helped me in battle."

This was the question he had been hoping his father could answer for him in his first letter home. However, with his father gone, Bishop Clovis was probably the next best person for Godfrey to confide in. In a lot of ways, Bishop Clovis was probably the more qualified person to consult, he thought. The reality of the loss of Godfrey's father was only now just beginning to sink in, but with so much going on there was little time to contemplate this latest death.

"The gods have their purposes," Clovis answered. "Sometimes we only see those purposes in hindsight. But I don't think the gods give us any challenges we are not ready to face. You seem quite adept at using that blade in more situations than simple combat anyway."

"That's true," Godfrey acknowledged, thinking back to Tancred's almost frightened expression as he waved Uriel in front of him.

The thought of Tancred reminded him that he had left Madeline in the corner alone. He turned back, searching for her, but she was gone. Scanning the crowd, he still could not find her among them.

"Excuse me, Bishop," Godfrey dismissed himself, going back the way he had come.

Walking slowly through the great hall, he did not see Madeline anywhere in the room. Was she using her magical abilities to hide? Why would she hide from him?

He retraced his steps back to the tower his and Madeline's rooms were in. Not finding Madeline in either his room or hers, he climbed the ladder to the tower roof. She was there, watching the men of Pavik departing through the gate they had entered only shortly before.

"You did not even say hello to your father," Godfrey observed.

"He seemed rather busy." She brushed off the comment, attempting to restrain the emotion in her voice.

"I suppose asking for your father's permission to marry you is off the table now." Godfrey gave a humorless smile.

"It seems that way." Madeline's tone was evasive.

"What if we eloped?" he asked.

Blushing, Madeline averted her eyes. Stung, Godfrey wondered why that was not an option. There did not have to be so much ceremony and ritual with everything.

"How long until your father figures out you aren't heading back to Pavik?" Godfrey changed topics.

"Traveling with the army," Madeline thought for a moment, "I'd say we have about a day or so before he reaches the site of the attack."

"He'll think you've been killed." Godfrey began thinking through the possible implications. "Or he'll think you've been captured."

"Some of the men of Pavik saw me here," Madeline assured him. "Once Father comes across the attack site, someone will come forward and tell him I'm here."

"Then he'll march right back here and fetch you," Godfrey finished, exacerbated. "Why don't you just save him the trouble, and catch up with him? You could take Moon Frost; Walaric's not using his horse here at Narlstad."

"I don't plan to be here by the time Father and his men sort out where I am versus where I am supposed to be," Madeline divulged. "Godfrey, remember Farthest Thule…"

A loud creak came from the trapdoor behind Godfrey, startling both Madeline and him. Turpin opened the door, revealing his head. Clambering up through the portal, Turpin looked at the two of them disapprovingly.

"This is no time to be getting romantic," he scolded them. "You know, Godfrey, the longer we stay in Azgald, the harder it will be for you to reclaim Bastogne."

"I know," Godfrey begrudgingly admitted. "But I already said I'm not going back until my crusading vows have been fulfilled."

"Yes," Turpin agreed. "But right now, even with Conrad the Wolf back, we only have a little under twenty thousand crusaders here at Narlstad. The castles we took in the Eastern Marches were small. Morgan the Bloodied assures me that the fortresses in the Northern Marches are much more formidable. They will not be taken so easily."

"And Morgan the Bloodied can't spare any of his Silver Suns to help after you did so much for him?" Madeline crossed her arms.

"No." Godfrey frowned. "They can't afford to only leave behind token garrisons in their newly won fortresses. They'd lose their castles just as quickly as they regained them. What about King Lothar's army?"

"Word is they have taken heavy losses." Turpin grimaced. "The King is currently gathering more men at Pskov."

"Godfrey…" Madeline's expression was determined. "I think we should go looking for Farthest Thule. It's the best chance we have for getting any kind of help attacking the Northern Marches."

"The crusade can't get lost looking for something we don't even know is there," Turpin countered.

"I'll go," Godfrey declared. "Turpin, you lead the men in my place until I return. Madeline, I'll need you to guide me to the Wyrmwind Peaks."

"I thought you'd never ask." Madeline could hardly contain her excitement.

Chapter Twenty-Two

"You can't wait?" Walaric exclaimed, sitting up in his bed in the infirmary. "I can feel my legs again. The doctors say with a few more days of rest I should be able to walk. After a couple of weeks maybe I can travel again."

"It's not that we want to leave you." Godfrey frowned, exchanging a glance with Madeline. "We've just been at Narlstad for a while already, and the crusade needs to move on."

"We spoke to Bishop Clovis," Madeline added. "He will stay with you until you are fully recovered, then he'll help you link up with us again."

"And you're pretty sure you can find Farthest Thule?" The tension in Walaric's voice eased off. "And you can bring an army of elves back with you?"

"We have no idea how long this will take," Madeline confessed. "But we are pretty sure Wyrmwind Peaks is the best place to start looking."

"That's why we can't wait any longer." Godfrey spread out his hands in an apologizing gesture. "Who knows what will happen to the crusade if we are gone too long."

"The only thing we know for sure is that it's not going in a good direction now," Walaric agreed. "Bringing in some help may change that."

"I really wish we could wait for you," Madeline sighed.

"It's all right." Walaric waved dismissively. "Really, don't worry about me."

He laid himself back down in his bed, getting more comfortable.

"Oh Madeline," Walaric added. "You can take Moon Frost with you."

"Thanks, Walaric." Madeline squeezed the acolyte's hand briefly before turning to leave. "I know there's not many horses to spare right now."

"That's why I'm letting you borrow Moon Frost," Walaric said. "There's not many to spare. I feel a lot better knowing Moon Frost will be with you than some knight I don't know."

"We'll see you again soon," Godfrey promised.

"Yeah." Walaric cracked a smile. "Don't do anything foolish without me."

"How could anything foolish happen without you?" Godfrey winked before leaving the infirmary.

Setting out from Narlstad, Godfrey followed Madeline to the Wyrmwind Peaks. He rode Baruch while she rode Moon Frost. A sadness lurking in the back of his mind threatened to seep through his whole being. He suppressed the feelings of remorse by focusing on the trees on either side of the road. Madeline had been ambushed here not long before. Vigilance was required now.

"How are you doing?" she asked over her shoulder after a long period of silence.

"Well," Godfrey answered without thinking.

"You haven't said anything about your father's death," she noted. "Are you sure?"

"What is there to say?" Godfrey shrugged. "I have lost a lot of people I loved lately. Is there anything left to say?"

"How did he die?" Madeline slowed her horse to ride beside him.

In that moment, he realized he had been hiding his feelings of grief ever since he first heard his father died. Godfrey had kept busy as his father himself had suggested when his mother died. He had tried not to think about it. King Wilhelm's seizure of Bastogne had overshadowed Duke Ulric's death. The pain from that wrong transformed into an anger that made Godfrey's jaw tighten. That anger was something he could focus on. He could eventually correct the wrong that caused it—once the crusade was over.

"Bishop Clovis tells me he died peacefully in his sleep." Godfrey frowned. "I wish I could have been there. But so much has happened here too."

"But you still miss him dearly." She nodded in understanding. "I can tell he meant a lot to you."

Godfrey nodded but said nothing. Swallowing hard, he hoped she would not notice. The pair rode in silence for a while.

"Right now I am a knight without a lord," he said. Then after a pause he added, "I have no lands or titles; only my crusading vows."

"You're like a paladin," she observed. "You are a lone warrior with only your patron god for your lord."

"Exactly," he agreed. "Did you ever hear the Tale of Cheldric?"

"Is that the one where King Lambert's nephew dies with an arrow through the heart?" She tried to recall the details.

"That's not how he dies in the version I know," he replied, frowning. "Anyway, Cheldric is mostly worried about doing his duty to the King, right?"

"Yes," she agreed.

"He goes through a lot of really hard things because that's what duty is all about," Godfrey continued. "Right now my duty is to the gods while on crusade. I promised to go through some really hard things, but the gods will reward my faith in the end."

"They always do." She made a pious gesture.

They continued riding side-by-side in silence again. The forest was quiet. After debating the issue in his head for some time, Godfrey decided it was actually warmer than when he first arrived in Azgald, though not by much.

Pulling back on Moon Frost's reins, Madeline gestured for Godfrey to halt. She looked to her right, and he followed her gaze. A narrow dirt path led off the main road.

"There." Madeline pointed to the path. "That will take us north up to the Wyrmwind Peaks."

Godfrey had not spotted the path the first time he went down this road in search of Madeline, nor on their way back. It was much darker when he was on this part of the road the first time, so he was not surprised he had missed this detail. He also had not been looking for such paths the first time, he reminded himself.

"Well," he said as he took the lead down the path. "There's not much chance we'll run across your father on this little trail."

"That is to our advantage," she agreed. "The road is mostly through wilderness from here. If we continue on narrow horse trails like this, we will avoid most towns and castles, but it will be faster than the larger roads."

"Good thing we packed lots of provisions," Godfrey thought aloud, slapping one of Baruch's saddlebags.

The path was barely wide enough for the horses. Godfrey's cloak caught on a stray branch more than once. This road had been used so infrequently that the forest had almost entirely reclaimed it.

As evening drew closer, Godfrey's stomach began to growl with hunger. He sucked on his waterskin, hoping to stave off the sensation. It was something he had learned to do on many such treks as a squire. The emptiness of hunger would soon return, but Godfrey could put it off for a while this way.

"Let's stop and eat," Madeline suggested.

"Gladly." He immediately stopped and dismounted Baruch. "I was just thinking about dinner too."

Madeline dismounted Moon Frost and took a piece of tough salted beef from her bag. Godfrey, likewise, began chewing on a very similar piece of beef from his own satchel. The meat was sinewy, and he swallowed his bite hard. Reluctantly, he took another bite. This one was better. More of the beef strip was gristly sinew than not. He only finished eating it so that it would not go to waste. Still, it left him feeling sick rather than satisfied.

"Well…" Madeline's hands were on her hips. "Aren't you going to gather some firewood? I can set the blaze with my magic, but I can't get all of the wood myself."

"No fires." Godfrey shook his head. "We don't want to attract any attention."

With a sigh, she finished eating her strip of meat. She gave Moon Frost a handful of grain from one of her saddlebags, and Godfrey followed suit with Baruch. The light was quickly fading now. Godfrey unpacked Madeline's bedroll and laid it out for her before grabbing his own off Baruch.

"Thank you." She pulled the bedroll around herself.

"I think there was something in the code of chivalry about treating women nicely," he said, smirking.

"Isn't chivalry all about courtly behavior?" She cocked her head.

"Actually," he corrected, "it's mostly about combat etiquette. Show respect to enemy knights, restraint when dealing with prisoners. There's a lot more about challenging an enemy to a duel and resolving that in an honorable way than anything else really."

"Oh." Madeline had not considered much about chivalry outside of her own experience with it at court. "Did you think about how this must look to the crusaders?"

"How what must look?" he asked, surprised by the sudden change in topic.

"You lose your inheritance," she started. "You promise to continue on the crusade, but then you run off by yourself. Surely some of the other crusaders must think you've deserted."

"This was your idea," he countered. "Besides, I didn't run off by myself. I have you guiding me through the Nordslands."

"That's true." She smiled. "I'm just saying we should hurry. If we take too long, doubt will start to spread. Desertion is contagious."

"I know," he concurred, wrapping himself in his bedroll. "But Turpin is a stern disciplinarian. He won't suffer any desertions."

The next morning, Godfrey awoke to see Madeline approaching with her cloak bunched up like a sack. Stretching, he sat up. With a smile, she spread her cloak out on the ground next to him.

"They're ice berries," she explained, revealing a mound of glossy red fruit in the center of her cloak. "They're a bit sour even when ripe, but they're very nutritious."

"Thanks," he said, eyeing the berries.

Tentatively plucking a berry from the pile, Godfrey popped it into his mouth whole. He discovered the skin of the berry was tough and flavorless as he probed it with his tongue. Biting down on the fruit, he was surprised at how thin the berry's skin was despite its toughness. The sour berry juice immediately shocked his tongue. Instinctively, he almost spat it out, but he quickly became accustomed to the taste. Swallowing it, he noted Madeline was eating the berries two or three at a time.

"A bit sour is an understatement," he complained, grabbing another berry.

"You get used to it." She shrugged, popping a few more berries into her mouth.

"It's better than that cut of beef at least," he consoled himself. "Next time, we try some before setting out."

She nodded in agreement.

A distinct chirping started up from some bushes not far from them. As she had said he would, Godfrey had quickly acquired the taste for ice berries, but they were not very filling. Madeline's pile of foraged berries was quickly shrinking, and he yearned for something more than berries and trail rations.

"Are those pheasants?" He tilted his head in the direction of the chirping.

"I think so." She turned in the direction of the sound.

"If I had brought a bow." He gave a rueful smile. "But we can't waste too much time foraging."

"Watch this," she said, and raised her eyebrows mischievously.

Holding her hand out in front of her, she faced the bush the pheasants were in. She concentrated on her hand. A small white orb of flame appeared, hovering just over her palm. Godfrey was prepared for something like this, but he took a step back all the same. With a look from her, the fire orb shot out from her hand, igniting the bush. The chirping momentarily turned into a horrid shriek, then went silent.

"There." She turned back to him. "They're already cooked."

Godfrey stammered.

"I can't do that all the time," Madeline answered his unasked question. "It's like running. If I do too much all at once, I get tired. But the more I do it, the easier it gets."

"I see…" He hesitated.

"Go on." She indicated the burned-out bush and pheasants. "Get them before they get too cold."

Godfrey and Madeline continued along the trail for another four days. Remembering her prior warning back at Narlstad, he did not even think of trying anything unchivalrous with her. She occasionally used her fire spells to catch some animal to eat, but he grudgingly suggested she not use them too frequently, to avoid unwanted attention should anyone happen to be nearby. Second-rate trail rations would have to be their main food source.

Eventually, the two reached another larger road. Madeline told Godfrey it was the road to Pskov. They followed it west for two days before diverting to another horse trail moving to the northwest. After two more days on this trail, they reached a river.

"This is the Irelven." She indicated the swift current. "This river serves as the boundary between Azgald and the Five Clans."

"There is a ford we can cross just a little upstream." He pointed. "We must be cautious crossing it."

"Also," she said, pointing to some distant mountains beyond the tree line, "those are the Wyrmwind Peaks. Another day and we'll be at the mountains."

"And Farthest Thule is somewhere up there." He took in the grandeur of the tall, distant mountains.

"This is only the southernmost part of the Wyrmwind Peaks," she said. "The mountain range extends north for more than a fortnight more."

"And what is beyond that?" he wondered aloud.

"As far as we know, more mountains." She frowned. "Much more beyond that, and we will have reached a land where there is snow all year long. It is too cold for men to stay for long, so anything farther than that is unknown to us."

"Hence *Farthest Thule*," he finished her thought.

Godfrey began crossing the babbling ford at a prudent pace with Madeline following close behind. One misstep and Baruch could be swept out from under him. When he was a squire, Fallard had told him more than one cautionary tale concerning the dangers of crossing streams and rivers too quickly.

At two thirds of the way across the ford, Godfrey heard several distinct twangs. He was confused as much as startled, unable to identify the sounds. A second series of twangs, and Godfrey saw the accompanying volley of whizzing crossbow bolts this time. The darts were coming from the woods on the other side of the bank. Spurring Baruch forward, he drew his sword.

Meeting an ambush head-on was always Godfrey's first response. If he'd had a javelin or a bow, he might have fallen back to seek cover. But as it was, with more of the river behind Madeline and him than not, and no cover until they reached the shore, charging forward to neutralize the threat was the only immediately available option.

Even at the best spot he could find to ford, the river was perilously deep. Baruch's charge through the water was labored and ineffective. The steed did not make it far.

Three bolts drove through Baruch one after another as fast as Godfrey could count them. Throwing him from the saddle, Baruch reared before crashing on his side into the water. Godfrey plunged into the water face-first. The frigid, murky current stung his skin. Pushing himself back to the surface, he coughed up the water caught in his lungs. He choked a moment more before regaining his bearings. The water was up to his armpits. There was no sign of Baruch.

Moon Frost was also nowhere to be seen. Madeline was next to the shoreline drenched from head to toe. Gouts of white-hot flame leapt from her outstretched fingers into the trees as she shouted incoherently. The hidden crossbowmen replied with squeals of surprise and sharp pain.

Sluggishly, Godfrey waded through the Irelven to catch up with Madeline. He still had Uriel in hand, and he unslung his shield from his back. As he progressed towards the shore, the water grew shallower. By the time the water was down to his shins, his movement was relatively unimpeded though his soaked clothing still weighed him down.

Madeline shot the white flames wildly from her hands at anything that moved through the trees. An orc in heavy mail armor rushed her, but she turned her fire on the unfortunate creature as soon as it caught her eye. The orc barely had time to gasp as it was incinerated.

Two more orcs came at her from her left and right sides simultaneously. Madeline launched a fireball at the one to her left, but the one to her right quickly closed in on her, raising its sword. With hardly a second to spare, Godfrey launched himself at the orc. Tackling the beast to the ground, he pummeled its face until it went limp.

Surprised, Madeline looked down at him and offered her hand. Taking it, he stood. His breathing was heavy. She was pale and shivering. The smell of scorched wood and burnt meat filled his nose. Knowing what that meaty smell was made him gag.

"I thought you were dead." She looked him over.

"I'm not hurt," Godfrey replied. "But the horses…"

"I know." She frowned.

Madeline froze in place at the sound of movement. Godfrey turned in the direction of the sound. A tall woman in dark robes carrying a jeweled staff emerged from beyond the burnt foliage, flanked by a party of orcs with swords and crossbows.

"That's Nera," Madeline whispered frantically. "She's the Great Witch of the North."

"You were right, Urzg." Nera turned to the orcs' leader. "A fledgling sorceress has been burning her way through the woods."

Urzg and his oath-warriors looked at the witch nervously. Their faith in their mistress and their own prowess was great, but they also saw what Madeline had done to their kin. Orcs were not fools.

"She's all spent now," Nera reassured the orcs. "Take her."

Madeline gave Godfrey a nervous smile, confirming Nera was right. Raising his shield, he stepped in front of Madeline to protect her. There were ten or so orcs with Nera. They wore more armor than most orcs Godfrey had seen, and they carried themselves with a confidence he was unaccustomed to seeing in their race. Still, he was far more worried about the witch than the orcs.

A pair of the orc oath-warriors stepped in to meet Godfrey. He struck out at one, but the orc deflected his blade with a parry, and offered an immediate riposte. Unprepared for the disciplined strike coming from an orc, he felt the sting of the blade run across his shoulder. Feinting, Godfrey slashed the orc's face, dropping it. The second orc thrust its blade at him, and he barely parried the blow. Their blades scraping against each other, Godfrey exchanged several blows with the second orc and a third that had taken the place of its fallen companion.

A blow to the helmet dazed Godfrey momentarily, but he cleaved into the torso of one of the orcs with a slash. Using his momentum, he thrust towards the next orc. Uriel hissed as the blade plunged into the beast. As Godfrey turned to the remaining orcs, their confidence vanished.

With a smirk, Nera waved her staff. Mimicking the motion of the staff, some unseen force lifted Godfrey off the ground and threw him into a nearby tree. He fell to the ground hard, the wind knocked out of him. Every part of him ached. Lying on his belly, he tried to stand, but he could not move. For a long moment all Godfrey could do was breathe motionlessly on the ground.

"Check him," Nera ordered one of the orcs. "Make sure he's dead."

Complying with its lady's command, an orc crunched through the snow towards Godfrey. The creature stopped and hunched over his prone form, sniffing suspiciously. After a moment, the orc stood and gave him a sharp swift kick. Anticipating this, Godfrey gritted his teeth to avoid crying out. Satisfied Godfrey was dead, the orc returned to Nera.

"Such a disappointing end." Nera huffed contemptuously. "Well, Alvir will be happy to know you're dead at least."

Screaming, Madeline ran toward Godfrey, but the orcs intercepted her. They dragged her in front of the witch. Realizing her struggle was useless, Madeline stopped resisting.

"What do you want with me?" Madeline glared at Nera defiantly.

"You will help me awaken Vozzab." Nera smirked.

"The legends…" Madeline's eyes narrowed in understanding.

"Magic runs through your blood," Nera continued. "And dragon-slayers are also in your blood, Madeline of Pavik. Yes, we have sought you long, but we only had to wait for you to come to our lands."

With a swift gesture, Nera signaled for the orcs to take Madeline away. Nera followed her and the orcs. Having watched the exchange from the corner of his eye, Godfrey realized they were beginning to leave. He attempted to stand, but only managed to raise himself up with one arm. He collapsed, losing consciousness.

Godfrey awoke several hours later. It was dark. He was still in the woods. The fires had put themselves out long ago, and the scent of smoke and burnt flesh had dissipated.

Standing, he heard the current of the Irelven behind him. He remembered where he was.

"But how can I chase after them on foot?" he muttered.

Wiping dried blood from his nose, Godfrey limped in the direction he thought Nera had taken Madeline. He had no way of knowing if this was even really the right way. They could have turned onto a path Godfrey could not now see. He did not even know where they had gone. His only clue was something about awakening someone named Vozzab.

After fumbling through the dark for longer than even Godfrey thought was rational, he tripped over a fallen tree branch. He fell with his head hitting the mud first. Only his spangenhelm's flared nose guard prevented any serious injury to his face. He stood. Kicking the branch, he screamed at the top of his lungs.

He could not follow Madeline. She was captured with no chance of rescue. Walaric was back at Narlstad. Baruch was dead. His father and mother were dead. Godfrey could not even begin to try to find his way back to the crusade. He had not the slightest clue how he was going to find Farthest Thule.

Silently, he cursed himself for letting Madeline talk him into such a vain and foolish quest. He should have stuck with the crusade. That would have been far more practical.

Godfrey had let some stupid notion of being the champion of the gods trick him into believing fate would somehow lead him right to Farthest Thule. He had thought he could just walk into the city gates unopposed. The elves, with their millennia-long lives and wisdom to match, would surely listen to a pair of human youths. Or so Godfrey had thought until now. Now it all seemed so foolish. Hot tears of rage burned in his eyes at not thinking this through further.

"What am I supposed to do now?" He shook his fist at the sky.

The stars stared back cold and silent.

The orcs dragged Madeline through the woods. Tripping over a tree root, Madeline stumbled a few paces as the orcs gruffly shoved her on. The brute Nera had identified as Urzg grunted something to the witch Madeline did not quite understand. Glancing back at Madeline, Nera halted, and the orcs followed suit. Procuring a set of copper manacles, Nera removed Madeline's gloves, and bound her wrists with the curious object.

"Copper drains your powers," Nera responded to Madeline's bewildered expression. "You'll find that as long as these manacles touch your skin, you won't be able to burn any more of Urzg's oath-warriors."

"I didn't know copper could do that." Madeline looked at the manacles skeptically.

"There is a lot about magic Azgaldians don't know." Nera sneered. "They put so much emphasis on restraint. It's no wonder a young sorceress like you has no idea how far your powers could extend or what limits you really have."

Madeline frowned.

"Did your parents instruct you to hide your powers because people would not understand?" Nera rolled her eyes. "Have you ever been called a witch? People fear magic, and they should. But in the Five Clans, magicians have power. In your home, you must either conceal your powers or live as an outcast."

"Suffer not the witch to live," Madeline muttered.

She remembered the ancient commandment. Witchcraft was rare, and old laws concerning magic were not always strictly enforced. Yet there was a certain truth to Nera's words as Madeline had told Godfrey back at Vindholm. Even if there was much Madeline would disagree with Nera on regarding religion, leadership, and a thousand other topics, she was right about Azgaldians' fear of magic.

"But look at you," Madeline continued. "Aren't witches like you exactly why people are afraid of magic? You abuse your powers to scare your subjects into submission."

"And King Lothar's armies don't scare his subjects into submission?" Nera countered. "The only law in this world is force. A shame you were not born into Clan Black Dragon. I could have reached you much earlier, shaped you into more than you are now; constrained by dogma."

"What do you intend for me?" Madeline asked. "You can't possibly think I'll willingly help you awaken Vozzab?"

"You don't have to be willing to fulfill your role in awakening Vozzab." The slightest hint of pity betrayed Nera's voice. "All the same, it's the most important service anyone could ask to render for the children of the gods."

Madeline shuddered at the far-off look in Nera's eyes as she made that statement. The witch came to herself, shaking her head. With a guttural command, Nera resumed the march. The orcs followed, shoving Madeline along with them.

Nera and the orcs stopped their march well after dark. Some of the orcs began chomping down on maggot-infested bread, while others drank foul-smelling ales from flasks. However, Urzg shoved Madeline against a tree trunk at the edge of their campsite without the slightest hint of compassion.

"Not so tight," Madeline complained as Urzg bound her to the tree.

Urzg snorted in reply as he tightened the rope around Madeline.

"Nera called your soldiers oath-warriors." Madeline looked into Urzg's pale eyes. "Why?"

"When an orc host assembles for war..." Urzg's reply was gruff; his tongue not accustomed to speaking in Madeline's language. "Most orcs must be forced to fight for their chieftains. Oath-warriors train every day to fight for their chieftain, and are eager to honor their oaths to fight for the chieftain and the tribe. Because of their oaths, the tribe gives them the best weapons and armor it has."

"It separates the honorable from the base," Madeline deduced. "It's like the Nordsmen's berserkers or Azgald's knights. They train harder for war than the commoners and occupy a place of privilege because of it."

"Orcs don't have mercy," Urzg laughed. "We do not spare the weak because of pity. The weak are to be enslaved to serve their betters. Woe to the vanquished."

"Perhaps that's why the orcs here are enslaved to the Clans." She gave Urzg a hard look. "Anyone can destroy something. Not everyone can build something to last. That takes a bit more virtue than simple conquest."

Urzg spat contemptuously. With a grimace, the orc turned and walked away. She had struck the orc chieftain's pride in a way neither had anticipated.

After two days marching through the Wyrmwind Peaks, Madeline caught her first glimpse of what she guessed was her destination. It was a fortress with high walls and tall towers, its appearance not sinister like a castle of Nordsman construction, yet too fine to have been built by the men of Azgald.

"We aren't going to Drammon?" Madeline gasped, recognizing what this might mean for her beliefs about Farthest Thule. "The elves built this."

"Olso Fortress has changed hands many times after the elves abandoned it," Nera confirmed. "But not even the elves knew what has been resting in the caverns beneath."

"Vozzab is in a cave under the castle?" Madeline gave the slightest tremble.

"I'll show you." Nera smirked.

Alvir, Nera, Warden Tarik, Urzg, and a few dwarf and goblin miners led Madeline into a vast, dark cavern deep below Olso Fortress. The miners shook in apparent terror. Madeline could hardly blame them for not wanting to be down here. It took what appeared to Madeline to be the strongest forms of persuasion Alvir and Nera could think of to convince the miners to lead them to this place after they discovered it. And to say that this pair knew some strong forms of persuasion would be an understatement.

Alvir smirked at the miners' discomfort. What a rare reversal, dwarves quivering underground. Still, Madeline found nothing funny about the irony of their situation.

"I told you." Nera wagged her finger at Alvir. "I saw it in the runes. I saw it in the clouds and entrails. I knew he would be down here."

"I didn't doubt you," Alvir protested, throwing up a placating hand. "Miners, you are dismissed. Go."

The dwarves and goblins hastily obliged. Scrambling back up the rocky tunnel whence they came, the miners were gone a moment later. They did not even bother looking back. Alvir snorted. Madeline probably would have followed the miners if Urzg had not had such a firm grip on the copper manacles which had bound her wrists since she was first captured.

The High Warlord took a step forward. Gusts of hot, steamy air pulsed rhythmically through the cavern. As Alvir brandished his torch out into the darkness, Madeline spotted what had spooked the miners so much.

It was gargantuan. Matte black scales covered its face, while a single, thick, bone-colored horn protruded from its snout. Its leathery wings were folded around its body, and the creature's eyes were closed.

"What a sight to come home to." Alvir peered at the slumbering dragon. "This will change everything. All the clans will bow to us. Azgald will be destroyed."

"And that is only the beginning," Nera concurred.

"And now what do we do with it?" Tarik asked nervously.

Urzg's grip on Madeline's chain tightened. She saw the look in the orc's eye. She saw the same look in Warden Tarik. They knew just as well as Madeline that whatever scheme Alvir and Nera were planning was pure madness.

"Show some respect for this child of the dark gods," Nera hissed.

"How do we make use of the dragon?" Alvir insisted.

"It will take a great deal of preparation to rouse him from his slumber," Nera explained. "This creature might normally sleep up to a thousand years before hunger awakens him."

"Him?" Tarik asked.

"This is Vozzab," Nera replied. "There's no doubt about it. Look at the scar across his snout where the angel, Othniel, struck him in battle."

Alvir nodded appreciatively. Madeline was somehow not surprised the witch knew so much about dragons, and she too knew the legend of the titanic duel between the angel and dragon. It was a tragedy Azgaldian children were told from an early age, though Madeline suspected Nera had a different perspective on the story.

"Vozzab's home is supposed to be here in the Wyrmwind Peaks," Tarik agreed.

Urzg nodded in assent, his nerves visibly beginning to calm.

"So we need to…" Alvir began.

"Prepare a great sacrifice." Nera frowned. "Propitiating a dragon is a very precise ritual. If any detail concerning the ceremony is out of place, Vozzab will not accept."

"And if he doesn't?" Madeline asked.

"Then all our lives are forfeit." Nera shrugged. "Not just yours."

The beast was as majestic as it was large. It was as ancient as it was deadly with its razor-sharp claws and bone-crushing teeth. Did Alvir really believe he and Nera could control a creature that could wound the gods themselves? Their plans depended on such audacity. Madeline was just as astounded by their hubris as she was by the dragon himself.

"How long?" Alvir took another step closer to the dragon.

"I began making the necessary preparations as soon as we told the miners to begin excavating the tunnels," Nera answered. "A few more days is all it should take."

The High Warlord stretched his hand out and patted the dragon's nose. Tarik gasped in surprise at this brazen gesture. Urzg took an instinctive step back, and Madeline's legs felt weak. Only Nera appeared unmoved. Rubbing the dragon's hard scales, Alvir himself appeared to momentarily question whether he was simply displaying his bravado or growing mad. Vozzab did not stir.

"So why is it you need to sacrifice me specifically?" Madeline's curiosity got the best of her. "That is why you have been trying to capture me, isn't it? You need to sacrifice me to Vozzab, right?"

"We cannot just awaken Vozzab," Alvir noted, slowly removing his hand from the dragon's cold face. "We need to make sure he serves us when he does awaken."

"You are an ideal sacrifice because of the deeds of your ancestors." Nera turned to Madeline. "If we sacrifice a person who has slain a dragon or is the descendant of someone who has, then Vozzab will agree to do our bidding. A dragon also loves magical blood spilt in his name. So you see we have two very good reasons for electing you to this honor."

Both Clansmen and Azgaldians considered it prestigious to marry into the families of dragon-slayers; Madeline knew that much. Over the course of several generations, there seemed to be no shortage of lords or ladies who did not have some trace amount of dragon-slayer in their blood. However, Madeline supposed that a direct line descendant such as her might be considered a purer sacrifice. She just had to take Nera's word on the magical blood part.

"The Duchy of Pavik borders on Clan Black Dragon's holdings," Madeline observed. "My father won't be long once he finds out you have me."

"Were you not listening?" Nera shot back. "It will be far too late by the time he arrives. His whole army will be able to do nothing against Vozzab's strength."

"In fact," Alvir thought aloud, "I would love to see the look on your father's face when he comes to rescue you, only to find a dragon waiting for him instead."

"I'll send word to the Duke of Pavik demanding a ransom in return for his daughter," Tarik offered.

"Yes," Alvir agreed to the scheme. "Of course Tancred would never pay a ransom, but he would certainly march on anyone who took his precious daughter."

Madeline was not going to argue against the High Warlord's cruel reasoning for extending her life. More time meant a greater chance for her to escape. She would think of something before long. Getting rid of these cursed copper restraints would be the first step. At first she had not noticed any difference with the manacles binding her wrists, but after a while they'd left her feeling agitated, thirsty, and itchy. She had no desire for any sort of copper jewelry if she made it through this.

"You live for now." Alvir pointed at Madeline. "But you will die knowing Vozzab's first victims will be your father and his men."

Chapter Twenty-Three

The wind howled around Godfrey as he trudged through the scattered snowdrifts adorning the Wyrmwind Peaks. His cloak flapped like a banner caught in the storm raging about him. Blinding snow obscured his vision. He had lost Madeline's trail a few days prior after recovering her gloves back in the forest. Now he wandered through the icy mountains aimlessly. Godfrey knew he had to find shelter, but all he could see was white as the snow stung his face.

Hunger pangs stabbed at his stomach. He had eaten very little since Madeline's capture. Most of the trail rations were lost with Baruch back in the Irelven, and foraging took time Godfrey did not have. Only his own force of will kept him going. Slipping on a patch of ice, he knew he was quickly succumbing to fatigue.

He tried to lift himself, but his arms gave out. Covering his face with his cloak, he took a deep breath, which came dangerously close to becoming a yawn. His eyelids were just too heavy to keep open anymore. His heavy cloak was the only thing separating his face from the elements. The wind continued to howl relentlessly.

"Gods," Godfrey muttered. "I am out of food. I don't know where I am even supposed to be going anymore. You've taken everything from me. Now take me."

His fingers and toes growing numb, he relaxed as if he were going into a deep sleep. That was how he would think of death. It was cold. Yet he counted the gradual loss of feeling in his extremities as a mercy. Death would be painless enough.

As he drifted in and out of consciousness, the last thing he was aware of was the howling wind of the snowstorm. It momentarily changed pitch to become more like a shriek. The wind died down, but fitfully shrieked once more before giving out entirely. Now Godfrey could die in peace.

He awoke to the sound of a crackling fire. He smelled some sort of vegetable broth cooking in a pot over the hearth. Looking about himself, he discovered he was lying in a large bed with a fine royal purple blanket covering him. The gilded furniture and decorations in the room around him were of extreme craftsmanship. Godfrey's cloak, armor, shield, and sword were set neatly in one of the corners. He was about to stand, but he stopped when he heard the sound of feet ascending a set of nearby stairs from outside the room.

The door creaked on its ornate brass hinges as someone entered the room. Godfrey sat up, surprised to see a tall, thin man with long, white hair enter the room. On closer inspection, Godfrey saw the man's ears were pointed.

"You're…" Godfrey began.

"I am called Luka." The creature's voice was melodious. "And, yes, I am an elf. What is your name?"

"Godfrey de Bastogne," he answered cautiously as he assessed his situation.

The elf wore only a cloak, a tunic, and trousers, but a long, curved falchion rested in a scabbard attached to his belt. Unarmed, and unarmored, Godfrey was at the elf's mercy. He hoped Luka remained friendly.

"You have no need to fear." Luka threw up placating hands, sensing the attention Godfrey gave to his sword. "You are my guest here."

"I'm in Farthest Thule?" Godfrey looked about incredulously.

"No," Luka chuckled. "You are still far away from there."

"Then where am I?" Godfrey asked.

"You are in the Watch Tower of Uvalin," Luka answered, leaning over the hearth.

The elf poured some of the broth from the pot into a small bowl. He handed the dish to Godfrey, who hastily began to drink the near-scalding liquid. It washed through him, invigorating every inch of muscle in his body. In retrospect, he was surprised the broth did not burn his throat, mouth, and lips, considering how hot it felt in the bowl.

"Our legion was headquartered at Olso back when the Empire still ruled these lands," Luka continued once Godfrey had his fill. "My flying cataphracts were stationed here. Long ago, I led a cohort of griffin cavalry on patrol through these mountains hunting dragons and other such beasts."

"My mother said ancestors of mine were griffin-riders," Godfrey said, clumsily searching his memory for any relevant details she might have told him.

"In later years." Luka nodded. "When the Empire's power was in decline, and fewer legions could deploy flying cataphracts, we trained men as well as elves to ride griffins. Where is your mother from?"

"Here in Azgald," Godfrey answered eagerly. "But it was my father's family that had the griffin-riders. That's why the griffin is our family crest."

"Yes…" Luka's gaze was lost in Godfrey's shield, as if recovering some forgotten detail. "Men are still patriarchal like that, I suppose. Where is your father from?"

"The Duchy of Bastogne back in Lortharain." Godfrey frowned. "But my mother and father are dead now, and the King has seized the Duchy for himself."

"Then you are an exile?" Luka sat on the bed next to him.

"Not exactly." Godfrey had not thought of himself as such before now. "I was on crusade up here in the Nordslands when my father passed away, and King Wilhelm stole my inheritance."

"I am also not exactly an exile," Luka divulged with a sad smile.

"Then you could not take me to Farthest Thule?" Godfrey's hopes were dashed.

"I could not do that even if I were in the city's good graces." Luka stood again. "It is not our way to let the other races venture among our people since the fall of the Empire."

"But you brought me to your tower."

"I found you alone in the storm about to die of cold," Luka explained. "When I saw the griffin on your clothing, your shield, your necklace… I had questions I needed to ask. Now I have my answers."

"What does my father's family have to do with griffin knights in the Wyrmwind Peaks?" Godfrey responded with a puzzled expression.

"Men are so short-lived," Luka sighed. "You do not know the songs of your families. You do not know their stories."

Godfrey gritted his teeth at the elf's patronizing tone.

"Elinor Bellator and Tristan Galeo." Luka grew visibly frustrated as Godfrey failed to recognize those names. "Those were two of your ancestors. I trained them to be griffin cataphracts in Bastogne after my legion disbanded. We fought a war against a mad king, destroyed his undead minions, helped forge the Kingdom of Lortharain from the ashes."

Luka's story sounded vaguely similar to the myth about the necromancer Lycus Godfrey had heard alongside stories like the Tale of Cheldric as a boy. Godfrey assumed Luka's version was probably closer to the truth, since apparently he had been a living participant in those events. Luka must have been both very old and very well-traveled.

"Please," Godfrey cut in. "I left the crusade to persuade the elves of Farthest Thule to help us. The crusaders are few and the Clansmen are many. We sacrificed so much not just for Azgald, but for everyone the Nordsmen might attack if left unchecked. I lost my friends, my steed, and my inheritance while away from my family on the gods' errand. The Nordsmen have captured my lady, and a witch called Nera is trying to awaken someone called Vozzab. Is there nothing you can do?"

"Nera is trying to awaken the dragon?" Luka froze in place. "That is what she has been doing at Olso."

"Vozzab is a dragon at Olso?" Godfrey tried to keep up with the details. "How do you know Nera has been there?"

"My eyes see far indeed." Luka grabbed Godfrey's empty bowl, setting it on a table. "Put on your arms and armor. Then come with me to the aviary."

Standing, Godfrey felt fresh, as if he had not spent the last few weeks out in the wilderness. He pulled on his hauberk with ease, and was surprised to find Luka sliding his tabard over the chainmail. Luka handed Godfrey's belt and sheathed sword to him.

"Time is of the essence," Luka chided. "Do not marvel that an elf would debase himself assisting a man in donning his armor."

He helped Godfrey finish dressing, and the two exited the room. Godfrey followed him up several flights of stairs running along the walls. As Godfrey glimpsed through a window on the way up, he saw that the tower overlooked a sheer cliff face on the side of a mountain. He pulled away, his legs trembling. He was too high up. Trying to forget what he saw, he focused on the immediate task of following Luka up the stairs.

Reaching the top of the stairs, any fear of heights Godfrey felt was quickly forgotten as he saw what lived in the aviary. Nestled on a large, straw bed, a majestic white griffin cocked its head at them. The resemblance the creature bore to the griffin in Godfrey's vision was uncanny.

"I saw this griffin before." Godfrey took a reverent step towards the creature.

"This is Spathi." Luka gestured to a few other empty nests. "He and his brother and sisters serve as my eyes and ears in the Wyrmwind Peaks. Spathi found you in the snowstorm. He saved your life."

"Thanks." Godfrey bowed.

To his surprise, the griffin nodded in reply.

"Griffins can't speak," Luka explained. "But they are very empathetic creatures. You'll find they have an intelligence to match as well."

Luka reached for Godfrey's hand, and set it on the griffin's beak. Spathi chirped in reply. Luka removed his own hand, and the griffin playfully nipped at Godfrey's finger. Recoiling, Godfrey turned to Luka.

"Spathi seems to like you well enough," Luka noted encouragingly. "But you will also find griffins to be as proud as they are strong. Respect Spathi, and he will respect you. Disrespect Spathi, and his beak and claws will teach you your folly."

Godfrey extended his hand with the palm out. Spathi sniffed it, barely touching the palm with the tip of his razor-sharp beak. Sensing the griffin's approval, Godfrey stroked the side of Spathi's head. The white feathers were soft yet firm. Godfrey continued petting for a few more strokes before turning back to the elf.

"Training a flying cataphract to legionary standards would normally take several weeks from dawn to dusk each day," Luka reminisced. "Most candidates failed in their training, and truly mastering the art of flying cavalry is a process that often takes years. However, I fear we do not have that time. Your training with horses will have to suffice."

Stunned, Godfrey did not know what to say. Though the loss of Baruch was still fresh in his mind, Spathi was a magnificent creature, and he already felt a bond with the griffin. Tears welled in his eyes.

Luka retrieved a saddle of elvish make, and allowed Spathi to sniff it. Standing, Spathi looked from the saddle to Godfrey, and pawed at the saddle in understanding. The griffin then gave Luka a long, sad stare.

"We never ride the same wind twice." Luka scratched Spathi's feathery feline ear. "I will miss you too, friend."

Seeing the exchange between griffin and elf, Godfrey was reminded of his own love for Baruch. Could he really accept such a gift? He knew how hard it was to be parted from his own faithful steed.

"Let me show you how to properly harness a griffin." Luka offered the saddle to Godfrey. "It's a bit different than a horse."

Luka mostly pointed and offered corrections as Godfrey did the majority of the work. It was a teaching philosophy similar to Fallard's. Learn by doing. Godfrey had grown to appreciate that method. He would retain the lesson better that way.

"Why are you doing all of this?" Godfrey asked after the saddle was securely harnessed. "You're making a great personal sacrifice for someone you don't even know."

"Spathi's brother and sisters will find mates in due time." Luka caressed Spathi. "Griffins are not so uncommon they cannot find their own kind. I'll see to raising the next generation of griffins as I have in the centuries since returning here. One day their numbers may be great again. Your need right now is greater than mine. And Spathi himself seems to be very fond of you."

Luka's expression grew sterner and less whimsical. He stopped petting the griffin, and looked at Godfrey with a piercing gaze.

"Though you are generations removed from your ancestors…" The elf was looking at something deep inside Godfrey. "I see not just Elinor and Tristan's image in you, but their courage, determination, and spirit."

"They must have been great people."

Godfrey thought on his more immediate relatives. Perhaps his father's courage, determination, and spirit were traits he gained from his father and his father's father before that. Godfrey's memory of his father was of a man like Cheldric. When Godfrey was young, and he imagined the knight in the story, it was his father's face Cheldric wore. That face was something Luka apparently saw in both Godfrey and this long-dead Tristan.

"I trained your ancestors to be flying cataphracts," Luka went on. "I fought alongside your family long ago, Godfrey de Bastogne. They helped me see that right and wrong go beyond duty to lords and kin. And you are right. If Vozzab is set loose, all that is good in the Nordslands will suffer for it. A knight such as you wielding a holy blade, mounted on a griffin stands a chance."

"You saw Uriel?" Godfrey asked.

"I had to search you." Luka made an apologetic gesture. "I had to know who Spathi brought to our home."

"Griffins and magical swords in and of themselves are pretty rare and powerful." Godfrey frowned. "You said with their aid I only stand a chance?"

"Not a good one," Luka admitted. "Hunting dragons was a task which normally required the combined efforts of an entire flying cataphract cohort. With one bite, claw, or gout of flame, Spathi and you will die. But Spathi is faster than Vozzab. Fly high against the Sun if possible. Dive in behind the dragon as fast as you can, and keep flying after you strike."

"All right." Godfrey nodded, exhilaration shortening his breath. "It sounds a bit like jousting. There's just a few more things to remember."

"And it's much faster," Luka cautioned. "Be aware of everything around you. Not just to your front, sides, and rear, but look above and below as well. You will not be fighting on a plane but in a sphere."

Godfrey nodded, beginning to grasp what combat in the air might be like.

"One last thing," Luka added. "You will lose speed as you climb, and gain speed in a dive. If you need to get away, dive low and fly close to the ground. Take courage. Go now. Spathi will find the way."

Spathi turned to face one of the large openings in the aviary's wall. The griffin screeched. The noise reminded Godfrey of a large eagle or some similar bird of prey.

"Thank you so much," Godfrey said, mounting Spathi.

Raising a hand in farewell, Luka took a step back. The time for words had passed. Godfrey spurred Spathi on. The griffin howled again as he pounced out of the aviary's opening.

Lurching out into the air, Godfrey felt the sickening sensation of freefall abruptly cut short as Spathi's wings caught the breeze. The griffin beat his wings hard as he climbed higher into the sky. For a moment the griffin struggled, and Godfrey thought Spathi might not be able to carry his weight.

Godfrey's heart pounded. His hand trembled. He was afraid to look. Yet Spathi did not fall. Realizing he could not hope to ride into battle like this, Godfrey ventured to crack open his eyes. The mountains were tall and steep. Snow covered the tops of most of them. Behind them, the Watch Tower of Uvalin grew ever more distant. The similarity of seeing the Wyrmwind Peaks from above in reality to his vision back in the Temple of Spes was too great to be coincidence. Godfrey began to take courage as he realized this was where Loxias wanted him right now.

After reaching an impressive height, Spathi took to gliding on the air currents. Once Godfrey's breathing was under control, and his hand stopped trembling, he began to appreciate just how small he was from such a high vantage point. The sight reminded him of how he felt out on the sea.

"We should probably practice a few maneuvers before we face Vozzab," Godfrey shouted over the wailing wind.

With a shriek, Spathi went into a steep dive. Godfrey's stomach reeled. This was not exactly what he had in mind. Screaming, he held onto the reins as tightly as he could. Godfrey's vision was quickly filled by the sheer face of a cliff.

"Up," he bawled, pulling on the reins. "Up! Up! Up!"

Rolling away at the last second, Spathi began to climb again. Godfrey shifted his weight to the right, and the griffin banked accordingly. He shifted to the left, and Spathi changed direction. A broad grin creased Godfrey's face.

"Now we're getting somewhere, Spathi." Godfrey let go of the reins with one hand, patting the griffin. "Let's try this again."

Pulling on the stirrups with his legs, he hoped Spathi would go into another dive. The griffin understood. Ready for the rapid descent this time, Godfrey's fear transformed into excitement. Whooping, he tugged on the reins. The griffin went into a loop. With a tug on just one of the reins, Spathi rolled on his side.

The thrill of flight made Godfrey oblivious to everything else. The rolling, spinning, diving, these were sensations he had never even dreamed of before. It was something beautiful he was sure no mortal men had experienced in centuries. To think that there had once been hundreds if not thousands of men who flew on griffins like this. Godfrey's thoughts sobered as he remembered the task he still needed to accomplish.

"Luka said you could find the way," he said as Spathi glided low through a mountain pass. "Let's get to Olso. If we're lucky, we can defeat Alvir and the dragon, and maybe save Madeline too."

Screeching, Spathi flapped his wings. The griffin climbed over the tops of the Wyrmwind Peaks, and banked hard to the left. So much rested on Godfrey's shoulders. Even with such incredible fortune, he was more certain than ever that he was flying to his death.

Chapter Twenty-Four

Turpin rose from his seat at the campfire. The look on Varin's face was grim as he stood before Turpin and the other knights in the camp. Turpin exchanged uneasy glances with Karl the Hammer and Sir Rodair in the fading light.

"You're sure it's him?" Karl asked the ranger.

"How long have we traveled with the men of Pavik?" Varin cocked an eyebrow. "I know what Lord Tancred and his men look like."

"Thank you," Turpin replied. "Have the scouts watch their approach, but don't interfere unless they show signs of aggression."

"Of course, my lord." Varin bowed before disappearing into the dusk outside camp.

"Inform Conrad the Wolf." Turpin looked at Karl. "Have the boy meet us here."

Using his maul to help him stand, Karl the Hammer set off to the other end of camp at a brisk pace. Turpin turned his gaze to the fire. Brooding over the frustrations Tancred would undoubtedly cause made the chaplain's jaw tighten.

"What do you think?" Rodair looked at Turpin quizzically.

"I am uncertain." Turpin shook his head. "I don't think Tancred is out to attack us. But he is probably upset that we did not tell him about his daughter being with us back in Narlstad. He must have come back here looking for her."

"It will make him more upset to learn she went off to the Wyrmwind Peaks with Lord Godfrey," Rodair noted. "He will probably want to kill someone after that."

"Probably," Turpin snorted in agreement.

By the time the Sun had fully set, Turpin caught sight of Tancred approaching between the tents. Conrad arrived at Turpin's tent with Karl just as Tancred's and his retainers' faces became visible in the yellow glow of the fire.

"Where is Phillip d'Artois?" Tancred asked, searching the crusaders' faces.

"We had to leave him and his men back at Pskov," Turpin answered. "He was wounded on the way to the Northern Marches. Ambushes have become pretty regular these days."

"I know you." Tancred's expression grew angry as he recognized Turpin. "You're the chaplain who was with that stupid boy Madeline had gotten herself mixed up with."

"Be careful how you refer to Lord Godfrey." Turpin indicated Karl and Rodair. "You are in the presence of his loyal knights."

"*Had* gotten herself mixed up with?" Conrad repeated.

"Look," Tancred took a deep breath, "I know Godfrey ran off with Madeline from Narlstad, but I'll withhold my chastisement concerning your complicity there for the time being. Nera, the Witch of the North, killed him on his little adventure with my daughter, and now she is holding Madeline hostage at Olso."

A passing footman stood frozen in his tracks upon overhearing what Tancred had just said. Sir Rodair's mouth hung open. Karl the Hammer was on the verge of tears. Turpin could hardly believe what he had heard. The boy had been his last link to… Turpin shook his head, dismissing the thought.

"That is quite regrettable." Turpin was able to conceal all but the slightest quiver in his voice at the news of Godfrey's death.

"There's more…" Tancred held up a finger.

"I am sorry for your misfortune," Turpin cut in. "But you have done as much to hurt this crusade as help it, if not more. These men of Bastogne will not help you any further."

"What about revenge?" Tancred replied, gesturing out to the woods beyond the camp. "High Warlord Alvir is the husband of Nera. Both of them are at Olso right now."

"Attacking Olso now would be saving Madeline and fulfilling our crusading vows," Conrad noted.

"There is a very large silver mine underneath Olso Fortress," Tancred continued. "Its capture would be a huge blow to the Clans, and Azgald would gain just as much as the Nordsmen would lose. Help me do this. Please."

Turpin's eyes remained fixed on the fire. The embers smoldered and crackled. So much had been lost already on this expedition. Was there still a point in continuing?

"We will avenge our lord." Turpin nodded. "We will not do this for what your duchy would gain, your daughter's life, or even the crusade. We are going to avenge Godfrey with the deaths of the witch and her husband. And then we are leaving this cursed land."

After Madeline had been shown the sleeping dragon, she was taken to a cell at the top floor of a tower. A pair of Nordsman guards searched her, and took most of what few valuables she had on her. They tore from her finger a ruby ring that once belonged to her mother. They snatched away a necklace her father had given her on her birthday last year. She was sure she would never see these things again.

Losing these possessions pained Madeline, not because she had a particular attachment to jewelry, but because of the memories of the people she associated with the gifts. Though she wanted to scream at these rough men, to resist, and try to hold onto these things, she knew such efforts would be futile.

To Madeline's surprise, the guards' initial discovery of the ring, necklace, a bracelet, and a purse full of coins, distracted them from making a more thorough search. She held her breath as the guards ripped away these last two items and walked out of the cell bickering over how to divide the spoils. As they slammed and locked the cell door behind them, Madeline breathed a sigh of relief.

Once the door was locked, and she was sure there would be no intrusion, she removed her hairpin from the back of her head. It was bejeweled, and the guards would have confiscated it on those grounds alone had they noticed it during their search. However, her hair was an unkempt mess from her fall into the river, capture, and forced march— which helped conceal this last piece of jewelry.

Removing the hairpin revealed that the portion which was normally visible while worn was actually the hilt of an ornate dagger. She twisted the dagger's blade, unscrewing it from the hilt. On the reverse end of the blade was a small lock pick.

Madeline's father had given her this multifaceted tool for just this sort of moment—when she might need to escape imprisonment and fight her way out. Knowing how few friends her father had outside Pavik made her retrospectively wonder why she had not been taken hostage sooner. Not that she regretted any missed opportunities along those lines.

Madeline began working the lock pick against her restraints with practiced ease. Her father had repeatedly lectured her that brave knights might not always be able to save her from misfortune. She would never again complain about her father's paranoia in making her practice removing chains and fetters from her wrists since she was a little girl.

With a heavy clang, the copper manacles fell from her wrists. Already Madeline could feel the magic beginning to surge through her veins again. With a snap of her fingers, a small flame flickered briefly above her hand. Madeline was satisfied that she could call up much more than that in an instant if she wanted to.

She could barge out of her cell right now, incinerating the door then everyone and everything that got in her way. She frowned at this thought. She remembered passing many guards and armed servants as she was brought up to the tower. Such an escape attempt would undoubtedly be short-lived. The conflagration would attract Nera's attention, and Madeline knew the witch far outclassed her abilities.

What of stealth? Simply by holding her breath and concentrating, Madeline could deaden all the sounds around her while turning invisible as she picked the lock to the cell door. She would still need to deal with the guards at the cell door, but from there she could possibly sneak out of the tower. The only drawback to this plan was that she could only remain invisible for as long as she could hold her breath. She had to escape not just the tower, but navigate the keep and climb over the inner and outer walls, or somehow get through the gates while remaining undetected as well. Though Madeline might make it farther this way, she also saw her recapture as inevitable in this instance. What she needed was a distraction.

Looking out the window to her cell, Madeline had a good view of the fortress walls and surrounding countryside. Her father would be coming with an army soon, she was sure of that much. That would be the opportunity she would wait for.

Madeline screwed the blade of her dagger back onto its hilt. Instead of replacing it on the back of her head, this time she hid the dagger up her sleeve. She would not risk losing this valued possession, and doubted the guards would search her again.

Picking up the manacles, she could feel the magic beginning to drain from her again. She grimaced, but let them hang loosely from her wrists. With a silent prayer, she hoped her distraction would come before the sacrifice.

Spathi flew nonstop from the Watch Tower of Uvalin to Olso Fortress. Though this was by far the fastest way Godfrey could imagine covering such a great distance, passing through the high mountain air like this left him stiff with cold. Still, he was grateful for Luka's gift.

By the time they reached Olso, the fortress was only illuminated by pale moonlight. Godfrey preferred it that way. He doubted any sentries would expect an intruder coming from above, and cover of darkness helped all the more. Surprise was on his side.

In the distance, Godfrey made out the torches of what looked like several thousand men approaching Olso. He doubted the warriors in the fortress saw the approaching army yet, but they would soon. He could spend little time speculating whether the army was friend or foe. There was no way of telling from this distance in the dark, and his other priorities would be only more pressing if these were enemies.

Godfrey had Spathi circle over the fortress a couple of times as he tried to determine the best point to infiltrate. The rectangular keep had one large tower on each corner. A pair of sentries stood watch from the roof of each. Yet only one tower had light emanating from the window at the highest interior level.

"You think something important is happening in that one?" he asked Spathi, pointing out the tower in question.

Swooping in towards the roof of the tower Godfrey pointed out, Spathi crushed one of the unsuspecting guards with his talons as he landed. The Nordsman sentry died with a sickening crunch of bones. The second sentry cried out, but Godfrey ran him through with his blade. The disturbance did not go unnoticed, and Godfrey soon heard shouting from the other towers.

"Keep them busy," he told the griffin as he dismounted.

With a screech, Spathi launched himself at the sentries on one of the other towers. Seeing a trapdoor on the roof, Godfrey flung it open before sliding down the ladder into the tower. He hit the floor hard. The room was small, with a wall and heavy wooden door dividing the area from the rest of the level. The furniture was sparse, and only a couple of torches provided light to the interior.

Another pair of startled Nordsmen stared at Godfrey as he sprang at one of them. A quick thrust from Uriel ended the first guard. Godfrey swung at the second guard, but the

Nordsman already had his sword out. Their blades clashed as metal scraped against metal. The Nordsman swung at him. Taking a step back, Godfrey dodged the attack. Lunging forward, the Nordsman struck again. Blocking with his shield, Godfrey found himself backed into a corner.

Most Nordsmen Godfrey had fought were raging brutes like the orcs who fought beside them. This one was older, grizzled. He still fought with the ferocity of his kin, but the impetuosity in the typical Nordsman fighting style Godfrey could normally take advantage of was replaced by the kind of skill that only came with experience.

The impassive expression with which the Nordsman observed Uriel's glowing blade unsettled Godfrey all the more. He could see a certain degree of fear written across most of his opponents when confronted by Uriel, but not this Nordsman. This Nordsman was made of sterner stuff.

Godfrey struck out, but the Nordsman parried, and offered an immediate riposte. Godfrey blocked again with his shield. Feinting, he was sure his next attack would hit. The Nordsman surprised him with a perfectly timed block with his own shield.

This Nordsman was watching the position of Godfrey's feet, hands, how he shifted his weight before each movement. It was just as Fallard had trained Godfrey to do as a squire. Godfrey rarely needed to watch his foes' movements so closely, given the predispositions of most of his enemies in the Nordslands, but he found this Nordsman to be every bit as skilled as another trained knight.

With an overhead strike, Godfrey surged forward. As the Nordsman lifted his shield to block, he was forced to yield ground. Breaking free from the corner, Godfrey struck again as he attempted to get around the man's defenses. Stepping away, now the Nordsman had his back pressed against the door to the next room.

A deafening crash startled both Godfrey and the Nordsman. After a second and third crash, Godfrey recognized it was stone-throwers hurling their payloads against the battlements. The Nordsman clearly knew the sound too. Olso was under siege.

With a roar, the door behind the Nordsman exploded in a shower of splinters and flame. The force of the blast threw him forward. Unprepared for this inexplicable event, Godfrey fell on his back with the enemy on top of him. The Nordsman was limp, with dozens of door fragments piercing his back. Godfrey pushed the corpse off him and rose to his feet. To his surprise, Madeline stood in the open doorway before him. She returned an equally shocked look at him.

"You're alive?" she asked, helping him to his feet. "What are you doing here?"

"Rescuing you…I think." He brushed himself off after sheathing Uriel.

The two exchanged a long kiss. For Godfrey it was still too brief, but they were not out of danger yet. Once they were out of Olso, then they could celebrate.

"This way," Madeline said, and tugged Godfrey to a set of stairs leading down.

"No." Godfrey resisted Madeline's pull, indicating the ladder. "We need to go up. I have some help there."

"The dragon is down in the mines." Madeline pointed to the stairs. "With your magic sword, we could kill Vozzab while he still sleeps."

"The castle defenders should be getting ready to repel an assault at the walls soon." Godfrey considered the bombardment taking place outside. "This may be our best chance."

Drawing Uriel, he led the way down the spiral stairs in the center of the room. Madeline and he had not made it far when they heard another set of footsteps coming up the stairs. Godfrey signaled for her to halt, but it was too late. Nera stood in front of Godfrey with her jeweled staff pointing in front of his face.

"You again," Nera snarled, taking another step up the stairs. "It's time for the ritual, Madeline. But I'll make sure your knight dies here first this time."

Madeline launched a burst of flame from her hand over Godfrey's shoulder. The witch caught the fire with the end of her staff, but Godfrey saw a narrow opportunity. With a quick slash of his sword, he cleaved Nera's staff in two. The sudden discharge of radiant magical force threw him on his back, while the witch tumbled down the stairs. Standing, she screamed as she shot bolts of arcane energy from her fingertips.

"Not that way." Godfrey ran up the stairs, narrowly avoiding the eerie glowing projectiles. "Gods above, hurry!"

Madeline was already running a few steps ahead of Godfrey. A beam of the strange magical substance singed his cloak as Nera's attacks wildly bounced off the walls. Upon reaching the top of the stairs, Madeline bounded for the ladder. Godfrey stopped in front of the room's only table for a moment. It was heavy, and solidly built. Sheathing his sword one last time, he had an idea.

Flipping the table over, he shoved it down the stairwell. Nera cursed, but Godfrey did not stay to see what happened exactly. It was a desperate move, and he did not want to catch a magic bolt in the face if it did not work.

Ascending the ladder, he found Spathi had returned to the top of the tower. Godfrey shut the trapdoor behind him. Madeline looked between the griffin and him, astonishment overtaking her.

"This is just like in your vision," she gasped.

"There's no time." Godfrey mounted the griffin. "Let's go."

She took Godfrey's hand, and sat on Spathi just behind him. Spathi leapt from the tower, soaring through the night sky just as Nera threw open the trapdoor. Spathi went into a quick dive to gain speed, and just missed colliding with the parapet as he flew over the fortress' inner wall. Nera blindly hurled a fireball after the griffin, but Spathi was too quick and the lighting too poor. Godfrey could not help but laugh as he realized they really had escaped.

Alvir walked over Warden Tarik's broken form as he surveyed the room before him. Dozens of large, wooden splinters perforated the Warden's back. Alvir sighed. There was a loss not easily replaced.

Alvir took a moment to wipe the blood from the ax in his hand with a rag. It was the same ax he had murdered his brother with, months previous. He'd struck down several Azgaldians and crusaders with it in the last hour on Olso's walls. It would taste more blood before the Sun rose.

In front of Alvir, Nera sat on the floor with the pieces of her broken staff in hand. She looked at him with tears streaming down her face. She shook her head helplessly.

"The Duke of Pavik brought some crusaders with him," Alvir said, frowning.

"I know." Nera did not look at him. "That boy, Godfrey de Bastogne, took our sacrificial victim away."

"We've suffered a few setbacks tonight." Alvir indicated the scene around them. "Right now the siege goes poorly, but we can repel the assault on the walls with some effort."

"The staff held a vast reserve of my powers." Nera threw the pieces against the wall. "It will be difficult to replace."

"Are you spent?" He concentrated on her expression.

"I can't cast any more spells until I've rested." Nera shrugged.

Alvir's grip on his ax tightened.

"You did everything you could," he reassured his wife. "But there is one last service you can perform for me tonight."

"You need me to complete the ritual." Terror struck Nera's voice as she grew pale. "If the slightest thing goes wrong…"

"We are both of Clan Black Dragon," Alvir cut her off. "You have the blood of a dragon-slayer in you. Your blood will have to do."

Nera attempted to rise to her feet, but he shoved her to the ground. Having cast so many spells in her efforts to stop Godfrey from rescuing Madeline, she was utterly exhausted. She could hardly move at all.

"Vozzab," Alvir invoked the dragon's name. "Son of Yoan, hear my prayer. Accept this sacrifice, and lend me your strength."

With a stroke of Alvir's ax, Nera's blood splattered on the floors and walls as she screamed. Alvir waited a moment as the last of his wife's vitality drained from her. A moment passed with no discernible change. Doubt began to creep into his mind. He had not brought her down to the altar they had set up in the dragon's cavern as should have been done, but she was of appropriate lineage, and the prayer was simple and direct. With the enemy at the walls, there simply was not time to do everything properly.

"For what it's worth," he sighed, staring down at the dead witch, "I am sorry it had to be this way."

Something rumbled deep under the earth. The tower around Alvir shook with a roar that was felt more than heard. He rushed to the window as he heard the ground in the courtyard begin to crumble. A chasm opened in the courtyard leading down into the mines below. As the dawn broke, the dragon's black silhouette filled the sky.

Vozzab spread his wings as the battle below came to a standstill. Looking down on the embattled men and orcs on the fortress walls, the dragon roared again. To Alvir's horror, Vozzab swooped down, devouring all within his reach with his snapping jaws and raking claws. The dragon did not make any distinction among his victims.

Alvir had gone too far. His wife had been right about the ritual. He had no control.

Hearing movement behind him, he turned to see Urzg ascending the stairs. The orc's expression was unreadable as he surveyed the scene of carnage. Urzg looked past Alvir out the window to behold the further destruction the dragon was causing. The orc grimaced, recognizing Alvir's blunder.

"Never fear," Alvir reassured him. "This war isn't over yet. Come, we're leaving."

Chapter Twenty-Five

With Spathi circling over the army attacking Olso, Godfrey quickly recognized they were a combination of the men of Pavik and crusaders. Though it was still dark, he spotted Baldwin's group, Conrad's, and his own Bastognians all encircling the fortress. Godfrey was about to bring Spathi down in the camp of his own men when Madeline tugged at his cloak.

"We need to see my father," she insisted. "He came here for me."

Godfrey's heart stopped for a moment at this suggestion. He would have preferred to go back to Nera. Begrudgingly, he veered the griffin towards the Pavikian encampment.

Several siege engineers stopped in their tracks as the griffin flew over the trebuchets and catapults launching stones at Olso's walls. Some of the men aimed crossbows at the griffin, but lowered their weapons as they saw Godfrey and Madeline riding the creature. Landing in front of Tancred's tent, the pair dismounted Spathi to see the Duke of Pavik rushing out to meet them.

"This is what you came to the Wyrmwind Peaks for?" Tancred pointed at the griffin with an accusing finger.

"Not exactly," Godfrey admitted with his eyes downcast. "But it's the best I could manage."

"Godfrey just saved me, father," Madeline reminded Tancred. "Nera and Alvir were going to sacrifice me to awaken a dragon, and destroy your army. The ransom was a ruse."

For a moment, Tancred stood speechless. A range of emotions ran across his face. His daughter had nearly been sacrificed. He had been conned into a ruse that nearly destroyed him with all his men. This night could have turned out very differently.

"Where is the dragon?" Tancred looked to the besieged fortress.

"He is in the mines under the keep," she answered. "It's Vozzab."

"The angel-slayer." Tancred grimaced.

Madeline nudged her father, indicating Godfrey with a cough. Tancred looked at him as if seeing him for the first time. All of the dismissive pretention and suspicion Godfrey had grown accustomed to seeing in the man's expression was gone.

"I will not forget this," Tancred promised, clasping Godfrey's hand. "We are about to assault the walls. Go to your men. Lead them well. Slay your dragon."

"If we get Alvir here too, the crusade is over." Godfrey nodded as he mounted Spathi.

Hoping to cause as little panic as possible, Godfrey opted to have Spathi trot through the attackers' camp as opposed to flying through the midst of them. All who saw the peculiar sight of Godfrey riding a griffin immediately stopped what they were doing, staring in disbelief. The Pavikians maintained a respectful distance from Godfrey and the griffin, but the mood was different when Godfrey entered the Bastognian camp.

The crusaders excitedly shouted Godfrey's name as they saw him. Sir Rodair, Varin, Karl the Hammer, and dozens of others Godfrey had come to know over the course of the crusade practically swarmed him. Spathi hissed at the attention, and the crusaders backed away a step.

"Lord Godfrey." Turpin's jaw hung open for a moment.

In an instant, his eyes narrowed and he clenched his teeth.

"Tancred beguiled us again!" he spat. "He told us you were dead and tricked us into coming here like at Epsberg."

"No." Godfrey waved, dismissing the notion. "The witch left me for dead, and her neglect is the only reason I am here now."

Turpin nodded in response. He bowed his head and the crowd of knights and men-at-arms followed suit.

"The men are yours to lead." Turpin gestured to the crusaders.

"Thank you, Chaplain." Godfrey nodded before addressing the crusaders at large. "Men, I was hoping to bring you reinforcements, an army. Instead, I have but a single griffin and news that other lords might withhold from you for fear of what it might do to your spirits."

The celebratory mood among the crusaders died down.

"High Warlord Alvir and his wife are in that castle." Godfrey pointed to the fortress keep. "She is a powerful witch, but she is far less of a concern than what lies beneath Olso. The witch, Nera, captured Lady Madeline with the intention of sacrificing her. That sacrifice was meant to awaken an ancient dragon and bind it to High Warlord Alvir's service."

The crusaders listened to Godfrey with mouths hanging open or grim expressions.

"I have thwarted their plans by rescuing Lady Madeline," Godfrey continued. "The dragon will not serve Alvir now, and still slumbers in the mines beneath the castle. Even with the thunder of our siege engines, the beast has not awoken yet."

A few nervous chuckles rumbled through the crusaders.

"But it may yet awaken in the course of battle." Godfrey shook his head. "I cannot deny that possibility, given the prophecy uttered by my own mouth."

Many of the crusaders glanced around nervously as they too remembered Godfrey's prophecy. He himself thought it had been fulfilled when he confronted Tancred, and prevented a battle between some of the crusaders and the Silver Suns. Yet there was an uncanny resemblance between the events of the last few days and Godfrey's vision in the temple. Prophecies had been known to come to pass in both literal and figurative interpretations.

"Right now, focus on our goal." Godfrey gestured to himself. "If we slay Alvir here at this castle, the Clans will once again be divided and leaderless. Our crusade will be over, and then we can liberate Bastogne from King Wilhelm's oppression."

Several crusaders nodded in approval.

"With the gods on our side," Godfrey brandished Uriel, "how can we fail?"

A cheer erupted from the crusaders. A horn blew from somewhere in the Pavikian camp, and the stone-throwers ceased their bombardment. For an instant, silence overcame the camp.

"Siege ladders," Turpin ordered, and the crusaders sprang into action.

With Godfrey tugging on the reins, Spathi kicked off the ground. The griffin circled over the field a couple of times. With the Sun still slumbering behind the mountains,

Godfrey had difficulty making out much of what was happening on the ground. However, with a little effort, he spotted where the crusaders were beginning to place the ladders against the battlements.

He directed Spathi to a section of wall near the ladders. Swooping down on the parapet, the griffin's momentum knocked several Nordsmen off the wall altogether. Spathi's talons raked at the defenders and his beak tore into anyone close enough. In just a few short moments, Spathi had felled nearly a dozen warriors.

Any Nordsman who attempted to face the griffin from the front was almost immediately eviscerated. Godfrey quickly realized his own attacks should concentrate on Spathi's flanks, where the griffin was more vulnerable. With Spathi's merciless frontal attacks and Godfrey striking at anyone on the sides, they had soon cleared a small section of wall of any resistance. Crusaders began pouring over the parapet, taking advantage of the gap the two had created.

"I think we can do more good in an area with fewer friends," Godfrey noted as the wall quickly became crowded with people he did not want to see hurt.

Kicking off the wall, Spathi flew low with outstretched claws over the Nordsmen. The griffin tore into the enemy ranks from above, striking as much fear as physical damage. Godfrey spotted another section of wall where the crusaders were struggling to gain a foothold as the Sun began to crest over the Wyrmwind Peaks. Godfrey urged Spathi to attack, but the griffin gave a disheartening warble in reply.

"We have been at this for a while." Godfrey frowned empathetically. "And you've been flying almost continuously since yesterday. Let's go back to camp, and rest."

Flapping his wings, Spathi climbed higher in the air. As they turned back to the crusader camp, a terrible rumbling shook the earth. Godfrey's mouth hung open as the ground in Olso's inner courtyard fell into a deep chasm. Shooting out of the chasm with great flaps of his leathery wings, Vozzab looked down on the men and orcs fighting on the walls. Somehow the dragon did not appear to have spotted Godfrey and Spathi yet.

"It looks like we have one more thing to finish before we can rest," Godfrey sighed.

Madeline watched Godfrey ride Spathi out of the Pavikian camp. She waved in farewell, but Godfrey did not see. An emptiness filled her at the thought that maybe she would not see him again. She knew enough about war to understand that even those favored by the gods were not invincible. After all, she had thought once before that he had died.

Madeline ran after him for a few steps, but stopped. Godfrey had a duty. He had men to lead. There was a role for him to fulfill. What was her role in all of this?

Eyeing a heavy hand-ax lying on top of a stack of crates near a tent, she briefly considered taking it. Fortune favored the bold. Could she disguise herself, and join in the coming melee? Though some women were known to be legendary fighters, their examples were few and far between. Madeline had devoted much of her time to scholastic pursuits, and little to the physical training required to excel in close combat. Taking the ax would not end well for her.

As she thought of ways she could or could not contribute to the coming fray, her father blew his horn. With the assault signaled, the siege engines ceased their bombardment, and the men began to charge the walls. The warriors roared as they rushed to battle.

"I want to help." She tugged on her father's cloak as he drew his sword.

"I want you to wait here until this is over," Tancred replied, rejecting her offer, and pointing to his tent. "I lost you once already. It won't happen again."

"But," Madeline insisted, "I have magic. It has grown so much even in just these last few weeks traveling with Godfrey."

"The Clan warriors will try to capture you if they see you," Tancred countered. "Don't jeopardize yourself after all you went through."

"My fire has more than one use," she interjected. "Let me use it."

Tancred gestured to her. She followed him to the edge of the Pavikian camp. Grabbing a Bastognian banner marking the boundary between their camps, he pulled it out of the ground. He offered no explanation to her stunned silence as the two stared at each other for a moment.

"Stay to the rear of the men," he ordered his daughter. "There will be wounded among the dead."

Nodding in understanding, she watched her father join his retainers as they marched into battle. Taking a deep breath, she followed them at a distance. The clash of metal against metal rang from the fighting atop the wall. Screams of the wounded and dying followed as well.

Already the ground was littered with the bodies of the fallen as Madeline approached. Many of the bodies lay still, but some gasped, moaned, struggled to move. A pair of Pavikian warriors carried their thrashing comrade past Madeline, a crossbow bolt lodged in his eye. She froze at the ghastly sight. Shaking her head, she reminded herself this was exactly the sort of thing she should expect to see here.

Kneeling next to a man attempting to pull an arrow from his neck, she grabbed hold of the shaft, and yanked out the projectile. Blood spurted from the wound as the embedded arrow was dislodged. Letting out a cry of pain, the wounded man looked at her as if she were mad as she laid her hands on the wound. A soft, subdued glow emanated from her hands as the injury to his neck sealed itself.

"Sorcery?" The man stared at her in confusion as his hand explored the new skin covering what should have been a mortal wound.

"Fortune's kiss," Madeline answered. "You have a second chance. Go and fight."

Barely understanding, the man stood. He picked up his spear and shield, and with one last puzzled look back at her, he cautiously marched back to the battle.

Madeline found a dozen others like the first wounded man. With a touch of her hand, she let her fire heal wounds that would have otherwise killed or crippled these men for life. She found this use of her fire much more satisfying than its destructive use. To see the pain leave their eyes, the bewilderment at the restoration of their bodies, that was a gift she never should have concealed. Some of the men she healed were just as scared as they were confused by these miraculous acts of mercy, but none resisted her touch, nor did any try to restrain her efforts.

Here, Madeline treated wounds worse than the one Walaric had suffered back near Narlstad. She hardly understood how her own powers worked to begin with, much less why they were more potent now than before. The best she could figure was as she had guessed all along; the more she used her magic, the more powerful it became and the easier it was to use.

Kneeling over a man she knew was already dead, she laid her hands on him all the same. Despite her best efforts, the wound would not close, and the man would not stir. Cold and lifeless he remained. Now she knew the limits of her power. Still, she had to try. With a heavy sigh, she walked to the next fallen warrior.

With dawn fast approaching, Madeline's strength was almost spent from healing so many wounded men. Like her more destructive form of the fire spell, the healing variant sapped a portion of her strength too. However, she found her healing fire was not as taxing as the consuming fire.

As the first light of dawn broke over the mountains, she caught a glimpse of Spathi and Godfrey flying over Olso's walls. She smiled a tired smile. Godfrey was alive. She could think of a sight no more glorious than what she saw now. What else mattered?

What relief she felt was swept away with the rumbling of the earth. She fell. She was so tired. The flapping of immense wings blew Madeline's hair out of her face. She looked up to see Vozzab fill the sky. The dragon opened his jaws and let out a deafening roar. Panicking, warriors leapt from Olso's walls as Vozzab swooped down upon them from on high.

The dragon crushed Nordsmen and Pavikians, devoured orcs, and ripped apart crusaders. All fled before the dragon. Vozzab's fury was primal. His fiery orange eyes knew no friends, only prey.

Screeching, Spathi dove onto Vozzab as the dragon occupied himself with the helpless men and orcs. The griffin tore into the dragon's back with his talons. However, Vozzab's black scales were hard, and breaking through was difficult. Godfrey was about to strike at Vozzab's spine with Uriel, but the dragon shook the griffin off.

"Fly," Godfrey screamed, hoping to gain some distance before the dragon could attack.

Rolling, the griffin flew hard with Vozzab in pursuit. Godfrey had Spathi stick as close to the ground as he dared, remembering that climbing would lose them speed. Snarling, Vozzab let loose a gout of orange flame from his mouth. The fire washed over the inner courtyard as Spathi turned sharply around the corner of the keep. Godfrey risked pulling the reins to have Spathi climb as they circled the keep. Vozzab lumbered around the corner just behind them, digging his claws into the building itself before he launched himself at Godfrey and Spathi. The dragon's jaw snapped inches behind Spathi's tail. Godfrey's hand began to shake, but he gripped his sword tightly, and steadied his breathing.

Spathi dove with Vozzab just behind. The griffin screeched as Godfrey took a steep angle towards the inner courtyard wall. He pulled the reins hard, and Spathi climbed, dodging the wall with not a moment to spare. The dragon, reacting too slowly, crashed through the wall. Stone crumbled and hurtled through the air with the men and orcs that stood atop the battlements a moment before.

The dragon lay inert, covered in rubble from the broken wall section he had crashed through. Blood trickled from his snout, but the dragon did not lie still for more than a moment. He shook himself off, a cloud of grey dust falling from his bruised form. If a dragon's visage could possibly look even more malicious than it naturally did, Godfrey would have sworn it did in that moment Vozzab looked up at him as he and Spathi desperately climbed higher into the air.

Shooting more gouts of flame up after Godfrey, Vozzab stretched his wings. Launching himself off the ground, he pursued his quarry with outstretched claws. Turning to face the Sun, Godfrey prayed Loxias would not let him falter now. Vozzab squinted as he turned into the bright morning rays.

"Just a little bit farther," Godfrey urged Spathi.

Below, the battle for Olso Fortress resumed. Baldwin de Ghend and Torcul's crusaders still struggled to maintain a foothold on the outer wall, but in other sections the battle turned more in the crusade's favor. The Pavikians were the first to pour through the breach in the inner wall created by Vozzab, but the Bastognians were not far behind. The men of Errans had breached the outer wall, and Conrad directed his knights to aid Baldwin's group on their flank. The Clan defenses were beginning to fail, and soon only a few groups of berserkers and orcish oath-warriors offered any real hope for their success. Sensing ultimate victory was near, the crusaders took up a hymn as they slaughtered their foes. The sight was the first bit of comfort Godfrey had taken in a while.

With Godfrey pulling on the reins, Spathi made a tight overhead loop. The Sun was in the dragon's eyes, and Vozzab turned his serpentine head behind himself too late as the griffin attacked his back with beak and talon. Godfrey swung his sword, but Spathi could not get close enough for him to land a blow. To further Godfrey's frustration, the griffin did little damage to the dragon's back before they were forced to pull away by Vozzab's sweeping claws.

The scales were too hard. Though Spathi's beak and claws were easily the match of any man's armor, they could only chip away at Vozzab's back one scale at a time. Uriel could slice through the scales with ease, Godfrey was sure of it. If he could just get in close enough to strike.

"Gods above," Godfrey muttered as an idea crossed his mind. "May no one sing a shameful song about me."

Spathi and Vozzab circled. The griffin was more agile and was coming up on the dragon's tail again. Seeing this, Vozzab twisted in midair and tried to catch the griffin in a deadly embrace. Godfrey had hoped for this response.

Time slowed. Godfrey signaled for Spathi to dive, but Godfrey leapt from the saddle. Spathi screeched in protest but was forced to continue in his dive to avoid the dragon's reach. For a moment, Godfrey was suspended in freefall. He had known he was going to die falling, but he had never imagined it would be from such heights.

As Vozzab turned to follow the griffin, he was caught completely unprepared for Godfrey to abandon his mount like this. Godfrey narrowly slipped past the dragon's scarred jaws and grasping claws as the beast dove after Spathi. Grabbing hold of the dragon's soft underbelly as he passed, Godfrey plunged Uriel deep into Vozzab's breast. A second, then third thrust from the blessed blade; Godfrey knew he was going to die in this moment. He just wanted to make sure the dragon did too.

Steaming blood flowed freely from the wounds Godfrey dealt. Vozzab bellowed in rage, confusion, pain. Not since his battle with the angel, Othniel, had Vozzab appeared so unsure of his immortality. Godfrey dealt a fourth strike as he made his peace with the gods just as Vozzab flung him off his chest. This final blow went to the dragon's heart.

The last thing Godfrey was sure he heard was the sickening crunch of bones as Vozzab crumpled to the ground. Sliding across the mud, Godfrey's head hit something hard. He instantly went blind at the impact, and tasted blood in his mouth. Godfrey was dead.

At least, Godfrey was sure he was dead. A distant voice pleaded with him, begged him not to be dead. It was Madeline's voice. Warmth washed through Godfrey. It was faint. It was just enough to restore sight to his eyes.

Madeline was cradling his head. Tears were streaming down her face. Another faltering spurt of warmth, and Godfrey could feel her hands on the back of his head. He tried to speak, but could not move his tongue. Her eyes darted, focusing here and there as she saw he was alive. A final burst of warmth from Madeline, then her already-fair skin drained completely of color. She pulled back, gasping through extreme exertion.

"If only I could always awaken to such a vision of beauty," Godfrey managed, coughing up blood.

"You may yet still," she cried.

The damsel stood and pointed up at Olso's keep. Looking down from the keep's parapet stood Duke Tancred of Pavik waving the blue banner of House Cretus. It was Godfrey's banner. There was no mistaking the white griffin rampant emblazoned upon it. It was only now that he realized the ancient symbol of Godfrey's house was personified in Spathi. And there was Tancred atop the keep, declaring Olso to be Godfrey's prize. Was this what the gods had had in mind for Godfrey all along? Tears streamed down Godfrey's face like never before.

"Victory?" Godfrey asked.

"Victory," Madeline reassured him.

Turpin and Varin approached him from the ruined form of Vozzab, son of Yoan.

"Victory," Godfrey sighed.

Turpin nodded, nursing a wound. Spathi landed on the ground close to Godfrey. Folding his wings in close to his body, the griffin rubbed his head against Godfrey's chest. Godfrey smiled his first genuine smile in a long time.

The battle was over. Every orc and Nordsman was either dead or had managed to flee through the chaos of Vozzab's attack. All that remained were the crusaders, Tancred's army, Madeline, and the griffin.

The gods had led Godfrey here to this very spot. He saw their hands in it now. Yet, looking over the bloodied forms of those with him, he realized much tribulation and uncertainty would still follow. Closing his eyes, he bit his lip then slowly exhaled. He was so tired.

As a thank you for purchasing this print copy of *The Griffin Legends: Godfrey's Crusade*, here following is a bonus short story set a few years prior to the main events of this novel. *The Joust* features someone you previously met, Karl 'The Hammer.'

<u>The Joust</u>

The crowd screamed ecstatically as Karl rode atop his horse onto the tournament field. Damsels declared their love for him. Young boys waved toy wooden swords at him. Smugly, he waved to the commoners present in the stands before bowing his head to the nobles seated in a raised gallery in the center. Despite his fatigue, it was hard not to get carried away in the crowd's euphoria.

Still, his hot breath washed back over his face as it hit the inside of his great helm. He blinked away droplets of sweat trickling down his brow as the late afternoon sun gleamed in his eyes. His body aching from the day's earlier matches, a single thought persisted in his mind. Just one more.

He offered a silent prayer to Helios, Tyche, Yael, Atniel, and any of the other gods, demigods, and angels of the celestial realm that were inclined to listen. He needed strength, dexterity, clarity of mind, and a bit of luck to pull this off.

From the opposite end of the field, Karl's opponent appeared. He was another knight weighed down by heavy chainmail whilst sitting atop his steed. His face, like Karl's, was obscured by a flat-topped great helm. The knight's heraldic tabard and shield were his only identifying marks, a black lion rampant emblazoned upon a white field distinguishing him from his peers. Karl immediately knew the man: Sir Melcho of Elgun. This would be a tough fight.

After the other knight paid his respects to the audience, he stopped just short of the wooden rail that bisected the tournament field. Sir Melcho waited on one side of the field while Karl waited at the other end with the rail in between the two combatants. A herald bustled to the center of the field and stood just to the side of the rail facing the audience. The herald was a portly man who walked with unusual precision and purpose for a man of his size. Gesturing for silence, the herald persuaded the audience to settle down, at least a bit.

"On this end of the field," the herald bellowed, indicating Karl. "We have Karl the Hammer riding Epono, undefeated here on their native soil!"

More cheering erupted from the audience. Karl raised his lance in response. Even more roaring rang out from the crowd. They loved the spectacle. He smirked, wishing the adulation would never end. Sensing the tension in his horse's muscles, Karl pulled back on the reins to prevent him from galloping off prematurely.

"Almost," Karl whispered in Epono's ear, rubbing the beast's neck. "You know the signal."

The herald waved again, and the excitement subsided. Turning to the other knight, the herald cocked his head as he indicated Karl's opponent.

"And over here," the herald pointed to Melcho. "We have Melcho of Elgun riding Morvach, hailing all the way from the Kingdom of Ogledd."

If the audience's response to Melcho's raised shield was any less enthusiastic, it was only because Karl's fame in Bastogne was greater. Karl estimated Melcho was just as, if not more, skilled at jousting than he was. Karl's mind raced as he thought about how he would try to counter the tactics he had seen Melcho using throughout the competition.

"So the day's tournament all comes down to this," the herald continued in his bellowing voice. "More than a dozen knights have competed on this field today. And now we are down to these two champions. Karl the Hammer, Duke Ulric's personal retainer, will face off against Melcho of Elgun, slayer of the cyclopean minotaur, Rodark. Who will come out victorious and claim today's prize money? After three passes, we will find out!"

The herald raised a small flag with Duke Ulric's heraldry: a white griffin set against a deep blue field. He stepped back from the rail several paces. Karl tensed. Gripping his lance and shield as tightly as he could, he nodded to himself as his plan of attack solidified in his mind.

The herald looked from one end of the field to the other. He waved the flag in a downward stroke, and both knights spurred their steeds across the field. The mounts thundered as galloping hooves churned the muddy earth. Lowering their lances, the knights closed the distance between them in just a few heartbeats. Hoping for a torso hit, Karl aimed his lance under Melcho's shield, but was deflected by Melcho's lance. Instead, Karl's lance struck Melcho's shield with a heavy thump before bouncing off while Melcho's lance shattered in a spray of splinters as it struck Karl's shoulder.

Grunting in discomfort, Karl was glad these lances were blunted. He slowed his horse down to a trot as he reached the end of the field. Tears welled in his eyes as the pain still throbbed throughout his entire left arm. It could have been worse.

The herald returned to the center of the field and consulted with two squires as Karl and Melcho assumed opposite starting positions for their second pass. Melcho's squire handed his liege a fresh lance as Karl rolled his shoulder in an attempt to work out the pain. After a few deep breaths, Karl's shoulder felt a bit better. Shake it off, Karl's father used to tell him. The words rang in his mind after every injury he had received, even years after the old man's death.

"Strike to the shield," the herald announced after he finished with the squires. "One point for Karl. Strike to the shoulder. Two points for Melcho. Broken lance. One point from Melcho. Current score: one to one."

The herald raised his flag again. Should Karl attempt a head strike? The head was a small target—easy to miss in the split-second Karl had to attempt his blow, and an easy strike for an opponent to deflect. Most knights would not even try it. But it was worth the most points.

Resuming his position out of harm's way, the herald signaled the second pass. Breathing heavily as their horses raced towards each other, Karl aimed his lance for Melcho's head. Melcho deflected Karl's weapon with ease, sending the shaft flying out of his hand before hitting Karl's collarbone.

Karl cried out at this blow. Epono whinnied sympathetically. Karl's only comfort came in the knowledge his father was not alive to hear his cry. Silently cursing the old man, Karl shook his head. Even now, Karl could not escape the memory of his father's rebukes.

The knights resumed their original starting positions as the herald consulted the squires once more in the center of the field. Grimacing, Karl nodded as a grizzled man-at-arms named Fulcher handed him his lance.

"A bad pass, my lord." Fulcher frowned.

"Indeed," Karl murmured, noting the displeasure on some of the damsels' faces in the crowd. "I need to win this."

"Try to keep your head, sire," the man-at-arms warned.

Karl scoffed at the irony of Fulcher's words. So much was at stake. Epono snorted as if sensing his master's contempt.

"You're right," Karl admitted, deferring to the grizzled warrior's experience. "It's time to focus on the task at hand."

"Strike to the torso," the herald announced. "Five points for Melcho. Lost lance. One point from Karl. Current score: six to zero. Melcho leads."

"Gods be with you, sire!" Fulcher withdrew several paces.

"Fortune favors the bold," Karl muttered. "One more try, Epono."

The herald raised his flag once more. Karl determined the exact motions he would make, and he repeated them over and over again in his mind. He was sure he would win this pass if he timed everything just right. Yet there was no room for mistakes.

The flag dropped one last time, and Karl and Melcho raced towards each other. Karl aimed for Melcho's chest but raised his lance at the last possible second. Melcho's lance fell just shy of blocking Karl's strike to the head. Splitting on impact, Karl's lance sent Melcho reeling backwards off his horse. Melcho landed on his back with a hard thud.

"Karl the *Hammer*!" The herald gestured as if swinging an invisible mallet in both hands.

Standing, clapping, whistling, and screaming their approval, the audience completely drowned out the herald's final score. No one needed to hear it. Karl won back all the points he needed and more with the head strike and de-horsing his opponent. Raising his shattered lance, Karl forgot his inner demons as he let the crowd's praise carry him away.

Sitting in his tent, Karl counted out his prize money. The silver coins clinked against the table as he poured them out of the bag Duke Ulric had given him during the award ceremony. He scowled. It was still not enough. He knew it would not be.

"What troubles my gallant knight?" a red-haired maiden asked as she entered Karl's tent.

"Dadin." Karl smiled at the young woman.

"I slipped away from Auntie," the maiden said. "I have just a few minutes."

Dadin extended her hand, and Karl kissed it. Returning his smile, she sat in the chair next to Karl's. For a moment the two just looked at each other. Then Karl's gaze turned back to the coins piled on the table. Her smile faded as Karl gave a heavy sigh.

"For all the tournaments I've won, I'm afraid I still don't have enough money," he conceded.

"You're the most popular knight in Bastogne's tournament circuit," Dadin countered. "Maybe the most popular in all of Lortharain. If that's not enough to win father over, I don't know what will be."

"Any self-respecting lord would want to know I can provide a future for his daughter." Karl pointed an accusing finger up in the air.

"You're one of the Duke's retainers." She shook her head. "There is a secure enough future in that. When are you going to ask father for my hand?"

Karl delayed his response for longer than he knew he should have. He shifted uncomfortably in his seat. So much business had to pass through fathers.

"What about becoming a Royal Guard first?" he asked at last. "The new King, Wilhelm, he is expanding the Royal Guard. If I were to join their ranks, your father would have to accept my marriage proposal. There's no more prestigious position in all of Lortharain."

"I suppose so." Dadin's eyes turned to her hands.

"Winning this tournament qualifies me to participate in the joust at Roun," Karl said. "The grand prize is a position in the Royal Guard. If I can beat Melcho, I know I can beat all the competitors at Roun."

"You're unhappy with Duke Ulric?" she asked.

Karl stared at his shield resting against the table at which he sat. As a retainer in Ulric's household, Karl's shield and surcoat bore the same markings as the Duke's. He furrowed his brow in contemplation.

"Is this really fair to him?" Dadin persisted. "You have vows of fealty to think about."

"I'm not unhappy in the Duke's service," Karl replied. "We talked after the award ceremony. He gave me his blessing. He'll allow me to compete at Roun. Besides, the Duke's son will be coming of age in a few years. He'll be able to fill my place. I have to think of me and of us. This is just the opportunity of a lifetime, and I think I stand a good chance at getting it. Imagine, me, a Royal Guard."

"I know you'll get it." The smile returned to Dadin's face. "Just promise me you'll speak to my father once you win your next joust."

"I promise." Karl kissed her hand.

"When are you leaving?" Dadin asked.

"Tonight," he said, releasing her hand. "Roun is a long journey, and the joust is soon. If I delay, they will start without me, and there can be no late entries."

She stood then put her hands on her hips. For a moment, Karl could not read her expression. He stroked his beard in uncertainty.

"Then let me wish you luck." Dadin offered her hand.

Karl took it, and she pulled him into an embrace. The two shared a long, passionate kiss.

The road to Roun was little more than a muddy, cold trail in the woods. The scent of decaying leaves wafted through the crisp autumn air as Karl rode Epono down the path. Occasionally glancing to either side of the road, Karl kept an eye out for sudden movements. Orcs, trolls, wargs, and other, far worse monsters were known to ambush unsuspecting travelers. Yet even Karl's keen warrior mind could not always remain alert to danger.

"I know she wants me," Karl confessed to Epono. "But lots of women do. Is it fair to let this one tie me down while there are so many other opportunities?"

The soft clopping of hooves was the steed's only reply.

"Of course you're right." He huffed. "An opportunity like Dadin is a rare one. But give me a year or two in the Royal Guard. Let me settle down into that, and then I can think about marriage and children. Besides, the Royal Guard opens up many opportunities regarding beautiful maidens."

The horse snorted.

"I'm not making excuses." Karl bit his lip. "And I'm not just trying to avoid talking to Dadin's father. I just have to focus on getting to a higher station in life before I let a family drag me down."

He looked about at the trees on either side of the road. The leaves had all changed colors and were beginning to fall. Karl swallowed hard.

"She'll wait for me," he reassured himself. "She's waited this long."

Epono made no reply.

"This isn't about my father," Karl insisted. "Everything I ever did disappointed him. It didn't even bother me by the end of his miserable life. I knew he wouldn't approve no matter what I did. Marry Dadin? Join the Royal Guard first? Wait for a maiden of higher birth to come along? Whatever decision I make, I'm sure his shade will scowl at me from the Abyss."

Epono's ear twitched at Karl's rising frustration.

"Oh, what do you know?" Karl threw his hands up. "You're just a horse!"

The knight rode in silence for a long time. Epono would get over it. The horse knew his master. Karl need not apologize, he silently reasoned.

The Sun was beginning to set, and Karl shivered as a cold breeze rustled through the trees. Something prowled in the forest up ahead. Unsure of what it was, Karl stopped Epono. He squinted in an effort to find what had caught his eye. The sound of soft footfalls approached from somewhere nearby. Tilting his head with a sudden jerk, he strained his ears in an effort to locate the source of the sound. He gripped his lance, ready to strike. Unlike his jousting lances, this weapon was not blunted but rather ended in a sharp, heavy spear-head.

A woman emerged from a fork in the road so suddenly Karl's heart pounded in his chest at the sight. He took several deep breaths as he calmed himself. She was no threat.

She was old, frail, dressed in dark peasant garb, and a fresh cut across her forehead glistened with coagulating blood. Karl eyed her suspiciously.

"Sir knight!" she cried out, taking a few hurried steps towards him. "Thank the gods you're here. Sir knight, help!"

"What is wrong, old woman?" Karl tensed slightly at her apparent distress.

"Down there," she gasped, pointing to the path she had come from. "About five miles from here, there's a death knight. It's blocking the road and killing anyone who won't flee from it. You have to help!"

The words *death knight* sent a chill down Karl's spine.

"Aren't you a serf?" he asked. "Who gave you permission to leave the manor? How do you know it was a death knight?"

"I know it was a death knight." Her eyes narrowed.

There was a certain weight of authority in the woman's voice that made Karl momentarily recoil. This was not how a peasant should speak to a noble. Yet Karl thought better of mentioning this.

"How did you escape then?" Karl raised an eyebrow.

"I fell off the path," the old woman said. "I went down into a ditch. The monster didn't follow me."

Karl nodded in understanding. He began to relax. There was no need to get involved here. He certainly did not need to throw his life away confronting a death knight for this old peasant.

"Well then you're safe." He shrugged. "Find another way home."

"Find another way home?" she repeated, a stunned expression crossing her face. "You mean you're going to let that undead monster go unchallenged?"

Sighing, Karl gritted his teeth. He did not have time for this. He owed this peasant nothing. This was not his fight. No sense in dying here.

"I'm in a hurry," he spat, not caring what the old lady thought of him. "There is a joust at Roun. I have to be there."

"A joust?" The peasant's voice grew shrill. "A place to win accolades from fair maidens? Is that all you care about?"

Karl paused, once again taken aback by her boldness. That cut deeper than he would have thought. Clearing his throat, he regained some of his composure.

"Winning this joust at Roun will earn me a place in the King's Royal Guard," he explained. "I can't pass up this chance."

She gave a cold harsh laugh. It almost seemed unnatural. Shifting uncomfortably in his saddle, he grimaced as he began to see the irony of his words.

"If I make any delay they will start without me." Karl's excuses began to seem weak even to him. "I'm sorry. Another knight will have to help you."

Karl spurred his mount forward, which moved only after neighing in protest, but the old woman blocked his path. She stuck her finger out at Karl's shield, indicating the griffin rampant emblazoned upon it. Her face was cross. She reminded him so much of his father, always telling him what to do without any thought about his own desires. What about his plans? His needs?

"You are a knight of Duke Ulric," she objected. "You have a duty to your lord and this realm. I may not be a fair damsel, but I am in distress. Roun and whatever prizes may be there can wait."

He frowned. His horse nickered. Refusing to meet her gaze, Karl looked around in embarrassment. He stammered for something to say, but the words would not form. This was just like so many confrontations he had had with his father. He could still hear his father's words about duty and honor ringing in his ear. How many times did he accuse Karl of hubris, vanity, or something similar?

Her eye finally caught his. The old woman's gaze penetrated Karl's very soul. Squirming in discomfort, Karl realized his father had been right all along. How could he have been so selfish?

"I was there." Her expression softened. "I was there at Fuetoile Keep when you were dubbed a knight, Sir Karl. You were a different man then, not so conceited or prideful."

"I made an oath to the Duke that I would defend his realm." Karl looked off at something distant as he remembered the day she spoke of. "How could I have forgotten?"

"If you face the death knight, the gods will smile on you for it," she promised. "The gods will bless you for your sacrifice."

"Who are you to speak in the name of the gods?" he asked.

"I'm just an old woman sent here to remind you of duty and loyalty," she said.

Karl was about to call her a liar, but before he could respond, the old woman began walking down the road in the direction he had come from. He gaped at the sight. The audacity!

It was now just him, his horse, and a fork in the road. He looked longingly down the path to Roun. Setting his jaw, he turned away from what could have been.

"She's lost her mind." Karl shook his head, coming to himself. "Come on, Epono. Let's go see what this is all about."

He turned his horse and spurred him down the fork in the road. Grimacing, he pondered the life in the Royal Guard he was now turning his back on. There might not be a chance like that again. But duty called.

"No regrets," he told his mount, setting his eyes on the path ahead.

As Karl went farther down the trail, he found the earth increasingly covered in frost. The air was much too cold even for autumn. Epono's breath came out of his nostrils in steamy gusts. Finding consolation in the shaft of his lance, Karl grasped it so tightly he began to lose the feeling in his hand. His mouth was dry, and his heart raced. He knew what lay ahead.

The horse stopped in his tracks in front of some dense undergrowth. The image of a shadow reaching out in malice entered Karl's mind. His father's ghost now stood before him. For all of Karl's accomplishments in the tournament field, he could think of nothing to say to please the old man. His mouth moving desperately trying to utter something to dispel his father's scowl, Karl could say nothing. Nothing. His father bowed his head in shame and walked away muttering to himself.

The ghost faded away into thin air just as Karl reached out to stop his father from leaving. He suddenly felt very small. How did he think he could ever be a Royal Guard, a knight, or even a man? The old woman was there now, laughing over the broken forms of Epono and him.

Whinnying with bulging eyes, Epono reared. Snatching the reins, Karl narrowly avoided falling from the saddle. The world around him came back into focus. Adjusting himself in the stirrups, Karl patted his steed.

"No more evil thoughts," Karl attempted to soothe his horse as his own voice still shook. "It's okay. We'll do it together. You don't have to worry."

After passing a patch of obscuring brush, Karl's heart jumped in his throat as he saw the creature. The old woman was right. It was a death knight.

It was a skeletal figure with withered skin clothed in tarnished chainmail and a battered spangenhelm, sitting atop an undead horse. The undead steed was likewise little more than bone and dried flesh with a stained black caparison as its covering. The death knight's torn black tabard was too filthy and worn for Karl to make out any heraldry that might suggest the creature's former allegiance. Now it served the dark gods, and that was all that mattered. It must be vanquished.

Time itself slowed as the monster's pin-prick glowing eyes made contact with Karl's. No words were exchanged as they stared each other down. There was no need. Each knew the other's intent.

"Gods help me," Karl prayed.

The death knight readied its lance. Karl readied his. There would be no spare lances, only one pass, and one of the two would be destroyed in the end. Karl knew that much.

With a yell, Karl spurred his horse towards the death knight as it silently mirrored Karl's actions. He had just a few heartbeats to decide where to aim. His heart pounded so loudly in his chest, Karl could hear nothing else.

This was it. Time stopped altogether. The image of Dadin's face flashed in Karl's mind. There would be no wedding now after this final joust. No more competitions or prizes. No entry into the Royal Guard. It would all end here. Instead, he would sacrifice whatever future he had in the name of duty to the Duchy of Bastogne and Kingdom of

Lortharain. It would be a good death; worthy of bards' songs.

Karl aimed for the creature's chest, and it lunged with its lance to block his strike. Then Karl tilted his lance up towards the death knight's head at the last second, just as he had in his final pass against Melcho. The monster's skull shattered, and its spangenhelm went flying, but the sharp kiss of cold steel bit into Karl's gut as its spear cut into him. Karl fell out of his saddle as the death knight and its steed collapsed in a heap of bone, dried flesh, and rust-stained armor. Unholy ethereal fumes hissed from the inert pile before going silent forever.

Clutching his side, Karl lay sprawled on the ground for a long moment. Blood began to gush from the wound. His toes and fingers grew numb. He was dying.

"Gods help me..." Karl sputtered up blood. "Don't let me die."

His vision blurring, Karl barely recognized the old woman standing over him. His thoughts grew muddy and confused. He blinked, unsure if his eyes deceived him.

"What?" Karl managed to gurgle.

The old woman said nothing but pressed her hand over Karl's wound. Warmth flashed through Karl's innards, and the taste of blood disappeared from his mouth. His vision was clear.

It was no longer a peasant with a sagging wrinkled face standing over him, but a glorious winged angel in brilliant white robes. Her dark lustrous hair cascaded over her statuesque head and shoulders. The celestial creature's eyes remained old and wise, but the fresh cut to the angel's forehead was now a thin scar.

"Yael!" Karl cried in recognition. "Guardian of the Golden Tree?"

"I heard your prayer at the last joust." The angel nodded curtly. "The gods love you and have greater works for you to accomplish still."

He heaved himself up into a sitting position as he looked over the gut wound that was no more. Standing, he surveyed the ruined form of the destroyed undead. Already the air was beginning to warm. He knelt before the angel, Yael.

"Rise." She gestured with one hand while handing him Epono's reins with the other. "And never forget a joust's true purpose."

About the Author

I'm thrilled you're here, about to go on this crusade with me. It's been a long pilgrimage already, writing this book. It started as a few short scenes I typed out during my freshman year of college when I probably should have been studying. Looking back on it, the first draft wasn't exactly what I would call good now. I spent the rest of my undergraduate chasing girls, playing video games, and wondering why my grades weren't better.

I had this story in the back of my mind, but I wasn't sure how I wanted to change it in the second draft, so I kept putting it off. In 2014, I had my bachelor's, and I decided to start writing again in earnest. There were only two problems. I now had a wife and a small baby to provide for, and I also decided to pursue a master's degree at this time. Though this meant that the next draft took another five years to complete since I scrapped most of the ideas from the first draft outside of a couple characters and the setting, I think the work in front of you is much more mature thanks to my experiences in the interim. My master's degree gave me a much greater depth of historical and literary knowledge to draw inspiration from, and my time as a husband and father working through grad school broadened my personal experiences enough to give my characters the depth they deserved.

I've always wanted to be an author. My wife shares in this ambition for herself, and we intend to make this book the first in several series of books set in this world we've created. If you enjoy what you read, please post a good review online. That will help us bring more books to you more quickly. Thanks!

www.thegriffinlegends.com

CPSIA information can be obtained
at www.ICGtesting.com
Printed in the USA
LVHW052036090122
708114LV00019B/1882

9 781087 982045